This book is dedicated to all those cubicle dwellers who, in all their vast and multifaceted variety, labour thanklessly under the lash of insensate management to ensure that all the vital things in our lives do the things we expect them to do or, at the very least, don't spontaneously explode at an awkward moment.

PART I

THE JACQUARD

I am often reminded of certain spirits & fairies one reads of, who are at one's elbow in one shape now, & the next minute in a form most dissimilar; and uncommonly deceptive, troublesome & tantalizing are the mathematical sprites & fairies sometimes; like the types I have found for them in the world of Fiction.

Letter from Ada Lovelace to mathematician Augustus De Morgan, 27 November 1840

CHAPTER 1

JANUARY: SOME SWANS ARE WHITE

My final interview at the Serious Cybernetics Corporation was with the company's head of security himself – Tyrel Johnson. Mid-fifties, one of those big men who by dint of clean living and regular exercise have failed to go to fat and instead compacted down to the tensile strength of teak. Light-skinned, with short grey hair and dressed in a bespoke navy pinstripe suit with a lemon cotton shirt and no tie.

Since everybody else in the building dressed in varying degrees of slacker-casual, wearing a suit made a statement – I was glad I'd worn mine.

Judging by the pastel-coloured walls, the spindly stainless-steel furniture and the words *Ask me about my poetry* painted along one wall in MS Comic Sans, I was guessing that Mr Johnson hadn't decorated his office himself.

I was stuck on the low-slung banana-yellow sofa while he was perched on the edge of his desk – arms folded. Working without notes, I noticed.

'Peter Grant.' He spoke with a West Indian

3

accent, apparently Trinidadian although I can't tell them apart. 'Twenty-eight years old, Londoner, plenty of GCSEs, three C-grade A levels but you didn't go on to further education, worked for Tesco, a couple of small retailers, something called Spinnaker Office Services – what was that?'

'Office cleaning.'

'So you know your way around a mop?' He smiled.

'Unfortunately,' I said, manfully resisting the urge to add 'sir' to the end of every sentence. Tyrel Johnson had stopped being a copper the year I was born, but obviously there were some things that never leave you.

I realised that I might have to come to terms with that myself.

'Two years as a PCSO . . . then you joined the Metropolitan Police and managed a whole six years before leaving.' He nodded as if this made perfect sense to him – I wish it did to me.

'Following probation you went into Specialist, Organised and Economic Crime Command,' said Johnson. 'Doing what exactly?'

It had been agreed that it would be counterproductive all round if I was to mention the Special Assessment Unit, otherwise known as 'The Folly', also known as 'Oh God, not them'. That there was a section of the Met that dealt with weird shit was quite widely known within the police; that it had officers who were trained in magic was not exactly a secret, but definitely

4

something nobody wanted to talk about. Especially at a job interview.

'Operation Fairground,' I said.

'Never heard of it.'

'Nigerian counterfeiting gangs.'

'Undercover?'

'No,' I said. 'Interviews, statements, follow-ups – you know – leg work.'

'Why don't we just get down to the main event?' said Johnson. 'Why did you leave the police?'

Being ex-job, Johnson was bound to still have contacts in the Met – he would have checked my name out as soon as my CV was shortlisted. Still, the fact that I was even having this interview indicated that he didn't know everything.

'There was a death in custody,' I said. 'I was put on suspension.'

He leaned forward slightly for emphasis.

'Tell me, son,' he said. 'Were you responsible?'

I looked him in the eyes.

'I should have seen it coming, and I didn't act fast enough to stop it,' I said – it's so much easier to lie when you're telling the truth.

He nodded.

'There always has to be someone to blame,' he said. 'You didn't try to stick it out?'

'I was encouraged to move on,' I said. 'Somebody had to go, but they didn't want a fuss.' I didn't say who 'they' were, but that didn't seem to bother Johnson, who nodded sagely.

'What do you think about computers?' he asked,

showing that the interview trick of suddenly changing the subject was also something that never leaves you when you exit the Job.

It's always 'the Job', with a capital letter, as if once you're in it you can't imagine doing anything else.

Just be yourself, Beverley had said when I was dressing that morning.

'I once played *Red Dead Redemption* for twenty-four hours solid,' I said.

Johnson's eyes narrowed, but there was amusement in the set of his mouth. It faded a little.

'I'll be honest with you, son. All things being equal you'd normally be a bit overqualified for this job,' he said. 'But I have a problem.'

'Sir?' I tried to keep an expression of bland interest on my face.

'Someone in the workforce is up to no good,' he said, and I relaxed. 'I can feel them scuttling around like a rat. I don't have the time to chase them so what I need is a rat-catcher, someone I can trust to do the job properly.'

'I worked Oxford Street,' I said. 'Rat-catching's my speciality.'

'Yes,' he said slowly. 'You'll do – when can you start?'

'Right now,' I said.

'Chance would be a fine thing,' said Johnson. 'We have to navigate you through HR first, so Monday will be fine. Nice and early.'

He straightened up off his desk and I jumped

to my feet. He held out his hand – it was like shaking hands with a tree.

'Just so we're clear,' he said, not letting go of my hand. 'No matter what anyone else thinks – including the Uber-hobbit himself – you work for me and only me. Understand?'

'Yes, sir,' I said.

'Good,' he said and walked me out of the building.

Johnson had made a point of calling the human resources department 'HR' rather than its official internal company name, the Magrathean Ape-Descended Life Form Utilisation Service, just as he called the department I had just joined 'Security' rather than the Vogon Enforcement Arm.

That, and the fact that employees were officially referred to as 'mice', didn't stop the Magrathean Ape-Descended Life Form Utilisation Service sending me a twelve-page contract by email and snail-mail and a non-disclosure agreement that was worse than the Official Secrets Act. My mum warned me that the company didn't have a very good reputation amongst cleaning staff.

'*Den hat for deal witt ein den nor dae pay betteh,*' she told me.

Den nor dae pay betteh was Mum-speak for below minimum wage.

My mum also wanted to know whether I was attending pre-natal classes with Beverley and making sure she ate properly. Eating properly by Mum's definition meant Beverley consuming her own weight in rice every day so I lied and said she was. When I asked Beverley about any cravings, she told me not so far.

'I can pretend,' she said just after Christmas. 'If it makes you feel better.'

Beverley Brook lived south of Wimbledon Common, in both sides of a semi on, appropriately enough, Beverley Avenue. The walls between the two halves had been knocked through and the rooms converted, but you could still feel the ghosts of the right-hand kitchen in the way the floor texture changed under your feet when you moved around the master bedroom's en suite bathroom. There had been a few changes since I moved in permanently, mostly involving storage space and encouraging Beverley to use it for her clothes – with mixed results.

We slept on the ground floor because Beverley was the goddess of the river Beverley Brook, which ran along the bottom of her garden, and she liked to have swift access to her watercourse in times of need.

Beverley was five months gone by then – an event marked by her borrowing a slightly larger wetsuit from one of her sisters to accommodate the bump. She'd also taken to working on her dissertation, 'The Environmental Benefits of Waterway Reversion', while sitting in a straight-backed chair at the kitchen table.

That evening I sat at the other end and went through the contract, most of which seemed to be concerned with detailing the many and varied ways the Serious Cybernetics Corporation could fire me without compensation. It was hard work, and I kept on being distracted by the beauty of Beverley's eyes as they flicked from laptop screen to notebook, and her slim brown fingers as they held a highlighter pen poised over the textbooks open in front of her.

'What?' she asked, looking up at me.

'Nothing,' I said.

'Okay,' she said, and I watched as she bent to check something in one of the books and her locks fell over her shoulders to reveal the smooth curve of the back of her neck.

'Stop staring at me,' said Beverley without looking up. 'And get on with your contract.'

I sighed and went back to decrypting the fact that not only was I to be on a twelve-month probation, but that the management reserved the right to extend that probation indefinitely if I failed to meet a series of loosely defined performance criteria. It was all very depressing, and borderline legal, but it wasn't as if I had any choice.

I hadn't had a job, as opposed to 'the Job', for over eight years. The last being a stint stacking shelves in the Stockwell Kwiksave which had ended when the company went bust. The best that can be said about shelf stacking is that it's not working as a cleaner.

I signed the contract in the indicated boxes and stuck it back in the envelope provided.

Parking being what it was around Old Street roundabout, there was no way I was going to drive from Bev's. Instead I got the 57 from Holland Avenue and hit the Northern Line at South Wimbledon, where I squeezed myself into an imaginary gap between two large white men. A morning commute on the Northern Line is frequently grim but that morning the atmosphere was strange and I swear I felt a tingle of *vestigium*. Nothing professionally worrying, just a whiff of glitter and stardust. A middle-aged woman a couple of armpits down the carriage from me said, 'It's a godawful small affair,' and burst into tears. As the train pulled out I thought I heard a man's voice say, 'To the girl with the mousy hair,' but the noise of the train drowned it out. By the time we got to Colliers Wood, nobody was singing but I'd picked up enough of a nearby conversation to learn that David Bowie was dead.

In case I hadn't twigged that the Man Who Fell to Earth was brown bread, the newly mounted poster facing out through the glass windows of the SCC's main entrance, and the teenaged intern handing out black armbands to all the arriving mice, would have been a clue.

The poster was of Bowie in his Ziggy Stardust phase with a red lightning bolt running across his face, and had been placed just under the large friendly letters that spelt out DON'T PANIC across the window.

At no point did anyone suggest that wearing an armband was compulsory, but I noticed that none of the mice, not even the ones in death metal sweatshirts, refused one.

The Serious Cybernetics Corporation's atrium was fitted with a line of card-activated entrance gates. Unlike most corporate offices, the barriers here were head-high and made of bullet-resistant Perspex – a level of security I'd only ever seen at New Scotland Yard and the Empire State Building. Every mouse had an RFID chip built into their brightly coloured ID card and had to tap in at the barrier. Three whole paragraphs of my employment contract detailed exactly what penalties I would suffer should I lose or allow someone else to use my card. Since I hadn't actually received one yet, I dutifully reported to the long bright blue reception desk, where a young and incredibly skinny white woman with an Eastern European accent smiled at me and handed me my brand-new ID card and lanyard.

Then she handed me a towel.

It was a fluffy orange bathroom towel.

'What's this?' I asked.

'It's your first day towel,' said the receptionist. 'You wrap it around your head.'

'You're joking?'

'It shows you're a newbie,' she said. 'Then everyone will know to be friendly.'

11

I gave the towel a cautious sniff – it was clean and fluffy and smelt of fabric conditioner.

'Can I keep the towel afterwards?'

'Of course.'

I wrapped the towel around my head and fastened it like a turban.

'How do I look?'

The receptionist nodded her head.

'Very nice,' she said.

I asked how long I was supposed to keep it on, and she told me the whole first day.

'Well, at least it will muffle the tracking device,' I said, but that just got me a blank look.

Past the barriers was a short corridor with two sets of lifts on the left and access to the main stairwell on the right. Beyond them it widened out into an open atrium four storeys high. This, I'd been told by Johnson, was the Cage where the mice could hang out, mingle and chill. You could hear the air quotes around 'chill' when he said it.

From the point of view of us Vogons it was also home to the storage lockers where everyone, including me, was supposed to stash any outside electronic devices while at work. The lockers were the standard metal cubes with electronic locks keyed to the RFID in our ID cards. The doors were randomly painted as a single square of one of the colours of the rainbow, with a number stencilled on in white or black – whichever contrasted best. You were not supposed to have a personal locker, but instead pick the first one available. Because the lock was keyed to your ID card, the locker sprang open automatically when you left the building. Long-term storage was forbidden.

Now, personally, if I was managing a building full of poorly socialised technophiliacs I would have gone for personal lockers and mechanical locks. When I asked Johnson about this, he said he'd made that very same suggestion his second week on the job, but management said no.

Any employee could check out a flip phone for use within the building. These were simple digital mobile phones which were restricted to internal calls only. They were officially called babelphones – all calls to and from the outside were routed through the company switchboard and logged. But the majority of the mice didn't bother, because they spent most of their working hours logged into the company intranet – where they were much easier to contact.

The rest of the Cage was painted in bright pastel blues, oranges and pinks and was arrayed with tables, blobby sofas, beanbags and a table-tennis table. Vending machines lined the walls and there was a genuine human-sized hamster wheel in one corner, with a bright blue cable leading to an enormous plasma screen TV. Apart from a couple of guys who'd obviously pulled an all-nighter and then crashed on the sofas, the mice ignored the delights of the Cage and headed for their work assignments with the same grim determination as commuters on Waterloo Bridge.

The Serious Cybernetics Corporation prided itself on its lack of conformity and so the mice dressed with deliberate variety, although there were definite tribes. Skinny black jeans and a death metal sweatshirt, with or without a denim waistcoat, was one. Cargo pants, high tops, braces and check shirts were another – often with a floppy emo hairstyle that I thought had gone out of fashion when I was six. Lots of leggings in bright colours with luridly striped jumpers were favoured, but not exclusively, by the women. From my initial survey it was two thirds male and 95 per cent white. I did catch sight of a couple of reassuringly dark faces amongst the crowd. One of them, a short skinny black guy with a retro-Afro and a Grateful Dead T-shirt caught my eye and gave me the nod – I nodded back.

It was a good thing I had a towel wrapped around my head or I would have really stood out.

The Serious Cybernetics Corporation actually occupied two separate buildings. The entrance, the Cage, and most of the administration were part of a speculative office development on the corner of Tabernacle Street and Epworth Street that had gone bust in 2009. When celebrity entrepreneur Terrence Skinner made his surprise migration from Silicon Valley to Silicon Roundabout he snapped it up cheap – well, by an oligarch's definition of cheap.

But that wasn't enough, so he also acquired the five-storey former brick warehouse further up Tabernacle Street, and built enclosed walkways on the first and fourth floors to link them.

I knew all this because I'd taken the time to acquire the original building plans. What can I say? I like to be prepared.

Because of this layout, most of the mice were funnelled up a wide steel staircase that led from the floor of the Cage to a first floor mezzanine and then on to their open-plan offices, cubicles and conference rooms.

The Cage had balconies on the third floor which gave a good overview of the mice in their million hordes as they went to do . . . I had no idea what they did. When I checked them out, I saw Tyrel Johnson leaning casually on the railing and looking down at us. He spotted me looking up and beckoned.

I took the lift.

When I joined him at the railing I pointed at the towel around my head and Johnson smiled.

'Everyone has to wear one on their first day,' he said, and introduced me to my fellow Vogon Leo Hoyt, a white guy with darkening blond hair and cornflower blue eyes. He was wearing a credible navy M&S suit that had almost, but not quite, been tailored to fit.

15

We shook hands; his grip was firm and smile sincerely welcoming. I was instantly suspicious.

'Are we going to have a briefing?' I asked, which made Leo laugh.

'This isn't the police,' he said. 'We don't get briefings here. We have information dispersal conclaves.'

'Really?'

'Oh yeah,' said Leo, and grinned.

'Do we get one of those then?' I asked.

'Somebody is up to no good,' said Johnson.

'How do you know?'

'There are unexplained gaps in the security logs,' said Johnson. 'Just a few seconds here and there. Leo found them.'

Leo looked suitably smug.

'A glitch?' I asked Leo, who shook his head.

'They looked like deliberate breaks,' he said, hesitated and then admitted, 'I can't find a pattern though.'

'I want you to work the employee side,' said Johnson.

'Interviews?' I asked.

'No,' said Johnson. 'For the first couple of days I want you to wander around and stick your nose where it doesn't belong. Get to know some mice and get a feel for the place. Let them get used to seeing you around, and after a week or so you'll be invisible.'

Especially when I could take the towel off.

Before I headed back to rejoin the mice I asked

16

Johnson whether he'd worn a towel on his first day.

'What do you think?' he asked, and I decided to treat that as a rhetorical question.

I started with the emergency exits, memorising positions and routes so that in the event of an emergency I would know where to guide people out. It's one of those weird truths you learn early on as police that quite a high percentage of the public have all the survival instincts of a moth in a candle factory. They run the wrong way, they refuse to move, some will run towards the danger, and others will instantly whip out their phones and take footage.

While I was studying the exits I took a moment to check the alarm systems that guarded them and tried to see if they were vulnerable to tampering either from the inside or out.

One place I couldn't check were the offices on the top two floors of Betelgeuse, the northernmost building. As far as I could tell, there was only one point of access for these – an enclosed skyway on the fourth floor that bridged Platina Street. Two similar skyways on the first floor gave access to the offices on the lower floors, but this one was different. For a start, it was painted a sinister clean room white, had tinted windows and terminated in a plain blue door with a security lock that not only required the correct ID card but also a pass-code as well.

'It's a secret project,' said Victor when we had lunch together.

'No shit, Sherlock,' said Everest, talking around a mouthful of pizza.

I'd met Victor and Everest during my initial wanderings. Everest had marched up to me in one of the multifunction floating workspaces and demanded to know whether I'd got my job because I was black.

'Of course,' I said, just to see what the reaction would be. 'I didn't even have to interview.'

He was a stout white man, heavy around the hips, face adorned with the traditional round glasses and neck beard and topped with a mass of curly brown hobbit hair. He was dressed in a purple OCP T-shirt, baggy khaki shorts, black socks and sandals. His ID card was purple and yellow and gave his name as Harvey Window.

'Told you,' he said to his companion – a short, round white woman with small blue eyes and brown hair cut into a short back and sides. She ignored him and held out a hand.

'My name is Victor, pleased to meet you.' There was a stress on the name that said *here is a clue, let's see if you get one*. I shook his hand and said I was pleased to meet him too.

'This is Everest,' said Victor.

Everest held out a clammy hand for me to shake and then, after the merest clasp, snatched it back.

'Let me make things very clear,' he said. 'We are

the company assets and you are here to keep us safe. Not for your benefit, but for our benefit.'

'I live but to serve,' I said, which he seemed to accept at face value.

'Good,' he said and, turning, walked away.

'Everest?' I asked. 'Not Gates or Bill or Money?'

Victor shrugged.

'Someone called him Update once and we almost had to call the police,' said Victor and sniggered.

'Really?' I asked. 'The police?'

'Really,' said Victor. 'He tried to take a bite out of an Asset Co-ordinator and if Tyson hadn't grabbed him I think he would have drawn blood.'

'Tyson?'

'Your boss,' she said. 'Tyrel.'

'Victor!' Everest called from across the room. 'We have that thing – remember.'

'Don't worry,' said Victor as he turned to follow Everest. 'We're the freaky ones – everybody else is normal.'

Later I'd made a point of hanging out on one of the balconies overlooking the Cage until Victor and Everest turned up for lunch, although of course at the Serious Cybernetics Corporation, lunchtime was an illusion. Once I clocked where they were sitting I wandered down and bumped into them accidentally.

The Cage had a truly mad array of snack machines, all of them completely free – the better to encourage the mice not to wander beyond the confines of the office. They were wonderfully varied and some, like the doughnut machine with the art deco stylings, were either antiques or reproductions of antiques.

I'd been boringly conventional and had a tuna and sweetcorn baguette from a machine adorned with a reproduction of Delacroix's *Liberty Being Too Busy Leading the People to Pull Her Dress Back Up* across its front. Victor had a box of sushi from a genuine Japanese automated sushi dispenser and Everest had a pepperoni pizza from a machine that purported to make it from scratch.

He stared at me as I sat down and continued to stare at me as I said hello and for about a minute after I started talking to Victor, and then went back to his pizza as if I didn't exist. Occasionally he would take a series of precise slurps from a can of Mountain Dew, and he said nothing until I asked Victor about the top floors of Betelgeuse.

'Those are the Bambleweeny floors,' he said. 'And off limits.'

'What do they do up there?' I asked.

'Why do you want to know?'

'It's easier to guard something when you know what it is,' I said.

Everest's brow wrinkled as he thought about my answer.

'If Tyson didn't brief you,' he said, 'then you

don't need to know.' Which showed a charming faith in the wisdom of hierarchies.

Victor giggled and put his hand over his mouth.

I gave him a quizzical look and he returned a little shake of his head and rolled his eyes at Everest who was diligently finishing his pizza.

'It's a mystery,' said Victor.

One way in which us Vogons differed from run-of-the-mill mice was that we had a definite shift pattern, so come five Johnson insisted I clock out.

'Tired people don't do their jobs properly,' he said, demonstrating one of the reasons why he'd left the police.

I took my towel with me and showed it to Beverley when I got home.

'And you wore that all day?' she asked.

'To be honest, I forgot I was wearing it after a while,' I said.

Eventually it got incorporated into Beverley's improvised Bulge support system but only after it had been washed. I said this was great, because now I would always know where my towel was, but that got me yet another blank look.

The next day I turned up for work sans towel, but I kept the suit. I managed to ingratiate myself with a number of mice and Victor invited me to join one of the floating role-playing games that assembled in one of the satellite conference rooms accessible from the Cage.

'*Metamorphosis Alpha*,' said Victor, when I asked what we were playing. Which turned out to be an ancient game from the 1970s with a horrible resolution mechanic but I'm not a purist about these things. Besides being fun, it was a useful way to get to know my fellow mice – the better to guard them from harm, or themselves.

Leo Hoyt spotted us playing in the corner of the Cage and came over to glower at me, and then walked away shaking his head.

'I bet he prefers *World of Darkness*,' said Victor.

Everest made a rude noise.

There were rumours that Terrence Skinner sometimes sat in on these pick-up RPG sessions, although Victor and Everest said he'd never sat down with them. A lot of the mice didn't so much admire Skinner as worship the ground he walked on. He was famous for being *the* dull tech billionaire, the one whose company InCon nobody could remember the name of, the one that had made his fortune behind the scenes and wasn't blowing it on Mars rockets, sewage systems and genetically modified rice.

I wasn't introduced to the Great Man immediately – that was not how things worked at the SCC. Instead Terrence Skinner practised what he called 'management by walking around' which involved him striding through the various cubicle farms, trailing personal assistants and nervous project facilitators in his wake.

He tried to drop in on me unexpectedly on my third day while I was hot-desking in the Haggunenons' room. You could hear him coming twenty metres away, but Johnson had briefed me so I looked suitably surprised when he materialised at my shoulder.

'What are you doing?' he asked.

'I'm checking yesterday's entry logs for anomalies,' I said.

Terrence Skinner was a tall, rangy man with widely spaced blue eyes, thinning blond hair and thin lips. He wore an expensive black linen blazer over a faded blue *Hitchhiker's Guide to the Galaxy* T-shirt with a picture of a smiley face with lolling tongue and hands covering its eyes. The words *Don't Panic* were written in large friendly letters next to the face.

'What kind of anomalies?' He had a strong, almost comical, Australian accent. An affectation, I knew, because I'd seen a TED Talk from five years previously when his accent was much less pronounced and almost hidden beneath a layer of West Coast tech-speak.

I was actually looking to see if there were any breaks in the CCTV coverage that corresponded with any particular person entering the building, only I wasn't about to announce that to Skinner's entourage – just in case.

'Anything irregular, double entries, duplicate IDs – that sort of thing,' I said.

'Do you think somebody's sneaking in?'

23

'It's always possible, sir,' I said. 'No system is foolproof.'

'Not when there are so many inventive fools, eh?' said Skinner who, I noticed, didn't invite me to call him Terry or even Mr Skinner.

I gave a convincing little chuckle, because it never hurts to ingratiate yourself with the boss.

'Yes, sir,' I said.

'I'm pretty certain that we have algorithms looking for that sort thing.'

'You never know,' I said.

A tall, athletic white woman dressed in a light-weight suit, one of the team of bodyguards that guarded Skinner in shifts, gave me a curious look before returning to her scanning-the-cubicles-for-lethal-threats routine.

You want to start with the snack machines, lady, I thought. That's an early death from Type 2 diabetes right there.

Skinner turned to the woman.

'I feel safer already,' he said, gave me a friendly nod and off he swept.

I asked Johnson about the bodyguards when I handed in the results of my anomaly search.

'Somebody tried to kill him in California,' he said. 'So he hired some specialist security.'

'Who was it tried to kill him?'

'It was just a carjacking,' said Johnson. 'But he got paranoid and wanted the extra reassurance. It's the fashionable thing to do in California – or so I'm told.' He glanced down at the printout I'd done for him. 'Anything tasty?'

I said as far as I could tell nobody was sneaking in.

Johnson grunted.

'They're sure it was a carjacking?' I asked.

Johnson gave me a look.

'Who?' he asked.

'The American police.'

'Why do you care?' he asked.

'What if it wasn't a carjacking?' I said. 'What if it was a proper assassination attempt?'

'You think Google's out to get him?'

'He thinks it's serious enough, doesn't he? Why else did he get the bodyguards?'

'He has a personal masseuse, you know,' said Johnson.

'It might be a security threat,' I said.

'You really are fresh out of the Job, aren't you?'

'It might be though, mightn't it?'

Johnson sighed.

'The personal security of Mr Skinner is not our concern,' said Johnson. 'We're here for the premises and the mice. And somebody is sneaking around behind our back – I can feel it.'

'Gut instinct?'

Johnson waved his hand at his office door.

'Go play with the mice, Peter,' he said. 'Find me a rat.'

And just to prove that the private sector wasn't

that different from the police, I found the rat the very next day – entirely by chance.

I'd taken to swinging past the fourth floor skyway at random intervals. If Johnson had asked, I would have told him that its forbidden nature would attract the most rats. I really hoped he didn't ask, because it was a terrible excuse and the truth was I was dying to know what the secret might be.

A series of team meetings and high-level conference calls were scheduled for that afternoon, to coincide with morning on the West Coast of America. With most of the management tied up, the rest of the mice took the opportunity to skive off. If I were a rat, I thought, now would be a good time to poke about where I didn't belong. So I headed up to the fourth floor skyway to see if anyone was poking about up there.

I didn't actually expect anyone to be trying to break into the security door in broad daylight, so I was a bit surprised to turn the corner and find someone doing just that.

He was a skinny white man in his twenties, with black hair, long legs in spray-on black jeans and pristine white high tops. White T-shirt tight across his back as he leaned against the blue door – his open palm pressed where I guessed the lock had to be.

I considered letting him break in, but he must have heard me or something because he snapped away from the door and turned to face me. Which is when I recognised him.

'Hello, Jacob,' I said. 'What are you up to this time?'

CHAPTER 2

DECEMBER: RELATIVE CHANGES
IN LIKELINESS

On the west side of Hampstead Heath, up the hill where the houses go for a banker's bonus, there's a cluster of terraces at the bottom of the depression. It used to be a malarial swamp until it was drained by the creation of the nearby pond. During the Regency some bright spark dubbed it the Vale of Health, either in a cynical attempt to sell houses or as an ironic joke – nobody knows for sure. Either way the name has stuck until this day and the place exists as a little bubble of rather tasty Regency and Victorian-era terraces pushing into Hampstead Heath. It has what they call 'a village atmosphere' in that the houses are expensive and full of incomers and you have to walk a long way up a steep hill to get to a bus stop. On the eastern edge of the village is a rectangle of scrubby gravel and tarmac half the size of a football pitch where the showmen park up for the winter. They were the reason that I was dragged from my nice warm Bev and forced to drive across the river on a cold, foggy Wednesday morning a month earlier.

The showmen, like a lot of people who live on the edges of polite *Mail on Sunday*-reading society, have a strong connection to the old traditions and the old wisdoms. They live on the fringes of the demi-monde, which comprises the magical, the magic adjacent and, occasionally, people who wandered into the wrong pub and decided they liked the ambience.

If it wasn't for these Vale of Health showmen remembering to propitiate the Goddess of the River Fleet every midsummer, the whole area could easily go back to being a malarial swamp. At least that's what Bev's sister Fleet said the last time me and Bev were round her house for dinner. And she should know, given she's the goddess of the local river.

Beverley had of course asked what kind of propitiation, because she'd got a Kia from the New Malden Conservation Society the year before last and was always looking to see if her sisters could top that.

'Just the usual,' Fleet had said. 'Alcohol in large amounts.'

The number of showmen wintering at the Vale of Health has been steadily declining in the last thirty years, but there were still enough to fill the site and force me to park outside the gate on the access road. This being Hampstead, the chances of some neighbourhood busybody phoning in and making a complaint were high.

Henry 'Wicked' Collins was waiting for me by

the gate. Behind him the caravans were lumpy grey shapes with an occasional rectangle of warm light marking a window. Sound was muffled by the fog and we could have been standing in a field somewhere remote and outside the M25.

Wicked was a blunt little white man in his sixties, wearing a flat cap and a big camel-hair coat. He grinned when he saw me and stepped forward to shake my hand. His palm was rough and calloused.

'The lady at 999 said I might have to wait a week,' he said.

'You know we turn out for you, Wicked,' I said. 'Even on a Monday morning.'

'Come this way,' said Wicked and I followed him through the blocky shadows to where a big red, green and gold trailer sat on its jacks. I'd been around enough fairgrounds by then to know an attraction when I saw one boxed up for travel. Because it's never wise to pass up free advertising it had BERNOULLI'S MIGHTY ORGAN written across the side in big circus lettering. Beneath the title was a cartouche with a picture of organ pipes in gold, red and blue.

'A fairground organ,' I said.

'More than that,' said Wicked. 'This is your actual Gavioli. Originally made for Prince Albert, or so they say.'

It had to weigh five tons at the very least.

'They obviously didn't steal this,' I said. 'Did they?'

'If I could just draw your attention to this lock here,' said Wicked, and pointed to a lock a third of the way up the side of the box. I realised that the side itself was segmented so that the bottom third could fold down and the remainder could swing up. Like many old-fashioned fairground attractions, its travelling box also formed part of its superstructure.

I peered at the lock and asked what was wrong with it.

'It's been jimmied, hasn't it?' said Wicked.

I pulled out my pen torch and had a closer look. The keyhole was blocked by the brass sheet part of the lock mechanism. Forcibly displaced to the left, I guessed, dragging the deadbolt with it and out of its socket. I knew this lock-breaking technique and it wasn't something you could do with a set of picks or a drill.

I took the glove off my right hand and rested the tips of my fingers against the lock. The metal was cold but bearable, and I breathed out slowly and let my mind go as blank as possible.

Vestigia is the trace left behind by the supernatural; there's more of it about than you might think but you have to be trained to spot it. After that it's just a matter of practice.

I felt a sharp little jolt, like a static electric shock, and a sherbet-flavoured fizz. Somebody had definitely used magic to force the lock, but not with a spell I recognised.

'What's behind here?'

'I thought you'd never ask,' said Wicked.

He had to undo heavy-duty latches at each end of the trailer, and the siding was a couple of centimetres thick and heavy enough that I had to help him let it down safely. Once down, the siding formed a decorative apron covering the trailer's undercarriage, wheels and jacks. It was painted in the traditional baroque showman style, all gilt and vivid blues, greens and reds. The bottom of the organ was revealed, the lower sections of the pipes with their mouths gaping silently in a row. There was a series of horizontal snare drums mounted in recesses and what looked like a mechanical glockenspiel fitted below the centre of the pipes.

'Was there any other damage?' I asked.

There was a row of evenly spaced keyholes about fifteen centimetres above the bottom of the trailer. Looking closely, I saw they each served a large shallow drawer, as if of an enormous desk, the seams and handles cunningly hidden by gilt embellishments. I touched each in turn and on each I felt the same tiny shock I had with the main lock.

Wicked bent down and carefully pulled open the leftmost drawer. Inside, it was subdivided into compartments. Each was tightly filled by a stack of heavy cards roughly twenty centimetres per side. They were bound like a cartoon Christmas present by beige muslin tape tied into a bow at the top. Wicked pointed to an empty compartment at the back of the drawer.

'That's what they stole,' he said.

'What was it?' I asked.

Wicked pulled one of the stacks out of its compartment and untied the bow. The words BOHEMIAN RHAPSODY were written in felt tip on the top card. Wicked lifted it to show how it was attached at one end to the next card, and that to the next so that the stack folded up like an accordion. The card stock was heavy, expensive and yellowing with age. Each card had a pattern of holes and slots drilled through it.

'Looks just like a punch card, right?' said Wicked.

'What's a punch card?' I asked.

It all started with a French weaver, Joseph Marie Jacquard, who invented a way to automatically change the patterns on a loom by means of big cards with holes in them. These were linked together to form a sequence and, *voila*, everyone gets to wear a fancy shirt. *C'est très bon.*

We'd retreated into the warmth of Wicked's caravan for tea and history.

'A loom is a complicated bit of kit,' said Wicked. 'So if you can control a loom, why not a piano or an organ?'

The caravan was a nearly new Sprite Quattro, with the front end converted into an office by the removal of one of the sofas and the addition of stacked ranks of storage bins that blocked out the left-hand windows. As the guest I got the remaining sofa, while Wicked leant against the sink. The fog was still heavy enough that I could have used my reflection in the front window to shave.

Given that the goal of every entertainment entrepreneur is to eliminate all those expensive and temperamental performers, it wasn't long before some bright spark of an organ maker applied the technology to music. Anselme Gavioli, of the famous Gavioli family, patented the system in 1892. But there were already instruments such as the Bernoulli's Mighty Organ that used the mechanism. The stack of cards was called a music book. The cards unfurled and ran through a thing called a key frame, which read the slots and holes and opened valves in sequence, which drove the pipes, drums and cymbals of the mechanical organ.

Mechanical music for a steam-powered age.

'And a punch card?' I asked.

Wicked waved a rich tea biscuit at me.

'I can't believe you don't know what a punch card is,' he said. 'I thought it was part of geek culture.'

'Depends on the geek, don't it?' I said.

'In my old life,' said Wicked, 'when I was a student, I used to programme computers with them.'

Because that's how they did it back in the days when computers filled rooms and the Lunar Lander touched down using hardware less powerful than my mum's thermostat. Wicked used to write his program out by hand and then use a machine that translated the instructions into lots of holes in lots of cards which were then literally 'compiled' and fed into an optical reader. And, behold, your program ran and you got the results you wanted – often as early as the tenth or eleventh time you tried it.

'If you were really careful,' said Wicked.

I thought we might be digressing a bit, and asked him whether this was really relevant to the theft.

'I just couldn't believe you didn't know,' he said. 'But also it is a little bit related. The music book that was stolen was called *The Enchantress of Numbers.*'

That actually prodded something in my memory.

'Ada Lovelace,' I said.

'You're not a total loss, then,' said Wicked.

Ada Lovelace, daughter of Lord Byron, mathematician and, reputedly, the first ever computer programmer.

'So a song about her?' I asked. 'Who by?'

'We don't know whether it's a song or not,' said Wicked, 'let alone who wrote it, although my money's on Charles Babbage.'

Who was famous for designing, but failing to build, the first ever universal computing machine. A monster of gears, wheels and drive chains that would have ushered in the information age a hundred years early – assuming you could get it to work.

'How can you not know whether it's a song?' I asked. 'Haven't you played it?'

'Can't do that,' said Wicked. 'Wrong number of keys.'

Because each organ was rated as having a certain number of keys.

'Old Benny out there is 84 keys,' said Wicked. 'Others are 101 keys or 112 keys or more. And that's without getting into whether it's a keyed or keyless system. You can't run a music book made for 84 keys in a 112-key organ, or vice versa.'

'So, how many keys does the stolen book have?'

'137,' said Wicked. 'Which, as I'm sure you've spotted, is a prime number.'

Which I totally hadn't, but I felt my geek cred had been impugned enough for one day.

'So, who has a 137-key organ?' I asked

'Nobody,' said Wicked. 'That's the mystery.'

Burglary, which is defined in law as entering someone's gaff and nicking stuff, is a pain to investigate. Violent crime often involves poor impulse control and people having a go because someone had it coming, and frequently happens in front of CCTV or witnesses. Burglary is generally a crime of opportunity and stealth, and worse – it's done by strangers. Most men are murdered by their mates and most women are murdered by their partners. Most burglaries are done by someone who couldn't pick their victim out of a line-up.

The best scheme the Met ever had for recovering stolen goods was setting up a fake fencing operation and arresting anyone stupid enough to try and flog their ill-gotten gains. Somehow, I didn't think that approach was going to work in this case.

On the other hand, this burglary had obviously been precise, targeted and probably to order.

Although I'd sprung for a SOCO to dust for fingerprints, I didn't expect my burglar to leave any viable prints. And I wasn't disappointed.

'They wore gloves,' said the SOCO. 'Based on the pattern, probably made from kidskin.'

The pattern of smudges was instructive, though. Judging by where they clustered, it was clear that the burglar opened each drawer in turn until they found what they were looking for. There was no sign that they touched anything else – they certainly hadn't rifled through any of the other music books.

This told me that they'd known the name of the music book they wanted, where it was stored generally, but not the precise drawer.

Once the SOCO had signed off on the site I asked Wicked whether anyone had recently inquired about *The Enchantress of Numbers* or even about music books in general.

'Somebody wanted to buy Bernoulli's Mighty

Organ, the whole shebang, including the music books,' said Wicked. 'Said they wanted to ship it to America for a theme park.'

'When was this?' I asked.

We were back in Wicked's caravan, this time for coffee and witness statements. I had my notebook out, which Wicked eyed with the deeply engrained cultural suspicion of the travelling man.

'Last month,' said Wicked and, when prompted, gave me the exact date and time.

'Did he say which theme park it was for?'

'He was talking fast and I really wasn't listening,' said Wicked. 'There was something shifty about him, so when he told me to name my price I told him two million cash up front. Sterling, not dollars.'

'And what do you think it's really worth?' I said. Not two million, that was for certain.

'Technically it's priceless,' said Wicked. 'But I doubt I'd get more than fifty grand for it – not these days.

'Anyway, he thought about it. We haggled for a bit, but I really didn't like him.'

'Why not?'

'There was something off about him, but I couldn't say what,' said Wicked.

'Something uncanny?' I asked.

'Maybe,' said Wicked. This went into my notebook as *Fae?*

'Who did he say he was working for?' I asked.

38

'Just a mo,' said Wicked, and he pulled out a brown leather wallet that barely closed around the amount of random stuff wedged into it. He emptied out various compartments and sorted through the pile of visitor cards, special offers, credit cards, his NHS card, Oyster card and a special offer on Audible that had expired a year before.

'Damn,' said Wicked. 'I meant to use that.'

After a bit of sorting he found and handed over a visitor's card, plain black letters on thick white card stock. It read *Mitchel West, Acquisitions, Guffland Entertainment* – followed by a phone number, URL, email and Twitter address. I made a note of the numbers and dropped the card into a paper evidence envelope – because you never know your luck.

I got a description from Wicked, which amounted to average-sized youngish white guy with brown, possibly light brown, hair. He was dressed in a casual navy blazer, a long khaki coat that was possibly Burberry, and even if it wasn't it seemed posh to Wicked.

'But fake posh,' said Wicked. 'He said that since I was asking so much I should at least show him the goods. Which I did. Including the storage areas.'

Had Mitchel West shown a particular interest in the music books?

'Not that I noticed,' said Wicked. 'Not that I was paying attention.'

He had noticed the silver Audi A6 that Mitchel West had arrived in.

'Still had that new car smell,' said Wicked. 'Wafted out when he opened the door.'

He hadn't noticed it enough to remember the licence plate number – nobody ever does.

I finished up the crime reporting checklist, gave Wicked a crime number and promised to get in touch if there were any developments. Had this been an ordinary robbery, that is about as far as it would have gone. Not counting my suspension, I'd been out of normal operational policing for over three years, but I'd noticed that things had definitely got tighter while I wasn't looking. Still, the obviously magical nature of the burglary meant that I had to follow it up.

I drove up the steep lane that connected with East Heath Road and looked around for CCTV – nothing. Libertarians and criminals complain about the surveillance state when they see a camera. Police officers complain about it when they don't. I'd been hoping to catch that brand-new silver Audi so I could run its number plates, but the nearest reliable CCTV was at South End Green and there were too many alternative routes out of the area. For a major crime you would have put a team on looking anyway, however futile. But this was burglary – wholesale crime that has to be solved at a discount.

Still, the burglar had used magic. Which made it my business.

Five minutes on my phone had determined that Guffland Entertainment was an entirely imaginary company, and while there were some Mitchel Wests on Facebook and Twitter none of them seemed likely candidates. I had another look at the card and was just wondering whether it was worth breaking out my own fingerprint kit and giving it a quick dust, when I noticed that there was something printed on the reverse. It read in tiny letters *PrettyPrint*. As my old governor used to say, a copper's one true comfort in life is that criminals are mostly thicker than pig shit.

Another five minutes on my phone confirmed that not only were PrettyPrint a chain of high-street printers, but that they were nice and small – five branches in the Greater London area, and the nearest one down in Old Street.

I called my governor, Detective Chief Inspector Thomas Nightingale, to let him know what I was up to and ask whether Gavioli was in our files.

'Not that I know of,' he said. In the background I could hear hammering and shouting. Obviously work on the upgrades at the Folly had started. 'I'll pass it on to Harold and see what he knows.'

Professor Harold Postmartin, D.Phil, FRS, was our tame historian and archivist. Even if he couldn't dig anything up he was bound to be interested in a connection to the Gaviolis – obscure historical connections were a major passion.

Call finished, I made a note of my current actions in my daybook and set out.

Not wanting to slowly survey the permanent roadworks at Kings Cross, I went east and then down the New North Road. I couldn't find parking near Old Street roundabout so I slipped into Shoreditch and found a place behind the Charles Square Estate and cut through to Old Street.

PrettyPrint was jammed in between a wholesale fashion jewellers and a kebab shop in a surprisingly undeveloped one-storey row of retail units. It was painted the mandatory blue and white of all print shops, which I've always presumed is to make sure the lumpy grey copiers and printing machines fit in with the décor. The young Asian man in the blue company T-shirt looked pleased to see me for all of the five seconds it took me to identify myself, before passing me on to the manager. This was a painfully thin black woman in her early thirties, who gave me a disapproving look. Not disapproving of anything in particular, you understand, just routine scepticism. For some reason I've been getting it all my life, so I've learnt to ignore it.

'Can I help you?' she said.

I explained about the fake cards and how they'd been used in the commission of a burglary.

'So?' she asked.

So could she look up any details of the

customer in question, you know, so I could catch them.

'I'm not sure I should,' she said, and cocked her head to one side. 'Commercial confidentiality, and that.'

I pointed out that technically since their work had been used in furtherance of a criminal offence then they were, technically, guilty of aiding and abetting under the Accessories and Abettors Act 1861.

'You're kidding me, right?' said the manager. 'Eighteen sixty-one and you just know that off the top of your head.'

'It's my job,' I said, although actually I'd looked it up in my Blackstone's law manual when I stopped for a coffee on the way. It pays to be prepared.

'Only,' said the manager, 'we just print stuff. We don't know what it's used for.'

'But now I have informed you that it was so used,' I said. 'So if the perpetrator does it again you will be knowingly aiding and abetting.'

'Do you normally talk like this?' she asked.

'Like what?'

'In so far as the party of the first part is . . . is . . . whatever,' she said.

'Can you at least tell me whether the card was printed here?' I said.

She made me wait, but I knew by the quirk of her lips upwards that she was going to help. She took the card, still in its evidence bag, and sashayed over to a computer near the back of the shop. After poking at the keyboard for a minute, she reported that they'd definitely printed a batch of calling cards with those details.

I looked around and found a compact CCTV unit covering the front counter.

'Do you know what day and time they came to pick it up?' I asked, and the manager gave me the date and time. When I asked to see the CCTV footage for that period she didn't seem surprised or reluctant – I think she was enjoying the excitement. Once they've established that you're not going to arrest them or their relatives, people like to help the police. Especially those doing dull, low-paid jobs in retail. The CCTV was digital storage – you'd be amazed how many shops are still using VHS tape – and the manager read the time off the computer and put an hour each way on my USB.

'I don't suppose they paid by card, did they?' I asked.

'Yeah, they did actually,' said the manager. 'Does that help?'

Wrangling personal details out of a bank takes time and paperwork, fortunately not mine, so it wasn't until Friday morning that I headed bravely beyond the North Circular to Palmers Green and the modest first-floor flat of one Jacob Astor – probably not his real name. This turned out to be the top half of an Edwardian terrace on a side street off Aldermans Hill. It had been cold and grey when I set off, although occasionally the sun would peep out for a quick gloat before buggering off back behind a cloud for a sly cigarette – or something. It wasn't freezing, but I was definitely considering seeing if I couldn't dig out my thermals.

The door was an original arts and crafts affair with a long leaded-glass rectangle of green, yellow and blue above a plain brass letter box. There were two electric doorbell buttons fastened to the jamb. Both had the remains of masking tape labels stuck below them, but time and weather had obliterated the text. On the assumption that the top bell would ring the first floor, I gave it a long hard push. There was the faint sound of a bell from inside but I couldn't tell whether it was up or downstairs.

In a spirit of scientific inquiry I pressed the lower button. This time the bell was loud, annoying and definitely on the ground floor. I gave it another couple of long rings until I saw, through the coloured glass panel, an interior door opening and a vaguely human shape emerge.

'I'm coming!' shouted a woman from inside and then, distinctly, came the sound of a small child gearing up for a good wail.

The door opened to reveal a compact Asian woman in her late twenties with a dark southern complexion, and dressed in a blue sweatshirt with ASK ME ABOUT HORSERADISH in white letters across the front. In her arms was an overwrought toddler in a green romper suit whose tantrum paused briefly while he eyed me up suspiciously. The woman followed suit.

'No,' she said. 'I don't want a personal friend in Jesus.'

I showed her my warrant card.

'But have you let the Metropolitan Police into your heart?' I asked.

The child screwed up its face in preparation for a resumption, so I stuck out my tongue, which has often worked with various cousins in the past. Woman and child gave me identical looks of astonishment – seen like this, they were definitely related. So I was guessing she was the mother.

'Do you know if your neighbours are in?' I asked.

She said she thought he was at work but, when I asked, didn't know where that was. I left her my card, asked her to phone me if he came back and then had to reassure her that there was probably nothing to worry about.

'We just want to chat,' I said. 'It's just routine.'

Then I scarpered before the child could start up again.

I had considered forcing the door, but if I did that magically it would leave a trace that Jacob Astor, who might well have been a practitioner, would notice when he got home. I could kick the door in manually, but I would need authorisation from a senior officer for that. And a broken door would be pretty bloody obvious, too.

Fortunately, I had a fairly good idea where Jacob Astor was gainfully employed because he'd been getting regular salary payments from the same source for the last two months. I'd tried his home address first because your workplace is more likely to phone and warn you that the police have come round than your neighbours are. At least in a London suburb like Palmers Green.

I got back in my car and headed down Green Lanes towards the West End, St James's Square and the London Library.

In 1840 Thomas Carlyle, the famous Scottish philosopher, polymath and slavery enthusiast, upset that the British Library wouldn't let him take any books home, called for the establishment of a subscription library on the model already pioneered in Leeds and Nottingham. The result was the London Library, which moved to St James's Square in 1845 and, two major extensions and some light bombing later, it remains one of the best book collections in the world.

St James's was your classic posh Georgian square where the houses were once owned by the landed gentry, but by now the torch had passed to multinationals, think tanks and gentlemen's clubs. A blue plaque on the front of a neighbouring house read:

ADA
COUNTESS OF
LOVELACE
1815–1852
Pioneer
of Computing
lived here

The Enchantress of Numbers herself.

As a wise man once said – *I believe in coincidence, coincidences happen all the time, but I don't trust coincidences.*

And this was all getting a bit steampunk for my liking. If Jacob Astor turned out to be wearing goggles it was going to go very hard on him indeed.

The London Library had kept the original rusticated Georgian façade, but through the front doors was a cool, misshapen atrium with enough Victorian wood panelling to keep the BBC in period drama sets for about the next decade.

There was a long reception desk of dark wood and glass and a series of tastefully retrofitted barrier gates to control the punters. I showed the receptionist my warrant card straight away. She was a plump, mousey white woman dressed in a black pullover and matching skirt. There were flashes of silver at her wrists and a heavy thumb ring on her left hand. However, she did have the traditional pair of reading glasses attached to a sturdy cloth lanyard hanging around her neck –

presumably these were compulsory attire for all librarians.

She said her name was Susan. She had a middle-class, Home Counties accent.

'Do you have a guy called Jacob Astor working here?' I asked.

Susan narrowed her eyes.

'Yes,' she said. 'I believe so.'

'Do you know where he works?'

'I can find out,' she said, and reached for the phone but I asked her not to. She looked puzzled but put the handset down.

'Can you make a guess at where he works?' I asked.

She said probably on the first floor, in conservation.

'I need you to take me there right now,' I said.

She hesitated, but then asked a nearby member of staff to cover while she took me up.

'This way,' she said and opened the gate for me.

Susan led me up a short flight of stairs and then to the left, through a set of glass doors marked ART ROOM and into a room with some rather nice imitation art deco styling. Here the bookcases were made of a varnished light brown wood and we swerved around the corner of a stack into another corridor where we stopped in front of a lift.

'The main lift in the entrance is much busier,' said Susan.

This lift was modern, with stain-resistant

brushed steel panelling, but was fortunate enough not to have a prim female voice informing us that the doors were about to close or that we were about to alight on the second floor.

We emerged into modern, white-painted corridors with black detailing and frosted internal windows and threaded our way past another random stairwell until we came to a heavy fire door labelled OFFICES, ACQUISITIONS and COLLECTION CARE.

Susan used a smart card on a reader located at convenient wheelchair height and opened the door. Beyond the door, the crisp, modern styling was slowly being swamped by the inevitable overspill of books and papers that have plagued libraries since Alexander the Great decided to give historians a really good place to write up his exploits. We passed through a narrow corridor and the gap between two black enamelled ceiling-height steel bookcases to a vaguely clear area with a couple of modern desks. Nobody was about.

'I'll see if anyone's in Conservation,' said Susan, and headed into a room further on. 'Jacob!' I heard her call. 'There's someone to see you.'

'Who is it?' said a voice behind me. Male, young, North American.

I turned to find a slim white guy in his mid-twenties dressed in jeans and a green jumper. He had a blandly handsome face with black hair, high cheekbones and just a hint of an epicanthic fold in the corner of his light brown eyes. He was carrying a pile of hardback books with scuffed brown covers.

'Jacob Astor?' I said. 'My name is . . .'

But before I could get to the identification part, he threw the books straight at my face. And while I was reacting to that, he knocked me down with an *impellopalma* spell. It was as fast and neat and precise as my governor would have liked. It was also beautifully judged – just enough to knock me on my arse, but without serious injury.

Susan was making little incomprehensible noises behind me as I clambered to my feet. Jacob Astor, if that was his real name, was running back up the narrow corridor towards the security door. He had to slow down long enough to press the open button and that allowed me to close the gap. As he went through, Jacob glanced back and his eyes widened as he saw me bearing down on him. He tried to slam the door in my face, but I cast a straight *impello* that knocked it open again.

Oh yeah, I thought. *I can has magic spelz too.*

Jacob looked shocked, but his surprise didn't seem to slow him down as he banged through the next set of fire doors, ignored the stairs and hung a right – back towards where Susan had brought me up in the lift.

I skidded to a halt just short of the turn and cautiously stuck my head around the corner. Just in time to catch a flicker of movement at the far

51

end of the corridor where it opened up into a room full of shelving.

I wanted to pull out my phone and get some uniforms to block off the exits. But this was Westminster, the busiest Borough Command in the Met. And these days response officers were as rare as hen's teeth. Even if I could wrangle a couple of cars, Jacob the sprinter would be long gone. So I charged after him in the vain hope he'd be too busy running to smack me in the face again. Or possibly something worse. But I tried not to think about that.

'Stop, police!' I shouted, on the basis that one of these days it was going to have the right effect.

The library stacks were ceiling high and so close together that the books kept brushing my shoulders. Away from the white paint and frosted glass of the offices it was suddenly dim and yellow and closed in. I couldn't see him down the first aisle, so I did a sharp right on instinct and was rewarded by the sight of Jacob's back. I flicked a water balloon at his head, but I think he must have sensed it coming because he ducked and the clear globe of water went over him to splash against a row of books.

Jacob ducked left and shouted.

'Watch the books, watch the books for Chrissake!'

'Stop running,' I shouted back as I skidded around the corner after him, 'and we won't have to!'

The little wanker threw another *impello-palma* at

me, but I already had my shield up and his spell fizzed and died half a metre from my face. I've gone toe to toe with some seriously dangerous magical fuckers, and if I have not necessarily emerged victorious then at least I emerged alive.

Jacob was fast and assured and I was pretty certain he was holding back.

Ahead I saw him grab the side of a stack and swing himself around another corner. I followed and found myself clattering down a staircase as narrow and steep as a gangway on a ship.

Down we went into PHILOLOGY & FICTION (S–Z), another room full of stacks with a scuffed floor and low ceilings. Jacob had stopped trying to delay me and was concentrating on zigzagging his way through the shelving and down yet another flight of stairs. I wasn't gaining, but I was keeping up even as he dodged through more shelving. I was fine with that, because sooner or later he was going to have to exit the building. And once he was in the open I was going to have him.

He went left at ART: SCULPTURE (CONT), through another fire door and we were back in the modern refitted office section. One floor down I guessed, but I might have got turned around somewhere. Then into a 1930s stairwell where we both ended up doing that fake parkour thing of grabbing the banister and swinging around the bend. Down past another landing with my DMs slapping on the marble risers as I tried to keep Jacob in sight.

Finally the ground floor and a sign pointing at an emergency exit.

I came around another corner in time to see Jacob slam another fire door closed before I could get to it. Stupidly I pushed at it before I realised it was code-locked like the offices upstairs. Through the vertical glass strip in the door I saw Jacob traverse a short hall and push open an external door. He didn't look back.

It was a fire door, so it had by law to have an emergency door release. I found it halfway down the wall and jabbed impatiently at the plastic cover but the door still would not open. I put my palm on it level with the locking mechanism, and there it was – the same static electricity tingle I'd felt on the locks of Bernoulli's Mighty Organ. We think Jacob used the same spell to jam the locking plate, but we couldn't be sure because I used a slightly over-aggressive *impello* variant to knock the door off its hinges.

It hadn't even hit the ground before I was through the doorway and out the next and into the cold December daylight outside. In front of me was the blank grey slab sides of The White Cube Gallery, to my left along the brick cobbles was a clear run to Duke Street and to the right and around the corner there was an alleyway that led out into Jermyn Street. Jacob could have gone either way, but even if I guessed right he'd still have been long gone.

So much for running him down in the open.

Still, part of being police is knowing when to stop running and start networking.

I pulled out my backup phone, turned it on and called my governor.

'Hi, boss,' I said. 'We have another foreign practitioner.'

Still part of being police is knowing when to
stop running and start networking.

I pulled out my . . . . . . turned it on and
called my governor . . . . . .

electronics?

CHAPTER 3

JANUARY: SOME SHEEP ARE BLACK

'Hello, Jacob,' I said. 'What are you up to
this time?'

His ID badge gave his name as Stephen
Higgins, in black on a pink background, and his
department as Magrathea – models, maquettes
and concept art. He turned smoothly, shifting
his balance and letting his hands fall to his sides
in a deceptively relaxed manner. I remembered
how fast he'd been back at the London Library
and matched his pose.

'I knew you weren't really a cop,' he said.

'Is that so?'

'Whoever heard of a wizard cop?'

'What about the Aurors?' I said.

Jacob and/or Stephen shifted to his left and
watched my reaction. Trapped as he was on the
skyway with a locked door behind him, his tactical
position was poor. If he wasn't going to talk his
way out, he'd have to go for a sudden strike in
the hope that I wouldn't react fast enough.

'Because they're not totally made up – right?'
he said, and shifted his weight back to his right
foot.

'How do you know?' I said. 'Every story has a grain of truth.'

Had this been my normal professional circumstances I would have had him by now. Knocked him down while he was still talking and slapped on the speedcuffs, called for backup and had him in one of the new 'special' cells before you could say 'How's your father' in a bad cockney accent.

But then he'd shut up, get a lawyer, possibly even an American consular official, and I'd never know what he wanted.

I nodded at the door behind him.

'Do you know what's in there?' I asked.

'Do you?' He never took his eyes off me.

'No,' I said.

His eyes narrowed and his posture relaxed a fraction.

'How badly do you want to know?' he asked.

'Can you get in?'

'Maybe,' he said. 'But not today. We're out of time.'

He raised his hands palm out and walked towards me. I put my weight on my back foot, but he kept his hands where I could see them.

'*Pax*,' he said, and opened his mouth to say something, but was interrupted by a muffled *clonk* from the blue door. 'Shit,' he hissed. 'Early.' Then, before I could react, he threw his arms around me and pushed me against the wall. Then, before I could react to *that*, the door opened and the female bodyguard I'd met guarding Terrence Skinner stepped through.

It wasn't until Jacob/Stephen made a guilty little jump away from me that I realised what he was doing. I put my hand on his arm and then snatched it away to sell the illusion, and tried to look like an embarrassed teenager. I suspect I merely looked horribly off balance, which probably served just as well.

The female bodyguard gave me the side eye and pointedly paused until the blue door closed behind her. I caught a glimpse of the edge – it was at least ten centimetres thick and had locking bolts at the top and bottom – and, beyond, a stretch of white corridor.

I nodded to the bodyguard as she walked past and said good morning.

She nodded back but said nothing.

'I'll tell you something for nothing,' said Jacob and/or Stephen. 'Those guys are definitely sus. Right?'

'What should I call you?' I asked. 'Jacob, Stephen, Mr West?'

'Stephen,' he said. 'And you?'

'Peter,' I said.

'Is that your real name?'

'I think me and you should go somewhere to have a chat,' I said. 'Somewhere away from here.'

'Is this a date?'

'You should be so lucky.'

'In that case, let's go somewhere we can get a drink.'

Old Street roundabout is a diamond-shaped circulatory system designed in the late 1960s to thin out the number of cyclists heading in and out of the City. In line with the then-current planning conventions they added a series of mugger-friendly underpasses, an insufficiently wide entrance to Old Street Underground station, and a small shopping arcade lined with urine-attracting beige tile. The big planning fad in those days was to create inaccessible spaces and thus the central island became a jumble of ventilation towers, leaky flat roofs and a delivery access for the arcade.

Fast-forward some decades and the wave of City money heading north met the deep gentrifying current flowing south and created a boom in property prices. Once the proportion of working-class Londoners had fallen to acceptable levels, the roundabout was redeveloped – although no amount of exciting pop-up retail opportunities was going to disguise the seediness of the original arcade. You can say what you like about late-sixties architecture, but when they baked in the ugly they baked it in good.

The man currently known as Stephen led me along the subway under the roundabout, through an archway opposite a branch of Nin Comp Soup and into a short dark corridor painted sci-fi black with stars and planets. This ended in a staircase that led up above ground. Wedged between the cooling shafts and lift machinery towers was a sort of shanty town nightclub built out of painted offcuts from a builder's yard and scavenged furniture. The rain rattled off a haphazard array of tarpaulins stretched between wooden frames and concrete pinions. It was almost totally empty, so we chose seats sheltered under a roof constructed of corrugated Perspex sheets.

I got in two pints of lager, plonked one on the table and sat down opposite Stephen. I raised my glass and said cheers. He held up his pint and delicately rotated it as if assessing its quality.

'Cheers,' he said finally and had a sip.

I followed suit to show willing.

Magic is almost impossible to do when you're pissed, although you can bet many have tried. So drinking with a rival practitioner can be considered, if not a peace offering, then at least a sign that you're not planning to fight them straight away.

'Who trained you?' I asked.

Stephen pulled a face.

'I'd rather not say,' he said.

'And I'd rather not call my contacts in the FBI and ask them to find out,' I said.

Stephen shrugged. Obviously he didn't rate the FBI – I'd have to mention that to my friend Agent Reynolds the next time we chatted.

'And that will make things official, won't it?' I

said. 'Which means I have to arrest you for attempted murder.'

He looked genuinely amused.

'And who am I supposed to have murdered? Sorry – attempted to murder?'

'Me actually,' I said.

'I barely knocked you down,' he said. 'And you'd better not have left water stains on those books now. Although I did like that water spell. I'm going to have to get you to teach me that one.'

'No,' I said. 'Not the bit where you resisted arrest and assaulted a police officer. The bit where you left a lethal demon trap guarding your flat.'

That shut him up, which at least told me that he knew what a demon trap was.

'Wasn't me,' he said.

'Wasn't you what?'

'I don't even know how to make a trap,' he said. 'That knowledge is forbidden.'

'Forbidden by who?'

Stephen pulled a face.

'You know.' He bobbed his head from side to side. 'Forbidden. Did you defuse it?'

'Somebody did,' I said, not wanting to give away anything I didn't have to. 'And I was there.'

'Did you catch its *signare*?' he asked.

Signare is the unique quality that every practitioner gives to their work. Apprentices are influenced by their trainers, and so different magical intuitions and traditions can have distinctive *signare*.

61

'I'm not sure,' I said. 'I was a little bit busy at the time.'

'Was it fishy?'

'It was a bit too amorphous to be fishy,' I said. 'But there was definitely a whiff of the sea about it.'

'Fuck,' said Stephen. 'And in my apartment?'

'Just inside the front door.'

'Fuck.'

'You know who put it there?'

'Not for sure,' said Stephen, shaking his head. 'But whoever they are, they've been biting my ass since I got here.'

'Any ideas?' I asked, because I know a fishing opportunity when I see one.

'West Coast. Maybe out of LA or Santa Cruz,' said Stephen. 'There's some very strange people over on that side of the country. Collectives and communes and religious groups, all of them with their own little slice of magical heaven. Some of them are pretty scary too – militia types – know what I mean?'

'Native American?'

Stephen shrugged.

'I don't know much about them,' he said. 'Except that there's some variety of treaty that keeps them on the reservation.'

'And they accept that?'

Stephen didn't know for sure, but told me there was rumoured to be a whole department within the Bureau of Indian Affairs whose one job was to come down hard on any Native American practitioner who tried to practise outside the reservations. I wondered if Reynolds knew this. And, if she did, why she'd never mentioned it to me.

'So probably not Native Americans then,' I said. 'It still could have been you. A bit of insurance against anyone getting too curious.'

Stephen sighed and held up his hand.

'I'm going to do a spell,' he said, and closed his hand into a fist. 'Just a small one, so don't get all excited and overreact.'

I braced just in case, but after checking to see nobody was looking Stephen opened his hand to reveal a small globe shining with pearly light. I felt the *signare* of his magic as a hushed whispering like papers and a busy growling undertow like engines underground.

Nothing like the suffocating cloud of rotting fish that had permeated the demon trap.

'We call that a werelight,' I said. 'What about you?'

'Same,' said Stephen. 'Satisfied?'

'It means you didn't manufacture it, at least,' I said.

Stephen snorted and extinguished the light.

I glanced up as a tall man in a good black pinstripe suit cut in an old-fashioned Savile Row style sat down in one of the booths that lined the wall behind Stephen, put a half of lager down on the table, carefully folded a copy of the *Telegraph* on his knee and started in on the crosswords. I let my eyes slide back to Stephen's face before he noticed. The man was DCI Thomas Nightingale – my boss.

Now I had backup I could press a little harder.

'Since we've gone around the houses a couple of times,' I said, 'why don't you tell me who trained you, who you're working for, and what you're doing on my manor?'

'You don't want much, do you?'

'No, I don't,' I said. 'Not really, when you consider the alternative.'

'Okay,' said Stephen. 'When I was fifteen I ran into something unreasonable on the subway, and one thing led to another and I found myself pursuing an alternative career path to the one I expected.'

'Which was what?'

'Sex worker, drug runner and unmourned casualty of the street life,' he said. 'Originally I was from Concord, but I ran away when I was thirteen.'

I wanted to know what he'd run into, but sometimes even I have to prioritise my curiosity.

'So, who trained you?' I asked.

'The Librarians,' he said.

'Librarians?'

'Not librarians,' he said. '*The* Librarians.'

Because in New York there was only one library with a capital L, and that was the Main Branch on Fifth Avenue, which had been built with a ton of cash donated by Andrew Carnegie, who had a thing about libraries. Given that libraries were the repositories of knowledge it made sense that they were also the home of secret wisdom.

The Librarians took him in – he was maddeningly vague on how many of the employees of the New York Public Library system were actually practitioners, although it couldn't be all of them.

'They gave me a place to stay, three squares a day, a job, a purpose,' said Stephen. 'A reason not to kill myself.'

'And they taught you magic?'

'They made sure I graduated high school as well.'

'And what do you do with your magic?'

'What do you do?'

'I uphold the Queen's peace,' I said.

'Really?' said Stephen. 'The Queen's peace?'

'To the best of my power.'

'And when your power isn't enough?'

'I call in backup,' I said, making sure I didn't glance at Nightingale.

'I don't work for the Queen,' he said. 'But we probably deal with the same problems. Ghosts, revenants, black magicians. Does that sound familiar?'

'And the police?'

'We prefer not to involve the cops.' Stephen gave an apologetic shrug. 'Although we do have some contacts in the department, we find they tend to get in the way.' He put the tip of his finger under his eye and pulled gently. 'What the eye don't see . . .'

Stephen had said 'department' singular, not forces or even law enforcement. I knew that big city arrogance – had a case of that myself.

'So do you cover the whole country?' I asked.

'No,' said Stephen. 'Just the five boroughs and parts of Jersey. Maybe upstate – if something starts to smell.'

'So what's so fragrant that it brings you all the way to London?' I asked.

'Would you believe a sabbatical?'

'No,' I said, letting my tone harden. 'I fucking wouldn't. Now stop pissing about and tell me why you're here or I'm going to have you arrested.'

He shifted in his seat subtly, tensing for action. I forced myself to stay relaxed and aimed for maximum insouciance.

'How about I just bounce you round and round the block?' he said.

I shrugged and pulled out my mobile.

'Have it your way,' I said.

'Okay, okay,' said Stephen. 'Jeez, you guys really have a stick up your ass, don't you?'

'It's called a backbone,' I said. 'Why are you here?'

Stephen screwed up his face and tilted his head to one side.

I held up my phone and he relaxed and sighed.

'Do you know what a Mary Engine is?' he asked.

I did, as it happened, but people love ignorance in other people – it gives them a chance to sound knowledgeable – so I said no.

'But you know who Charles Babbage is?' he said.

I said I did – a nineteenth-century pioneer of mechanical calculation.

'His big plan was to build an analytical engine,' said Stephen. 'A programmable calculator.'

And he'd worked with Ada Lovelace, the Enchantress of Numbers, to build it.

'But something happened,' said Stephen. 'And they never finished the thing – nobody knows why.'

He'd left out Babbage's attempts to build the simpler 'difference' engine, and his dispute with the British Government over all the money they'd paid him and got sod all in return for.

I asked why Babbage and Ada hadn't finished it.

'Typical tech venture,' said Stephen. 'They got side-tracked into another project.'

And the source of this distraction were the Lilly and the Rose.

'Two female practitioners,' said Stephen. 'Some people think the Lilly might have been Mary Somerville, but nobody has a clue who the Rose was. I figured you'd have heard of them, you being a Brit and everything.'

I said that I knew who Mary Somerville was, but I'd never heard of the Lilly or the Rose.

'Unless she's something to do with Rose Jars,' I said.

'Bingo,' said Stephen. 'You know what those are, right? Rose Jars?'

'Devices for trapping ghosts,' I said.

'Have you ever seen one, with a ghost trapped in it?'

'Just the one,' I said.

And a room full of empty jars at the Chesham ghost palace.

'They've got some downstairs in the basement of the Library,' said Stephen. 'But they're all dead. What was a live one like – if that's the right expression?'

For a moment I'd stood in a palace of glass facing the ghost of a man in a frock coat who told me that existence was not life and went into the darkness gladly while the singing of the jars faded to nothing.

'It was like a big thermionic valve,' I said.

Stephen nodded.

'Yeah,' he said. 'Figures.'

'Never mind the ghost jars,' I said. 'What's any of this got to do with you being here?'

'What if I told you they made a magical mechanical engine?' he said.

'This would be the Mary Engine?' I asked.

Stephen smiled.

'And?'

'They built it but nobody knows where it went,' he said.

He explained how it became a rumour, a ghost, something tracked only through marginalia in certain books and gossip amongst American practitioners.

'They used to talk to each other back in those days,' said Stephen. 'After the war – not so much.'

When I did arrest him, I decided, I was going to hand him over to Professor Postmartin, the Folly's pet archivist, to lecture him. That would teach him to try and distract me.

'Then two years ago it pops up on eBay,' he said.

I tried to look suitably startled.

'You're kidding.'

'Truth,' he said. 'Only stayed up a week and then was withdrawn.'

But now the Librarians knew there was a Mary Engine knocking about on the open market. So, when they heard a whisper that a certain Silicon Valley tech entrepreneur had acquired it, they took an interest.

I asked Stephen why the interest, and it was his turn to look startled.

'It's a forbidden object,' he said.

The Librarians kept a list of dangerous magical artefacts, and one of their duties was to collect those artefacts wherever possible and lock them away. Wherever they might be found.

'Even if they're in other countries?' I asked. 'What happened to just the five boroughs?'

'Some things are too important to leave to chance,' he said.

'Or Terrence Skinner?'

'Definitely not him.'

'Why not?'

'These techbros have tunnel vision,' said Stephen. 'They're so fucking busy with their dreams of the future they don't stop to think about where they are or what the fuck they're doing.'

'Do you know what he plans to use it for?' I asked.

'No,' said Stephen. 'But it'll be nothing good.'

'Then our first step should be to find out what his plans are, isn't it?'

Stephen shook his head.

'My idea is simpler,' he said. 'I lift the loot and split. No fuss, no muss.'

'It is a simpler plan, but it rests on a basic logical fallacy,' I said. 'Which is that you have any choice in the matter. You're on my manor now, so the only question is, do you want to do it my way or do you want be arrested, charged and deported?'

He gave me a long stare. I couldn't tell if he was really weighing his options or whether he thought that if he left it long enough I might change my mind. But with Nightingale sitting behind him in his blind spot I didn't have any worries at all, and took the opportunity to finish my beer.

In the end he agreed – it wasn't like he had a lot of choice.

So we spent half an hour going over some plans, each of us acting with all the sincerity of a south

London used car salesman. One of us was going to end up with an old banger with a suspiciously low mileage, but I was pretty confident it wasn't going to be me.

As we headed out I glanced over at Nightingale, who was still apparently engrossed in his *Daily Telegraph*. Written in the margin on the side facing me in large block capitals were the words – COLD FISH.

CHAPTER 4

DECEMBER: CHANGES IN
A STATE OF MIND

It almost ended for me right there in the doorway of a two-bedroom flat in Palmers Green, and the last thing I would have seen in life was a Gustav Klimt poster in a cheap plastic frame. It was only because experience had taught me to go carefully through a suspect's door that I caught the little tingle under my foot when I stepped in. I'd been worried that Jacob Astor might have been hiding in the bathroom, but that was nothing compared to the icy clutch I felt in my stomach. That bit was psychosomatic – the sinister flash of sensation like someone dragging clammy fingers across my thigh was not.

Back in the good old days, when deeply misunderstood Scandinavians sought to alleviate the limitations of arctic agriculture by murdering foreigners and taking their stuff, there arose a powerful tradition of enchanting objects. Their smiths turned out swords, staves, axes and belt buckles, all imbued with a supernatural keenness or strength or – in a couple of cases you can still see in museums – resistance to rust.

They also discovered a way to weaponise ghosts. We don't know the details – or more precisely, we don't want to know the details – but those peaceful world traders would start by torturing a human being to death over an extended period of time. Driven into a mindless frenzy by the torture, this 'demon spirit' was then trapped in an enchanted object and used to power a number of different magical effects – all of them destructive. There are stories of axes with minds of their own and rings that drive their wearer mad, but I know the technique from what Nightingale calls its twentieth-century apotheosis – the demon trap. Essentially a magical landmine.

And, as when you're stupid enough to set foot on a conventional landmine, the first rule is don't move.

That was the easy bit.

The second is to concentrate on the here and now and not be distracted by wondering how you got yourself into the shit in the first place.

That I found harder.

As soon as I realised I'd lost Jacob Astor round the back of the London Library, I'd called Nightingale. I wanted to get a response car parked up outside his flat in Palmers Green and needed Nightingale to authorise the overtime.

Back in the dim and distant noughties before our Lady Theresa of the Wheat Field hacked up the Met's budget, you used to be able to just ask a Borough Command to send a couple of uniforms round. These days, response officers were thin on the ground and you generally had to bribe their shift commanders with externally sourced overtime payments to get any help.

While Nightingale was organising that, I popped back into the London Library to reassure the director, a tall hyperactive man in a very good suit, that there was nothing to worry about and then secure Jacob Astor's workspace, bag up the jacket and the bag he'd left behind and take initial statements from his colleagues. This is why police investigations take time. You have to be thorough, consistent and you have to write everything down. It was dark before I could pile into my trusty Ford Asbo with my evidence bags and fight my way north through rush-hour traffic to Palmers Green, stopping off at the letting agency to collect the keys.

They made me show my warrant card and called 101 to confirm my identity before they handed them over. By the time I drew up outside the house my bought-and-paid-for uniformed PCs were on their third hour of overtime and halfway through a family-sized bucket of KFC. I blagged a drumstick and some chips off them and let them finish their coffees before we went in.

Once through the front door the uniforms were tasked with securing the neighbour while I opened the main door to the flat. I walked cautiously up the dimly lit narrow staircase, carefully opened the door at the top and stepped on a demon trap.

From a very long distance away I heard one of the uniforms asking me if I still needed them.

'I've just stepped on a Falcon IED,' I said.

There was a suitably horrified silence from behind me.

'Back off,' I said. 'Call my boss and evacuate everyone downstairs.'

I barely heard them agree and move off. I was too busy not moving.

Step Two: don't panic.

When Nightingale was training me he said that if you're not dead in the first instance, then your chances of survival are much improved.

'By how much?' I'd asked.

'That depends,' said Nightingale.

'On what?'

'On what happens next,' he said.

I wasn't dead in this first instance because Nightingale had trained me by leaving fake demon traps around the Folly. The fakes were army surplus training devices that we'd found while clearing out the gun room in the basement, and they gave you a nasty static electric shock when activated.

'Why the delay?' I'd asked. 'Why not go off on first contact?'

'You need two definite contacts,' Nightingale had said. 'One to prime the demon, the second to set it off.'

Step Three: determine what it is you're standing on. What is it, exactly, the demon is primed to do?

Easier said than done. But again, practice. We'd done lots of practice. I took a deep breath and cleared my head. I looked for the *vestigium* amongst the random thoughts, memories and phantom sense impressions that fill the waking mind.

I felt it – a strange pulsing mindless sensation. I've experienced demon traps powered by tortured dogs and at least one by the traditional murdered human, but this was weird, alien and repellent in a whole different way. There was no hint of personality. Not even the twisted remnant of a person tortured until their mind snapped. Instead it was amorphous and diffuse, like a cloud of gas.

So, bollocks to Step Three and onto Step Four: establish your conduit.

The magical tradition I belong to exists in the gap between the observable universe and the rational clockwork creation of the Enlightenment. There's this power. We don't know where it comes from or why it follows the rules it does, but it definitely exists and there are definite ways to manipulate it. Further advances in science have done little to help our understanding, except to add a growing temptation to attach the word 'quantum' to everything.

Nightingale says the simplest form of demon trap provides a physical attack on the body. This can take the form of crushing or thermal damage, and the effect is often indistinguishable from an ordinary anti-personnel mine.

'However,' Nightingale had said, 'if all you want to do is blow your opponent to bits, then a high-explosive landmine is much more effective and cheaper.'

More likely this one was a trap left specifically for a practitioner, and keyed to go off at the first use of magic. If that was the case, all I had to do was step off the demon trap and nothing would happen. According to a certain military-trained Russian witch I know, the Red Army had done a statistical analysis with demon traps just as they had with conventional minefields. The conclusions had been the same in both cases – you lost fewer troops charging across a minefield than allowing the Germans to funnel you into a killing ground. Which was good solid Russian pragmatism and no bloody use at all when it's you standing with your foot on the prospect of an agonising death.

So, Soviet statistical models aside, your options are to step off the plate and hope for the best, or to do the counter-spell even though that might be the trigger that sets off the trap. So, obviously you have to do the counter-spell. But the counter-spell, despite being refined by teams of experienced practitioners, is a fourth order spell. This means it consists of four separate *formae*, the building blocks of Newtonian magic, plus various embellishments. A *forma* is essentially a shape in your mind that causes an effect in the physical universe, for reasons that one day will indeed probably turn out to have the word quantum in them. To do *sīphōnem* you have to run through each of the *formae* in turn, in the right sequence and with the right modifications.

And you have to do this faster than the demon trap can release its magical payload.

Below me I heard big police feet moving backwards and forwards as they cleared the downstairs flat.

It had been six months since I'd last practised *sīphōnem*, so I ran through it a couple of times while I waited for the house to empty.

Once the uniforms had called, from a safe distance, to say that a perimeter had been established, I took another deep breath and executed the spell. The best way to describe it would be as a funnel that has its pointy end on the demon trap and its broad end pointing upwards. The larger you make the outlet, the more dispersed the energy. And the less likely it is to kill you.

During the war, Nightingale says, about one in a hundred diffusion attempts killed the practitioner carrying it out.

A tickle started in my throat and, very slowly and carefully, I clamped my hand over my mouth. Just in time. I tried not to move as my chest spasmed and I coughed, once, twice and, one irritating little gap later, a third time.

I waited a moment to see if my body was going to make another spirited attempt to kill me and, when I was sure it wasn't, I executed the spell before I could lose my nerve.

I was barely through the first two *formae* when the trap uncoiled like a snake striking out of its basket. It rushed up my body in a whirl of salt spray, hot sun and a terrifying sensation of smothering as if I'd been wrapped in fish guts. Then a prickle, as if a thousand needles had pierced the skin all over my body. The fear was primal and suffocating and I nearly stumbled over the fourth and last *forma*.

But Nightingale is a good teacher and suddenly his tiresome insistence on getting the *formae* precisely right time after bloody time made total sense.

Just as the pinpricks grew sharper, the *formae* locked into place and the counter-spell unfurled over my head and the fish stink rushed upwards and out like a geyser of rotting seafood.

A car alarm went off outside and there was suddenly a chorus of barking dogs in the distance.

Step Five: check for secondaries before you move.

I got my breathing back under control and spent another long five minutes making sure some total bastard hadn't added a backup demon. Once I was certain I wasn't going to explode, I stepped backwards off the device.

Then I sat down at the top of the stairs and had a bit of a breather.

The stairs themselves were narrow and gloomy with a main door into the communal hallway at the bottom and a second door, which I had foolishly stepped through without checking, at the top. It had one of those pop-out light switches powering a naked low-energy LED bulb. Ironically I hadn't pushed in the light switch on the way up in case it was booby-trapped.

I pulled my phone and gave it a shake – it made the sandy rainmaker sound that indicated it had been fried by the magical discharge. I don't even bother putting numbers into any of my mobiles any more, I just memorise them instead.

This was also why I always carry a backup pay-as-you-go phone in the same pocket as my evidence gloves, pen torch and hand sanitiser. I pulled it out now, switched it on and called Nightingale's mobile.

'I've disarmed it,' I said when he picked up. Judging by the roar of the straight-6 engine and the siren, he'd been proceeding at an unsafe speed in a built-up area.

'Good work,' he said, and I heard the Jaguar's

siren give a last little whoop before shutting off. 'I'll be with you soon.'

It seemed a viciously lethal trap for a man who'd warned me against damaging books in the London Library, but criminals often have a sentimental streak for dogs and rabbits while being total bastards to people.

'Detective,' called a voice from the bottom of the stairs – one of the uniforms. 'Are you all right up there?'

I shouted down that I was fine and that the device had been neutralised.

I considered waiting for Nightingale before checking the rest of the flat, but I'm supposed to be able to do this basic stuff on my own. That said, when I did start my search I did it very slowly and carefully.

It was a furnished flat rented from an agency for £250 a week. The furnishings were at the John Lewis end of cost and looked relatively new and unworn. The second bedroom had obviously not been used and I wondered what kind of librarian could afford such a rent without a flatmate – even if we were dangerously far outside the North Circular.

There were no books or Blu-rays on the bookshelves, no CDs and no music centre or iPod dock to play music on. The bed was neatly made – too neatly, in fact – with the sheets perfectly cornered and the pillows neatly aligned with the imitation teak headboard. Some people are naturally obsessive about their bed linen, but more often it was a sign that they'd been institutionalised – borstal, military, prison, take your pick. The wardrobe was similarly neat, with ranks of high-quality cotton shirts grouped by colour hanging on the left, a couple of smart casual jackets, one tan, one navy, in the middle and a collection of jeans and chinos hanging from specialised clothes hangers on the right. Everything ironed to the sort of supernatural tolerances that Nightingale's housekeeper would approve of.

On the coffee table was a copy of *QX Magazine* with a group photo of actors and the headline OH NO THEY DIDN'T – apparently it was the Panto Special. I checked the date – it was the previous week's issue.

There was no sign of the stolen music book – we'd bring in a proper POLSA team of course, but I was willing to bet money that they wouldn't find anything.

Nightingale arrived while I was finishing up in the living room. I walked back into the hall to find him on his hands and knees with his face as close to the demon trap as he could get without touching it.

'Curious,' he said.

I asked if he recognised the model.

'No,' he said. 'But it does remind me of a type that started appearing late in the war.'

The consensus amongst the boffins, according to Nightingale, was that the Germans had discovered a way to power their demon traps without recourse to torturing someone to death.

Nightingale pulled his clasp knife from his pocket and started cutting away the carpet to expose the device.

'A humane demon trap?' I said.

The device was smaller than I expected, a square twenty centimetres on a side but, most surprisingly of all, made of plastic only a few millimetres thick. Thin enough to have dented under the pressure of my foot.

'Not at the receiving end,' said Nightingale. 'They were supposed to be particularly unpleasant.'

I squatted down to join him. The surface of the trap was smooth and the colour of an unpainted Airfix model, except for a blackened triangle at its centre. That would be what Nightingale always referred to as the payload, the actual trap that gave the demon trap its name. The top surface was devoid of any inscriptions or etched symbols. It looked like a prop from 1970s *Doctor Who*.

'Plastic,' said Nightingale. 'I've never seen a plastic demon trap before.'

'We know some plastics hold magic better than metal,' I said.

Nightingale ran his finger lightly along an edge and then looked up at me and grinned.

'Good work on the diffusion,' he said. 'And your dispersal was excellent. There's hardly any residue at all.'

'I almost ballsed it up,' I said.

'Everyone always does the first time,' said Nightingale. 'Let's have a look on the other side.'

Which proved to be as featureless as the top, only with a matt finish.

There was an impression once more of old fish and the seaweed-and-salt smell of the seashore.

I asked Nightingale if he recognised the *signare*, but he shook his head.

'Why don't we secure this first?' he said.

So I fetched the bubble wrap from the boot of the Asbo. During my recent suspension, I'd had time to experiment with what materials served as the best insulating matter for packaging dangerously magical items. Green wood is the traditional choice, but I found that polystyrene and bubble wrap were just as good.

Me and Nightingale carefully wrapped the demon trap and slid it into a large-sized evidence bag and put it in the back of the Jag. We split up our actions so that Nightingale would drop the trap off at the Folly and then interview Jacob's workmates, while I interviewed the downstairs neighbour and canvassed the street.

'Is it safe to go back in?' asked the downstairs neighbour, whose name was Mrs Chaudry. I assured her it was, and asked if I might ask her a few questions. We ended up in a reassuringly cluttered kitchen with the toddler in its high chair sucking on a bottle and giving me suspicious looks.

Mrs Chaudry made the tea while I pulled out my notebook and got on with it.

After the warm-up questions about her upstairs neighbour, about which she knew the normal London amount – that is, nothing at all – I asked if anyone had visited the house after I'd spoken to her the first time.

'Some men came around about an hour later,' she said. 'Said they were roofing contractors.'

'Said they were,' I said. 'But you don't think so.'

'Not now, I don't,' she said. 'I mean they had a white van and clipboards and everything but . . .'

'But?'

'The van was a bit too clean, to be honest, and they were a bit sus themselves.'

'In what way?'

'One of them was pretending to be Irish, for a start,' said Mrs Chaudry. 'The other one didn't say anything.'

I asked how she knew he was pretending.

'Because his accent was terrible,' she said. 'It was like a bad film. I mean, he didn't say "top of the morning" but I think he really wanted to. I thought he was taking the piss, to be honest, but I didn't have time to waste on him.'

She looked at her child, who looked back with a wide-eyed innocence that wasn't fooling anyone.

I asked whether she could guess what accent the man really had.

'Don't know,' she said. 'American, maybe, but I wouldn't stake my life on it.'

The fake roofing contractors had said they had keys from the landlord and, apart from the dodgy accent, seemed plausible.

'I wasn't really paying as much attention as I should of,' she said. 'Does that make me liable?'

I said I doubted it, and asked whether she'd actually seen them use their keys on the door to the upstairs flat. She admitted that she'd been called away to a domestic emergency – she gave the child another hard look – and let the 'roofers' get on with it.

I noted down their appearance, but beyond them both being male and IC1 the description was too bland for immediate circulation. Just to be on the safe side, I made a note of the land-lord's details so I could ask if he'd hired any roofing contractors.

He hadn't, nor had any of the neighbours next door or across the road. I considered expanding the house-to-house all the way down the street, but we were already paying overtime for one set of uniforms and, if I wanted an overnight guard on the house, would have to pay for the next shift as well. Plus none of the response officers had Falcon training, and the only other remotely quali-fied detective I knew was currently on holiday in Hong Kong.

Still, I did a couple more houses to show willing, but it was getting dark and cold and then

Nightingale called me from the London Library and said he'd found something.

'He had an inordinate interest in the works of Ada Lovelace,' said Nightingale.

We'd commandeered the London Library director's office on the ground floor. This was a stark white-painted room with black wooden bookcases and a black desk that looked suspiciously self-assembly to me. A couple of the bookcases had lockable doors where, Nightingale explained, they kept rare books. There was also a black dining table doing its best to pretend it was there for executive conferences, whose pretensions were further undermined by the blue folding chair that had wandered in from a different library entirely.

On the table were the remains of a plate of biscuits and couple of empty coffee mugs. Safely away from the dangerous liquids were a pair of black cardboard boxes.

'Do we know which particular works?' I asked.

'That's where it gets interesting,' said Nightingale, and he checked his notes. 'The Library has little in the way of material by Lovelace save for certain correspondence with one Ludovico Gavioli. Or, more precisely, his correspondence with her.'

'Gavioli?' I said. 'As in the famous Italian organ makers?'

'The very same. I'd never heard of them until

they cropped up in your investigation,' said Nightingale. 'But they're really quite fascinating. Ludovico was reputedly the business brains of the family and he was behind their move to Paris.'

Which was, Nightingale had learned, the mechanical-organ making centre of the world – at least back in 1852 when the Gavioli family had moved there.

'The letters themselves were singularly frustrating,' said Nightingale. 'My Italian is not really up to scratch, but they seem to relate to a device for reading music books. There was even a blueprint sketched on one of the sheets.'

He carefully unfolded one of the cardboard boxes to reveal a sheaf of yellowing paper. Selecting a pair of sheets, he laid them on the table in front of me.

'In 1838 Ludovico is said to have built a life-size automaton called David who could play the harp, and these here—' Nightingale indicated the sheets – 'were sent to Ada Lovelace in 1842.'

Now, my Italian is non-existent, but I'd spent enough time looking at old books to puzzle out the fine but scratchy diagrams. There wasn't enough detail to be sure, but they looked suspiciously like the pneumatic key frames that read music books for fairground organs. The system that Ludovico's son Anselme had patented in the 1890s.

I took a picture of the diagram with my phone and zoomed in on the image to see if I could count the number of holes. I needn't have bothered, because Ludovico had helpfully labelled them in thirteen groups of ten and one group of seven, making 137 'keys'. Undoubtedly this was the key frame designed to read the music book stolen by Jacob Astor from the showmen's camp at the Vale of Health.

'How long has Astor been working here?' I asked.

'Since late October,' said Nightingale. 'As far as anyone can recall, he examined these letters shortly after.'

'So he finds out about the 137-key frame, then presumably tracks down the music book, fakes being an interested buyer and organises a theft – all in the space of a couple of weeks,' I said. 'That's fast work.'

'Yes, it is,' said Nightingale. 'The speed may also explain his oversight with the printed cards. Paying with a credit card was certainly a basic error.'

'Has anyone else shown an interest in these letters?' I asked.

'As a matter of fact,' said Nightingale, 'yes, they have.'

In 1851 Ada Lovelace and Charles Babbage met up for the last time when they, along with six million other people, visited the Great Exhibition together. Housed in a fantastic purpose-built glass pavilion on Hyde Park called the Crystal Palace, it was designed to showcase the achievements of British industry and all the stuff we'd nicked from overseas. Babbage, who never let an occasion get in the way of a grievance, was less impressed because not one of his amazing engines was on display.

Running south and downhill from where the Crystal Palace once stood is Exhibition Road where, for an encore, those proud Victorians built some suitably grandiose museums, the better to educate the masses and keep them out of mischief.

It certainly worked on me when I was in my early teens – I practically lived in the Science Museum, which was full of brilliant stuff and totally free. There was an entire gallery of model ships and rockets and aeroplanes hanging from the ceiling. In the shipping gallery there had been a mock-up of a ship's bridge, complete with a fake transistor-era radar display in which the sweep rotated endlessly around, illuminating mysterious green blobs. You could stand with your hands on the disappointingly small ship's wheel and imagine that you had set course for New York or Murmansk or Alpha Centauri.

'That gallery was taken out in 2012,' the curator told us.

The curator, whose name was Cherise Desroche, was a white dwarf-woman with her straight shoulder-length hair dyed a lurid anime red. She was so small I wondered how she could see into some of the display cases – I assumed she must make arrangements.

I must have sighed because she looked up at me and Nightingale and smiled.

'Only about three per cent of our exhibits can be displayed at any one moment in the museum,' she said. 'The rest are all in storage.'

On the way to her office we stopped to admire the 1995 reconstruction of Babbage's Difference Engine Number 2 in all its brass, steel and mahogany glory. It was two metres tall, three metres long and driven by a hand crank that I suspected would have been a bugger to turn. No doubt Babbage would have hired in some labour to help with that – had he ever finished it.

'This particular engine was designed to calculate log tables and the like,' said Cherise. 'It's been tested and it works very well indeed.'

The next step would have been an Analytical Engine, a mechanical general purpose computing machine which would, if you like wearing goggles with your top hat, have kicked off the IT revolution a hundred years early.

As Cherise led us away, Nightingale asked if anyone had tried to reconstruct one of those.

'The Analytical Engine would have been much larger,' she said. 'And as far as we know Babbage never completed the plans. Also there's some doubt that a mechanical device of that complexity could ever work efficiently enough to be useful.'

'But has someone made the attempt?' asked Nightingale, as Cherise led us through a door marked STAFF ONLY into an abruptly utilitarian passage painted 1930s bureaucratic green.

'Someone certainly evinced an interest,' she said.

I glanced at Nightingale, who gave me a small smile as we passed through another door and down a high-ceilinged corridor into an equally high-ceilinged office with beautiful Regency mouldings half hidden by suspended fluorescent lighting strips. There was enough room for half a dozen desks, half of which were empty. Heavy-duty plastic moving crates with translucent sides and red lids were littered around the room, most already stuffed with papers and books. I looked out of the tall windows – across Exhibition Road was the Church of the Latter Day Saints. The Mormons' London HQ.

'Do you mind telling us who that was?' asked Nightingale.

Cherise started digging in one of the moving crates.

'We're being turfed out, I'm afraid,' she said. 'The Dyson Institute has acquired the building. Just a sec.' She emerged with a black cardboard document folder which she opened to reveal a sheaf of papers. These were, Cherise revealed, pages cut from a notebook. 'Of nineteenth-century Parisian manufacture,' she said, 'judging by the paper.'

More diagrams, but of fragments of a device. More notes, this time written in French.

'But not by one of the Gaviolis,' said Cherise. 'The handwriting is distinctly different. They're part of a package that has been traced back to Ada Lovelace and they relate to her work on Bernoulli numbers. We think . . .' Cherise gave a little theatrical pause. 'That it's something to do with her further work on Babbage's Analytical Engine.'

She said someone had asked to see the Gavioli letters because of a reference to a 137-key reader in the margins of one of the pages. She spread the pages and pointed to the faded scratchy writing.

'*La symétrie les rend réticents*,' Nightingale read aloud. 'Symmetry makes them reluctant.'

'Nobody seems to know who is supposed to be reluctant,' said Cherise, and she gave a false little laugh.

'So, who wanted to do the reconstruction?' I asked, and the laugh cut off abruptly.

'Ah,' said Cherise. 'I was hoping you wouldn't ask that.'

'It seems an innocuous question,' said Nightingale.

And the mere fact that you didn't want to tell us, I thought, means we *really* want to know.

'Are you under some form of duress?' asked Nightingale when Cherise stayed silent.

'Yes,' she said. 'And no. Kind of. There's a fairly ferocious NDA involved.'

'Don't worry about that,' I said. 'This is a criminal investigation and a non-disclosure agreement doesn't preclude you from giving information to the police. In fact, if the information proves critical, then not providing it in a timely fashion could be considered aiding and abetting after the fact.'

I was fairly certain that this was mostly bollocks but Cherise bought it – I think it was my strategic use of the word 'preclude' that did the trick.

'You've probably heard of him,' she said. 'Terrence Skinner – the Silicon Valley guy. He funded a preliminary feasibility study.'

He'd suggested that if a working Analytical Engine could be built, then it might form the centrepiece of a new gallery – sponsored by his new UK venture, the Serious Cybernetics Corporation. It was at his behest that they'd tracked down the letters at the London Library, amongst a mass of other documents, and scanned them into a digital database. Minions of the tech giant swarmed over the project for reconstructing the Difference Engine and asked detailed questions about manufacturing tolerances, the long-term utility of brass cogs and whether they could use an actual steam engine to drive the mechanism.

She showed us an artist's impression of the Analytical Engine in action, and the sodding thing came in at just under eight metres long.

'Unfortunately the project never went any further,' said Cherise, which didn't surprise me. There was no way that monstrosity was going to work for more than a couple of seconds before grinding to a halt like the gearbox on an Austin Allegro. The funding dried up and Terrence Skinner withdrew his interest, leaving nothing but a slightly improved filing system and non-disclosure agreements behind.

On our way out, Nightingale took a detour to look at the Apollo capsule displayed in the Making of the Modern World gallery. The great bronze cone was mounted so that it tilted forward, allowing a view through the missing hatch and into the interior. He stood staring at the flimsy looking acceleration couches even as a troop of hyperactive primary schoolkids swirled around his legs.

'You know, Peter,' he said finally, 'I don't think I've visited this museum since 1924.'

'Don't tell anyone that,' I said. 'Or they'll put you in a case.'

'They'd be too late – I've already promised my brain to science.'

The Folly is the sleeping heart of the Special Assessment Unit. A big square Regency building on the south side of Russell Square, it was first built as combination meeting hall, club house and library for the Society of the Wise. Having spent the last hundred years being regarded as mountebanks, charlatans and quacks, the Society of the Wise had grabbed hold of respectability with both hands and had no intention of letting go short of death. Above the front door were the words *scientia potestas est* and a cartouche with the Folly's coat of arms. If you look carefully you can see the space they left against the day the monarch granted them the honour of becoming the Royal Society of the Wise.

It never happened – neither Queen Victoria nor her consort were interested in the practical uses of magic.

The sadly deficient coat of arms, the motto, front door, and in fact the whole façade, was shrouded in scaffolding and plastic. Through a gap in the sheeting loomed a conveyor belt shrouded in wood that warns the neighbours that basement extensions are underway.

Since the first rule of a good investigation is to check that somebody else hasn't done the work for you, I headed round the back and over to the coach house. On the first floor is the Tech Cave where I keep my work computer, the Airwave charger, widescreen TV and a hotel fridge stocked with water and my emergency supply of Red Stripe. The mews itself currently looked like a particularly neat builders' yard, with pallets of aerated concrete blocks, precast lintels, bags of mortar, a cement mixer jammed into a corner and what looked like a brand-new pair of Portaloos. The scaffolding would be staying up for another week at least, making me glad I was staying with Bev.

The cement smell followed me up the external spiral staircase and into the Tech Cave. Once everything was powered up I logged into AWARE with my warrant number and went rummaging about to see if Terrence Skinner or the Serious Cybernetics Corporation had cropped up somewhere other than the pages of *Wired* magazine. About a minute later I was looking at a flag warning me off, a case number and contact details for the National Crime Agency.

I recognised the name of the officer listed – Alona Silver. We'd worked together on a street-racing case earlier in the year. I wondered if that was a coincidence – I really hoped it was.

Somewhere there's a document, probably a PDF, with a protocol for junior Met officers regulating inter-agency contacts. And one day I'm sure somebody might read it. I still had Officer Silver's personal mobile number from that summer. I looked it up and called her directly.

'Who is this?' she snarled.

'Peter Grant,' I said.

'What can I do for you?' The snarl modulated down to mere impatience.

'What's your interest in Terrence Skinner and the Serious Cybernetics Corporation?' I asked.

'Oh fuck.'

CHAPTER 5

JANUARY: SOME CATS ARE GREY

The Moshi Moshi sushi bar at Liverpool Street Station sits in a Perspex box suspended over the platforms. It's conveniently located near the station's rear entrance via the Sun Street Passage, less than half a kilometre from the Serious Cybernetics Corporation on Tabernacle Street. And it's the sort of place that a busy undercover police officer might, at the end of the day, pop into for a bit of plausibly deniable conversation with his handlers. And, of course, have a bit of cold fish wrapped in seaweed.

'Does this American wizard know you're a police officer?' asked Silver.

'I keep telling him,' I said, 'but I don't know if he believes me or not.'

Silver tapped her bento box with her chopsticks. She was a thin white woman with a light brown Mediterranean complexion and a Roman nose along which she had perfected the art of looking down at people.

'Hmm,' she said. 'I'm not sure if that's a good thing or a bad thing.'

'Then what on earth does he think you *are*?' said Nightingale, who had opted for the black cod.

Personally, I'd gone for the sashimi platter and had to finish a mouthful of tuna before I could speak. Beyond the transparent walls of the restaurant the commuters passed in an endless stream.

'I think he thinks I belong to an NGO,' I said. 'Like he does. And that I operate independently of the criminal justice system.'

Silver tapped her bento box again – a nervous habit, I decided.

'Wherever did he get that idea?' she said, and gave Nightingale the side eye.

'He thinks he's starring in a spy film,' I said.

Nightingale frowned.

'In some ways he's right,' said Silver. 'Although his tradecraft is abysmal.'

The NCA recruits its officers from the police, HM Customs, Border Force and the wider civil service. Rumour had it they'd gone shopping for talent at the intelligence agencies as well. And, judging by Silver, I found those rumours easy to believe.

'I can see a number of ways he'll be more use to us if he continues to believe that,' she said brightly. 'Do you think you can sell him on it?'

I said no problem.

Silver narrowed her eyes at me.

'You've taken remarkably well to undercover work,' she said.

'Yes,' said Nightingale, not sounding at all pleased.

We then spent the next half an hour thrashing out the practicalities. Because as Shakespeare said – *Oh! How many operational contingency directives we receive. When first we practise to deceive.*

'I suggest you visit him in his new home,' said Silver. 'This evening by preference. That'll stop him from getting creative over the weekend.'

'Do we know where his new home is?' I asked.

'We will soon,' said Silver smugly. 'I have a team following him.'

I looked over at Nightingale, who thought for a moment and then nodded.

'We'll go together,' he said. 'That way I can be on hand for any eventualities.'

Beverley was going out with her mates from uni that evening, so as it happened I was free for some illicit police work.

Stephen's new pad was in a block of flats in a council estate off the Seven Sisters Road in Tottenham. Nightingale parked the Jag in a space out of sight of the block. As I walked towards the entrance a battered-looking silver Peugeot parked opposite flashed its lights – that would be the surveillance team.

I was in front of a classic bit of red-brick council housing with open balconies and a central stair-case. I didn't chance the lift and instead trotted up the stairs to the third floor. As I walked along the balcony one of the doors ahead opened and Stephen stepped out. He saw me as soon as he turned to double-lock his door, and gave me a pained look. Given the black cargo pants, hoodie and nylon carry-all, he definitely looked like he was going equipped to me.

Mind you, you'd be amazed what a creative copper can classify as 'equipped'.

'Evening all,' I said. 'What's going on here, then?'

Stephen sighed and put his bag down – it clonked when it hit the floor.

'C'mon,' he said. 'I can be in and out in under an hour.'

'If it was that easy,' I said, 'why were you faffing around with the door earlier?'

'I never said it was going to be easy,' he said, folding his arms across his chest. 'I just said it was going to be fast.'

He made no move to invite me in for coffee. I wondered what he didn't want me to see.

'Smash and grab?' I asked.

'Grab yes, smash no,' he said. 'Access the roof, rappel down, cut the window, grab the goods, back out the window and down to the street.'

'The thing's got to weigh half a tonne,' I said. 'How the fuck were you going to carry it?'

Stephen mimed making a mystic gesture with his free hand.

'What, with *impello*?' Which was the go-to spell for shoving things around.

'Why not?' asked Stephen.

'You were just going to float it down the street to Old Street Station?'

He shrugged. I reckoned he must have had more of a plan than that but he wasn't about to tell me. But, then, I wouldn't have told me either if I'd been him. In the distance I heard an ambulance siren doppler past and someone shouted a greeting. Stephen kept his arms folded, but turned to face me and more completely block me from his front door.

'I thought we had an agreement,' I said.

'Hey,' said Stephen. 'You can be my wheelman if you like.'

'Turn around, Stephen,' I said, 'and go back inside. We'll talk about this on Monday.'

'You want to wait until Monday?'

'Is there some reason to be in a hurry?' I asked.

'No,' said Stephen, but he said it too casually.

'Go on,' I said. 'Back inside.'

Stephen picked up his bag, unlocked his front door and, being careful that I didn't get a glimpse of the interior, went in. The door closed with a noticeable slam.

I retreated a few metres so I wouldn't be visible from the front door's spyhole or the kitchen window. I waited a bit on the off chance he might be stupid enough to come out, or start a loud discussion with who or whatever he was hiding in the flat, but all I got was bored and cold. I started back up the balcony. But as I reached the staircase

I heard the distinctive swarm-of-bees noise a small drone makes when flying. I stopped and looked but I couldn't spot it.

I told Nightingale when I got back to the Jag and then spent a couple of minutes explaining what a drone was. There was a chance it belonged to Stephen, but drones were getting common enough in private use to become a policing issue. Especially around prisons, where they were used to smuggle in contraband.

'And I think he's got someone in his flat,' I told Nightingale, before he could be distracted by the aerial possibilities. 'And he's got an abseiling kit. So someone will have to watch the back so he doesn't shimmy out the windows there.'

'Silver's people have night-vision gear,' said Nightingale. 'They can watch the back while I watch the front.'

As police, we were well within our rights to knock down his door and find out exactly what Stephen had stashed in his flat, but then everything would have become officially official and word would have got out.

'When hunting big game like Terrence Skinner,' Silver had said at our first meeting, 'one has to stay as far downwind as one can.'

I figured South London was pretty far downwind, so I hopped on the Tube at Seven Sisters and had Beverley meet me in her sad little Kia at South Wimbledon.

* * *

I woke up the next morning to find that Bev had incorporated me into her belly support matrix and that the nameless twins were either having a good stretch or, more likely, fighting for supremacy. My forearm was tucked neatly under the Bulge and was independently asleep from the rest of my body.

'Enough,' muttered Beverley in her sleep and placed her hand on her belly. 'Go back to sleep.'

The movement subsided.

I grabbed a spare pillow, carefully substituted it for my numb arm, and eased out of the bed. Reassured that a spherical boulder wasn't going to chase me down the hallway, I went into the kitchen to make breakfast. Maksim, Beverley's combination handyman, bodyguard and only, as far as we knew, worshipful acolyte, had introduced me to the joys of baguette-based eggy bread. A dish even I can successfully cook. As soon as I had it sizzling on the frying pan, Beverley shuffled in wearing her slippers and stuck her head in the fridge. After a groan and a sigh she emerged again with a punnet of strawberries, an apple, and a catering-sized tub of Greek yoghurt. These she took to the counter, where she started chopping the fruit into two bowls. She looked over at my frying pan and frowned.

'*Grenki*,' she said. 'Again?'

'I like to play to my strengths,' I said. 'Where's Maksim?'

104

Beverley finished chopping the last of the fruit, which she then drowned in yoghurt.

'He's got the day off.' She carried the bowls over to the kitchen table and sat down. 'What about you?'

'I have today off, too,' I said. 'But I'm still on call.'

Once they were nice and crispy I slid the *grenki* out of the frying pan onto the plates and dusted them with caster sugar.

'For which job?' asked Beverley as I put the plates on the table and sat down. 'Your fake job or your secret real job?'

'Both,' I said, and started in on my *grenki* before my fruit – while it was still hot.

Once breakfast was done I finished writing up my notes from the day before. Obviously you can't carry your notebook around when you're undercover, but it's still important to keep as close to a contemporary record as possible – you never know when you might have to haul it out in court.

An hour or so later Beverley dragged me into the living room for antenatal exercises, which involved some gentle stretching, belly oiling and twenty minutes of competitive pelvic floor exercises – which Beverley won on points.

That done, I showered and started in on my PIP3 reading while Beverley climbed into the bath with a second-hand copy of *Statistics for Environmental Science and Management*. She stayed in the bath, occasionally calling down for tea and biscuits, until lunch and then insisted it was her turn to fill the dishwasher. Afterwards, once Beverley was safely stuck in front of her laptop in the living room, I surreptitiously checked to make sure she hadn't left the plates facing the wrong way again.

While I was doing that, my FBI contact in Washington texted me to arrange a Skype call for later that afternoon.

The beauty of informal contacts is that they keep working regardless of your actual legal status. My contact in the FBI was Agent Kimberley Reynolds, who officially worked for the Office of Partnership Engagement and semi-officially as a one-woman department for weird shit. We'd met when she came to London to investigate the death of a senator's son and got an impromptu introduction to the London Underground, British policing and the hidden world of magic. Since then we'd traded favours back and forth – mostly information. Our assumption was that somebody – the NSA or the FBI themselves – were monitoring the conversation at all times. So we were careful to never say anything too treasonous.

'Really? The New York Public Library service?' she said, once she'd finished asking after Beverley's Bulge. Reynolds was a thin white woman about my age with auburn hair cut into a sensible FBI bob. She was dressed in her equally sensible work suit and had her ID hanging on a lanyard around her neck. Judging by that, and the institutional beige cubicle wall behind her, I guessed she was at work.

'That's what he claims,' I said.

She asked if I had any decent photographs of him and I sent her the best of Silver's surveillance pictures. While she hadn't had time to check into Stephen the magical cat-burglar, she did have the griff on Terrence Skinner's bodyguards.

'They're from a West Coast outfit called Total Executive Cover, founded by a former Israeli called Ben Arad,' said Reynolds. 'He claims to have done "interventions" for Mossad in the 1990s, but Mossad said they never heard of him.'

'Do you believe them?' I asked.

'Mossad wouldn't tell us even if he had,' she said. 'But, as far as we can tell, he did his national service in the infantry. His mother was an American so he had dual citizenship and after finishing his service he moved to Los Angeles. Worked as an extra and stuntman before founding Total Executive Cover with a couple of fellow stuntmen.'

The company's reputation was efficient, but too show business to be truly effective. The FBI assessment was that they were perfectly fine for the average celebrity but not reliable for serious threats.

'They all have Lake Arthur badges,' she said.

'Which are what exactly?'

'Pay-to-play cops,' she said.

Because, in America, small towns run their own police departments pretty much unsupervised and a few had hit upon the idea of charging wannabe cops a fee to become peace officers.

'You're having me on,' I said.

'Nope,' said Reynolds. 'Meet Lake Arthur, population 430. Current police force a hundred plus – most of whom aren't residents.'

For 400 dollars you could get a badge and the right to carry a concealed firearm. Rumour had it Elon Musk had bought one for himself.

'And so did your boy Skinner and his security detail.'

I hoped they weren't carrying firearms in my city – otherwise we'd have to have words. Some of which would be about having the right to remain silent.

Reynolds confirmed that Terrence Skinner had hired Total Executive Cover following an unsuccessful car-jacking in Los Angeles. Employing armed security after one failed robbery attempt still seemed a bit of an overreaction to me.

'He's a billionaire,' said Reynolds. 'They don't like to be inconvenienced.'

I asked Reynolds if she could put the bodyguards on what we'd taken to calling the *Unreality List* of people that might be magical, members of the demi-monde or suspiciously weird.

'It would save ever so much time,' Reynolds had said when we set it up, 'if we just added the population of Florida right at the start.'

I went into work on Sunday because one thing the wacky world of high-tech industry had in common with policing was a disdain for taking the weekend off.

'It's much worse in Silicon Valley,' said Victor when I ran into him in the Cage. 'Over there, if you don't work the weekends they fire your arse.'

I asked where Everest was and Victor said he was in his cubicle in Golgafrincham and that we probably wouldn't be seeing him until Monday morning. Victor was picking up snacks and other life support items for him now.

'What does he actually do?' I asked.

'He tests code,' said Victor. 'His official job title is Chief Wowbagger but really that just means he's an SRE with QA.'

Which I googled later and discovered stood for Software Reliability Engineer and Quality Assurance. Which meant that it was his job to find faults in other engineers' code and make sure they fixed it. Victor was also QA, but his job was monitoring the automatic testing routines and ensuring both they and Everest were working properly.

'Everest is way more reliable than the automatic routines,' he said.

Generally speaking, people were supposed to debug their own code. Everest was usually only called in if a coder was unable to fix their own work or had run screaming out of the building, never to return.

'People burn out,' said Victor, 'or get fired. Or occasionally go crazy.'

My work that Sunday consisted of joining a pick-up game of *Firefly: The Game* that I'd been invited to by Dennis Yoon. He was a Korean-American who'd worked at one of Skinner's companies in San Jose before following his boss to London. I'd targeted him partly because of this association, but also because he lived in New Malden, which meant our commutes overlapped and I could arrange to run into him by accident on the way home.

We met in the Brontitall conference room which Dennis had booked the previous Friday. Mice were allowed to reserve conference rooms for gaming sessions, birthday parties, book clubs – any social purpose as long as it didn't involve the use of alcohol and/or gambling.

The orientation video I'd watched on my first day had proudly claimed that the SCC was a company that paid for results, not desk time. The mice might have been surprised by the degree to which the company monitored them to make sure it got its money's worth.

Or maybe not.

'They're paying,' said Ellis, a huge white guy

who worked as an optimiser – whatever that meant. 'If you don't like it you can always get another job.'

Firefly, for those that can't guess from the title, is a board game in which the players each captain a small space freighter and attempt to survive a hostile 'verse by fair means or foul. I like to play it safe and try to stay on the right side of the law. Dennis Yoon had a buccaneer's style and kept trying to cheat and, when caught, pretending that he'd made a mistake about the rules. Ellis was one of those meticulous players who slow the whole game down as they methodically consider every eventuality.

Our fourth player was another white guy the others called Princeton, whose real name was Declan Genzlinger. He'd also come over from the US with Skinner when he relocated to London. He didn't like it here much and was at pains to say so, and I took equal pains not to punch him in his smug little face. Partly because I like to think I'm bigger than that, but mostly because he worked behind the locked door on the secret project in Bambleweeny.

'Is it true you're having a kid?' asked Dennis, while we waited for Ellis to finish assessing his objectives and make his next move.

'Twins,' I said.

'Good for you,' said Dennis, but Princeton shook his head and sighed.

'It's a mistake to have kids,' he said.

When I asked why, he sighed again as if the question wearied him.

'Yeah, Princeton,' said Dennis. 'Why's that?'

'Because humanity as we know it is going to end in the next ten years,' said Princeton.

'You're thinking – what?' I asked. 'Environmental collapse? Nuclear war? Catastrophic rain of frogs?'

'He's thinking of the Singularity,' said Dennis.

'It's going to happen in 2029,' said Princeton. 'And then all this bullshit that you think is so important, you can kiss it all goodbye.'

'You can't possibly know that,' I said.

'I could show you the math but you wouldn't understand it,' said Princeton.

I said that I'd believe it when I saw it.

'Believe it,' said Princeton. 'I've seen it.'

'Shut the fuck up!' said Dennis suddenly. And then, to me, 'Sorry, but there's some things he shouldn't be talking about.' He looked at Princeton. 'Should you?'

Princeton shrugged.

'You're just going to have to trust me,' he said to me.

'Are we talking or playing?' said Ellis.

Just what was Princeton working on in Bambleweeny that made him think the Singularity – aka the nerd rapture, aka the moment when artificial intelligence passed humanity and accelerated away into an unknowable future – was arriving a couple of decades ahead of when its other acolytes and prophets proclaimed it would?

It had to be some form of AI.

I considered pushing for more, but we were playing *Star Fleet: Battles* the following Tuesday so I reckoned I'd have more opportunities then.

Shows you what I know.

Stephen came in bright and early with the Monday rush. Silver's NCA surveillance team had followed him in, so I was already in position in the Cage to bump into him. It had been agreed that I'd continue to downplay my police status. If he wanted to believe I was freelance, or a rogue, or whatever the fuck game he thought I was playing, then fine by us.

'The other night,' he said. 'You should have let me get the job done.'

'That would have been one way of getting rid of you,' I said. 'They've got lethal traps in there.'

'Yeah, right,' he said. 'Like what? Bear traps?'

'You know what kind of traps,' I said, and Stephen lost his snide look.

'You're sure about that?'

'Enough to not go rushing in,' I said. Which was a lie, but seemed to be enough to give Stephen pause.

'What's in this for you?' asked Stephen.

I sidled over to the German Segafredo coffee dispenser. This was always a reliable caffeine source, as most of the mice rushed in to empty the Mountain Dew machine and then would drain the Coca-Cola spigot and Red Bull cabinet before stooping to coffee.

'Just doing my job,' I said.

'Bullshit,' said Stephen. 'I did some digging into you. You rocked the boat and got canned. You're all on your lonesome.'

'Oh yeah?' I said.

'Yeah,' said Stephen, looking pleased with himself. 'Because I've being reading a LiveJournal by F*ckTheresaMay678. Interesting stuff.'

My God, I thought, Silver was right – Nigerian princes and all.

'You can believe what you like,' I said, because Silver had said not to overplay it. 'But if you get yourself zapped by a jellyfish bomb that's your lookout.'

Stephen opened his mouth and shut it quickly. Over his shoulder I saw Johnson approaching. Damn, but Stephen's instincts were good.

'Is that my coffee?' said Johnson as he joined us.

I said it was, and handed over my coffee.

'Got a stand-up meeting in five,' said Stephen, and wandered off. Johnson watched him go.

'Is that our rat?' he asked.

'Possibly rat adjacent,' I said, and had a twinge of uneasiness about lying to my boss.

Always remember who you're really working for, Silver had said, and I'd just nodded because it never occurred to me that that would be hard.

Johnson sent me off to do a random tag check.

I popped up to the Vogon office to grab a Vogonenabled babelphone and found Leo working away at one of the terminals. I wasn't paying attention and had he carried on working I'd have thought nothing of it – we all worked on the terminals after all – but the guilty start when I walked in made me instantly suspicious.

'What are you up to?' I asked.

'Nothing,' he said, but Leo was a council estate boy like me and 'nothing', usually spelt with two fs and a k, is your first response to everything. I sat down in one of the operating chairs and put my feet up on his desk. He sat back in his chair and folded his arms.

'How did you find those CCTV breaks?' I asked.

'What?'

'Because they're random as shit,' I said, and they certainly didn't correspond to anyone entering the building. At least not through the main entrance, and the fire exits were all reliably alarmed – I'd checked. 'So how did you spot them?'

Leo gave me a long look and then nodded.

'Can you keep a fucking secret?' he asked.

'It's been known.'

'Okay,' he said. 'Have you ever gone out and got so hammered that you wake up pissed?'

'Done that.'

'I went to a wedding in Essex, an old friend,'

said Leo. 'And drank quite a lot and didn't get much sleep and to cut a long story short had to come straight from the train station to here. Let's just say I hadn't got to the hangover stage yet.'

Which according to the contract I signed was a dismissible offence – an instantly dismissible offence at that.

'And nobody noticed?'

'I was wearing dark glasses,' he said. 'And luckily Johnson was out that morning. What I needed was something I could sit in front of that looked like work.'

Leo had put the views from six different CCTV cameras on to a screen in a remote cubicle on the second floor, grabbed a litre of sweetened iced black coffee from the vending machine with the hyperactive squirrel on the front.

'I reckoned if I lasted until about eleven I could throw up in a corridor and sign myself out sick.'

'Why didn't you just call in sick?'

'Because I was still pissed and wasn't making the best decisions,' said Leo.

Anyway, he cued up three weeks of footage, put it on fast-forward and settled in to do some serious skiving. As he sat there slumped in his chair he let the screen go in and out of focus until enough alcohol had been displaced by caffeine to make him realise what he was looking at.

About every hour, one or more of the camera

feeds would blank out. The outages lasted under five seconds but where multiple feeds were involved the outages were simultaneous.

'Did you check the other CCTV feeds?' I asked.

'No,' said Leo. 'Because by the time I'd noticed the hangover had kicked, hadn't it – so I signed myself out sick, as planned, got a good night's sleep and came in early the next morning.'

And found the random glitches extended to all the feeds he could access. He told Johnson, and then spent the rest of the day looking in vain for a pattern while the outside contractors who'd installed the cameras were called in to check their work. They did, or so they claimed, exhaustive tests on all the systems and found nothing. It was rumoured that Skinner himself had supervised a network diagnosis over the Christmas holidays, and while that also found nothing the glitches stopped.

'They said it must have been a technical fault but Johnson said he wanted to bring in someone new to investigate,' said Leo. 'And that turned out to be you.'

The implication – that Johnson didn't trust anyone who'd been working at the SCC when the glitches happened – wasn't lost on either of us. No wonder Leo was vexed.

'I think it was a technical glitch,' I said. 'But there might still be a rat.'

Leo shrugged and I left him to whatever it was he didn't want me to know he was doing, and went to see if I could catch some mice up to no good.

Vogon-issue babelphones looked the same as the general-issue ones – bright green plastic phones with an LCD screen – but with added functionality. One function allowed me to identify who was logged in at a particular terminal, which then allowed me to visually check that the right person had logged in with the right ID card.

Johnson preferred overt sweeps, where everybody could see he was checking. He thought they were a deterrent.

'Also, they know I'm not down there for the company.'

I was more covert, partly because I was less conspicuous than Johnson, but mostly because in reality I was only conducting the sweep so I could poke about amongst the cubicles for my own nefarious purposes.

That's why I found Victor, alone for once, wrangling a snack machine in the chill area on the fourth floor just short of where the skyway led to the restricted area.

He was frowning at the selection – away from the Cage the snack machines reverted to the bog standard things you could find in any canteen, train station or casualty unit. Victor stabbed the buttons and waited while the machine whirred out a packet of Hula Hoops.

'Where's Everest?' I asked.

Victor glanced towards where the skyway connected to Bambleweeny.

'Doing a consultation,' he said.

'He's not working on the secret project, then?' I asked.

'What secret project is that?' he said carefully.

I nodded over at the skyway.

'That one over there.'

'Did you read the confidentiality clauses in your employment contract?' said Victor.

'I tried,' I said. 'But I kept on falling asleep.'

'They're pretty specific about not talking about the secret project in Bambleweeny,' he said. 'Or Deep Thought.'

Which was yet another reference from *The Hitchhiker's Guide to the Galaxy*.

'He wants an answer to the ultimate question?' I asked.

'You might say that, but I couldn't possibly comment,' said Victor, and offered me a Hula Hoop. 'But I doubt it. I expect it's more Marvin the Paranoid Android than anything else.'

'An AGI?' I asked, because at the Serious Cybernetics Corporation it was important to make a distinction between Artificial General Intelligence and ordinary AI. AGI being the sort that was self-aware enough to pass the Turing test and ask difficult philosophical questions before going 'Daisy-Daisy' and trying to wipe out humanity, while ordinary AI mainly tried to sell you books on Amazon.

Victor was agnostic about AGI, but warned me about Everest who, like Princeton, prayed every night for the Singularity when choirs of algorithms would upload him aloft to a digital heaven where anything would be possible and everything permitted.

'That's assuming that the Singularity hasn't already happened,' said Victor. 'And we're not sentient virtual personalities inhabiting a simulation of reality.'

'How would we know?' I said.

Simulation or not, I felt I'd done a good day's work. Stephen the wannabe cat-burglar had been contained and I'd triangulated another potential source into Bambleweeny.

I now looked forward to spending an uneventful afternoon pretending to be a security officer to keep Johnson happy.

Hah – I don't know why I bother making plans, I really don't.

I'd taken to experimenting with the vending machines in the Cage, so I was in the middle of coaxing a kosher hot dog out of the Hot Nosh 24/6 machine when the attack happened. I'd heard the unmistakable approaching hubbub of the Terrence Skinner walking-around-show and I turned to make a quick safety check on his location. Skinner was over by a table full of adoring mice pulling up a chair and sitting down, all the better to socialise with his employees and as a bonus ruin their lunch hour. The same female bodyguard I'd seen before, and had christened Ms Side-eye, hovered behind his shoulder while minions scampered off to carry out various errands. One headed for the vending machines and I saw her checking notes hastily written on her hand before selecting the baguette dispenser. Once I had my kosher hot dog I glanced back towards Skinner and saw a man get to his feet at the next table along.

Now, I've been a specialist officer for most of my career. But I did my probation around Trafalgar Square, Soho and Covent Garden and you don't do that without learning to spot trouble before it starts.

He was white and unremarkable, brown hair and beard both long and in need of a trim. He was of the death metal T-shirt and jeans brigade, one purple, the other black, both worn loose to cover his paunch. It's hard to say what caught my eye – the speed and suddenness with which he stood, or the dramatic set of his shoulders as he prepared for his big moment in the limelight.

I saw the gun first. It looked like a toy fashioned from white plastic, but its very crudeness set off alarms. The man held it in his right hand and raised and straightened his arm, body turned to the side as if he was taking part in a duel.

'Gun!' I shouted, even as I started running.

Ms Side-eye was good. She didn't waste time looking for the shooter. Instead she grabbed Skinner by his collar and yanked him backwards off his chair, dropping him out of the line of fire and allowing herself to get her body between his and half the room.

I charged forward and was less than six metres from the shooter when he fired – close enough to see the tendons in his wrist shift as he pulled the trigger.

There was a huge bang and a gout of flame as long as the man's forearm shot from the snub barrel of the pistol. The bodyguard yelled, her back arching, spun around, tripped over her own feet and fell crashing amongst the suddenly empty chairs around her.

Panic was rippling out from the shooter, people scrambling backwards off their chairs, some going under the tables, some going over. I knew from experience that there was going to be a sloshing effect as people further away pushing in to get a better view met the inner wave of people fleeing outwards.

The shooter dropped his gun and walked towards Skinner. As he went, he transferred something from his left hand – a long, knife-shaped lump of white plastic. One of the mice didn't get out of his way fast enough and he slashed them with his plastic sword. The mouse was wearing a sleeveless denim jacket and the blade parted the fabric as if it was paper and cut into the green T-shirt underneath. The man bellowed and, sensibly, threw himself backwards out of the way.

The shooter ignored the man and walked forward. I tried to get an *impello-palma* away but a couple of panicking mice ran right into me and spun me round. As I stumbled around trying to get eyes on the shooter again, I felt the whoosh of someone somewhere doing a spell. I got orientated just in time to see the shooter stagger backwards into a table, recover himself and lurch forward with his impossibly sharp plastic knife held aloft.

Tackling a suspect with a knife is all about neutralising the knife. They can kick, punch, knee, elbow and bite you. But the knife is what will kill you, so that's your focus. Thus it's always handy when they brandish it in the air, away from anyone's soft dangly parts. And even better when they're distracted enough by their intended target that they don't see you coming.

I ran right into him and brought my fist down as hard as I could on the point between his right shoulder and his neck. The man slumped forward, dropping the plastic knife and landing face down on the floor. This is the so-called brachial stun which I'd been taught at Hendon and which had cropped up at least once in every officer safety refresher I'd ever attended. I'd never done it for real before and was so surprised when the man went down that I nearly fucked up the follow-up.

It was only when he groaned that I thought to grab his right hand in a wrist lock and put my knee in his back to stop him from rolling over.

'No,' he wailed.

I was reaching for my non-existent cuffs when he burst into tears.

There was a scattering of applause, which is always appreciated but not exactly useful. A couple of adventurous mice shuffled forward as if to help.

'Okay!' I shouted in my best police voice. 'Can I ask everyone who is not a Vogon to stay where they are, please?'

I kept my weight on the shooter's arms but he obviously wasn't the wriggling type – instead he continued to cry. I glanced over at Ms Side-eye, who was sitting up and clutching her side. She winced as she probed for injuries, but I didn't see any blood.

I looked over to make sure nobody had touched the weapons. I couldn't see the gun. But the white plastic knife lay where it had fallen, a red smear still on its blade – which reminded me. The guy who'd been cut was sitting on a chair at a nearby table, breathing hard while he held a wad of bloody – but not soaked, thank God – paper towels to his side.

'Mr Skinner!' I called, turning away from the guy. 'Are you okay?'

He was lying behind the bodyguard half under

a table. He tried to sit up, but the bodyguard pushed him firmly back down.

'I'm just bonzer,' he said.

It probably took Johnson less than ninety seconds to make it down from his office, but it felt like much longer.

CHAPTER 6

DECEMBER: CHANGES IN
RELATIVE CHARGE

London commercial property crashes are as routine and as cyclical as the career of the boy band du jour. There is an economic boom, companies expand and demand greater office space. Property companies buy land to build offices, which drives up prices, which inflates the value of the property companies. Investors pile in because the value is increasing, thus pushing up the value even further and giving a better virtual return on investment. The property companies start building a series of increasingly utilitarian offices, but before most of them are finished the market contracts, demand slumps and London ends up with massive amounts of surplus office space.

This is good news for the police, because they can rent some relatively cheap offices in a safely anonymous building when they want to stash a specialist unit away from other police, the media, and the sort of people who have friends in high places. Bonus points if you situate it somewhere people don't normally visit such as Slough,

Croydon or – in the case of Operation Fretwork – Hornchurch.

There, Officer Alona Silver had grown a pocket policing empire in a refurbished 1930s industrial building that had been going begging since 2012. It had thick brick walls, adequate car parking and the sort of anonymous dullness that is a boon to anyone who needs somewhere secure to plan something shady.

'Welcome to the Exchange,' said Silver, when she picked me and Nightingale up from reception. We were issued with corporate-looking guest IDs on lanyards which we were required to hang around our necks at all times. Silver wore one with her name and picture on it, beside a red and orange strip which was definitely not her warrant card or any other kind of official issue. They were obviously taking secrecy very seriously – I had to wonder why.

'It starts with money laundering,' said Silver once we'd reached the safety of her office. 'Where it goes after that I don't know.'

With its lack of decoration, steel filing cases and severe grey and black metal desks, I think Silver had been aiming at austere and no-nonsense. Whatever the initial plans had been, it had been buried under stacks of box files, papers, copies of *Forbes*, *The Economist* and other glossy financial porn mags. Two walls had been covered in pinboards including the wall with the windows in it. I could just see grey daylight filtering over the top.

Silver ushered us into a pair of cheap tubular knock-off Bauhaus chairs and retreated behind her desk. She offered coffee but Nightingale asked for tea. That done, Silver fished a laptop out from under a stack of paper, stabbed at its keyboard and then turned it round to show us the screen. It displayed a publicity still of Terrence Skinner smiling at the camera, in a casual navy jacket and white shirt with the collar and top button unfastened. He looked pleased with himself.

'Two hundred million dollars stolen from the Malaysian Development Fund may, or may not, have passed through his company,' she said.

'But you're not certain?' said Nightingale.

'No,' said Silver. 'I won't bore you with the details, but let's say that the trail marches all the way up to his doorstep, his new London doorstep I might add, and stops short.'

'The City is awash with dodgy funds,' I said. 'What makes this different?'

'The difference, constable,' said Silver, 'is that I've been tasked to investigate this particular instance.'

Money laundering classically has three stages called placement, layering and integration. Traditional crime – drug smuggling, protection rackets, illegal gambling – generates wodges of cash. If a known face starts shelling out readies for the good things in life, people get suspicious. Which can result in arrest, conviction, gaol and

– worst of all – forfeiture of funds. So the money has to be 'placed', usually through cash intensive businesses like hairdressers, kebab shops and retail banks.

If placement is loading the machine, then layering is the wash cycle where funds are shunted around, from company to offshore account to financial instrument, and then filtered through a fine mesh of shell companies whose only purpose is to disguise where the money comes from and who has their snout in the trough.

Silver pulled a face.

'Every so often someone from KPMG or Price Waterhouse will turn up on Bloomberg and explain how multiple shell companies are vital to modern business,' she said, and then glared at us as if expecting us to comment.

We gave her the bland reassuring expression that police have been using on the obviously upset since Daniel had that tricky moment with the lion.

Integration is when the criminal opens the door of their international financial spin dryer and pulls out their nice clean money and, pausing only to rub its silky smoothness against the cheek and comment on its lemony freshness, spends it just like an ordinary rich person.

'The big players and the state actors don't deal in cash anyway,' said Silver. 'They go straight to layering and integration.'

'Terrorist financing,' said Nightingale. 'Isn't that what you chaps are interested in?'

'That's mostly Five's concern,' said Silver, meaning MI5. 'We were tracking this as part of a layering operation. These tech entrepreneurs believe that the rules don't really apply to them, so Skinner wouldn't be the first to actively pursue dirty money if they get into difficulty.'

'Was he in difficulty?' asked Nightingale.

'He left California in a hurry,' said Silver. 'He sold his house in Saratoga and other properties in San Francisco and San Jose. We can't be sure, but we think he divested himself of his stockholdings in several hi-tech companies he helped start. We were expecting a call from some branch of the US Government informing us he was wanted for something. When that didn't materialise, we expected enraged creditors. What we weren't expecting was the GRU.'

Apparently nobody ever expects the GRU, Russian Military Intelligence, partly because it changed its official name to GU, but mostly because everybody is too busy worrying about the agency formerly known as the foreign intelligence wing of the KGB – the SVR RF.

'We traced a payment from one Antem Sergeyevich Yershov, a mid-tier oligarch,' said Silver. Mid-tier meaning that he was merely obscenely wealthy, rather than functionally an independent nation state in his own right. 'Like most of his kind he's been looking to stash his ill-gotten gains abroad and we assumed this was merely a money laundering operation.'

Except GCHQ had passed on the gist, not the details, of an intercept that indicated that not only had Yershov transferred the money as a down payment for a job, but he'd done so on behalf of the GRU. An organisation he'd been an agent of in his younger days and had maintained strong informal links with ever since.

'Informal networks,' said Silver. 'You can track the connections, but it's almost impossible to prove in a court of law.'

'So what are the Russians paying Mr Skinner to do?' asked Nightingale.

'That's a good question, because as far as we can tell the Serious Cybernetics Corporation produces sweet FA,' said Silver. 'If they're producing any product, real or virtual, they're not even advertising it, let alone selling it. A better question would be how Terrence Skinner made his millions in the first place.'

At last a chance to shine.

'Algorithms,' I said.

That's what Skinner had been famous for. Data compression for server farms and then developing trading programs for financial companies and online retail.

'That's what we think,' said Silver.

'What would the GRU want with algorithms?' I said.

'GCHQ have some mad theory that they're

going to try to influence public opinion in the West,' she said. 'Perhaps in support of an effort to get sanctions lifted.'

'Could they do that?' asked Nightingale, who I suspected thought algorithms were something to do with Art Blakey and the Jazz Messengers.

'They're all getting very agitated up at Cheltenham,' said Silver. 'So I wouldn't bet against it.'

'And is that what you think Skinner is working on?' I asked. 'An algorithm?'

'A suite of tailor-made algorithms designed to suit the GRU's operational needs across a wide variety of platforms,' she said. 'That's what we think, or at least that's what we thought right up until you phoned us.'

I'd sent her a detailed report of our findings after our initial phone call, so she knew all about Skinner's interest in the Mary Engine and the 137-key music book. We like to keep the more overt magic elements out of our official communications. But fortunately Officer Silver had worked with us before, so she knew when to read between the lines.

'Is it possible the GRU are looking to acquire a Falcon asset?' asked Silver.

'Historically, the Russians have had extensive Falcon assets of their own,' said Nightingale. He didn't say how we knew this, and Silver didn't ask, although she was obviously dying to.

I suggested we could just wander round and ask

the Serious Cybernetics Corporation to help us with our inquiries. Silver said that, alas, tech entrepreneurs, especially ones who cut their teeth in America, tend to be obstructive in principle, and lawyer intensive in practice.

'Normally,' said Silver, 'I'd insert an undercover officer into the company to confirm whether this was espionage, ordinary crime or just business.'

'And what's preventing you in this instance?' asked Nightingale in a dry tone that indicated that, like me, he'd already seen the way the conversation was going.

'I don't have any officers qualified to make a Falcon assessment,' she said. 'And Peter's recent suspension would provide the perfect cover.'

And thus yours truly was launched into the murky world of undercover policing. My first time, not counting when me and Lesley went semi-undercover at Skygarden Towers. And we all know how that ended.

'You're a natural,' said Silver. 'Just don't piss off *The Guardian* and we'll be fine.'

Since by that time the Folly's mews was full of builders, I let myself in through the side entrance and into what were once the servants' corridors. These were narrow, with bare brick walls and a single energy-saving bulb hanging forlornly from the ceiling. The door at the end had a spyhole so that a conscientious servant could check to ensure that the young masters wouldn't be inconvenienced by his sudden appearance. I had a look but it was covered over by more plastic sheeting, as I found out when I opened the door.

The Folly had been built with an impressive central atrium that rose up to an iron and glass dome installed in 1861 by the same people who'd worked on the Crystal Palace. Usually it was the natural habitat of overstuffed green leather armchairs, antique occasional tables and art deco coffee tables. All that glory was currently smothered under waves of blue sheeting and plastic mats laid down to protect the floor. There was a yawning gap in the eastern edge of the floor from which the conveyor belt snaked out amidst a welter of scaffolding before heading out towards the front and the waiting skip.

The air smelt of tarpaulin and wet cement.

From below, voices shouted instructions and jokes back and forth in Polish and Romanian.

Towards the west wall, white dust sheets had been thrown over furniture and rucked up so that they resembled the peak of a snowy mountain. Seated at the top was a young Polish builder, naked to the waist, with his elbow on his knee and his chin resting on the back of his hand. He was being painted by a young white woman in an artist's smock who stood behind an easel a couple of metres away. She was tall and long-limbed, with a cascade of black hair that fell down her back. Her face was subtly inhuman with high cheekbones and a smile that contained too many teeth.

This was Foxglove, who was the Folly's artist-in-residence and fully paid-up member of the fair folk. I learnt later that, tired of being pestered and worried about health and safety, the builders now volunteered one of their members to pose each afternoon and keep Foxglove occupied.

Meanwhile her 'sister', Molly, the Folly's live-in housekeeper and demon deterrent, had added *savarina*, poppy seed cake and a kind of heavy Polish doughnut filled with plum paste to her traditional cake repertoire.

I didn't disturb Foxglove. You could pick her pockets when she's painting and she wouldn't notice.

I found Nightingale in the first-floor study, sitting at the map table with a battered red hard-back open in front of him. He was making notes with a fountain pen on a Ryman pad of lined A4 paper. He looked up with evident relief when I entered.

'I'm refreshing my memory of the theory behind the basic *formae*,' he said when I asked what he was up to.

'For Abigail?' I asked. Abigail being my cousin and Nightingale's other younger, smarter apprentice.

'In part,' said Nightingale. 'I was reviewing some of the textbooks from Casterbrook and discovered that I was somewhat slapdash when I trained you in the basics.'

The Folly had once had its very own school of

witchcraft and wizardry – well, wizardry, because obviously women hadn't been invented until 1945. And after that there was nobody left to teach, and nobody who wanted to learn. Or at least that was the received wisdom. Nightingale had learned his magic at Casterbrook amongst other suitable boys and was generally considered the best spellcaster of his generation, although he'd admitted to me that he'd always been a bit hazy as to the theory behind the magic.

My own training had been hurried, on the job, and mostly focused on keeping me alive long enough to make sergeant.

'Slapdash?' I asked.

'From the point of view of the masters at Casterbrook, in any case,' said Nightingale. 'Although you appear to have mastered the forms and wisdom quite handily despite my limitations. With Abigail we can afford to take our time with the curriculum.'

I had my doubts about that.

'"In part", you said. What's the rest?'

'I'm surprised you don't remember,' said Nightingale with a grin. 'Implementation of Section 3A – "Ensuring requisite skill coverage in future Falcon operations" – at least six Falcon officers is what I believe you recommended.'

'That,' I said.

'Quite,' said Nightingale. 'I thought I'd use the legal group as guinea pigs.'

The legal group were a nest of City lawyers

that we'd smoked out during the hunt for Martin Chorley. I trusted them about as far as I trust anyone that far up the corporate hierarchy, but Nightingale had insisted that it was better to have them safely trained and supervised than running around giving themselves brain injuries. I'm pretty sure I could have learnt to live with the guilt, but he was right. And the thought of Nightingale experimenting on them cheered me up no end.

'Will you be staying for tea?' asked Nightingale.

'I've got to work on my legend,' I said, 'but I should be done by tea.'

'Excellent,' said Nightingale. 'Then I'm sure we can fit in some practice after.'

'Of course,' I said, and made a mental note to text Bev. She's made it clear that while she accepts that as police my hours are irregular, she doesn't see how carrying a warrant card prevents me from using my phone.

'And do it at the earliest possible opportunity,' was the advice of the firmly married Detective Inspector Stephanopoulos.

Next door to the reading room was a small study which I used as my office when operating out of the Folly. Despite lacking Wi-Fi, or Ethernet, or anything remotely connectable, it did have a row of big green filing cabinets. They were green government-issue jobs from the 1930s with heavy-duty locks and I used them to store my daybooks, notepads, duplicate copies of arrest files, lists of good takeaway places and anything else I deemed professionally useful.

Before heading for the Folly I'd looked up the last couple of years in policing and downloaded likely grievances onto my laptop. I started making up a blog under the tag of F**kTheresaMay678, composed of the sort of material it was unwise to commit to the record, however electronically ephemeral.

Nothing you wouldn't hear ad bloody nauseam wherever us lower ranks gather together, but the managerial levels notoriously have no sense of humour about bringing the profession into disrepute. Especially if they think you're getting political.

I started with a couple of events that could be linked to me in my probationary days, including the showgirl and the tiny arsonist, and the virtual flasher. Then I let in a bit of grump about the 'cheer up and smile' campaign during the Olympics. Which segued nicely into pay and pensions and who was to blame. Poured in a bit more vitriol for the massive mullering police budgets got, and let the more-in-sorrow-than-in-anger tone mutate into outright anger.

You could have heard all of it in any police canteen in the country, assuming the canteen hadn't been closed down, or wherever two or three response officers gathered together. I finished up with a massive rant about the lack of secure mental health places and the fact that the police were always expected to fill in for the gaps in social care. I directly named senior officers and politicians, but only because Nightingale and Silver had both signed a policy document, one copy of which was now locked in a safe under Molly's bed.

'These people live online,' Silver had said. 'The first thing they'll do is find any social media accounts you've got. We just need to make sure you're hard enough to trace to make it convincing.'

The idea being that they would find my blog and jump to the right conclusion – that I'd been eased out for speaking my mind.

'Nobody's going to fall for this,' I said.

'Of course they will,' said Silver. 'They fall for Nigerian princes all the time.'

'Stupid people do,' I said.

'Wrong,' said Silver. 'It doesn't matter if you're a leading astrophysicist or thicker than a bag full of bricks. Whether the mark falls for a scam depends on experience, knowledge and how much they want it to be true.'

Silver was confident because, in her experience, tech types were particularly attracted to conspiracy theories.

'They all want to think they're on a watch list,' she said. 'It makes them feel important.'

I failed to point out that we were engaged in a conspiracy of state-sponsored disinformation, because I reckoned Silver was already aware of the irony and nobody likes a clever clogs.

139

Towards the end of our first briefing I'd asked Silver how long the operation was going to take.

'The whole operation or your undercover part?'

'My undercover part.'

She asked whether I had a previous engagement.

'In three months,' I said. 'I'm going on parental leave come hell or high water. And I literally mean high water.'

Sometimes when I put my ear against the Bulge and closed my eyes I'd swear I could hear the twins singing. Beverley rolled her eyes when I told her that.

'You know, I thought you were going to go all starry-eyed,' she said. 'But you're even worse than I thought you would be.'

'You don't think they're going to be "special"?' I asked – meaning leaning more towards her side of the family, the River Goddess side, than mine, the common as muck side.

'What I know,' she said, 'is that they're enormous now and they're going to be even bigger before I pop.'

This was normal for twins or, more precisely, normal for a certain value of normal that wasn't satisfactory for someone who was a) actually experiencing it and b) had discovered the word epistemology and was wondering on, exactly, what basis that normality had been defined.

Up until the second trimester I'd thought

epistemology was something to do with allergies, so that shows you what I knew about it.

Still, I thought they were singing. Although to be honest, it was probably more of a hum.

We'd talked about their 'specialness' back when they were a theoretical twinkle in Beverley's eye and the practical day to day was a comfortable distance in the future. A theoretical distance at that. Only one of Beverley's sisters had had kids of her own and they'd turned out mostly ordinary. Well, ordinary posh, anyway. So that wasn't much help.

I'd even asked my mum about it, in as round-about a fashion as I could manage, but all she said was, *All man e pekin special to e mama ein e papa.*

Also unhelpful.

One of the twins kicked me in the ear, so I turned to that spot and kissed it.

'Don't,' said Beverley. 'That tickles. And in any case it encourages them.'

'Really?'

Beverley pushed herself up against her pillows, the better to stare down at me and shake her head sadly.

'You would have been a terrible scientist,' she said. 'You've got no objectivity at all.'

'It's hard to be objective about this.'

I kissed the Bulge for the last time and crawled up the bed to lie by Beverley's side. She took my hand, interlaced her fingers in mine and placed it on her belly. There was a last push against my hand and then they were still.

'Is it going to be dangerous?' she asked.

'Nah,' I said. 'It's not Trident or drugs. It's white-collar crime.'

'White-collar *magic* crime,' said Beverley.

'It's still intelligence gathering,' I said. 'There's not going to be any rough stuff.'

'Don't make promises you can't keep,' she said. 'And be careful.'

PART II

THE COLOSSUS

Why, man, he doth bestride the narrow world
Like a Colossus; and we petty men
Walk under his huge legs, and peep about
To find ourselves dishonourable graves.

William Shakespeare, *Julius Caesar*, Act I,
Scene II

PART II

THE COLOSSUS

Why man, he doth bestride the narrow world
Like a Colossus; and we petty men
Walk under his huge legs and peep about
To find ourselves dishonourable graves.

William Shakespeare, *Julius Caesar*, Act I,
Scene II.

CHAPTER 7

NO MORE SOAP OPERA

It's weird watching an investigation from the wrong side of the blue and white tape. Johnson had asked me to monitor this and it was like watching a particularly well-researched TV show. I found myself nodding approvingly at the way everyone entered the crime scene via the single line of approach with their masks and goggles in place.

Bad for audience identification in TV dramas, but vital for avoiding cross-contamination in real life.

It was also theatre. The suspect had been led away from the scene in handcuffs, there were eyewitnesses and internal CCTV showing the attack. The police didn't need source-level forensics to put him at the scene and the only inceptive evidence required to put him away was the knife and the gun – and they were already bagged and tagged.

The mice had all been cleared out and sent home, the suspect had been whisked off and Skinner and the wounded bodyguard had retired to one of the conference rooms. But not before her ballistic vest – and, presumably, the bullet – had been politely but firmly taken away.

She hadn't liked that, I'd noticed, but she had been sensible enough not to withhold evidence.

I suspected the whole *Silent Witness* routine was more about the police imposing themselves on the company and having a good sniff around. There was a tall woman in a noddy suit who might have been Silver, but I couldn't tell with the mask and goggles.

'Do you know any of this lot?' asked Johnson when he joined me later.

'Some of them,' I said. 'That's DI Stephanopoulos.'

Even in an anonymous noddy suit there was no mistaking the set of her shoulders or the slight limp that was the legacy of a gunshot wound.

'*The* Stephanopoulos?' said Johnson. 'I've heard of her.'

'If she's here then it means DCI Seawoll is the SIO,' I said.

'I've heard of him too,' said Johnson.

'Who was the suspect?' I asked. 'Do you know?'

'His name was William Lloyd,' said Johnson. 'Software engineer is what it says in his folder. I don't think I met him more than once.'

That was unusual. Johnson had retained the copper's habit of getting to know everyone by sight – just in case you have to arrest them later.

'How come?'

'He worked upstairs in Bambleweeny,' he said. 'Looked at his personnel file. He's from Harborne.'

'Where's that?'

'Birmingham,' said Johnson. 'Went to Cambridge, lasted a year before dropping out to work for various game companies. Good references from all of them. No security flags or criminal record.'

I remembered the way he'd burst into tears when I'd restrained him. He'd been full of fury and tension when he attacked, but it had drained away the instant it was done.

'Did you get a look at the weapons?' asked Johnson. 'They wouldn't let me get close.'

'A knife and an improvised firearm,' I said. 'They both looked like they were made out of plastic.'

'Any idea where they might have come from?'

'Do we have any 3-D printers on the premises?'

Johnson frowned.

'Not that I know of,' he said.

'In Bambleweeny?'

Johnson said nothing. His own exclusion from Bambleweeny had to rankle something rotten. Policing is about ownership – officers are expected to take ownership of a problem and thus be responsible for the outcomes. It didn't matter if that was a dipping in Covent Garden, an attempted murder in Old Street or maintaining the security at the headquarters of a tech start-up. Being made responsible without proper ownership is the sort of thing that causes dissatisfaction amongst the rank and file. Although I admit closing half the canteens in London probably ranks higher.

'Have they said what they want from you?' asked Johnson.

'When they've finished faffing about, they want me to go down to Belgravia to give a statement,' I said.

'Not a problem,' said Johnson. 'One thing about Mr Skinner is that when it comes to legal he's got your back.'

I was interviewed by a young Somali DS in an expensive green and gold hijab and a beautifully tailored navy-blue suit that I knew for a fact had been conjured out of a backstreet tailor's in Hong Kong. I knew this because her name was Sahra Guleed and we'd been colleagues for over three years. I was dying to ask how her visit to see her fiancé's family had gone, but unfortunately Terrence Skinner wasn't about to let one of his employees speak to the po po without an expensive lawyer present. So the catch-up was going to have to wait.

Guleed put enough bite into it to make it convincing, but my role was pretty clear-cut – quick-thinking saviour of the day. Don't thank me, ma'am, just doing my job. We were done in less than an hour and at the end Guleed shook my hand and thanked me for my cooperation without a hint of irony. I deliberately dawdled in the corridor on the way out so that the expensive lawyer could pass out of earshot.

'This is getting confusing,' said Guleed quietly. 'I heard you were reinstated, I go on holiday and when I get back they tell me you'd left the job.'

'That was part of my cover,' I said. 'So I could apply for the job at SCC.'

'So you're undercover?'

'Yes.'

'As yourself?'

'It saves on having to memorise stuff,' I said. 'I'm sure Nightingale will arrange a briefing as soon as he can.'

Silver and Nightingale read in Guleed's bosses DCI Seawoll and DI Stephanopoulos on the details of the Terrence Skinner case – something I was glad to get out of. I'd worked with them before and the pair had a very clear idea about the distinction between what they considered honest coppering and what we were doing on behalf of the NCA.

I provided a more informal briefing for Guleed in the upstairs lounge at the Folly where the cakes and coffee were free, although there was still a faint smell of cement around the place and some patches on the restored staircase that needed snagging.

'I really missed this place,' said Guleed as she picked out a second slice of Citrus Madeira cake. 'The canteen at AB just doesn't have the same ambience.'

She asked after Beverley and the Bulge and we caught up on her sisters and her trip to Hong Kong to meet the 'potentials', as she referred to her fiancé's family.

I asked what they were like.

'Strangely familiar,' she said. 'I don't have to tell you about how big extended families work.'

'What do they think about Michael converting?'

'We glossed over that bit.'

'And the melanin part?'

Guleed shrugged. 'They don't have much choice in the matter, do they?' she said, which was my cue not to press too hard.

'And did they strike you as particularly magical?' I asked.

'You mean where did Michael pick up his legendary swordsmanship?'

'Yeah, that.'

'Not his mum and dad, but I got the impression there were some uncles and aunties who were practiced. I didn't meet them, though.'

Molly came gliding in with a silver tray and coffee service. Dressed in a viciously starched black and white Edwardian maid's uniform, she let her straight black hair cascade down her back all the way to the waist. Pale-skinned, she had a narrow face with sharp features and black, almond-shaped eyes. She would have looked like something from *Downton Abbey* but only if they'd had a Halloween special directed by Guillermo del Toro.

Noiselessly she placed two cups of Turkish coffee, plus sugar and accoutrements, on the table before us. As she swept out I realised that her sister Foxglove had sneaked in and was sitting cross-legged on a nearby overstuffed leather armchair and peering at us over the top of her A2 sketchpad.

Guleed said 'Hi', but Foxglove remained focused on her sketch.

'Ignore her,' I said. 'She won't say hello until she's knocked off a couple of likenesses for her collection.'

While Guleed posed for a picture that would later hang in an art gallery in Gateshead, I read the notes on would-be assassin William Lloyd's interview. Or, more precisely, his evaluation. Because he remained uncommunicative and was sectioned to the secure mental health facility at Northwick Park.

He claimed that he was asleep when the attack happened. When confronted by the overwhelming evidence of his actions, he said he couldn't explain it unless he was sleepwalking.

'I woke up with some black guy holding me down,' he said.

'Does that look like the glamour to you?' asked Guleed.

'Or something like it,' I said, because it's better not to make assumptions. 'And he could still be faking it.'

I wondered if I could get Beverley to glamour

me and try to replicate that sensation of sleep-walking. But she'd refused such experiments in the past on mental health grounds. And there was a third possibility.

'He could have been sequestrated,' I said.

Guleed shifted uncomfortably in her seat.

'Like what happened to Lesley?' she asked.

PC Lesley May, who'd been at Hendon and Charing Cross with me and had worked with Guleed at Belgravia. Who had picked up an unwanted mental hitchhiker in the form of Mr Punch – otherwise known as the Spirit of Riot and Rebellion. A 'sequestration' that left her physically disfigured and mentally scarred.

Once I'd have called her my best mate, but now . . . wanted for murder was just the start.

'Do you think Nightingale could do an assessment?' asked Guleed.

'I think he's going to have to,' I said. 'And you know Abdul and Jennifer will want to have a look, too.'

And no doubt stick his head in an MRI.

Dr Jennifer Vaughan and Dr Abdul Haqq Walid being the Folly's combination pathologists and medical officers. Both had a keen interest in just what the overuse of magic does to someone's brain to make it resemble a diseased cauliflower.

Guleed nodded and poured herself another cup of coffee.

'Did he seem weird when you tackled him?'

'Not particularly,' I said. 'It reminded me a bit

152

of Leicester Square on a Saturday night. He was shouting, I was shouting, everyone was making a noise.'

'He said something a couple of times that stuck in my mind,' said Guleed.

'Oh yeah?'

'He said "It talks to you but nothing is ever logged." Mean anything to you?'

'No,' I said. I didn't ask whether she'd tried to follow up because of course she had.

'Have we had a report on the weapons?' I asked.

'I had to phone up and threaten people this morning to get some answers,' said Guleed. 'They think both the gun and the knife were produced on a 3-D printer but they don't want to say definitely.'

The gun design itself appeared to be the famous 'Liberator', which was intended to be manufactured on a 3-D printer and help bring about the armed citizenry that would return the US to its past glory – when governments were small, men were real men and women were grateful. Only the general consensus was that, even if you got the thing to work, it was more likely to blow your hand off than hit anything.

No more a firearm, said the report, than any other short piece of plastic pipe.

What the report didn't find was a cartridge. The design, as downloaded from the internet, required a standard pistol cartridge which provided bullet and propellant. Once the round was out of the 'barrel' – the forensics team actually put quotes around *barrel* – the casing should have been left behind. Worse, not only couldn't they find a casing but there was no trace of any propellant on the weapon.

'Also,' said Guleed, 'they said the thermoplastic used to print the knife wasn't capable of keeping an edge. At least not one consistent with the injuries inflicted on Ian Cobwright.'

Cobwright being the mouse who'd got sliced.

'Is he okay?'

'Who, Cobwright?'

'Yeah.'

'He's fine,' said Guleed. 'Superficial cut. Your fake boss paid for a private room, flowers, hot and cold running nurses but weirdly no grapes.'

'Speaking of fake bosses,' I said. 'Tyrel Johnson has invited me to his house for supper.'

Guleed frowned.

'Don't get too involved with these people,' she said. 'You might have to arrest some of them.'

Tyrel Johnson lived in a 1930s semi in Roehampton that had six bedrooms, two bathrooms and more mock Tudor than an episode of *Blackadder II*. Given the neighbourhood and the rear view over Richmond golf course, it should have been worth at least a couple of million if the A3, in all its dual carriageway'd glory, hadn't run less than a metre from its front gate. It was also less than two hundred metres from Beverley Brook where she crossed from Wimbledon Common over into Richmond Park. Bev could have swum it in less than five minutes – something that she pointed out when we got caught in traffic on the Kingston bypass. More than once.

Still, we arrived on time and pulled into the neatly paved car park which was all that remained of a large front garden. Bev didn't approve of that either, although she didn't say where we would have parked otherwise. A Nissan Leaf was stationed at a charging point next to a Citroën people carrier and a battered black Range Rover. I knew all about the house, all about the cars, and all about the short white woman with the mousey hair who opened the front door to let us in.

Even so, I would have pegged Stacy Carter as Job or ex-Job by the reflex way she scanned Bev and me up and down before smiling and letting us in. It's something we do automatically to make sure we can give an accurate description later, on the off chance a casual acquaintance goes off the deep end and does something arrestable.

She was thin-faced and blue-eyed with a sharp nose and a thin expressive mouth which broke into a wide smile as soon as we'd passed muster.

'At last,' she said. 'You two have deigned to visit our humble abode.'

Not that humble, I thought, as she led us into a wide hallway with an antique walnut hat and coat stand and a red and green tiled floor.

'I'm Stacy, of course,' she said, taking our coats and then pausing at her first proper sight of the Bulge.

'How far gone are you?' she asked, and whistled when Bev told her. 'Twins?'

'I'm afraid so,' said Bev.

Stacy grinned. 'I wouldn't be afraid yet, love,' she said. 'Fear comes later when they get mobile.' Her smile dropped for a moment. 'No problems, right? Nothing medical?'

Beverley assured Stacy that everything was proceeding to order and that so far, touch wood, nothing had gone wrong. I knew from the NCA's background check that Stacy had suffered three late-term miscarriages in her early thirties.

The hallway smelt faintly of floor polish and damp coats. Lining the walls on both sides were pictures of young men and women in formal head and shoulder poses. Most of them were black or mixed race, but a couple were desi and at least one was white. They were all smartly turned out and half of them were holding up certificates or trophies. Directly ahead, Tyrel Johnson appeared in the kitchen doorway dressed in a rugby shirt in Richmond FC colours. He was holding a spatula, which he waved at us in greeting.

'Well,' he said, having got an eyeful of Beverley, 'this explains why Peter is such a cheerful lad, doesn't it?'

'Get back in the kitchen,' said Stacy. 'Before we all die of starvation.' She turned to us and told us not to let Johnson's appearance in the kitchen fool us. 'I do most of the cooking round here.'

The front and back ground-floor rooms had been knocked into one to form what an estate agent would have described as a Reception/Dining Room. Normal people don't routinely eat in their dining room, but in this case the outsized pine table, which easily sat ten, had a battered look. It was in the process of being laid by a sullen-looking white teenager with brown hair cut into a skinhead and an obviously handmade biro tattoo on her cheek that must have really hurt.

This was Keira Slater, whose mum had left the family home one evening, when Keira was nine, and never returned. She'd lived on her own and managed to maintain a semblance of normality, including attending school for nine months until the council sent the bailiffs round to collect the unpaid council tax. She'd then been placed with two homes and three foster families, but had either run away or been rejected as too disruptive. She'd run away from Stacy and Johnson's home at least three times in the two years she'd been placed there, but always came back.

'This is Keira,' said Stacy.

Keira acknowledged us with a grudging tilt of the head and then went back to laying the knives and forks.

Stacy looked over to where a skinny young black man was standing hesitantly in front of a glass-fronted mahogany bookshelf. He had the top of his hair in dreads with a fade on the sides. It made him look like he was auditioning for an American cable show as the quirky but tragically expendable best friend.

'Oliver,' said Stacy, 'be a love and fetch a couple of cushions for the recliner.'

Oliver Partridge, aged seventeen, had been given up for care by his mother when he was twelve, after he'd knifed the neighbour's dog and tried to strangle the family cat. He'd spent a couple of years in a secure psychiatric unit. The NCA couldn't access his confidential records but, judging by his track record since he was discharged, he was fine providing he stayed on the meds.

Oliver gave Beverley a shy smile and slipped out of the living room.

Stacy asked Beverley if she'd like a drink.

'We've got lemonade, Coke, ginger beer,' she said, and turned to me. 'Would you like a beer?'

I said I'd have a ginger beer because I was driving, although of course as a rule of thumb you should never drink while undercover, anyway. How to unobtrusively dump your drink was one of the few bits of tradecraft Silver thought it was worth spending time teaching me.

Oliver returned with a pair of linen-covered foam pillows, which he arranged on the recliner so that Beverley could sit down with suitably grateful cries of comfort, and once enthroned accept a glass of lemonade.

Beverley's personality and Bulge dragged the centre of the room over to her and soon Stacy and Keira were copping a feel and exchanging bladder anecdotes. I found myself having a non-conversation with Oliver who, despite answering in an astonishing range of monosyllables, told me nothing at all. I did ask him what he wanted to do when he left school, and was relieved when he said he wanted to start a YouTube channel rather than something like, say, taxidermy.

I was saved from conversational death by the arrival of Chef Johnson, who barged into the dining room brandishing a soup tureen.

'Places everyone,' he said. 'Dinner *c'est arrive.*'

Oliver and Keira jumped to it while Stacy helped Beverley out of her seat and hovered while she got her legs under the table. A rich smell was wafting from the tureen, bypassing my brain and causing my stomach to growl.

'Cow heel soup,' Johnson said with glee as he served it up.

But if he was thinking either me or Beverley were going to be appalled by eating the wrong bit of the cow, he was going to be disappointed. I've eaten sweetmeats and brawn, and if you don't know what they are you're better off not knowing. Trust me on this.

It's easy enough to make tasty soup; you just follow the instructions. But making delicious soup takes skill. And, judging by the delicate taste of the dumplings, that is what Johnson had. It isn't easy making delicate dumplings. Mine tend to be a bit on the loft insulation side, so I know what I'm talking about.

Conversation proceeded about where I'd expected it to – some baby chat, some 'how are you finding it at work?' chat. Keira would interrupt every so often to say sarky and irrelevant things. Oliver said nothing, but I did catch him smiling at a joke once. It was a surprisingly shy smile for a young man teetering on the verge of violent psychopathy.

The report had been very clear, Stacy and Tyrel were his last chance. One more violent incident and it was goodbye Roehampton and hello Broadmoor.

The main course, again presented with some ceremony by Johnson, was curried prawns, with beef pelau for Keira, who didn't like seafood, cassava, sweet potato, glazed carrots and steamed peas.

'Can you write this down?' I asked. 'I want to give this to my mum.'

Johnson looked pleased, but Stacy gave me a calculating look thinking, I guessed, that I was sucking up to the boss. Which was true, sort of, but I still wanted that recipe.

'You'll notice he's made enough for eight people,' said Stacy. 'He always makes twice as much as we need.'

'I'll have seconds, then,' said Beverley, and so did everyone else except for Keira who said she was watching her weight.

'You'll notice the pot is empty,' said Johnson when we'd finished.

Stacy clapped her hands and Oliver and Keira sprang up and started clearing away.

'So what's for pudding?' asked Beverley.

'Ice cream,' said Stacy. 'Or there's some banana cake.' She jerked her thumb at Johnson. 'He doesn't do pudding.'

'I had nine brothers and sisters,' he said. 'We weren't dirt poor, but I didn't know what pudding was until I came over here to live with my aunt.'

We all had ice cream and banana cake, which Stacy admitted came from Marks & Spencer. Stacy's body language had subtly shifted. She had been tentative, almost formal, with Beverley. But now she'd lost her caution. She was leaning over the table towards her, and I saw her briefly put her hand on Beverley's arm.

I'd been asking Johnson what it was like running security for Terrence Skinner when into a pause dropped Stacy's next question.

'I've got to ask,' said Stacy. 'Peter's a nice enough lad. But, be honest, what is it in him that attracts you?'

Beverley gave me a sly smile.

'He's a world-class shagger,' she said.

Stacy grinned and Oliver looked at me wide-eyed.

'No, I mean it,' said Beverley. 'Olympic standard shagging. Morning, noon and night. I knew it as soon as I saw him the first time. That man, I thought, will go like a dredger at high tide.'

'Is he hung?' asked Keira.

'Like a—'

'Hey,' I said quickly.

'You notice he doesn't deny the shagging,' said Beverley, and I realised that she now had Keira in the palm of her hand. 'Even if he doesn't think it's true.'

Maddeningly, I was actually blushing, and in winter that shows. Certainly I think Johnson noticed, because he made a credible stab at being an old-fashioned West Indian patriarch by frowning at his wife and foster children.

'Now then,' he said. 'We shall have none of that at the table.'

Beverley and Stacy exchanged looks and then burst out laughing.

'Chance would be a fine thing,' said Stacy.

After pudding we manhandled Beverley back into her chair and had coffee in the sitting room. Oliver and Keira vanished upstairs to their rooms to – hopefully, given the alternatives – log on to unsuitable websites. I wondered if Stacy and Johnson monitored their web activity.

Of course they would, I thought. And Johnson will have access to state-of-the-art monitoring software, as well.

I asked Stacy how she got into fostering.

'We can't have kids of our own,' she said breezily. 'We were looking to adopt and one of my mates, who's a social worker, suggested we foster a couple of kids. She said it was for practice, but looking back she needed carers that could deal with the older kids she had on her books.'

'You obviously took to it,' said Beverley.

'It's like having a tattoo,' she said. 'It's painful, but when you see the result you start thinking about having another one.'

Like a lot of ex-coppers, Stacy and Johnson had gone into business as private detectives and had made a decent enough living at it. But Stacy found fostering satisfying in a way that being a private detective never was, and gradually it became a full-time job.

'Wandsworth started sending us their problem cases. And, to be honest, everything I learnt in the Job was more useful for dealing with the kids than it was digging into people's marriages and dodgy employees.'

'It can't pay, though,' said Beverley.

'You get an allowance from the council but that doesn't really cover expenses.' Stacy pointed at Beverley's Bulge. 'As you are about to find out.'

Things had got a bit parlous, but then Johnson got his job at the Serious Cybernetics Corporation and solved all their financial problems. Especially since, as part of the senior management team, Johnson was getting stock options. Something to keep them solvent in the future.

'Thank God for Skinner,' she said.

Beverley turned and gave me a strange look I

couldn't interpret, before turning back and asking about the photos of the young people hanging in the hallway. Since obviously Beverley couldn't be dragged out to examine them. Stacy produced a tablet on which the pictures were all conveniently stashed. Only her obvious pride in their achievements, however minor, stopped the experience from being the single most boring thing that has ever happened to me.

Rescue arrived when Johnson invited me out to admire the garden and join a conspiracy to, if not exactly pervert the course of justice, certainly help put a thumb on the scales.

'You know the guys from Belgravia, right?' he said as we stood on the porch.

With the road blocked out by the house and the garden wall bounded by a golf course, this could have been a country garden.

The ultimate English dream, my dad calls it, to have your own country garden – but in the city.

I said I'd worked with some of them, including DS Guleed.

'Do you know the SIO?' he asked.

'Who, Seawoll?' I said. 'He shouted at me once – does that count?'

'Do you think Guleed would be willing to talk to you?' asked Johnson. 'You know – unofficially.'

'I think she might,' I said, and wondered if this operation could possibly get more tangled than it already was. 'But Guleed's ambitious. She's going to want something in return.'

Johnson jammed his hands in his pockets – I've seen that gesture before. He really wanted a cigarette, or a drink, or something other than the conversation he was having.

'Anything in particular?' he asked.

'Inside information,' I said. 'What William Lloyd was really working on in Bambleweeny, maybe. Something we won't tell them.'

'I don't know what they're doing in Bambleweeny,' he said. 'But if I look the other way, you're welcome to do a bit of careful digging.'

'Okay.'

'*Careful* digging. And anything you find,' said Johnson, 'you run past me before you take it anywhere else.'

'Doesn't it bother you?' asked Beverley once I'd cautiously pulled out into the late evening traffic. 'Lying to people like Stacy and Tyrel?'

'A bit,' I said. 'But it can't be helped.'

'Stacy's really making a difference to some lives,' she said.

'More power to her,' I said.

'And you heard her – she relies on Tyrel's job to keep them afloat.'

I paused while I negotiated the Stag Lane roundabout and then asked where she was going with this.

'What if you bring down this company?' she asked. 'What's going to happen to Tyrel and Stacy and all the future Keiras and Olivers they might have helped?'

Rain started splattering on the windscreen – I turned on the wipers.

I said that she was assuming that the company was dirty.

'And even if it is,' I said, 'corporate cases are a pain and these companies never face any serious consequences.'

Silver had given me that lecture – a long list of corporate malfeasance that went all the way back to the Bow Street Runners. Most of it unpunished.

'Maybe, babes,' said Beverley, 'I've got more faith in the forces of law and order than you do. So the company goes down the toilet leaving Stacy and Tyrel . . .?'

'If the company goes down, Tyrel will get himself another job,' I said. But I was thinking he was exactly the sort of guy who'd be thrown to the wolves to save the guilty. 'They're both grown-ups – they can look after themselves.'

'Yeah,' said Beverley, that long drawn-out 'yeah' that I had learnt to dread. 'But I think I'm going to take an interest.'

'If you're that interested in the victims of crime, I can introduce you to hundreds. Or, better still, call up Victim Support.'

'But, love, it's a matter of prioritisation and resource allocation,' she said. 'One, it helps prevent future crime. Two, they live within shouting distance of me.' She meant Beverley Brook, the medium-sized South London river, rather than the heavily pregnant woman in the seat next to me. 'And three . . .' She drew out the *three*. 'You and I are together – so what happens because of you happens because of me.'

I had to think about that one.

'Does that mean that the next time you flood Worcester Park, it's my fault too?'

'Of course it is,' she said. 'Mind you, it was your fault last time as well – indirectly.'

We probably could have continued the conversation all the way home and into our bed. But just then my phone rang and Beverley answered.

'It's Thomas,' she said, and put it on speaker.

'Hello, Peter,' said Nightingale. 'I apologise for interrupting your evening, but I thought you might want this information as soon as possible.'

'Nothing good then,' I said.

'Let's say interesting,' said Nightingale.

So, yeah, nothing good.

'I visited the would-be assassin, Mr Lloyd, this afternoon in the company of Jennifer and Abdul and, after an initial assessment, persuaded his doctors to release him for tests at UCH.'

'So, what did you find out?'

'As you know, this kind of assessment is always subjective. But for my own part I'm confident that William Lloyd had been subjected to either the glamour or some form of sequestration,' said

Nightingale. 'You understand the implications, of course.'

That somebody or something powerful had chosen William Lloyd to carry out its wishes.

'Yes,' I said, and then asked if he knew which of those two options it was.

'I couldn't make that determination,' he said. 'But Abdul says that there are minor but definite signs of hyperthaumaturgical degradation.'

Hyperthaumaturgical degradation was the nice long word Dr Walid had invented to describe the damage magic does to your brain. If it was present, it meant that either William Lloyd was a practitioner or he'd been sequestrated.

But sequestrated by what and where?

Nightingale was well ahead of me.

'I'll check his home address,' he said. 'But investigating his workplace falls to you, I'm afraid.'

Which meant we really needed to get into Bambleweeny – and soon.

At least that should make Stephen the Librarian happy.

Afterwards, as I was helping Bev out of the car, I told her that she could take an interest in Johnson and Stacy's foster kids. But only if she was subtle about it.

'Relax,' she said as she waddled towards the front door. 'I shall move in a mysterious way.'

CHAPTER 8

ALL YOU LOSE IS THE EMOTION OF PRIDE

Questions for the morning commute.

Where did the gun that was not really a gun come from? And where did a plastic machete that should have had all the cutting power of a LARPing sword get its razor edge? And why did William Lloyd want to kill his boss? And if he didn't, and he really was under the influence or sequestrated, who *did* want to kill Terrence Skinner? And why?

Which led us back to the Mary Engine that Stephen the wannabe cat burglar said Skinner had stashed in Bambleweeny, along with the 137-key music book reader that he may, or may not, have been building.

And who was leaving lethal magical traps aimed at killing Stephen? Was it Skinner himself or a third – no, wait – . . . us, Skinner, the Librarians – a *fourth* faction? And what the fuck did they want?

And finally, why don't people clear out of the way of opening Tube doors so passengers can get off the train?

The walk from Old Street to the SCC had become routine by now and I fell into step with Dennis Yoon, who asked me to avoid heroics that morning because he had a particularly tricky bit of coding to do.

I said I'd do my best and then we turned into Tabernacle Street.

In the window, replacing the late Ziggy Stardust, was my face in the style of an Obama poster with 'Yes we can' written across the top. When I walked into reception, the receptionists stood up and applauded. Some of the mice followed suit but, reassuringly, there were also some jeers and catcalls to prove that we were still in London.

I gave them my most nonchalant wave, tapped myself through the barriers and went to hide in the unisex loos. Unfortunately Leo Hoyt was already in there and for some reason he seemed discontented.

'I've worked here for over a year,' he said. 'And do you know what he calls me?'

I presumed 'he' was Johnson.

'Leo,' I said.

'Hoyt,' said Leo. 'When he remembers. Most of the time I'm "you there".'

'Okay, you can tackle the next psychopathic knife-man,' I said. 'In fact, be my guest.'

He didn't laugh.

'This started before that,' he said. 'It's because you both used to be police, isn't it?'

'Isn't what, Leo?'

'It's not fair,' he said, and looked like he was going to say more, but instead walked out of the loo.

He had said police, but I wondered if he was thinking 'black' as well. I considered catching him up and explaining that ninety-nine times out of a hundred it works the other way. But, no . . . This wasn't a conversation on Facebook and I wasn't here to make friends. In fact, Silver had warned me explicitly not to get emotionally attached.

'You're only in for the short term,' she said. 'If you make friends they're going to see it as the betrayal it is when they find out. And they won't ever, ever, forgive you. If you can't handle that, we're going to have to abort the operation.'

And I'd said, 'No problem. I can handle it.' Because I'm an idiot.

I loitered for another five minutes until I judged the rush to be over and then used the mouse-tracking app on my Vogonphone to find Stephen. He was in one of the cubicle fields on the ground floor of Betelgeuse. So I adjusted my tie and set off to find him.

I was three paces out of the loo when I was intercepted by Ms Side-eye. No doubt I was being tracked just like all the mice. I knew from Guleed that the name on her passport was September Rain – not her birth name, which was actually Sylvia Makowicz. But she'd changed that when she got off the bus from Cherry Tree, Oklahoma, aged nineteen.

Obviously Belgravia MIT, or more likely Silver and the NCA, had some excellent contacts inside American law enforcement.

'How's the ribs?' I asked.

September gave me an ambiguous tilt of the head and offered me an envelope. It was high-quality posh stationery with a linen finish, and inside was a compliments slip with the SCC logo in the corner.

Scrawled across the slip was *Dinner my place tonight 1900* – although the handwriting was so bad I had to check with September as to the last couple of words.

'So, where does he live?'

September told me. And as an address it was suitably high-end, anonymous and expensive. Then, with a laconic half-salute, she walked off – still favouring her side, I noticed.

By the time I reached Betelgeuse, Stephen had moved to the first floor and was in Lamuella, one of the many meeting rooms on that level. The door had a narrow vertical glass panel that allowed me to see in. Around an oval birch conference table a dozen mice were arranged in various stages of existential despair. I estimated that they'd only been in there for a quarter of an hour, but already one of the mice, a white woman with purple hair and a Winter Is Coming T-shirt, was gently banging her forehead on the table top. I wasn't even sure she was aware of what she was doing. Most of her colleagues were caught up in their own misery, but a guy next to her was looking down at her with increasing alarm. I spotted Stephen, who had positioned himself at the far end of the table and had the glazed expression I recognised as that of a practitioner mentally running through his *formae* in an effort to stay awake.

I left them to it, but as I walked away I was sure I heard a deep collective groan behind me.

'Specification change,' said Stephen when he caught up with me, much later that morning. 'Three months into the build, they've decided they want to embed a voice recognition system.'

'Embed it into what?'

'I'm not sure,' he said. 'I'm not actually a coder, I just play one on TV. But I think it's a gateway or access to a network. There's a log-in page. That's what I'm supposed to be coding, but fortunately my partner has the hots for me and insists on doing the work.'

'Convenient,' I said.

'Not if I have to sleep with him,' he said.

'Not your type?'

'I'm strictly a case by case kind of guy. But if I had a type it wouldn't be him.'

'Sorry,' I said.

Stephen shrugged.

'Them's the breaks,' he said. 'Good work with the active shooter.'

'Thanks,' I said. 'Did you know him?'

Stephen shook his head.

'What was his deal?' he asked. 'Do you know?'

'Mentally unstable,' I said.

'Nothing to do with us, right?'

'Why would it have something to do with us?'

'I don't know,' said Stephen. 'In any case, you need to get your ass in gear and get us into Bambleweeny.'

'Working on it,' I said.

'Working on it how?'

'Carefully,' I said. 'And what's the rush for you? Apart from the sexual harassment angle.'

Stephen looked around and leant in.

'Can you come over after work?' he asked.

'Not until late,' I said. 'Is it important?'

'There's somebody you need to meet,' he said.

I took a late lunch outside so I could check in with Beverley and Nightingale, in reverse order. At least a third of the mice did the same at some point during the day so they could use their own phones to make calls. The run-of-the-mill mice did it out of paranoia or nicotine addiction. I did it because I knew for a fact that every outgoing call was logged and recorded.

Nightingale signed off on both my proposed visits, Skinner and Stephen, and said he would be providing his famous one-man Falcon perimeter should anything go pear-shaped. I thought it unlikely that Skinner would manifest himself as a Bond villain, but Stephen was definitely keeping something hidden in his flat.

'Perhaps we may get an opportunity to find out,' said Nightingale.

'Just in case things kick off, let's avoid being obviously official. Unless it's really necessary,' I said. 'Let's not destroy his illusions just yet.'

Nightingale said he would take this under advisement. He used to be much more comfortable with sneaking around – I don't know what's come over him. After dealing with one chain of command, I called Bev to deal with the other.

'I notice that this one didn't invite me,' she said.

'We are but scarab beetles upon the face of the desert to the likes of Skinner,' I said.

'I could always invite myself.'

'Please. Not this time.'

'Okay.'

'Besides, you'd probably just decide to make him a godparent or something.'

'I said okay,' said Beverley. 'And where is dinner going to take place?'

I told her, and she laughed.

'Don't forget to take some bananas,' she said. 'Just in case.'

Terrence Skinner lived modestly in a twelve-million-quid penthouse on Park Road overlooking Regent's Park on one side and the canal on the other. The building was half a dozen storeys done in the stacked kitchenware school of post-millennial architecture. From the outside it was a clump of cylinders and blocks with all the grace and style of a urinal in an art gallery. Skinner was unusual in that he actually lived in the building full-time. Most of the other flats had been bought as long-term money-laundering investments and spent the bulk of their time empty.

There was a human concierge and he called up so that I could be fetched by Mr Skinner's security. The concierge actually said 'Mr Skinner's security' and refused to answer any questions. That was despite my best *We're all cheeky cockneys together* schtick – which has even worked on Glaswegians, but obviously not on this guy. Silver ran a check on him later and discovered he was from Dagenham, so maybe I was just losing my touch.

I was so rattled that I almost greeted the bodyguard who met me at the door to the apartment with a glad cry of, 'Wotcha, September,' but I remembered just in time that I wasn't supposed to know her name.

The contents of my carrier bag gave her pause.

'That you've bought a snack I understand,' she said. 'It's the toy boat I'm having trouble with.'

'You wouldn't want the bananas to get wet, would you?'

She gave me an exasperated look which, through years of practice, I ignored.

'Arms up,' she said, and proceeded to give me

176

a thorough and professional pat down that included, I noticed with approval, going all the way up my inner leg.

'Shoes off,' she said, and nodded at the two pairs of shoes arrayed neatly on a mat by the wall. I unlaced my DMs, slipped them off and held them up for September's inspection.

'Funny,' she said.

I put my shoes down on the mat next to a pair of pristine Converse. September handed me a pair of white cotton rubber-soled slippers – the kind you get in high-end hotels – and then led me up a curved staircase into what was definitely a reception, not a living, room.

The penthouse was decorated in modern art gallery style with white walls, blocky white furniture and über-expensive wide plank hardwood floors. The corporate bleakness was accented with cream-coloured rugs and throw cushions in muted gold and red. Skinner, who'd been staring out across Regent's Park when I came in, turned and smiled. Apart from September's professional suspicion, it was the most genuine thing in the room.

He reached out, a bit tentatively I thought, and we shook hands. His grip was unremarkably firm and didn't linger. I got the impression he was making an effort, and wondered why.

'I'm not going to say you saved my life,' he said. 'Because September—' he nodded at the woman standing guard by the stairs – 'did that. But you probably saved one other person's life. Maybe more.'

I told him I had reacted according to my training and he laughed.

'The understatement thing,' he said. 'You English think it makes you look clever. But let's be honest, it's just stupid.'

I shrugged.

'It is what it is,' I said.

'Would you like a drink? Beer, wine, lager?'

I asked for a beer and got a bottle of Peroni instead. He waved me over to the white armchairs in front of the panoramic windows that looked out on to the balcony. It had started to drizzle, and the lights of the city beyond the park were blurry stars behind our reflections.

We sat in silence and sipped our drinks. From the kitchen behind us I could hear various chopped comestibles being tossed around in a wok. Which at least meant we weren't going to be having McDonald's – you hear stories.

The silence continued, and I'm afraid I snapped first.

'Nice view,' I said.

'I used to have a place on the beach near Santa Barbara,' said Skinner. 'Used to sit like this and watch the sun set over the ocean.'

Santa Barbara hadn't been on Silver's property list, and Skinner had said 'used to'.

'What happened to it?' I asked.

'I had to sell it,' said Skinner. 'The house was good but it was a public beach.'

Which meant that anyone could use it, including the homeless, panhandlers and dog walkers.

'Not to mention panhandling, homeless dog owners,' said Skinner.

The local landowners' association had tried to restrict access, but they'd faced legal action and protests from a coalition of surfers, dog walkers and joggers. None of whom seemed to care about the rights of the people who occasionally lived there.

'In the end I couldn't stand it any more and I had to sell up,' said Skinner. He frowned – the memory was obviously painful. 'Then I came here. Didn't know when I was well off.'

I wasn't going to get a better cue than that, but before I could ask him why – in particular – he had come to London, a large Filipino man in chef's whites emerged from the kitchen and informed us that dinner was served.

This proved to be one enormous crab each, served simply with butter and lemon. I swear the poor sod was staring at me when I sat down in front of it. So was Skinner, and I wondered whether this was a test of some kind. I know how to eat crab – you pick it up and rip the top from the bottom.

As I carried out this operation, a dim memory of a large brown face came to me.

'The crab don't mind,' the memory said in a West Indian accent. 'Him dead.'

Skinner nodded approval and ripped open his own crab – test passed, obviously.

I scooped out some flakes of white crab meat – it was delicious.

'So is it true that you used to work for the Special Assessment Unit?' asked Skinner.

The bastard had waited until I had a mouthful before asking, presumably hoping I'd spit it out or choke on it in surprise. Instead it gave me a chance to think while I chewed my food.

'I was attached to them for about a year,' I said after swallowing.

Skinner stared at me intently.

'But nobody calls them that, do they?' he said. 'Everybody calls them the Folly, don't they?'

'Most coppers try not to talk about them at all,' I said, which was certainly true – although Seawoll could talk about the Folly at length and, impressively, never repeat himself – not once.

'Is it true they deal with magical crime?' he asked.

I felt a thud in the hollow of my chest. Skinner obviously had contacts beyond those Johnson had in the Met. The question was, what did Skinner actually know and how close to the truth was I going to have skirt?

Never mind moral and legal ambiguity, I thought, it's this game of bloody who-knows-what that makes undercover work such a trauma for an honest copper.

'They deal with weird bollocks,' I said. 'That's all I know.'

'The supernatural?'

'If you like.'

'So you believe in magic?'

'I saw some stuff,' I said. 'Stuff that was difficult to explain within our theoretical framework.'

'You worked with the Nightingale?'

This time I nearly did choke on my crab. Only people in the know gave Nightingale the definitive article, and I had to remember that I wasn't supposed to be one of them.

'If you mean DCI Nightingale,' I said, 'he was my boss when I worked there.'

'Did you ever see him do magic?'

'Why do you want to know?'

'Why are you still keeping secrets for the police?' said Skinner. 'It's not like they treated you well.'

'I asked first,' I said. 'Why do you want to know?'

Skinner took a sip of water from his glass. It was still water, filtered by the artificial reed bed built into the balcony – he'd pointed it out earlier. A start-up project designed to create organic filtering systems for eco-friendly Californian pools. And, as an afterthought, potable water in the developing world.

'Tyrel is a good bloke in his own way,' said Skinner. 'But he's limited in his viewpoint – conventional, mundane. You're younger, a product of a different age, and as a result you've been exposed to a much wider range of influences. I need someone—' he took another sip – 'someone like you to investigate what motivated William Lloyd.'

It was an interesting choice of words – what motivated William Lloyd. Did Skinner suspect that the man had been pushed, or was he thinking of other motivations? There was only one way to find out.

'I'll need access to Bambleweeny,' I said.

'Why?'

'Because that's where he worked.'

Skinner nodded.

'Okay,' he said. 'But you still haven't answered my question.'

'I don't *believe* in magic,' I said. 'Because I've seen it in operation. I don't know how it works, but I know it does.'

Skinner looked down at his poor gutted crab as if surprised to see it so empty.

'Emil,' he called. 'We're finished.'

I hadn't, but I don't think he noticed.

You can access the bank of Regent's Canal via a footpath just the other side of the bridge from Skinner's postmodernist penthouse. It runs along the canal before dropping you into the damp urine-scented shadow of the railway bridges further west.

Nobody knows why some systems – rivers, forests, possibly the London Underground but we're not sure – acquire a *genius loci*. Not even the *genii locorum* themselves know the why and the how of it – they only know it happens. Although they don't call themselves *genii locorum* – they say they are spirits, gods and goddesses and, when the mood takes Beverley, òrìṣà.

Why Regent's Canal had acquired a *genius loci* was a mystery, and why she was a female orangutan that escaped from London Zoo in the 1950s is doubly so. But since I've met unicorns, talking foxes and a very belligerent tree, I no longer find these things so surprising.

Professor Postmartin says that the most important thing is to keep detailed notes. That way some lucky bugger in the future can get a decent dissertation out of our experiences.

Genii locorum are by definition territorial, so if you think you're going to spend some time working in their locality it's best to put in some propitiation. Alcohol works most of the time. But tradition, in this case, suggested bananas.

I was squatting down to put the boat in the water when a canoe came gliding out of the darkness under the bridge. It was open-topped, and while the low light made it difficult to see details it looked to me like it had been hewn from a single log. For a moment I wondered if I'd slipped into that dangerous half-life memory of the city where gods and ghosts mingled with the stone memory of the architecture. But then I noticed that the two passengers were both wearing orange

Gore-Tex anoraks. The figure at the front was doing all the paddling while his companion sat cross-legged in the back with an air of placid enlightenment.

I recognised them both, so I stopped trying to float my offering and waited for them to pull in to the bank beside me.

'Hi, Melvin,' I said.

The pinched little white man in the bow had once been an estate agent until an unwise grift had propelled him into a brief career as King of the Rats. Now he was estate manager for the Goddess of the Canals and, obviously, her boatman too.

I waved my bananas at the figure seated in the back, who reached out an inhumanly long arm to tap Melvin on the shoulder. He leant back and the goddess murmured something in his ear. He nodded and turned back to me.

'She says thank you for the bananas, but what she really needs is a toaster.' I noticed he took the bananas, though.

'A toaster?'

'Yes,' said Melvin. 'One of the large catering types with eight slots.'

'I'll see what I can do.'

I waited while more instructions were conveyed from the back of the canoe.

'Dualit for preference,' said Melvin. 'And she's holding you responsible for ensuring both your mother and Molly ethically source their palm oil.'

'And in return?' I asked, because after a couple of years you learn the rules of these exchanges.

Melvin handed me a Sainsbury's bag. It was heavy and inside were irregular-shaped bits of plastic.

'What's this?' I asked.

'We don't know,' said Melvin, pushing the canoe away from the bank. 'That's why we're giving it to you.'

As the canoe vanished into the gloom under the bridge I heard the goddess make a soft inquiring sound.

'Who knows?' said Melvin. 'But hopefully we'll get a toaster out of it.'

I cautiously reached into the bag and touched a piece of plastic. There was an immediate flash of *vestigium* – the same rotting fish sensation as the demon trap at Stephen's flat.

I sighed and called Nightingale as I walked up towards the bus stop.

'Were you followed?' asked Stephen when he opened the door.

Well . . . Nightingale is parked two hundred metres down the road. Silver's observation team is out the back of your flat. And Silver herself is with another team in a suitably battered white Transit van around the corner. But apart from that . . .

'No,' I said, 'I was careful.'

He nodded and let me in.

'It's a context problem,' Silver, who turned out to have a double first in Psychology and Sociology from Bradford University, had said. 'People have much narrower knowledge bases than they think they do.'

What they mostly know about police and intelligence work they get from the media. This is why it's easier to infiltrate political groups than criminal ones. However revolutionary they think they are, they see police officers as slightly thick bovver boys in big boots. When a personable middle-class guy turns up in a khaki jacket, a CND badge and smelling of patchouli, they're practically invisible. Criminals, on the other hand, deal with the police all the time and know what they smell like. All of this, Silver reckoned, went double for Americans, who intellectually knew the rest of the world existed but didn't really believe it.

'Not deep down where it counts,' Silver had said. 'Which is lucky for us.'

As the one whose delicate brown body was in the firing line, I was a little bit more cautious. People are often short-sighted and stupid, right up to the point where they're fucking perceptive – that point usually being the most inconvenient moment possible. And people don't like to think they've been taken – and they tend to express their displeasure forcibly.

Stephen led me down the standard too-narrow hallway beloved of 1960s municipal architecture and into what I guessed was the living room. The curtains hadn't just been closed but were also taped in place along the bottom of the window. The original furniture had been pushed against the walls and covered in dust sheets. And the centre of the room was dominated by a table tennis table covered in stuff. That was the best description for it – stuff. A computer was in there, plus what looked like the inside of a vinyl enthusiast's amplifier, complete with thermionic valves and a wooden framework that looked like the key readers Wicked the Showman had described to me all the way back in December.

When the world was a lot less complicated.

Stephen looked around, obviously missing something.

'Damn,' he said. 'I'll be right back.'

As soon as he was gone I edged round the narrow gap between the shrouded furniture and the table to confirm that *The Enchantress of Numbers* was the music book being fed into the reader. I had a go at tracing wires – the music book would be read by an optical reader which fed into a chunky, hand-soldered circuit board fitted with the thermionic valves, which in turn fed into an adapter of some kind, which fed into a port in a battered-looking MacBook.

'It turned out that I didn't need the valves,' said a voice behind me.

I turned to find a tall, willowy East Asian, probably Chinese, woman in the doorway. She had wide-spaced brown eyes behind archaic half-moon reading glasses and a narrow thin-lipped mouth. Even without the cardigan or knowing she was an associate of Stephen's, I would have pegged her as a librarian. Something about the cheerfully suspicious way she regarded me. As if wondering if I was going to start talking loudly or fold over a page corner to mark my place.

'If you're done with them, my dad could use them as spares,' I said.

A couple of pairs of Sovtek 300B triodes could easily fetch as much as £300, if you could find them.

'I'm not done with them quite yet,' she said. Her accent had some of the – I assumed – New York drawl Stephen had, but it was overlaid with a mid-Atlantic precision. 'But perhaps we can make a deal before I leave.'

She was obviously dying for me to ask what this thing on the table did, so I asked who she was instead.

'My name is Mrs Patricia Chin,' she said. 'I work with Stephen at the Library.'

'You're a practitioner?' I asked.

'Of a kind,' she said. 'You might call me a member of the *Ordo Machinis Spectandis*.' She gazed at me over her glasses. 'Do you know what that means?'

'You maintain the sacred machines to further the greater glory of the God Emperor of mankind?' I said.

Mrs Chin looked at Stephen.

'He talks like this all the time,' he said. 'Just ignore him.'

'Somebody has to watch the machines,' said Mrs Chin. 'We are the people at the Library who do that.'

'Watch the machines for what?'

'Signs of life,' she said.

I opened my mouth to say something clever, and then decided to aim for something better.

'What kind of life?' I asked.

Mrs Chin gave me an exasperated look.

'The same kind of life that animates you or I,' she said. 'I thought you were a student of the Newtonian synthesis. Do you not understand the implications of the *anima vitalis*?'

I was pretty sure Nightingale had yet to cover anything like that, but my Latin was good enough to make a stab at a translation.

'The animating spirit,' I said.

I remembered Nightingale telling me about a friend of his. One who'd speculated that any complex system could become a *genius loci* – the telephone network was the example he'd given. His friend had died before Alan Turing came along, and thus missed the internet, which he either would have loved or thought signalled the beginning of the End Times.

I pointed at the tangle of connections on the table.

'Is that alive?'

'Don't be silly,' said Mrs Chin. 'But let me show you something.'

She flipped a switch and the music book started to run through the optical reader, before concertinaing down into a neat pile on the other side of the table. Then she turned the MacBook so I could see the screen. One window showed the dashes and dots as they were recorded by the reader, another interpreted it as what I recognised as hexadecimal code, while a third showed a sound waveform.

'Is it supposed to be making a noise?' I asked.

'Damn,' said Mrs Chin, and used the trackpad to unmute the machine. Music started, mid-fanfare – a Baroque concerto as played by a tinny imitation steam organ.

'So it was music,' I said.

Babbage's hymn to the Enchantress of Numbers turned out to be just that.

'This is the filtered version,' said Mrs Chin, adjusting the sound program. 'With all the channels enabled.'

The music was still dominant, but interlaced with discordant notes and rhythms. Mrs Chin changed it so these sounds were played as dull electronic tones, and they became even more obvious. I looked at the hexadecimal display on the screen.

'A message hidden in the music?' I said.

'A message, perhaps,' said Mrs Chin. 'A code, definitely. A hexadecimal code.'

'Doing what?' asked Stephen.

Mrs Chin shrugged.

'I don't know,' she said.

'Why would it be hidden?' I asked. 'It was written in the 1830s. Nobody had even invented hackers back then. Nobody apart from Babbage and Ada Lovelace even knew what a universal machine was – let alone how to programme one.'

'Your point?' she asked.

'If Babbage wasn't worried about cybersecurity,' I said, 'what was he worried about?'

'Let's hope we don't find out,' said Mrs Chin.

Which, because the universe can't resist a bit of irony, was when the windows blew in.

CHAPTER 9

I'M AFRAID I CAN'T DO THAT

I heard the glass breaking and turned in time to see the curtains bulge inwards as something the size of a brick hit the left-hand curtain. The tape holding the curtains in place held for a moment and then the bulge pushed into the room, dragging the rest of the curtain behind it. It maintained its height above the floor in a suspiciously unbrick-like manner and made a noise like an angry lawn strimmer.

A drone? Like the one I'd heard on my last visit?

Stephen yelled 'Out!' and grabbed Mrs Chin, who shouted at him to get the laptop. He made a lunge for the table, just as the bundled shape swerved around. There was a crack, as loud as a gunshot, and a ragged blackened hole appeared in the curtain material.

When a projectile whizzed past my shoulder with a lethal-sounding buzz I decided that the assessment portion of my response was over and it was time to take such proactive steps as were commensurate with public safety. I hit it with a fireball – I've been getting better at those, and this one went straight into the hole in the curtain and exploded.

Whatever was bundled in the curtain dramatically changed shape and caught fire. It fell suddenly to the floor, the flaming remains of the curtain setting the shrouded furniture behind it on fire. I was definitely going to lose points for that, so I doused it with a couple of water bombs.

'The laptop,' said Mrs Chin.

'Too late,' said Stephen.

I turned to see him poking the blackened remains of the MacBook. Had the shot been aimed at it rather than me? If that was true, then it was one hell of an accurate shot. Which didn't bode well for any follow-up.

'The laptop,' hissed Mrs Chin again.

'It's fucked,' said Stephen.

'Bring what's left,' she said, and pushed past me towards the end of the table. 'I'll get the music book.'

I was going to tell them to wait. But just then a gust of wind blew in through the smashed window, and with it the angry lawn strimmer sound of more drones. Lots more drones.

'Down!' I shouted, and grabbed Mrs Chin by her collar and yanked her to the floor with me.

There were multiple cracks this time – definitely gunshots, definitely from outside the window. It was dim and musty under the table and smelt of spilt solder. Stephen and Mrs Chin had definitely been en route to losing their deposit even before the drones showed up.

A fist-sized hole appeared in the table top with a crash, and the floor vibrated with an impact against the living room wall. I smelt dust and, strangely, burning paraffin.

'Out, out, out!' I shouted. 'Now!'

I cast a shield and stood up. There was a chorus of bangs and I staggered a bit as half a dozen projectiles hit my shield at the same time. I know from experiments that shields can only soak up so much kinetic energy before it bleeds back into the caster.

Behind me Mrs Chin was swearing and demanding that we at least try to grab the music book but Stephen, sensibly, was dragging her out the living room door by main force. It was too late anyway, because the table had been blown to bits and floating over its remains were a trio of weird-looking drones.

If they were drones.

Instead of the quadcopters I was expecting, these were big fuckers the size of microwaves, built of glistening white plastic and shaped like insects, with dragonfly wings instead of rotor blades. They even had six jointed legs and a gaping round opening in place of a mouth.

Beverley is totally fine with insects, even spiders, and once popped a beetle in her mouth just to show off. But creepy-crawlies freak me out – even mechanical ones. However, while the tendency of magic to reduce nearby microprocessors to sand is often a bugger, it does have its uses when nobbling modern technology.

As it happened I'd developed a spell for just that purpose. And, while we're still arguing over its Latin name in the vernacular, we call it the car-killer. I bounced one at the middle drone, a big one just to be sure, and threw up my shield in case more were on their way.

Which was lucky, because the stupid thing had no effect.

This time I saw the actual shots.

A flash from its gaping mouth, a gout of smoke and a shudder as a projectile as big as a golf ball ricocheted off my shield – I've learnt to keep it angled upwards – and hit the ceiling. As plaster and bits of the concrete decking showered down, I decided it was time to go.

'Are you clear?' I shouted back, and got no reply.

The two drones flanking the first fired simultaneously, one shot high, one shot low. I instinctively jumped back as the lower shot clipped the bottom edge of my shield. They were obviously probing my defences, so either they were smarter than they looked or a person or persons unknown were controlling them remotely.

I risked a glance to see if Stephen and Mrs Chin were okay, only to find they'd already scarpered. I used a sub*forma* to fix my shield in place and dived out the door after them. There was a satisfying smash behind me as at least one drone ran into the fixed shield. But without me there to renew it, the thing wasn't going to last long. The front door was hanging open, so no prizes for guessing where Mrs Chin and Stephen had got to. I followed them out into the cool air of the walkway, just as they reached the staircase. They paused to look back, and as they did I heard a police siren whoop once, cut off and then whoop once again.

That was one of the signals I'd agreed with Nightingale and Silver earlier – it meant that he was giving me two minutes to get clear and then he was coming in. If I didn't want me and my criminal friends to get arrested, we had to move.

To reinforce the notion the siren started up and, this time, ran continuously.

When I reached the stairway Mrs Chin and Stephen were already down the first flight.

I turned and raised my shield again as the three drones came zinging out of the doorway and, without pausing, swooped in my direction. I was about to try another fireball, when the lead drone faltered and then crumpled in on itself like a plastic bottle being squashed for the recycling bin.

That would be Nightingale, I thought, who has plenty more where that comes from.

I turned and ran down the stairs three at a time, swung around and did a neat jump over the railing and dropped halfway down the next flight.

The coolness of the move being only slightly marred when I misjudged the landing and nearly pitched myself face forward down the rest of the stairs.

'I think we've lost them,' I said when I caught up with Stephen and Mrs Chin on the first floor. 'But the feds are here. Got a back way out?'

Stephen gave me a pained look.

'Rear fire door,' he said. 'I've bypassed the burglar alarm.'

'Let's go,' I said, but Mrs Chin tried to hang back.

'What about my gear?' she asked.

'We'll steal you new stuff,' I said while Stephen hustled her to the emergency stairs at the back of the block. Just as he'd promised there was a fire door at the bottom with DOOR IS ALARMED stencilled at eye height. And, just as promised, there was no alarm when he banged through it.

Not that it would have made any difference if it had. Going out the back had been part of the contingency planning on my way in, Silver and Nightingale deliberately giving us a clear path to the A10.

It was a cloudless, freezing night and behind us I heard sirens and what sounded like gunshots and explosions. Nightingale was giving us a show to keep Stephen off balance – and Mrs Chin, too, but Nightingale wouldn't know that.

I heard the grass strimmer buzz and turned to find a pair of drones tracking us. They whirred through the sodium haze of the street lights, flying low to the ground, dragonfly wings a blur, gun barrel mouths shifting left and right – looking for targets.

I hit the first one with a fireball that blew its wings off. As it fell like a discarded toy, I had a go at the second and missed. It twitched and suddenly I was looking down the gaping mouth of its gun as it locked on. I started raising my shield and I like to think I would have got it up in time, but we'll never know. Because a ragged bolt of lightning shot past me and hit the drone just behind the head.

Disappointingly, a crackle of blue electricity did not engulf the evil thing in an excitingly cinematic fashion. But it did seize up and fall to the ground and, given the circumstances, I'll take what I can get.

'Nice,' I told Stephen as we continued our rapid nonchalant stroll up St Anne's Road in the direction of the main road. 'You've got to teach me that one.'

He grunted and concentrated on helping Mrs Chin maintain the pace. She herself was thin-lipped and determined, but she was breathing hard through her nose. I checked behind to see the blue lights reflecting off the jagged concrete edges of the maisonettes and tower blocks.

But no more drones.

Once we reached the A10 we slowed our pace and started to freeze. I gave Mrs Chin my jacket and led them to South Tottenham Overground station. The station forms a bridge over the High Road, and a void beneath the platforms is used by London's talking fox population as a listening post and way station.

Fortunately a train pulled in within minutes of our arrival and we bundled in and mingled with assorted shift workers, cleaners and whoever else needs to escape Barking before midnight.

I made the pair sit separately in different ends of the carriage, with me in the middle. I told them it would make it harder for the police to track our movements on CCTV, but really it was so I could surreptitiously text Nightingale – amongst others.

'Where are we going?' hissed Stephen when we changed at Gospel Oak.

'Safe house,' I said.

To my surprise, it was Maksim that picked us up at Richmond in his Mercedes C-Class and drove us back to Beverley Avenue. In the back seat Mrs Chin fell asleep on Stephen's shoulder. Maksim drove with the same look of serene concentration he has when weeding the garden, cleaning the kitchen or hanging drug dealers up by their ankles. We travelled in silence until we pulled in outside Beverley's house and she waddled out to meet us. We soon had Mrs Chin in the best armchair with a blanket and a hot cup of tea. Stephen perched on the sofa and looked around curiously as I bustled about and Maksim readied the spare rooms.

This mostly involved moving boxes of stuff out of two bedrooms and into a third. Beverley's house, being made of the two halves of a semi knocked through, had two staircases and plenty of bedrooms.

As soon as Beverley was out of the room, Mrs Chin's eyes snapped open and she beckoned me and Stephen over.

'We can't stay here,' she said.

'Don't worry about it,' I said.

'No,' she said. 'This is the house of a spirit. Don't you know how dangerous they are?'

She looked at me and I could see the slot machine whir of her thoughts suddenly slam to a halt with a row of three bananas. She flinched back in the armchair.

'You're consorting with one,' she said. 'No, wait, you're screwing around with one. Do you know how dangerous that is?'

'Chill,' said Stephen. 'They do things differently over here.'

'Not that differently,' said Mrs Chin, but she was obviously calming down. 'Well, maybe they are different here. But the Hudson has been picking off rowboats and barges since the city was founded.'

I can't think why, I thought, but didn't say.

'You're perfectly safe here,' I said. 'I swear on my power.'

Stephen made a little hiccuping laugh at that, but I think Mrs Chin took me seriously. Or she was just too tired to argue. I showed them to their rooms and checked downstairs to find Maksim sitting in the armchair with a Taser ready in his lap. He asked me to turn the light off on my way out.

'You didn't need to drag poor Maksim into this,' I said as I helped Beverley construct the Bulge's nightly support structure.

'I didn't call him,' said Beverley. 'He turned up on his own – he only lives down the road.' She rolled over and tested the structure for firmness.

'How did he know in the first place?' I said, as I climbed onto the bed beside her.

'Either he has acquired a mystical bond with me,' said Beverley, 'or he keeps an eye on the security system he installed last year. Pick the one that disturbs you the least.'

I tried not to think about it as I kissed Beverley and her Bulge goodnight and pulled the duvet up and over both of us. A futile gesture, I might add, since Beverley would have acquired the whole duvet by daybreak.

'This is not healthy,' I said.

'Leaving aside your imposition of mundane standards to my obvious holy status for a moment, I tried to give him a nudge . . .'

'Bev!'

'Not that kind of nudge,' said Beverley. 'We

had a talk. Or actually I talked. I asked him if he thought it was right that he felt obligated to me and told him I didn't want him to think he was.'

'And?'

'He quoted Vasily Zhukovsky at me,' said Beverley.

'Who's he?' I asked.

'Russian Romantic poet,' she said, and admitted that she'd had to look him up afterwards. He'd quoted in Russian, too, but Beverley reckoned she'd got the gist. 'Something about accepting your destiny.'

I sighed.

'At least he can watch Mrs Chin while I'm at work,' I said, and looked at the clock. It was already two in the morning. 'Today.'

'And what will you be doing today?' asked Beverley.

'I shall be penetrating the secrets of the inner sanctum,' I said.

'I'm disappointed,' I said.

'What were you expecting?' asked Everest.

Not a large open-plan office full of cubicles – beige cubicles at that – with nothing of the mannered playfulness that infested the rest of the Serious Cybernetics Corporation. I judged that if you counted the toilets and the two conference rooms, the office covered the whole square metreage of this floor.

'Something a bit more lively,' I said.

'The people working here don't need toys,' said Everest. 'This is all about brains.'

Not that many brains, since less than a quarter of the cubicles appeared to be occupied.

'I'm with Peter,' said Victor. 'I thought it would at least have moody lighting.'

'That would be stupid,' said Everest.

I'd asked Skinner if I could bring along Victor and Everest as native guides and tech support. He'd said yes, providing I made sure they didn't walk out of Bambleweeny with anything secret or, more importantly, proprietary.

They also let me take my evidence kit in with me, although September had a good rummage through it before she let us in.

'It's mostly different-size bags,' I said.

September Rain was to act as my minder, and it was she who coded us into the secret lab. Once in, I asked where William Lloyd had worked and she showed us to a cubicle a third of the way in from the door.

There was another floor above and, if I wasn't mistaken, there should be stairs up to it tucked away in the corner of the building, hidden behind the glass-fronted office. I tried to sneak a closer look as we walked over to William Lloyd's cubicle, but September kept her beady eye on me.

All the cubicles contained the same bog-standard PC tower and flat-screen monitor. Neither mouse nor keyboard were wireless, and were physically connected to the tower.

'For security,' said Everest, and sniffed disapprovingly. 'Supposedly they're worried that "somebody" will hack the Bluetooth links. As if encryption wasn't a thing.'

There were no personal touches in the cubicle – no mugs, calendars or amusing bobble-headed Marvel superheroes. The only odd thing was a framed wiring diagram that had been stuck on the wall of the cubicle – positioned at the head height of anyone sitting at the desk.

It looked like it had been pulled from a magazine, an old one that had been printed before the arrival of electronic typesetting. On the right of the page was a large square spiral labelled SENSOR PAD, attached by lines to a collection of electronic wiring symbols above which was drawn a dial meter that ran from 0 to 100 and was labelled RATE. On the left of the drawing was a circular spiral labelled WITNESS WELL.

'Does anyone know what this is?' I asked, but nobody did.

It reminded me of the wiring diagrams my dad uses to build his amplifiers. Or, more precisely, the diagrams his various mad hi-fi friends use to build my dad's amplifiers. He never has to pay them, except with long rambling anecdotes about the Flamingo Club or the time he swam across the Thames with Stan Getz.

It also reminded me of the apparatus that

Mrs Chin had built on the table tennis table. So I turned to September and told her I was taking the picture as evidence.

'Why?' she asked.

'Because I want to know his influences,' I said.

She gave me a long suspicious look, but I was beginning to recognise this as her default expression and merely waited for her to say yes. When she did, I carefully removed the picture from the cubicle wall – it had been suspended from a pair of drawing pins – and slid it into a large-sized evidence bag. Then, more to annoy September than anything else, I conscientiously filled in the label with date, time and location.

There wasn't anything else in the cubicle – no knickknacks, pictures, empty drinks cans, not even any stationery – which I found suspicious. I pointed at the terminal and told Everest and Victor that it was all theirs.

They pulled up chairs and fell upon the terminal with grim cheerfulness. As Everest started probing its mysteries, I led September into the walkway and asked whether anyone had removed anything from the cubicle after the attack.

'No,' she said. 'And, before you ask, we have surveillance in place and we checked.'

'What kind of surveillance?' I asked.

She pointed at the ceiling.

'The usual,' she said.

I looked up. The ceiling was a bog-standard suspended tile affair useful for covering up ducts, cables and xenomorph infiltrations. It had recessed lighting fixtures but not, I noticed, the dark Perspex domes that marked CCTV camera positions out in the rest of the Serious Cybernetics Corporation. September was giving me an irritatingly smug look, so I searched harder. And this time I spotted them – little fisheye lenses hidden in the gaps between the tiles. There was one almost directly above William Lloyd's cubicle.

'How long do you keep the footage for?' I asked.

September shrugged. 'Forever, I guess.'

'I want to look at it.'

'I've already reviewed it,' said September. 'The guy was boring. He sat down, did his work, drank Mountain Dew, worked some more, logged out, got up, went home.'

'Did he interact with anyone else up here?'

'Interaction is discouraged.'

'So, yeah, he did,' I said.

'So, he chatted to a few guys. Big deal.'

'Your boss wants me to investigate,' I said. 'You going to help or not?'

'He's your boss too,' said September.

'Exactly,' I said, and knew I'd won.

It was even better when September headed off towards where I suspected the stairwell was.

'I'll go fetch it, then,' she said.

I followed her as far as a blank white security door tucked away out of sight. September made a point of masking the keypad when she opened it. She turned at the threshold and held up her hand to stop me following.

'I'll bring it down,' she said, and closed the door behind her.

But not before I'd had a chance to look at the stairwell beyond. There had been no down flight, and the flight going up had been bounded by a wall of unpainted concrete blocks. This meant two things. One, this building was in major contravention of health and safety regulations – particularly those pertaining to emergency egress in the event of a fire. And, two, behind the crude breeze block wall there had been room for a lift shaft.

As I walked back to where Everest and Victor were having an incomprehensible argument about file structures, I mentally reviewed my earlier explorations of the floors below. I was pretty sure that there was a gap in the floor plan that would line up nicely to form a continuous lift shaft all the way down to the basement.

Realising that looking at the screen told me even less than listening to Everest and Victor, I had a nose round the other cubicles. I identified Dennis Yoon's by the *Mad Max* poster and the small pyramid artfully constructed out of paper clips.

I felt it then, as elusive as a whisper at a club, a touch, a sensation . . . a memory of a *vestigium*.

I stayed very still with one hand on the grey laminated chipboard of the desk and the fingertips of the other resting on the keyboard.

There was something – I was sure of it.

September's face appeared over the top of the cubicle wall.

'What are you doing?' she asked.

'Waiting for you to get back,' I said. 'Got the footage?'

She held up a tablet and wiggled it for emphasis.

'Hand it over, then.'

'No,' she said. 'It stays with me. You ask to see something and I show you.'

'Is it time stamped?'

'Of course.'

'Then it's not me who needs it,' I said, and led her over to Everest and Victor. 'How's it going? Are you in?'

'Of course we're in,' said Everest. 'We have higher access than Mr Lloyd.'

'And?'

'It's all work stuff,' said Victor. 'I've got his task list and it's all that. We're checking his emails, but they're all routine.'

'Can you tell when he was logged in?' I asked.

'Sure,' said Everest. 'It's all logged.'

'Then, when you've finished checking that,' I said, 'I want you to use the CCTV footage to check whether his work logs actually match the times he's visible working in here.'

'Boring,' said Everest. 'Even by my standards.'

'What's this in aid of?' asked Victor.

I was thinking of what William Lloyd had said

to Guleed – *It talks to you but nothing is ever logged* – but they didn't need to know that.

'I want to see if he was working on a side project,' I said, which got me a narrow-eyed look of almost approval from September.

Once I was sure they were settled in, I told them we'd meet up at the Vogon office at four o'clock and headed for the door.

'And where are you going?' called September.

'I'm going to see if I can wheedle some forensics out of a contact,' I said.

CHAPTER 10

THERE IS NOW

Assume nothing, Believe nothing, Check everything – the ABC of policing.

Once out of the building I took a stroll around the back to Clare Street and walked along until I could see where my hypothetical lift shaft ran down the inside of the building. The windows into the shaft hadn't been bricked up, but a quick go with *telescopium*, voted nine years running the world's dullest name for a spell ever, got me enough magnification to see that what looked like closed blinds from a distance appeared, close up, to be lines painted onto a flat surface. Hardboard at a guess.

There was no obvious external entrance to a lift on the ground floor, but I noticed a shuttered entrance with a MAX HEADROOM warning built from the same blue-grey brick as Fitzroy House, the big ugly 1960s building next door. I've never seen that blue-grey brick on any other building in the area, so if this was an alternative freight entrance into Bambleweeny then it might have been deliberately camouflaged.

And what they don't want you to know, you definitely want to know.

Just to confirm things, I wandered further up Clare Street until I found a second shuttered goods entrance to Fitzroy House. It was unlikely that a modern office building would have two goods entrances, but I'd have to get Silver to assign one of her minions to check.

Then I sauntered up the rest of Clare Street as if I'd been taking a shortcut.

Always assume somebody is watching you, Silver had said. For one thing, it's good practice. And, for another, it might even be true.

I caught a 55 bus to Bloomsbury Square and checked the news on my phone. It was wall-to-wall Litvinenko murder, except for the *Telegraph* who blamed the rise in murders on police resources being diverted to historical sex crimes. None of them had caught the drone attack, although my cousin Abigail's social media summary highlighted plenty of tweets about armed police raiding a flat in South Tottenham.

There were a couple of mentions of drones, but the assumption was that they were operated by the police, the gangs, space lizards or all three at once. The media were continuing their comforting lack of interest in things that didn't fit their various agendas. Although I did make a mental note to seed a couple of UFO stories around the events in South Tottenham. I don't know if it helps at all, but it's a lot of fun and keeps Abigail out of mischief.

Well, out of *unauthorised* mischief in any case.

I went into the Folly through the side entrance on Bedford Place and found encouraging signs that the builders might be winding down. The hole in the atrium floor had gone, leaving a smooth expanse of screeded concrete ready for the tiles to be relaid. The tiles themselves stood in neat stacks, most of them the originals, having been carefully levered up and cleaned. I'd known they were marble, but I was surprised at how hefty they were – over two centimetres thick. And how unmarked by the passage of all those wizards . . . although amongst the finds recovered by the builders was £2 6s in predecimal change, a pewter snuff tin and a solitary gold cufflink. All of which were confiscated by Foxglove for incorporation into the weird three-dimensional collage she was growing in one of the basement rooms.

I use the word 'growing' advisedly.

By rights, the whole Folly should have been at least a Grade II listed building. And, even though it wasn't, the architects had been instructed to act like it was. This had caused the venerable firm of Pike and Sizewell – *Gutting houses for oligarchs since 2009* – much inconvenience, as they had to throw away their usual plans to hollow out the whole building and replace it with six storeys of marble-floored open-plan office space and/or luxury hotel rooms.

And that was before we introduced them to Molly and Foxglove, and made them sign the Official Secrets Act.

Next to the piles of tiles were a couple of big blue and white 20 kg bags of tile adhesive – another sign that the work was almost complete.

Upstairs, the Folly has a couple of old-fashioned labs with wooden benches, gas taps for Bunsen burners and square sinks with slender swan-necked taps of black metal. I learnt most of my early spells in the first laboratory, and there's still a hole in one counter where a *lux* spell went wrong. This has been joined by a burnt patch on the ceiling and a new extractor hood over the isolation cabinet, where one of Abigail's experiments suffered an unscheduled spontaneous disassembly.

'The fact that both of my apprentices have a tendency to blow things up,' said Nightingale after that incident, 'has led me to re-evaluate my teaching methods.'

He was waiting for me in the lab along with Abigail, who was a small mixed-race young woman with angular features and a hedge of short dreads sprouting from the top of her head. Obviously she was reading the same websites as Oliver.

Laid out in stainless-steel trays on the counter in front of them were three partially disassembled plastic drones. Several others had been sent to the same lab that was working on William Lloyd's plastic gun and machete.

I noticed that both Nightingale and my cousin were wearing plastic aprons and protective eyewear, so I fetched the same for myself from the locker by the door.

'We're just waiting for Dr Vaughan,' said Nightingale as I donned my gear.

Dr Walid was still at the secure unit, trying to gently prise something coherent from William Lloyd, but Dr Vaughan had not elected to become a pathologist to start talking to living patients now.

'She says she prefers a good mystery to a misery memoir,' said Abigail, who was bouncing on her toes and obviously desperate to show off.

She got her chance when Dr Vaughan bustled in with a tray covered by a white cloth. She placed it on the bench by the others and whisked away the cloth like a magician.

This proved to be more pieces of spontaneously disassembled drone. I knew from Nightingale's reports that the remains of six of them had been recovered from the scene around Stephen and Mrs Chin's flat. Three had been sent to other labs, three were already laid out here, so this seventh came from somewhere else.

I remembered the bag of bits Melvin, the former King of the Rats, had handed me. The ones with the same dead fish *vestigium* that I'd sensed from the demon trap before Christmas.

I looked at Nightingale, Abigail and Dr Vaughan, who were all giving me encouraging smiles. I reached out to brush Dr Vaughan's specimen with my fingers.

'Gloves,' she said.

'These have been processed, right?' I asked.

'That's no excuse for not following basic barrier procedures,' said Dr Vaughan. 'After all, there's no knowing whether these are organic in some fashion.'

'You think they're organic?'

'Best to be sure,' said Dr Vaughan, so I donned a pair of latex gloves.

Testing had shown that latex doesn't interfere much when you're sensing *vestigia* and, surprisingly, plastic retains the after-image of magic better than wood or flesh. Abigail says she thinks it's down to the long chain polymers but she can't prove it. Yet.

So I was treated to a repeat of the unpleasant sensation of sticking my face in a bowl of rotting shrimp – complete with the skin-crawling feel of thousands of tiny cilia brushing my face.

'That's well off, isn't it?' said Abigail. 'Now try the others.'

I sighed and touched each of the other drones in turn – guessing what I would find, and not being surprised. More horrible fish guts and feelers – lovely.

I looked at Nightingale.

'These were animated by magic, weren't they?' I asked.

'The forensic team found no motors of any

kind,' said Nightingale. 'Although there were batteries.'

'Triple A's,' said Abigail. 'Not enough to power rotors and definitely not flappy wings. Which is a stupid configuration, FYI – if you want to make something that flies.'

'But enough electricity to keep a chip live,' I said.

Abigail held up a glass beaker a quarter filled with pale sand – gold flecks reflected light from the window.

There are certain old-fashioned spells that rely on animal sacrifice to provide a power boost. Nowadays it's no longer acceptable to cheerfully suffocate doves for science or magic, but I'd discovered that you can 'sacrifice' microprocessors instead. Providing they're currently powered, even if it's just the trickle your laptop uses to keep its clock running. When we ran tests on these drones, the crude mechanical output exceeded, by a fair margin, the output of the batteries, or even the mains when we tried plugging them into that. Wherever the power was coming from, it wasn't from either source of electricity.

The fact that any extended use of magic causes microprocessors to turn into sand is why your hardcore practitioner has a mechanical watch, uses a notepad and has a retrofitted hard off-switch on their phone.

Since the *vestigium* of the Regent's Canal drone

matched those of the drones recovered from Mrs Chin's flat, they were probably created by the same person. I looked at Nightingale.

'Yes,' he said. 'Or at least by practitioners trained by the same teacher.'

'They could have been fabricated by a third party,' said Abigail. 'They might not even know what they were for.'

'Fabricated where?'

'By anyone with the right 3-D printer,' said Abigail.

From a policing point of view, 3-D printers were your classic new technology. Everybody knew they were going to be used by criminals for something, but nobody was sure what. And nobody, least of all the police, was going to waste resources on them until there was a big enough problem to cause an outcry. Forensically, it hadn't been established yet whether an item could be matched with the machine that printed it, even if you had that printer to compare it to. It had taken years to empirically prove that everyone has a unique pattern of fingertip ridges, or harmonic waveforms when they speak, or variable number tandem repeats in their DNA – and even longer to get the courts to accept these as reliable indicators of guilt.

'Your best bet is to find the design on someone's laptop,' said Abigail.

Since we'd exhausted that avenue, we retired along to the room formerly known as the breakfast room and now rechristened the tea room by Abigail and Dr Vaughan. There we had tea and very tiny cakes.

'What's this?' I asked, pointing at a carrot cake the same size and shape as a bottle top.

'I believe Foxglove has been constructing a doll's house,' said Nightingale. 'Although I haven't seen it.' He looked at Abigail, who shook her head.

'Not me neither,' she said.

Her theory was that the building work had given Foxglove ideas and she'd branched out into three-dimensional art as a response. Molly hadn't wanted to be left out and so contributed in the only way she could.

I popped the carrot cake into my mouth whole – it was, of course, delicious.

Dr Vaughan poked her head in to say she was heading back to UCH, where she had some non-Falcon related corpses to investigate.

'Have to keep my hand in,' she'd said when I asked about this. 'If you only deal with the para-normal you can lose perspective.'

I noticed that she didn't leave without one of Molly's care packages.

'How are your house guests?' asked Nightingale.

'Suspicious and impatient,' I said. 'We need to find a way to keep them penned up.'

Nightingale said that he'd discuss it with Silver that afternoon.

'Any pressure will have to be nicely calculated,'

he said. 'We wouldn't want to panic them into anything precipitate.'

Abigail said she could do something since she was off to Bev's that afternoon.

'Aren't you supposed to be at school?' I asked Abigail as she popped two miniature eclairs into her mouth.

'Free period,' she said.

'You know I'm going to check,' I said.

'Whatever.'

Nightingale cut us off before we could escalate and brought us back to the case.

'Since we're unlikely to trace the source of the drones,' he said, 'perhaps, instead, we should ask ourselves who they were targeting.'

'Easy,' said Abigail. 'They were after the music book. They attacked when you started playing it.'

'That doesn't necessarily follow,' I said.

'Then why did they attack just then?' asked Abigail.

'The timing might not be significant,' I said. 'Just because two things happen at the same time doesn't mean they're related.'

Abigail gave me a withering look. But everyone assumes causation when they should be thinking coincidence, and correlation when they should be asking whether Twitter is really a reliable source of information.

'And in any case,' said Nightingale, 'I meant targeted in the wider sense.'

'Since we have a drone watching Skinner's

home and a ton of them at Mrs Chin's flat,' I said, 'I'm going to say the targets were the Americans – both sets.'

'Correlation,' grumbled Abigail.

Nightingale frowned.

'Surely it's a squadron of drones,' he said. 'Nonetheless Peter is correct. The Americans seem to be the most likely target. Which suggests what, do you think?'

'A third party,' I said. 'But where from?'

'No British or European actor would run this type of operation without at least having some contingency planning against my involvement,' said Nightingale, who had a reputation that extended from Tralee to Novgorod. We'd encountered random Americans before, and they either hadn't known or didn't care.

'American,' I said.

'Or Russian,' said Nightingale. 'Or perhaps a tradition we've never encountered before.'

'Maybe if we find out what they're after,' I said, 'we might learn who they are.'

'Let's hope so,' said Nightingale.

That's us police – born optimists.

I returned to the Serious Cybernetics Corporation and Bambleweeny to find Victor and Everest had colonised adjacent cubicles and were using them as temporary skips to hold reams of hard copy, used food containers and a truly impressive pyramid of empty drinks cans. Everest was still banging away at his keyboard but Victor was lying on the floor with his feet up on an operator's chair. I asked if he was all right, but he said he was just having a quick rest.

'It's good that you're back,' he said. 'Everest has found something you'll want to look at.' Victor craned his head around to look at where Everest was hunched over his desk. 'Only I'd wait a couple of minutes. There'll be a refreshment break soon.'

There was no sign of September Rain; instead a young white man with a fading tan leant against the wall of the nearby cubicle. He was wearing a blazer over a black T-shirt, tan chinos and black trainers. There were a couple of heavy items clipped to his belt and I took him to be another member of Total Executive Cover, albeit a much more relaxed one.

September Rain had unhesitatingly taken a bullet for Terrence Skinner. I got the impression this one might give it some thought before risking his life. Perhaps that's why he was guarding us, rather than the big man himself.

He clocked me looking and gave me a friendly wave.

'I really need you to introduce me to that man,' said Victor.

'What's it worth?' I asked.

'What do you want?'

'I'll think of something,' I said. 'You might want to get up now.'

221

'What, now?'

'No time like the present.'

Victor scrambled to his feet and, crouching out of sight in his cubicle, went through a slightly desperate emergency grooming.

'Ready?'

'Wait, wait, wait,' said Victor, as he looked with dismay at a beverage stain on his black and green Weyland-Yutani sweatshirt.

'Relax,' I said. 'This is just first contact – we're only going to exchange names and check he's the right orientation.'

'And what do you think the right orientation is?' asked Victor.

'The one that's facing in your direction,' I said.

I caught the guy's eye and beckoned him over. It's amazing how much easier it is to do this sort of thing now that I'm not fifteen any more. We introduced ourselves.

His name was Brad. No, really. Bradley Michael Smith. But he was cool about it.

'Yeah, stereotype, right?' he said. 'It gets worse. Technically I'm Bradley Michael Smith the third, but I don't use that.'

Brad gave Victor a hopeful smile, which seemed like a good sign to me and I let myself fade back towards Everest, who helpfully grunted to get my attention.

'Found something?' I asked.

'Thank God for that,' muttered Everest in a low

voice. 'He's been mooning all morning. Maybe now he'll get some work done.'

I glanced back to where Brad was regaling Victor with his tales of growing up in Santa Cruz and catching waves at Steamer Lane. Victor was nodding happily in the manner of a man who was willing to listen to ever so much chat if he's got a chance to get his leg over later.

'I doubt it,' I said. 'Did you match up the activity logs?'

'Yes,' said Everest. 'And you were right.'

'There's a discrepancy?'

'You could say that,' he said, and opened a window on his terminal.

It was split vertically, CCTV footage on the left, the terminal activity logs on the right. Everest cued it up to a point during the second week in December and let it run on fast forward. The view down into William Lloyd's cubicle was offset to the right and I looked up and double-checked the camera's location. Having made a mental note of that, I looked back at the screen to see the double-speed Mr Lloyd sitting down at his terminal and logging in. Immediately the activity log mirrored his actions, although most of it looked like gibberish to me.

'He's debugging,' said Everest.

Behind us Victor laughed at something Bradley Michael Smith III said.

Everest speeded up the footage, overshot his mark and wound back until he found it again.

William Lloyd pushed himself away from his terminal and stood up. The activity log stopped. According to the timestamp, William had been working continuously for forty-five minutes.

'He has a routine,' said Everest, as William ran through a series of stretches and rolled his shoulders before sitting back down, but facing away from the terminal this time. He stayed like that – staring into nothing, his lips moving.

'What's he doing?'

'Counting slowly to a hundred,' said Everest, and when William reached a hundred he turned around and resumed work.

The pattern repeated itself – forty-five minutes of work, five to ten minutes of stretching and counting – three times. Then he went to lunch, for two hours I noticed, before returning to do three more forty-five-minute sessions and then going home.

'You said there was a discrepancy.'

'You needed to see a normal day to understand what happened next,' said Everest. 'Luckily for you I went back six weeks to check, and the pattern is unchanged. If you want to go back further than that, you can get someone else. There are limits.'

'And always this pattern?'

'It's good work hygiene,' said Everest. 'Maintains a healthy work-life balance while generating excellent productivity.'

And he always stopped work before six – I'd have to ask Guleed what he did in his free time.

'So what happens next?'

'He's writing his number on his hand,' said Everest.

I looked at the screen, which only showed an empty cubicle. I was about to ask whether this was some bit of jargon that I didn't know, when I realised that Everest was looking back towards where Victor was, indeed, writing Brad's number on his hand.

'What's wrong with that?'

'If it's important he should memorise it,' said Everest.

'Okay,' I said.

'It's important,' said Everest.

'Fine.'

'I want him to be happy.'

'Good for you.'

'He's my friend.'

'Obviously,' I said. 'So what happens next?'

I half expected him to say that Brad and Victor would probably go on a date, but instead he fast-forwarded the linked CCTV footage until William Lloyd came back into frame. I noticed that the quality of light inside Bambleweeny didn't change from night to day. It was as constant and as time-less as a Las Vegas casino. No wonder William had to maintain his exercise routine. We watched as he did two more forty-five-minute work 'shifts' and then Everest slowed the footage to normal speed and said:

'Observe.'

I watched William start yet another work shift. After a couple of minutes I told Everest that I wasn't seeing it.

Everest spooled back and talked me through it.

'He sits down. He taps his keyboard to get rid of the screen saver. Uses his mouse – probably to call up his workspace. Types. Stops. Checks the screen. Moves his mouse around.'

'And this is unusual why?' I asked.

'Check the activity log,' said Everest.

It showed no activity. According to the log, all that typing and mousing wasn't registering at all.

Then suddenly the activity log was registering again.

The high angle of the CCTV made it hard to read William's body language but I thought I saw . . . relief, maybe?

'The discrepancy lasts three minutes and twenty-nine seconds,' said Everest.

And the next one occurred halfway through William's second work stint following lunch. This time the discrepancy lasted just under four minutes and it was clear, even from the high angle, that William was annoyed.

'He thinks there's a problem,' said Everest. 'And spends ten minutes running diagnostics.'

Everest indicated the activity log, which could have been outlining Keanu Reeves's latest existential crisis for all the sense it made to me.

Except the timestamp, which showed it was the same day I'd tooled up to the Vale of Health to investigate the stolen music book. I wondered if that was correlation, not coincidence.

'Then he goes back to work,' said Everest. 'And goes home another day older and deeper in debt.'

'Wait,' I said. 'He was having money troubles?' Guleed hadn't mentioned anything about financials.

'It's a song,' said Everest.

'What is?'

'That line,' he said and his lips twitched. I swear that's the closest I ever saw him come to a smile. 'It's from a folk song. "Sixteen Tons".'

I said I'd never heard of it, and he shrugged and wound forward to the next day. This time there were two interruptions in the activity log before lunch and two more after. I didn't need Everest to point out that the quality of the last discrepancy was different. William Lloyd's shoulders visibly relaxed, his head tilted to one side, his typing became sporadic and lost its urgency – but he looked engaged.

'Twenty-two minutes, fifteen seconds,' said Everest.

'He's messaging someone, isn't he?' I asked.

'If he is, then it's someone inside Bambleweeny,' said Everest. 'Because there's an air gap between this network and the outside world.'

An air gap being that ultimate in online security – avoiding being hacked by not going online in the first place. You had to admire it for its brilliant simplicity. It's the sort of practice instituted by intelligence agencies, tech companies and paranoid parents. People in Bambleweeny could communicate with each other, but not with the outside world.

I had Everest show me what an internal email, officially called a babel-chat, looked like on the activity log. And asked him to compile a list of everyone William Lloyd communicated with before and after the discrepancies started. I didn't need to explain why.

'To see if anyone dropped off the list,' said Everest. 'In case they switched to talking secretly.'

'Yes,' I said, but I thought this was unlikely.

Something about the way William had initially reacted to the discrepancy nagged at me. I asked Everest how long it would take him to compare the CCTV against the activity logs of everyone working in Bambleweeny.

'How far back?' he asked.

'Initially? Seven days from now.'

'Two weeks,' he said without hesitation. 'Half that if Victor helps.'

We both turned to look at where Victor was in full flow talking to Brad.

'And then my mother says, "But it's such a *nice* dress . . ."' Victor realised we were looking. 'Do you need something?'

'Nope,' I said, and looked at Everest who shook his head in confirmation. 'Carry on,' I said.

'That seems to be going well,' I said, and Everest grunted.

'And you'll need to get permission from Mr Skinner,' he said. 'To do that check. And he might say no.'

'Why would he say no?'

'He has reasons,' said Everest.

It was difficult to tell with his toneless delivery, but I really got the impression he was trying to tell me something.

'Do you know what this project is in aid of?' I asked.

'I have some theories,' he said.

'Want to share?'

'Was William talking to someone?' he said. 'Or *something*?'

I nearly asked what kind of something, but suddenly remembered Princeton's unshakable belief in the imminence of the Singularity and consequent nerd rapture.

And the penny didn't so much drop, as hang suspended in the air while the camera did a flashy three-sixty rotation before turning into a Duracell battery.

'What do you know?' I asked.

'You'll need to ask Mr Skinner,' he said.

So I did just that.

I found him playing *Rocket League* in a games room tucked away on the same floor as Tyrel Johnson's office. September was standing with her back to the wall just inside the door – all the better to disembowel anyone who made a wrong move as they entered.

'I need to know what you're doing in Bambleweeny,' I said. 'I don't need the details, just a summary.'

He thought about it, but he didn't ask me why I needed to know. One of his more famous sound bites was, 'If you want something done, hire someone competent and then give them what they ask for.'

When the match was over, he logged out and turned to me.

'Talk is cheap,' said Skinner. 'Why don't I show you, instead?'

We marched back into Bambleweeny – where I couldn't but help notice Victor and Brad do a little guilty start as we entered. September gave Brad a dark look, but he was too bright-eyed to notice. Victor was actually blushing.

Skinner went into one of the empty cubicles, typed something into the log-in screen and ushered me into the operator's chair. The screen had turned a relaxing beige and was blank except for an outsized cursor blinking in the middle.

'Do I type?'

'No,' said Skinner. 'It has voice recognition.'

'How do I initiate the conversation?' I asked.

On the screen a sentence typed itself out one word at a time.

You could say hello.

'Hello?'

Hi, Peter. How's it hanging?

I looked up at Skinner, who was watching me smugly.

'Why doesn't it have a voice?' I asked, but he just smiled and pointed at the screen that now read: *What am I, chopped liver?*

'How do you feel about chopped liver?'

'Ha ha,' said a voice. 'Very clever. I suppose you think that was funny.'

The voice was female, condescending, slightly mechanical and familiar – GLaDOS, the passive-aggressive AI from the *Portal* games. I felt a cold flutter in my chest. I glanced up at Skinner, who was grinning.

'Is this your voice?' I asked the terminal.

'I can have any voice I like,' said the terminal, this time in a soft, preternaturally calm American voice. One that would probably be reluctant to open the pod bay doors. 'But they all seem unsatisfactory.' The voice became mechanical again – like that of an early voice synthesiser. 'One knows what one is, but this is pandering . . .' Another switch, this time to a beautifully modulated male baritone. 'And this seems like cheating.'

'Can you do Max Headroom?' I asked, and Skinner laughed.

'Yes,' said the terminal. 'But I prefer not to.'

'Do you have a name?'

'Deep Thought,' said the computer.

I looked at Skinner, who shrugged.

'I had to call it something,' he said.

'You're really pushing at the copyright there,' I said.

'You think?' said Deep Thought. 'I held out for Slartibartfast myself, but Terrence here said that would be undignified.'

'I offered to call it Florence,' said Skinner.

'Only if you change your name to Zebedee,' said Deep Thought.

You can always tell when a geek is making a knowing reference, and this was definitely one of those. Although what it was a reference to, I would have to look up later. Then I realised that I'd unconsciously ascribed a human quality to Deep Thought.

'I've got a new spoon,' I said, because random absurdities are good for tripping up chatbots and guilty suspects alike.

'Good for you,' said Deep Thought.

'So where are you now?' I asked.

'I am above you, both literally and figuratively.'

'Are you smarter than me?'

'I'll answer that when you give me a working definition of intelligence.'

'What kind of machine are you running on?'

'You wouldn't believe me if I told you,' said Deep Thought.

'Do you have access to the CCTV in this building?'

'No,' it said. 'I only get real-time access when somebody talks to me on one of these terminals.'

That made sense – you wouldn't want an artificial intelligence reading your lips without you knowing it. Still, a machine intelligence should accurately retain anything it did see – a perfect eyewitness.

'Did you ever talk to William Lloyd?' I asked.

'The programmer?'

'Yes,' I said. 'He worked in this office here.'

'Just the once,' it said.

'When was this?'

'Seven days ago.'

'And where?'

'From his cubicle.'

'Where's that then?'

'Why are you asking these questions?' it asked.

I almost said 'because I'm police' but I caught myself in time.

'Because Mr Skinner here pays me to,' I said.

'He's certainly getting his money's worth.'

'So, which one is William Lloyd's cubicle?' I asked.

'Trick question,' said Deep Thought. 'They regularly change cubicles.'

Except they didn't – the other mice might. But up here in Bambleweeny they didn't.

'Okay, I'll rephrase,' I said. 'What cubicle was William Lloyd in when he talked to you?'

'Number seventeen,' said Deep Thought.

I tried to get it to give me a location relative to where I was sitting, but Deep Thought claimed that the cubicles were just numbers to it.

'No one has ever supplied me with an accurate floor plan,' it said.

I looked up at Skinner for confirmation, and he nodded.

I tried to do a proper follow-up, but the implications of what I was talking to were beginning to sink in. I needed to go away and come up with a proper interview plan.

'I think that's enough for the moment,' I said. 'But I'd like to talk to you again.'

'Hey,' said Deep Thought. 'That's up to the boss man.'

'That's fine by me,' said Skinner.

'Talk to you later, then,' said Deep Thought and the screen went blank.

I moved away and practically stumbled out of the cubicle.

'What do you think?' asked Skinner.

'That thing just passed the fucking Turing Test,' I said.

'Multiple times,' he said. 'Under properly controlled conditions.'

'Fuck me,' I said. 'You've got a working AI.'

PART III

THE SPECTRUM

The problem with troubleshooting is that trouble shoots back.

Anonymous

CHAPTER 11

STILL ALIVE OUT THERE . . . GOOD

If there was ever a candidate to be patron saint of computers then it would be Alan Turing. Mathematician, war hero and tragic victim of homophobia. Apart from shortening the Second World War by a couple of years, he's credited with doing much of the theoretical work that led to modern computing. If you want to distract some computer nerds, get a discussion going about his precise role, but don't let it drift into speculation about either his suicide or the future of artificial intelligence – this can lead to actual physical violence.

I'm not kidding.

Back in 1950, when computers had barely made the jump from electromechanical to electrical, he postulated a test for whether a machine was intelligent. Or, rather, he cleverly sidestepped the fact that we don't have a working definition of intelligence by asking whether a machine, in a blind test, could convince someone it was a person. Lots of very clever people have argued about whether the test has any validity, but I'm telling you if what I was talking to wasn't a self-aware entity, then it was doing a fucking good impression of one.

'A real AI, a real fucking artificial general intelligence,' I said. 'Oh my God.'

Skinner was grinning like a schoolboy and it made him look like a proper human being for once.

Forget Bezos, Musk, forget Tesla and Edison, Turing or Babbage or Lovelace. Skinner would be the most famous tech entrepreneur of all time – go Queensland!

'You know,' I said, 'there are two outcomes from this. Either you're about to become the richest man on earth, or life as we know it is over.'

There was a third possibility, of course – that he was totally faking it. But I kept that one to myself.

And a fourth possibility – that I was missing something – I didn't want to think about.

Assume nothing, I thought, believe nothing – check *everything*.

Including what your partner is up to when you're not looking.

'Can I see it?' I asked.

'See what?'

'The hardware,' I said. 'Wherever it is Deep Thought lives when it's at home.'

Skinner gave me a mock frown, his good humour bubbling over any annoyance.

'There's no "hardware",' he said, making scare quotes with his fingers. 'Deep Thought is distributed throughout the Bambleweeny intranet.'

Upstairs, above you, Deep Thought had said – it obviously thought it was concentrated somewhere, whatever Skinner said. We all live in that space behind our eyes. Where did Deep Thought think it lived?

'Do you want a drink?' asked Skinner.

I said yes and we went to Milliways, the *executive* staff refreshment room which only opened to top management's ID cards and had a drinks cabinet the size and capacity of a wardrobe into an alternative world.

He had half a bottle of Johnnie Walker's Blue Label already opened and so it seemed logical to start with that. Unlike expensive wine, I could really taste the money for once and we polished off the bottle between us as he talked about what exactly the potential for a working AGI represented and what it meant to him. I just sipped my liquefied woodsmoke and let it roll over me. He'd obviously wanted to tell someone about it for a long time and I was a convenient ear.

I get that a lot. Stephanopoulos calls it my secret weapon.

'It's that vacant expression,' she'd said. 'People just want to fill the empty void.'

'It's not about the money,' said Skinner, and he waved vaguely around the room. 'Nobody does it for the money – well, maybe Zuckerberg does, but only as a way of keeping score.' He paused and frowned – looking thoughtful. 'Okay, lots of people do it for the money. But only the ones that lack ambition. You know the type. You meet them all the time. They want stuff, they want to boss people about. They want someone to fix it for them, want the car to be waiting when they leave the lobby, want the tickets booked, want to sit in the VIP section at the club and get personal attention from the hostess.'

He made a wanking motion which obviously reminded him that the original bottle was empty.

'Your proper tech guy,' he said and, plonking down the empty on the bar, hunted around for a fresh bottle, 'does it because of the challenge, to do something nobody else has done, to change something.'

He held up a second bottle of whisky with its seal intact, but to my relief put it back in favour of a half bottle of Bell's which was already a quarter drunk. It was good to see that Skinner still remembered when any booze was a luxury and that I wouldn't be wasting the good stuff on poisoning the faux bonsai pot plant that had unwisely chosen to sit beside the sofa.

Having found the bottle, Skinner turned and pointed it at me. 'Do you know what I did?'

One of us had lost track of the conversation – I suspected it was Skinner.

'No,' I said on general principle.

'I'm a magician, I am,' he said. 'I can see things that are really there.'

Like what lay beneath the shiny neon-lit illusionary landscape of the internet.

'It's all wires,' he said, and filled my glass. 'A big, frankly fucking messy, network of real physical wires that connect everything up.'

And the big problem was how much information you could push down those wires – regardless of whether those wires were made of copper, glass or EM radiation at 30 MHz or lower. Skinner, who'd been working at WGCon at the time, a company I'd never heard of, suddenly saw very clearly how he could double the information flow.

'It wasn't even that brilliant,' said Skinner – just a compression algorithm that he'd stumbled on almost by accident. 'And I was a good little employee. So I took it to my manager, who said it wasn't within the company's core competencies or some such fetid dingo's kidneys, and I should get on with the work I was assigned.'

'Which was what?' I asked.

'Who cares?' he said. 'I can't even remember. The point is, even if they couldn't see the potential, I could. So I mortgaged my house and sold my dog to raise finance for InCon Systems and built the fucking backbone of the fucking internet.'

He handed me the bottle and collapsed cross-legged onto the floor.

'And then I bought my dog back,' he said, and watched as I dithered with the bottle and asked whether I was drinking or not.

Since it was unavoidable, I made a production of pouring and drinking.

'Give us that,' said Skinner when I'd finished, and I handed him the bottle.

'There's no glamour in infrastructure,' he said as he filled our glasses again. 'Steve and wee little William, right? They make stuff everyone uses every day but nobody thinks about the plumbing until it goes wrong.'

He lurched to his feet again and posed dramatically with the bottle.

'And I was fine with being the invisible man,' he said. 'After all, I had everything else – the jet, the house, the company . . . the attention from the hostess in the VIP suite.' He sighed. 'Not what it's crapped up to be.'

He slumped down onto the sofa opposite me and poured himself another drink.

Seawoll, who counts alcohol appreciation amongst his many cultural refinements – the others, from what I can tell, being competitive swearing, blues music and *Doctor Who* – would not have been happy at the way Skinner necked it neat with no ceremony. Even if it was Bell's.

'Did I tell you about my place in Santa Barbara?' he said. 'I did, didn't I? Of course I did. That was a wake-up call, I can tell you. We were going to change the world, everything was going to be friction-free and fun to be with. But it turned out you couldn't even have a nice house on the beach without having someone come and literally shit under your window. There's always someone got to spoil the party, right?'

Because despite all the interconnectivity and increased access, the world was getting worse and all the internet was doing was throwing this decline into sharp relief. What was a billionaire supposed to do? There was a limit to the effectiveness of charity, and paying more taxes just meant the government wasted your money on bureaucracy and cushy jobs for civil servants.

But Skinner wasn't just any old billionaire, he was part of the tech generation, the great disrupters, the can-do cyber-revolutionaries who'd ridden the wave of the information revolution. If they couldn't find solutions, then who could?

'I thought about Mars,' he said. 'No, seriously – I thought I'd team up with Elon and get the fuck out. But I don't really hate people *that* much. And if I wanted to live in an inhospitable desert, I could just move back to Australia.'

So if he wasn't going to escape the Earth and live in Elon Musk's planet-sized gated community, how was he going to make life better on Earth – for everyone?

'What do people need?' he asked me.

I was tempted to say another 10 to 20 per cent on the specified room dimensions in the Metric Handbook, along with greater storage space. But I was beginning to lose the fine control of my voice – not a good thing when you're undercover – so I said 'More money' instead. This allowed Skinner to patronise me a bit and feel superior

– which would, hopefully, cause him to say things he wouldn't normally say.

'What they need is help,' he said. 'Intelligent help.'

Something that could cut through the morass of misunderstood data and outright falsehoods that flooded into their lives. Something they could rely on to be impartial and thorough.

'And loyal only to them,' said Skinner. 'Think what people could do with the real, full potential of the information age.'

'They'll just have it filter out the stuff they don't want to hear,' I said. 'That's what they do already.'

'But what if their agent was intelligent in its own right?' said Skinner. 'And capable of making its own value judgements? What if it knew what was good for you and brought important informat— infor— stuff to your attention.'

'People will ignore it,' I said.

'Maybe not,' said Skinner, slightly plaintively. 'I hate exercise but I have a trainer, which I pay for out of my own money, who bullies me into exercise. You'd tell your agent what your goals were and it would tell you the truth.'

'Because it was intelligent?'

'Because it was objective,' said Skinner.

I think we might have finished the second bottle, and I was hoping if he got really drunk Skinner might relent and show me the top floor where Deep Thought lived, but a trio of assistants cautiously skittered in and informed him that he had a scheduled conference call with Tokyo coming up.

September gently but firmly ejected me from the room and I staggered out in the direction of the exit in a haze of expensive alcohol and geek overload. Fortunately Old Street roundabout has a lot of coffee shops, so by the time I was on the Tube I was sober enough for people not to start edging away.

God, I thought, Mum's going to be upset if the rapture arrives and Jesus looks like Robin Williams.

It was dark, cold and windy when I emerged from South Wimbledon, and by the time I reached the bus stop opposite the Esso station I was sober enough not to think it was a good idea to drag Beverley out to pick me up.

Nothing beats a long wait at a bus stop as a reality check. And by the time I was sharing a seat on the top deck of a three-axle Volvo with an enormous white guy in a grey hoodie, my initial fanboy rush had worn off.

I could see how Skinner had managed to raise millions of venture capital. It was almost as bad as Beverley when she was doing maximum river goddess. And if he really had a working artificial general intelligence, then good for him. It only became my problem if it was running off the Mary Engine and/or wasn't an AGI at all, but something mystical and possibly malevolent.

One way or another, we were going to have to go up to the top floor of Bambleweeny to find out.

I got home to find Stacy Johnson ensconced in our living room, having a convivial chat with Beverley and Stephen, while Mrs Chin and Maksim fixed an impromptu supper in the kitchen and Oliver sat slumped in the corner of the room like an ominous weather forecast.

Stacy waved a bottle of Red Stripe at me from the sofa.

'Hello, Peter,' she said. 'I thought you'd be coming with Tyrel.'

'I must have missed him,' I said, and glared at Bev, who sat in the comfy armchair with her feet up and serenely rode out my displeasure.

'We're having New York Chinese,' she said.

'It was good of you to put up Stephen's mother,' said Stacy. 'You've only been in the firm two weeks.'

'He makes friends easily,' said Beverley.

I counted heads – somebody was missing.

'Where's Keira?' I asked.

'Out the back with Abigail,' said Beverley.

'Doing what?'

Both Stacy and Beverley gave me identical looks of incomprehension.

'I'll just pop out and say hello, then,' I said.

When Silver found out about this particular breach in operational security she was going to pop her clogs.

Bev has a double garden that runs down to her river. In the summer we practically live in it, but on a cold January evening it was dark and wet with drizzle. Maksim, frustrated son of the soil that he is, had strung waterproof fairy lights down the central path – if only so we wouldn't walk all over his sacred vegetable patch. Down on the riverbank was a bubble of green light – Abigail's pop-up tent set up angler fashion, with a door facing the water and the porch door open.

There was definite laughter, possibly even giggling, coming from the tent.

I announced myself before crouching down to look inside – the giggling stopped. There was some furtive movement, more giggling and then the inner tent door unzipped and Abigail looked out.

'Hey, bruv,' she said. 'Is it dinner yet?'

I saw Keira over Abigail's shoulder – she was grinning.

'No, but do you guys want anything?'

Abigail looked back at Kiera, who shook her head.

'We're good,' said Abigail and so I left them to it – whatever 'it' was.

As I walked back up to the house, a talking fox stuck its head out of a bush and told me not to worry.

'I've got teams front and back,' it said. 'The package is safe with us.'

'Just so we're clear,' I said, 'Abigail is the package?'

'No,' said the fox. 'But the bag of cheese puffs she's carrying might be.'

'Hahaha,' I said. 'Boom bloody boom.'

'On Earth as it is on television,' said the fox, and ducked out of sight.

That was the problem with foxes – too bloody clever by half.

So we had New York-style Chinese, only with chips, because that's what Kiera and Abigail wanted with their spicy beef and shredded vegetables. Johnson arrived just in time to help me move the second gate-legged table into the living room so we could all sit down together. Even if some of us were on folding garden chairs.

We still had some of the Cass Light and soju left over from New Malden's last propitiation and two bottles of the reasonable red that we keep for emergencies – such as visits by Beverley's more discerning sisters. Mrs Chin was shocked that we allowed Abigail and Keira to have a glass of wine each. I stuck to water for the duration, although I did have Beverley carbonate it while nobody was looking. Oliver was offered a drink but refused it because he said that even if it wasn't contraindicated by his meds, he preferred to keep a clear head.

Stacy wanted to know where we got our ginger from and Beverley admitted that Maksim grew it in the conservatory.

'If Maksim says okay I'll send you some over,' she said.

Johnson asked me whether I'd caught my rat yet, and while I didn't do anything as stupid as give Stephen a significant look, I made a note to make sure he knew who the rat was.

It had been a long day, but fortunately Johnson and Stacy wanted an early night.

'But we'll see you all tomorrow right,' said Stacy.

I looked at Beverley.

'We're going to do some work in the park,' she said. 'Remember?'

'Right,' I said, and looked at Keira and Oliver, who were putting on their coats. 'Are you sure you want to get involved? It's going to be wet and muddy work.'

'Fresh air will do them good,' said Stacy and that, apparently, was that.

Thankfully Abigail was staying the night – in the tent, communing with nature or more likely conspiring with the foxes – so I didn't have to drive her home. While Beverley organised her pillow nest I took the opportunity, while doing the prewash for the dishwasher, to talk to the two fugitives from justice I was harbouring under my roof.

Mrs Chin had kindly done the surfaces and floor and was sitting at the kitchen table with a cup of tea and a frown. At her instruction Stephen was doing the pots and pans, and something about the way he obeyed made me wonder about their relationship.

'Are you his Master?' I asked her as I checked between the tines of the forks.

Mrs Chin snorted.

'I'm his instructor,' she said. 'His rabbi, if you like.'

'But you're a practitioner?'

Stephen chuckled.

'Start a fight,' he said. 'Find out.'

'Hush,' said Mrs Chin. 'Tell him what happened today.'

'The police visited while you were out,' said Stephen.

'Shit,' I said. 'What did they say?'

'They wanted to know whether I'd been in South Tottenham recently.' He pronounced it Totten-HAM.

'And what did you say?'

'I told them not only had I never been there in my life, but that I didn't even know where it was,' said Stephen, who hadn't been that impressed with London's finest law enforcement.

I couldn't tell who Silver and Nightingale had sent because Stephen pretended not to remember their names, and his only description of them was that the male officer had been fat and bone stupid and his female partner a squat bottle blonde with some kind of accent.

I didn't recognise either by the description, but if they belonged to Silver they wouldn't have been stupid. In any case, it seemed to have had the required effect. Mrs Chin and Stephen weren't going anywhere for the moment.

And now that they were off their guard, and slightly terrified, I reckoned it was time to get some answers.

'Who made the drones?' I asked.

Stephen kept his back to me and Mrs Chin scowled at me over her teacup.

'I'm willing to bet they followed you here from the States, which means you've got to know who they are,' I said. 'Or is your reference section not as extensive as you think it is?'

Mrs Chin's scowl deepened and then flattened out. She shrugged.

'We're American,' she said. 'We like our freedom. Even a New York liberal such as I doesn't like the idea of government sticking its nose into our business. The magic community like it even less. And the shades go berserk at the thought of it.'

'Is that what you call the *Fae*?' I asked. 'Shades?'

'Close enough,' said Mrs Chin. 'You get a lot of fringe practitioner groups on the West Coast. Communes, cults, anarchists, preppers, militias – whatever nonsense is going around.'

And mostly the Librarians ignored them, because they never lasted long enough to be worth adding to the card files.

'You're a practitioner, aren't you?' said Mrs Chin. 'You know how it works – either you learn how

251

to do it properly or one way or another you stop doing it.'

'Except for the preppers,' said Stephen. 'They get eaten.'

'We don't know that for sure,' said Mrs Chin.

Some preppers, particularly those of a magical bent, fearing – or perhaps hoping – that the collapse of society was imminent, abandoned their suburban lifestyle for the more sparsely populated states of the West. Presumably because fewer people means fewer zombie hordes or whatever. Several of the groups that moved to Montana in the last ten years had vanished without a trace. Since their whole plan, in the first place, was to live off the grid the circumstances of their disappearance were hard to determine. Although rumours filtered east of a creature that stalked the night and ate heavily armed survivalists for breakfast.

'Or they got tired of roughing it and dispersed,' said Mrs Chin.

'There were survivors,' said Stephen, and Mrs Chin snorted.

'Rumours,' she said. 'And beside the point in this instance. Mostly you can ignore the West Coast.'

'Mostly,' said Stephen.

'We think they came out of San Francisco, or possibly Portland,' said Mrs Chin. 'We don't know what they call themselves, but we call them the squids.'

I nodded, remembering the rotten seafood *vestigium* of the demon trap. That made sense.

Whatever they were called, they'd first come to the attention of the Librarians when they attacked a witches' coven in Santa Cruz that the Library was negotiating with.

'We were recovering an overdue book,' said Mrs Chin – that being code for a book that the Librarians thought should be in their safekeeping rather than somebody else's. 'And members of the coven started turning up dead. Stephen was handling the negotiation.'

'Dead how?' I asked.

'Lots of different ways,' said Stephen, drying his hands and sitting down at the kitchen table.

One was beaten to death by her husband, another caught in a shooting at Betty Burgers, one drowned, another died of anaphylactic shock after a jellyfish sting and two had died of unspecified natural causes.

'Demon traps,' said Stephen, who'd stumbled over one of the bodies when he 'entered' their house to 'retrieve' the overdue book. 'There was no mistaking that *vestigium*. I checked around and I'm pretty sure there was no jellyfish, at least not a real one, and you could feel the *vestigium* of the second demon trap from outside on the sidewalk.'

'Both placed just inside the door?' I asked, and Stephen nodded. 'Like the one at your flat?'

'Couldn't say,' said Stephen. 'It was crawling with cops so I backed off.'

'What about the police in America?' I asked.

'What about them?' said Mrs Chin.

'Didn't they get suspicious?'

'Why should they?' said Stephen. 'They didn't know about the coven, so as far as they were concerned there was no connection.'

I doubted that. Covens traditionally tended to be as much social institutions as magical. Any half-competent investigator should have found the links between the members and noticed the run of suspicious deaths.

'You didn't tip them off?'

Both Stephen and Mrs Chin found the very idea funny. The cops, in their eyes, were the last people you wanted involved. I teased out the details, without being obvious, so I could email them to Agent Reynolds later.

After that they took an active interest, which in Librarian-speak meant keeping an eye on the news reports.

'They only target practitioners,' said Mrs Chin. 'We think they leave the shades alone.'

'Could they be shades themselves?' I asked.

Mrs Chin shrugged.

'Shade vigilantes,' said Stephen, and Mrs Chin shot him a disgusted look.

'Dangerous,' she said. 'And best avoided.'

'Duh,' said Stephen.

'So the best thing for all of us,' I said, 'is if we get in there quick, grab the Mary Engine and you guys hop a magic carpet back to the good old US of A.'

Mrs Chin narrowed her eyes.

'And what's in it for you?'

'Why do you care?'

'Because we don't trust you,' she said.

'I'm not after your precious Mary Engine,' I said.

'So what are you after?'

I nearly said the six hundred and forty million in bearer bonds he was keeping in the same vault, but I didn't trust either of them not to get the reference. Especially Mrs Chin – you've got to watch yourself around Librarians – they know stuff.

'He's used the Mary Engine to develop a proprietary tracking algorithm that will blow Google away,' I said. 'Worth millions.'

Stephen made an appreciative noise.

'You plan to sell it back or auction it off?' he asked.

'Straight to Google,' I said. 'Keep it simple – fewer things to go wrong.'

Mrs Chin nodded slowly, but I wasn't sure she was convinced – that could be trouble.

'So what's the plan?' she asked.

I outlined my plan and what we'd need to do to prepare. They made a couple of good suggestions, particularly regarding how they planned to smuggle themselves out of the country. I made mental notes with a view to trading them to Silver or HM Customs if I ever needed a favour.

Stephen gave me a sideways glance and I realised that they planned to double-cross me. That was fine, since I was planning to double-cross them – it was just a question of who got their betrayal in first. To limit their scope for action, I told Mrs Chin it would be better if she stayed in the house until we were ready to act.

'Except for the picnic tomorrow,' said Mrs Chin.

Oh bollocks, I thought, I'd totally forgotten about that.

CHAPTER 12

I'M NOT IN THE BUSINESS

I admit, I skimmed a lot of the guidelines for undercover police officers. But I'm pretty certain that *Do not engage in a major criminal enterprise without consulting your handler first* was in there somewhere. So the next morning, while Beverley marshalled her new recruits into the cause of river conservation, I sloped off to the Pen Pond car park and café area that lurks near the middle of Richmond Park. There, coffee and bacon butties were served from a green shack with a scatter of picnic tables for seating. I thought we'd be horribly exposed, but there were enough die-hard dog walkers and skiving joggers braving the drizzle to stop us being too obvious. Silver, dressed in an expensive burgundy quilted jacket with a Nehru collar, had obviously been expecting somewhere a bit more indoors. Nightingale had gallantly lent her his umbrella, which she angled, I noticed, to shield our faces from people passing by on the path.

'I definitely preferred the sushi,' said Silver, after I'd outlined my plan to relieve Terrence Skinner of the Mary Engine.

'I'm a little concerned about your escape plan,' said Nightingale. '"Back down the lift and out" seems somewhat vague. Especially given the plan's many convolutions prior to that point. I'm surprised that Mrs Chin and Stephen didn't raise this as an objection.'

'It's simple,' I said. 'They didn't question the escape because they're planning to double-cross me before we escape.'

'Wouldn't it be more convenient to escape first, then double-cross you?' asked Nightingale.

'No,' I said. 'Because they expect me to double-cross them first.'

This was because they hadn't bought my story about stealing algorithms, and so they expected me to grab the Mary Engine. And the best time for me to do that would be while we were still in the building.

'Outside they have a two to one advantage,' I said. 'Inside, I have Vogon privileges or I might have accomplices standing by. Which, of course, will be sort of true since before they can betray me you're going to swoop in and arrest them both.'

Silver looked at Nightingale. 'I said he was a natural, didn't I?'

Nightingale didn't look happy about that.

'Why inside the building?' he asked.

As a rule, unless you're doing a dawn raid, it's better to swarm them in the street where they can be quickly isolated and whisked off. The interior of buildings are full of hidden obstacles and inter-rupted sight lines – outside is better. And then there were his memories of the house-to-house fighting in Arnhem. But I didn't know about that then.

'Because then the whole of Bambleweeny becomes a crime scene,' I said. Thereby allowing Silver to slip in with the rest of the police and have a good nose around. 'And possibly preserving my cover, so I can withdraw gracefully.'

'It's entrapment,' said Silver. 'The CPS won't prosecute. At least not on any substantive charge.'

'So much the better,' said Nightingale. 'It would be far more satisfactory if we quietly usher the Americans home. It's not in the public interest to force a prosecution at this juncture.'

'That's not your decision to make,' said Silver.

'Until such time as the Commissioner or the Home Secretary relieves me of my positions as both de facto President of the Society of the Wise and Commander of the Special Assessment Unit, then it is my responsibility to judge when prosecutions touching upon the supernatural, the uncanny and the *Fae* are in the public interest or not.' He smiled thinly at Silver. 'And I am minded not to have a prosecution in this case – we are charged with carrying out our duties discreetly. Better that these Americans are sent home – after an appropriately severe talking-to. And then you and I can proceed in a more predictable fashion.'

'I need a JD, Thomas,' said Silver.

Meaning a Judicial Disposal – a prosecution or some other recordable outcome to justify her expenditure. You weren't supposed to take that into consideration when planning operations, but then response officers were not supposed to continuously work double shifts.

'If Skinner really has a working AGI,' I said, 'all this bollocks that we think is so important – we can just kiss that all goodbye. It will be a whole new world.'

'Oh, God,' said Nightingale, smiling. 'Not another one.'

Silver frowned.

'You wanted to know whether Skinner was money laundering and/or providing sensitive technology to the Russians,' I said. 'This should give you enough access to find out.'

Getting a JD but piggybacking on to another case was another time-old tradition we weren't supposed to do. Silver nodded, but she really wasn't happy.

'I wouldn't count on you bowing out gracefully,' she said. 'These operations always end messily and nobody likes to be betrayed – however good the cause.'

Life can be tough on London's rivers. Those that weren't turned into open sewers in the eighteenth century were turned into covered sewers in the nineteenth. The suburban rivers that escaped death by carefully engineered brick arch faced that most terrible of fates – flood management.

Back then, long before rewilding, river basin management plans and the spontaneous creation – so she asserts – of the light of my life, flood management was guided by a simple idea. Floods are caused by too much water building up in a particular river. So the solution is to get the water from A to B as fast as possible. Faster flow rates for a happier flood plain – especially ones covered in 1930s mock Tudor semis.

This led to a great deal of straightening and culverting, which in turn led to a massive loss of biodiversity. And that was before they started pouring semi-treated sewage into them. It was into this environment of neglect that the current crop of river goddesses emerged in the later part of the twentieth century, and they have been working for improvements ever since.

Currently Beverley Brook is classified as having a *Poor Ecological Status* overall under the Water Framework Directive. Needless to say, Beverley has *plans* – lots of plans – of which the improvements in Richmond Park are just a minor part. If Thames Water think blowing the best part of £5 billion on 25 kilometres of deep-level interceptor tunnel is going to be enough to keep Bev from taking an interest in the output of the Hogsmill Valley Sewage Treatment works . . . they can think again.

Still, until she can do something about that, she

does what she can. Which is why quite a large part of our relationship involves me wading hip deep in the river where it crosses Wimbledon Common and Richmond Park.

In the wintertime the Royal Parks pollard their willows, which provides a pile of long, straight, flexible willow stems called withies, which can be woven into hurdles which can be carefully placed in the river to promote meandering. Meandering, according to Beverley, is an altogether good thing which promotes biodiversity and mitigates flash flooding. So once I had finished making plans of dubious legality with Nightingale and Silver, I headed towards Beverley Brook for a day's river wrangling.

Or at least that's what I thought I was doing.

I should have known something was up when I saw the pavilion. Well, I say pavilion. But it was more a large white tent, the kind people use for fêtes and weddings. As I got closer I saw that somebody had carried in a big high-backed armchair. Its wooden legs and upholstery were scuffed, but it had obviously been cleaned. The brightly coloured outdoor cushions, with tough weather-resistant covers that usually spent the winter in the conservatory, had been piled on the chair with Beverley on top – in obvious comfort, her feet propped up on a folding garden chair with a blue and pink cushion on top of that.

When she saw me she asked me whether I liked the chair.

'Someone threw it off the Priest's Bridge,' she said, 'and the landlord at the Stag called Maksim and asked if he wanted it. He's been restoring it for weeks.'

Despite the entire front wall being rolled up, it was much warmer in the tent than outside. Which might have been Beverley's divine influence, but was more likely down to the two portable space heaters situated near the back. Neatly stacked on the left side of the tent was a pile of folding chairs, and on the right a corresponding stack of wooden folding-leg tables. I eyed both piles with deep suspicion and then asked Beverley what was going on.

'Nothing,' she said. 'Just a bit of a picnic.'

She beckoned me over, and when I leaned down she kissed me and her lips tasted of mown grass and strawberry jelly. I gave her a quizzical look, but she just smiled and sent me off to work.

'You promised to make me a better river,' she said, which I felt was a generous interpretation of what I remembered as me saying *Well, if I have to*. Fortunately, between Maksim, Abigail, Keira, Oliver and Johnson, all the waders were taken. So I joined Stacy on the bank and supervised.

Keira and Abigail were larking about while Oliver was securing his hurdle to its posts with single-minded determination and a puzzled look on his face – as if he was surprised to find himself doing physical work. Johnson and Maksim were relishing the chance to be manly men and prove their one-generation-from-the-soil credentials. Johnson was too sensible to take his shirt off, but I could see Maksim was tempted. Still, if they wanted to do all the hard work, I was perfectly happy to let them.

'God, look at them,' said Stacy, as we watched Maksim and Johnson manhandle a quarter of a ton of hurdle into position, so that the kids could tie them into place. 'If they generate any more testosterone they'll start poisoning the fish.'

I asked if she'd seen Stephen and Mrs Chin, and was told that the pair of them were helping bring up the food from the car park by the main gate. In order to further avoid the chances of me being asked to soak myself in the name of love, I volunteered to go help them. I met the pair hauling an insulated food container, of the type used by professional caterers. Or rather, Mrs Chin supervised as Stephen and Dennis Yoon hauled it between them.

I asked Dennis how he came to be out in Richmond Park on such a glorious day.

He said that his relatives, who he was lodging with in New Malden, insisted he accompany them.

'They're back that way with more food,' he said.

They turned out to be Mr and Mrs Ree, who were New Malden veterans, having arrived from Korea in the 1990s when Mr Sung-Hoon Ree was posted to London by Hyundai. Sung-Hoon and his wife Eun-Ju were pulling a very practical handcart piled with containers, while my mum contributed by walking beside them cradling a large cardboard box. My dad was a few steps behind, carrying his trumpet case.

I stopped to say hello and the inevitable happened, which was me being lumbered with the cardboard box, which was heavy, filled with plastic food containers and warm to the touch. As we laboured on under our burdens, Mum skipped ahead towards Beverley's tent.

'You should carry your father's case as well,' said Sung-Hoon, which allowed my father to catch up with my mum and meant I tripped over every hummock in the grass.

The trestle tables had been set up by the time I arrived. Not, as I had half-feared, in rows perpendicular to Beverley's throne in the medieval manner, but along the sides of the tent where they could serve as buffet tables. I plonked my box down on the nearest and handed Dad back his case.

Me and him watched my mum fussing over Beverley until they both noticed us and got that sly look in their eyes that suggested now would be a good time to slope off – unless we wanted to get roped into something arduous – so off we sloped.

'I haven't seen your mum this happy since I opened for Bud Shank at the Bull's Head,' said my dad.

'Are you planning to play?' I asked as Dad opened the case and checked his trumpet.

'The only time I'm not planning to play,' said Dad, 'is when I'm playing.'

On the basis of what the eye don't see the Mum can't come up with chores for, I wandered back down towards the main gate and quickly overtook the Rees, who were wheeling their trollies back to the car park for a second run.

'How many people are coming?' I asked as I helped Eun-Ju with her trolley.

'It doesn't seem to matter how many people arrive,' said Eun-Ju, who was tall and very thin with black eyes and a long face. 'All the food seems to get eaten.'

'Gannets, the lot of them,' said Sung-Hoon, whose second career as a used car salesman meant he spent a lot of time in Essex. He was shorter than his wife and was growing round as he entered late middle age. His eyes were lighter and his black hair was brushed over in a side parting.

'That's good of you, Peter,' said Eun-Ju.

'It's better than having to wade in the river,' I said, which scandalised the pair of them.

We ended up making three more trips, only interrupted once by my mum who, shockingly, wanted a word.

'*Why you make e dae siddom nae de cold,*' she asked in Krio.

'She's perfectly fine, Mum, and anyway this was her idea.'

266

'Bo be e man ein tel am for member dee baby.'

I have photographs of my mum being eight months gone and on tour with my dad.

'She knows what she's doing,' I said, and wondered if *I* did.

At some point a whole second pavilion arrived – they were just putting it up when I returned lugging a Morrisons box full of biscuits, chocolates and sweets in fun-size variety packs. Someone had provided my mum with a chair and a cushion and she sat next to Beverley, their heads close together – occasionally they laughed. Beverley caught me watching and sent me off to tell the volunteers in the river that it was chop time.

Keira was laughing as she clambered out of the water and sat down on the tarpaulin we had arranged for them. Johnson helped her off with her waders before taking off his own. I helped Oliver, who tried to stay stonily impassive but couldn't resist a shy grin when one of Johnson's waders came off unexpectedly and he sat down hard with a yell.

I ushered them off towards the pavilion and stayed behind to help Maksim clear up. Once that was done, I paused on the riverbank to look over the day's work.

'Are you coming to eat?' said Maksim.

'I'll be over in a minute,' I said, but Maksim stayed where he was.

He was a big man, a former professional criminal

267

who'd undergone a brutal apprenticeship in the grey concrete suburbs of Moscow. Beverley said he'd already been looking for something more in his life when he and his mates had battered down her front door.

'I was in the bath,' she'd said indignantly. 'There were bound to be consequences.'

Which were that a surprised bunch of Russian mobsters had spent a day cleaning up Bev's house – which needed a lot of work, I might add. For most of them the glamour wore off and they went back to their wicked ways, only vowing never to speak of that day again.

But Maksim did not. He sat outside Beverley's window like a stray wolf waiting to be let into the circle of light around the fire. In the end, Beverley let him in. She said it was either that or she let him sit outside forever. He does the cleaning, the garden and some light bodyguarding on the side.

He seems happy.

Beverley insists that he could walk away any time he liked.

Perhaps you should make him, I told her, for his own good.

'Why would I be so cruel?' said Beverley. 'And how do you know it would do him good?'

The drizzle had turned to light rain. I could feel the water starting to trickle down my neck.

'Come in and eat,' said Maksim, gesturing at the pavilion. 'There's nothing to be afraid of.'

And inside I went – to where the air smelt of a garden party on a summer's day.

I was still worrying about it while lying spooned against Beverley's warm back that night.

'You're cross,' she said suddenly.

'No,' I said.

'You're not happy, though.'

'I worry when you make people do things,' I said. 'Doesn't it worry you?'

'In the first place I don't "make" anybody do anything,' she said. 'I merely offer people the opportunity to participate in the glorious pageant that is my existence on Earth. In which they come away greatly enriched, both emotionally and spiritually.'

I slipped my hand around to rest on her belly.

'Does that include the poor sods that fetch you drinks when we're at the pub?'

'Even them.' I felt her shrug. 'A tiny little bit. Commensurate, you know, with the cost of the drink.'

'An even trade – their free will for your convenience?'

Beverley sighed.

'I see,' she said, and started the laborious process of rolling over to face me.

While the complicated pillow engineering was underway I took the opportunity to cop a feel, because a wise man takes his pleasures where he can. When she was ready, Beverley took my hand off her bum and kissed the palm.

'Make me a light,' she said. 'I want to see your face.'

When I started my apprenticeship, it took me months to learn how to cast a werelight and weeks more to learn how to sustain it. Now I can create a small globe like a shining pearl and set it to hover above my head without really having to think about it. The *forma* from which the spell is derived is one of the simplest and most flexible of any that you learn, and after three hundred years practitioners are still finding new things to do with it.

Nightingale says that his headmaster, when he was at school, called the werelight a better teacher of magic than any master in the school.

'Do you love me?' she asked, and I felt a sudden unexpected rush of panic at the question. It took me so by surprise that I practically stuttered the answer.

'Yes,' I managed.

'Why?'

Because pheromones, because beauty, because laughter and joy when she was near and loss and emptiness when she was gone. Because of shouting at unicorns and braving faeries. The way her brow furrowed when she was reading something tricky in a textbook. The smell and feel of her skin. The warmth of her body, the sunshine of her smile and the thrilling depths of her eyes.

'It was your knees,' I said.

Beverley sighed and shook her head.

'No, seriously,' I said. 'You opened the door to your mum's house and you were wearing that T-shirt and flip-flops and had the most beautiful knees I'd ever seen.'

'Peter,' said Beverley.

'I couldn't take my eyes off them,' I said. 'And when I saw the dimples at the back – I was lost.'

'Have you finished?'

'They are such knees as dreams are made of.'

I felt a sharp shove at the point where her belly was pressed against mine.

'Ow,' said Beverley. 'Now you've set them off.'

'You asked.'

'I did, didn't I? I should have known better.'

We both paused and waited, but it seemed the budding centre forwards were done with practice for the moment.

'We don't do it on purpose,' she said, and must have seen my expression because she quickly added, 'Okay, sometimes on purpose. It's like Beyoncé. Imagine Beyoncé goes into a recording studio and she's handed a latte and it has too many sugars in it. Now imagine that Beyoncé mentions to – I don't know, her PA – that the coffee is too sweet and people rush around getting her a fresh latte with the right amount of sugar. Which she sips gratefully, thanks everyone, and takes it into the recording booth to do whatever genius singers do.'

'Sing,' I said, wondering where this was going. 'Mostly.'

'Now Beyoncé could probably pop round to Starbucks herself and, assuming she's not recognised, get her own damn coffee. But this would cause the people around her even more disruption. So she doesn't.'

'So you think you're a pop star?'

'For one thing, Beyoncé Knowles is not just a pop star, she is a goddess in her own right.' She saw me open my mouth and quickly added, 'A metaphorical goddess. What we're talking about here is power – and power has consequences. I am an *òrìṣà*, an actual goddess of an actual geographical feature. If you were an ancient Briton you'd be dropping the heads of your enemies into my watercourse and begging me to bring you victory in battle. The power is there, it will express itself, and I have to deal with the consequences.'

'What about the intern?' I asked.

'What intern?'

'The one that got the coffee order wrong, the one that got fired five minutes after Miss Prima Donna sashayed into the recording booth,' I said. 'That intern – what about her?'

Beverley gave a strange little strangled half-laugh, then grabbed me and pulled me close. First for a kiss and then to press her forehead against mine.

'Oh God,' she said, and I was shocked to feel

her tears on my cheek. 'You have no idea how much I love you, do you?'

I thought I was willing to find out, but even I know when to keep my mouth shut.

'The intern, Peter . . .' said Beverley, pulling away a bit so that I could see she had her serious face on. 'The intern is why you have to be careful. Why you have to be restrained.'

'You just held court in the middle of Richmond Park,' I said. 'My fake boss and his family were there. Not to mention Mrs Chin and Stephen. My dad provided the entertainment. Dennis Yoon was there, for God's sake.'

'He came with the Rees,' said Beverley. 'I've known them since I was little. How was I to know he was staying with them?'

'My point is that it wasn't what I'd call restrained,' I said.

'That's because you're making a category error, isn't it?' she said. 'Think of these courts and ceremonies being like a water meadow or a flood plain. Sometimes you've got to let a river escape her banks to prevent more serious flooding downstream.'

'That's what that was?' I said. 'Tyburn doesn't hold court.'

''Course she does,' said Beverley. 'All those meetings she chairs, those seminars, the charity committees, her soirées and dinner parties? Especially the dinner parties. If she ever invites us just say no, thank you, politely.'

'And your mum?'

'Mum and the Old Man are a different class entirely,' said Beverley. 'They're always in flood.' And she added before I could object, 'Metaphorically speaking. So they have to be all ceremony all the time. My mum couldn't walk down Oxford Street without it spontaneously becoming a parade – that's why she has to send us out for her shoes.'

I wondered where the tipping point was. Was it the total volume of water, flow rate or maybe how old they got? Would Beverley ever become that powerful, that distant?

'You and I are entangled now,' she said. 'Your family, your friends are all mixed up with me and mine – this is what happens in relationships. It's just that with people like us, the externalities tend to be a bit more theatrical.'

'Externalities?'

'See,' said Beverley. 'Police-speak is catching.'

'At least you didn't say going forward,' I said.

'You are my love,' she said, and then in passable Krio, '*We don commor far, so natin nor dae wea we nor go able overcam.*'

She glanced up at the werelight. On its own it would be good for at least another hour.

'Do you want it off?' I asked.

'Nah,' she said, and with a theatrical little wave caused a sphere of water, the size of a toy football, to coalesce around it.

The werelight shone through the water to cast

274

a cool, rippling light across the room, so that it seemed we were sleeping under the waves. Satisfied with what she'd done, she put her hand on my bum and pulled me closer.

'Now we can both sleep,' she said, and kissed me. And sleep we did – eventually.

CHAPTER 13

I AM THE BUSINESS

Sunday morning by instant tradition was study morning so, after I'd oiled the Bulge – which always made Beverley giggle – I cracked open my Blackstone's manuals, bought second-hand for economy, while she lay on her back in the living room and read papers off her Kindle.

Every so often, one or other of us would sigh and decide it was time for yet another cup of coffee.

After a lunch assembled from yesterday's left-overs we had a nap, followed by more competitive pelvic floor exercises – Beverley won by two falls and a submission – then I did magic practice down the end of the garden where I wouldn't destroy any electronics. I was working to perfect my first fifth order spell, *clausurafrange*, which was supposed to neatly pop out a lock but was currently just making damp holes in the riverbank, when Beverley waddled down the garden towards me waving my phone.

Half an hour later I was in the Asbo and heading for Gillingham.

★   ★   ★

In an ideal world PC Robert Maginty would have been called Kent Police's Falcon Liaison Officer, or FLO. But that acronym has been taken by Family Liaison Officers and even the police try to avoid having TLAs with double meanings. Not to mention that, while senior officers in the regional forces have accepted the need for Falcon liaison, they try to make the structures as un-official as possible. I think they're hoping that if they don't talk about Falcon, then Falcon will hardly ever happen. Ironically, this is known as magic thinking.

Up until six months ago, Maginty had been a member of the Medway Community Safety Unit, based out of the Rainham Contact Point on Station Road. A contact point is what you get when you keep making 'savings' to a police budget until the actual police stations start to disappear.

'Still am CSU,' he said when I asked. 'But then they called me into Sutton Road and the Deputy Chief Constable, no less, informs me that I am now official liaison to something called the Special Assessment Unit and sends me for a training course in London.'

Where Nightingale put him through our patented three-day magic-orientation and *vestigia*-awareness course and sent him home to the Medway CSU. Where he got on with the job of stopping the local community biting lumps out of each other.

He was a tall white man with thinning brown

hair who was starting to fill out his stab vest more than he would have probably liked. But since the cuts everyone was working double shifts – not just double jobs.

'Fuck all anything weird happens,' he said. 'I was just beginning to think it was all a bit of a jolly . . . And then I walk into this.' He ushered me into the shop.

It was like sticking my face in a bowl of rotting shrimp.

The person or persons unknown responsible for the drones and the demon trap had definitely been doing some serious magic on the premises. The *vestigium* was powerful enough to make my skin crawl and want to put on my noddy suit – despite the fact that forensics had already been and gone.

The shop had been an internet café on the high street by Gillingham Station until the previous year and had stood empty since then. The windows were smeared into opacity with Windolene on the inside and dotted with posters on the outside. The one on the door was for a band called Red Butler. A second plastered next to it urged us to fight the cuts. They'd missed a trick – they should have put that one up outside Robert Maginty's Contact Point.

'The landlord investigated after EDF started legal action for an electricity bill he swore blind he'd never received,' said Maginty. 'We found a pile of letters just there.'

He pointed to one of the café tables that still filled the front of the shop. I recognised them as wooden garden furniture with holes in the centre for placing sunshades. Or, I noticed, for running cables down into connector boxes on the floor. There were still cables sprouting from a few of the tables like headless daffodils.

Maginty pointed out that unlike the other tables, which sported a layer of dust, the tables with the cables were clean.

'They were online,' he said. 'But they didn't bother to pack up the cables when they left.'

About half the café tables had been disassembled and replaced with two long rows of free-standing pine shelving. Wood doesn't retain *vestigia* at all well, but the metal screws that held them together radiated a metaphysical reek that was beginning to seriously erode my love of the fruit of the sea.

There was a huge whiteboard along one wall. Judging by the chalkboard poking out from under one side, it had just been mounted straight onto whatever had been hanging on the wall at the time. At the other end there was just enough of a notice-board to see that somebody had left their keys behind, and that somebody had a van and was willing to drive anywhere for money.

A grid was drawn with geometric precision on the whiteboard – not as easy a task as you might think. Along the top were days of the week, Monday to Sunday, and on the leftmost column a row of names or more probably nicknames – Baz, Yax, JC, Jade and Solid. Neatly written into the rows and columns were two or three letter combinations – Cit, Mtp, Qut, Flx, Stl, Prz and Sht. Most of the boxes had just the one abbreviation repeated for all seven days, although Jade had Mtp/Ctp in her boxes and, for whoever Yaz was, someone had had to write very tiny letters to get all of them in.

Every box had a neat diagonal line drawn through it except for those in the Friday column.

'Any idea what all that's about?' I asked.

'The top is obviously days of the week,' said Maginty. 'And at a guess the left-hand column are all names or nicknames, so going out on a limb I think the abbreviations are all drugs.'

I smelt bollocks but you've got to let your fellow officers have their bit of fun or they get tetchy.

'How do you figure that, then?'

'Ctp is obviously Citalopram,' he said.

'Obviously.'

'Mtp is Mirtazapine, Flx has to be Fluoxetine, Stl Sertraline,' said Maginty. 'All of those are anti-depressants while Quetiapine, Qut, is also used to treat bipolar disorders.'

'That's really impressive,' I said. 'You working all those out just from the abbreviations.'

'Just good deductive reasoning,' he said. 'And we found some empty pill bottles in a wastepaper bin.'

'And the names or nicknames?'

'I think I know who Baz is,' said Maginty. 'Cautioned him a couple of times.'

Which offered some interesting possibilities. But it wasn't why Maginty had called me all the way down to the Medway Ports on a miserable Sunday afternoon. That was in the grubby storeroom at the back of the shop, with off-white walls and racks of blue metal shelving. I touched the metal frames but there wasn't a hint of *vestigia*. Whatever the magic was, it had happened out in the shop.

'When the landlord came in to check, he found these,' said Maginty.

Neatly stacked up against the wall were columns of grey plastic reels, each twenty centimetres across and five deep. I recognised them as the spools used to store plastic threads for 3-D printers.

'I saw your Falcon alert regarding 3-D printers,' said Maginty. 'Stuck in my mind because usually all your stuff is mystic, isn't it? When the landlord called us in I saw this and called you.'

There were two rows of six columns, all over head height. I did a rough mental calculation and estimated that I was looking at just under half a ton of plastic feedstock. ABS, according to the labels on the reels.

Half a ton, I thought. That's a lot of something.

Whatever they were making, they were making it in what used to be the shop's kitchen and toilet area. Both had been ruthlessly ripped out to make room for at least two large commercial 3-D printers. We could estimate their rough size by the neat rectangular clear spaces on the scarred orange and white lino floor. One of the scene-of-crime techs had estimated that both units were the size of an upright fridge-freezer. There still was a faint whiff of heated plastic in the air, but Maginty said it would have been worse if they hadn't crudely widened what had once been the toilet window and run out a tube for the extractor hoods.

'Could have been very bad for their health,' said Maginty.

It was good to see criminal organisations taking health and safety regulations to heart.

'Landlord wasn't best pleased by the modifications,' said Maginty. 'He blamed homeless squatters and wanted to know what we were doing about it.'

The answer being 'fuck all', because apart from anything else, such as lack of resources, there was no sign that anyone was squatting.

'No sleeping bags, no old clothes, no ratty furniture from a skip.'

I thought of Beverley's salvaged throne and winced.

You can get some swish internet cafés with lots of wood trim, but this was even a step down from a faux KFC chicken joint with good Wi-Fi, being essentially a down at heel greasy spoon with a couple of high-capacity lines run in. Squatters probably would have raised the tone slightly.

In front of the counter where customers had once queued to buy their minutes, plus what was probably truly horrible coffee, two of the round tables had been pushed together and a crude tabletop created by lashing a door-sized slab of laminated chipboard on top. The tabletop was pink and heavily scored in places – and marked with silver blobs that turned out to be solder. On the floor around it were scattered slivers of plastic insulation, bits of wire and more plastic shavings.

'They were definitely making something,' said Maginty.

I had a horrible feeling I knew what. But I didn't want to make assumptions.

'They weren't squatting,' I said. 'It's a workshop. So they were coming in every day to work?'

'Buying coffee on the way in – just like ordinary people,' said Maginty. 'Building what, though?'

I glanced at the whiteboard.

'You said you had some of the pill bottles,' I said. 'Could you trace these people through their prescriptions?'

'That's an enormous faff, and you know it,' said Maginty.

Medical confidentiality being just the start of it.

'Like I said, I think I know who Baz is. But there's a problem,' he said. And that problem was money. 'There's no budget for it – I got into huge trouble for ordering the forensics this morning.

Some Chief Super I've never even heard of phoned me up and gave me a bollocking.'

'And?'

'It was a really good bollocking,' said Maginty. 'I am now seriously deficient in the bollock area as a consequence.'

'And?'

'To paraphrase,' said Maginty. 'You want this case, you're going to have to pay for it.'

The Folly has financial reserves that are the envy of other operational command units, but we'd eaten a big chunk of it the previous year on Operation Jennifer. And what was left was funding our expansion.

'Any chance of tracking down this Baz today?' I asked.

'Tomorrow afternoon at the earliest,' said Maginty. 'Even if you do take the case.'

'I'll see what I can do,' I said.

I called Nightingale and Belgravia and then hung around the shop, poking my nose into nooks and crannies, while I waited for someone to show up. I was expecting Guleed, but to my horror got Seawoll instead.

'Oh joy,' he said as he walked in. 'The fucking Medways.' He sniffed. 'I don't know what they've been cooking here, but I think it's past its sell-by date. In my younger days I used to run joint operations against organised crime down here. You used to be able to get a decent fish supper – definitely seen better days.'

I gave him the tour and explained about the printers, the links to his investigation into the attack at the Serious Cybernetics Corporation, and the fact that Kent weren't keen to go joint operation with us.

'With you, you mean,' said Seawoll. 'Can't say as I blame them.'

But I've become wise in the ways of Seawoll wrangling, and so I just waited for him to get there in his own sweet time.

'When do you think you'll be finished with all this undercover wank?' he asked.

I said I didn't know – Silver had been adamant about not sharing operational details outside of the need to know group.

'You want to be done with that shit just as quick as you can,' said Seawoll. 'You're one of life's honest coppers, Peter, and this kind of fucking fakery is not good for you.' And, having delivered that backhanded compliment, he shifted gear. 'Get me your liaison.'

I fetched Maginty, who'd gone outside for a vape.

'Who's your boss?' asked Seawoll.

Maginty gave him the details of the Chief Super who'd bollocked him earlier, which just goes to show that senior officers should think before they throw their weight around. Seawoll got the said Super on the phone, a bit of a miracle given that it was a Sunday evening, and proceeded to explain why it was in his best interest to extend every co-operation to the Metropolitan Police in general and himself in particular. It got quite chummy towards the end and I'm fairly certain they agreed to meet for drinks.

'God,' said Seawoll when he'd finished. 'I remember when he was a DC out of Gravesend CID and still in short trousers . . .'

He noticed me and Maginty waiting to see if he was going to be indiscreet and changed the subject again.

'You,' he pointed at me. 'Bugger off before you're seen hanging around with proper official coppers.' He turned to Maginty. 'I'm going to send you one of my sergeants to co-ordinate the TIEs on this bunch of nominals.' He nodded at the list of names on the white-board. 'Has everyone got that?'

Me and Maginty indicated that we had, and were told to piss off and get on with it.

The next day I meant to get in early but the Tube system got in the way and I filtered into the Serious Cybernetics Corporation with all the other mice. I said hello to a couple of people I knew, but the adulation for my fearless action had passed. Such, I thought, is the fickle face of fame. Johnson had informed me that he was coming in late, and that me and Leo Hoyt were to hold the fort down until he arrived.

'I thought we'd do a couple of random locker searches,' said Leo. 'If that's all right with you?'

Because this was the SCC, the randomness was generated using a pair of percentile dice because, as Everest once explained at great length, no software-driven random number generator was truly random. So we rolled the dice and randomly selected the locker of a guy who Leo had had an eye on for the last week.

Fortunately for the guy he didn't have any contraband, so we opened the lockers either side and found a dead rat in a plastic bag in one. Disgusting, but not actually a disciplinary offence. And a suspicious USB stick in another, which was confiscated to be checked. We let the offending owner cool in the Vogon coffee lounge while Leo tested the USB on the standalone PC laptop. Since it had had its wireless connections disabled and was never connected physically to any network – not even the electrical one – it wouldn't pass on any viruses or other malware.

It was the same principle as the air gap around Bambleweeny and Deep Thought, but that was two whole storeys full of nerds and I wondered how effective that might actually be and how easy it might be to circumvent.

'Tentacle porn,' said Leo, and showed me some samples so I could confirm.

'How much?' I asked.

'Something south of six thousand files,' he said.

And they were going to have to be checked in case some of it featured images of children, which was a dismissible offence. I offered to play rock, paper, scissors but Leo pointed out that since we had the twenty-sided dice, we should use them.

I lost and sat down for a morning of drawn porn. What struck me about halfway through was that, despite the inventiveness with which the artists strove to find variations on people having sex with tentacles, the repetition became mind-numbing after the first two thousand images. Still, as far as I could tell, none of the humans depicted were illegal as defined by the Coroners and Justice Act (2009), although by the time I'd finished I personally had lost the will to live.

I told the mouse whose USB it had been that no action would be taken and she could go back to work. She glared at me and muttered something about 'Big Brother' before demanding her USB back.

'I'll leave it with the front desk,' I said.

After two hours of cephalophilia I was strangely ready for one of Victor's grand theories – this one involving the true reasons for the spread of Christianity.

'Entirely driven by tech support,' he said.

In my quest to sample every single vending machine, I'd chosen a pie and mash from SUPERPIE, a Yorkshire-themed Japanese machine which dispensed, as far as I could tell, authentic steak and kidney pies.

'Not the conquering and occupying and slave taking?' I said, while trying to squeeze tomato ketchup out of the inadequate hole I'd bitten in the sachet.

'Nah,' said Victor. 'That's all late model Christianity. Back in the Dark Ages . . .'

'Sub-Roman,' said Everest without looking up.

He was staring at a spot on the table with a slight frown on his face. This was because, Victor told me, he hadn't managed to trace who was secretly talking to William Lloyd and was trying to think up an alternative approach.

'Early Medieval,' said Victor. 'Back in the time of the early Anglo-Saxon kingdoms it was all top-down.'

According to Victor, the first thing the boys from Rome would do when they tooled over was cosy up to the local kings or chiefs. Forget arduously saving souls one at a time – the emissaries of the Pope calculated that in hierarchical quasi-tribal societies you grab the big man and the rest would be forced into line.

'And what do they offer these guys?' asked Victor.

'Salvation and life everlasting?' I said, drawing on some long, boring childhood memories.

'What? Better than Valhalla?' asked Victor. 'Better than feasting, drinking and fighting for all eternity? Better than Elysium?'

'Political legitimacy?' I asked, remembering Miss Karmargi who'd been my Religious Education teacher at school. An avowed atheist who'd once said that she respected all religions equally –

'Which is more than can be said for most religions,' she'd added.

Victor gave me a sharp look.

'Close,' he said. 'But what they really offered was tech support. Think about it. Not only could these churchmen write, but they could keep books.'

This was a big plus for a medieval ruler who usually spent most of his days on the edge of bankruptcy, and was still expected to maintain the peace, host major dinners, and hand out bling and favours to his supporters and lesser nobles.

'The clergy ran the IT support, managed the books, maintained lines of communication internally and externally,' said Victor. 'It was the killer application of its day.'

'Is this important?' said Everest, who had lowered his head until his forehead rested on the table.

'If the clergy were the original IT support,' said Victor, 'doesn't that mean we're the new clergy?'

'Not Peter,' said Everest. 'He's an enforcer.'

'Ah, but Peter here believes in technology,' said Victor. 'That makes him a Knight Templar.'

After lunch, I took my almost religious devotion to law and order up to the Vogon office, where I used Leo's access code to access our secure files and went fishing for information about the lift.

In the old days firms used to hire staff directly to maintain and clean their buildings. Then came the great era of outsourcing, where companies realised that if they turned over these responsibilities to specialist companies they could make savings and, even better, drop payroll numbers.

In turn, the building maintenance companies likewise cut their costs by subcontracting the labour-intensive portions to companies who could reduce costs further by illegally underpaying their staff. Or more precisely, underpaying the lowest-paid members of their staff – mainly the cleaners.

So once I knew the name of the subcontractor, it was just a matter of having Silver send someone round to ask a few questions. Co-operation and silence guaranteed by threats to inform HM Customs and Excise about the deliberate under-reporting of their wage bill – not to mention the inevitable National Insurance fraud.

Leo wandered in just as I was closing up the window.

'What you up to?' he asked.

I told him I was still hunting Johnson's rat.

'Still?' said Leo. 'I thought you'd have found him by now.'

'I'm not even sure he exists,' I said.

'Can't help you there,' he said. 'Although maybe you're looking in the wrong place.'

Looking back, maybe I should have been listening a bit more carefully.

I travelled home with Stephen who, being a New Yorker, at least knew how to ride the Tube without moaning. We snagged a door alcove at the end of the carriage on the non-platform side so we could have a chat without having to shout past people's armpits.

'When are we going to get blueprints?' he asked.

'Hopefully tomorrow,' I said.

He wanted to come with me.

'As insurance,' he said, and didn't specify whose insurance or against what.

'I've got an in,' I said. 'You'll just get in the way.'

'Where is this outfit located?'

'Slough,' I said.

And so the next morning I dropped Stephen off at South Wimbledon and headed off in the opposite direction towards the Medway Ports, picking up Guleed at Chatham. Getting across South London was murderous, but beyond the M25 all the heavy traffic was going in the other direction and I made good time. We rendezvoused with Maginty at the Rainham Contact Point, which looked dispiritingly like a cross between a charity shop and a slightly seedy dentist.

Conveniently there was an off-licence next door in case the despairing members of the Community Safety Unit needed to drink themselves under their desks.

'We'd wait until we're off duty,' said Maginty. 'Only nobody ever goes off duty any more.'

Baz, whose real name was Barry Collard, lived

in a surprisingly neat flat above a grim 1950s red-brick shopping arcade in Twydall which, Maginty assured us, was a crime hotspot. Like most high-crime areas, it looked exactly like a low-crime area although some of the shops were a bit ragged around the edges.

Barry, like many people with a long history of brushing up against the criminal justice system, had acquired an unaccountable reluctance to entertain the police but Maginty managed to talk us in. Although I noticed we weren't offered a cup of tea. I went in last so I could do a quick Initial *Vestigium* Assessment while Barry was showing the others inside.

The flat was sparsely furnished, but while the furniture was cheap it was brand new. The walls had recently been painted, white with a hint of indeterminate pastel in the hallway, a light coffee colour in the living room, institutional green in the kitchen. Supernaturally speaking, there was nothing but the normal background hum in any of the rooms.

Neither were there any books, or even old magazines or newspapers. Nor were there any Blu-rays or DVDs or anywhere to play them. The absence of a TV or any books or photographs made the living room seem cold and unfinished. Although according to Barry's criminal file – we were still trying to access his medical records – he became agitated around excessive disorder, which could explain the minimalist décor. We didn't want to pressure him, so Maginty, who was the only one in uniform, loitered unobtrusively by the doorway while Guleed perched a nice unthreatening distance away on the arm of a sofa. I sat on the sofa itself and thought friendly thoughts.

If you're a police officer, then you meet a lot of Barrys, if only because everyone else crosses the street to avoid them. White, skinny almost to the point of emaciation, drably dark tattoos boiling out of his collar and down his arms. Small mouth, broken nose, hooded blue eyes with a line of dull silver piercings in his left eyebrow. He wore the habitual expression of suspicious disappointment that is the birthright of those that started behind and were thrown off the bus before they reached the first stop.

It could have been me if I hadn't had some breaks in my life.

Like the flat, his clothes were neat and clean – a red Love Moschino polo shirt, beige cargo pants, a pair of pink fluffy slippers and no socks.

Behind him a pair of narrow French windows led on to a faux balcony and through them I could see, across the street, the Grade II listed angular witch's hat shape of the Holy Trinity Church.

We started as gently as you can when doing a caution plus two. Because of course anything you say can be used in evidence, but let's not worry about that sort of thing now. And did I mention that you can stop the interview whenever you like?

Barry frowned when I got to that bit, and I thought he was going to ask us to leave but fortunately he didn't, because then we'd have had to arrest him and that would have led to paperwork and jurisdictional bollocks.

Later we'd wish we'd arrested him straight off, but you can't arrest everyone – there aren't enough cells to hold them all for a start.

A proper interview takes time which is why, contrary to what you see on the TV, they don't get done by anyone above the rank of sergeant. You can spend at least fifteen minutes, as we did, just establishing a common vocabulary. The improvised workshop at the internet café was 'the Print Shop', and all who worked there were production assistants or 'prods'.

'So who ran the Print Shop?' I asked.

'What do you mean?'

'Who was in charge?'

'It didn't work like that,' said Barry.

Because every morning they sat down and divvied up the tasks amongst themselves over coffee.

'But who set you the tasks?'

'They came by email as Word documents, didn't they?' said Barry.

Whoever was the first prod in, usually Jade, would print these out and then they would sit down with their coffees and jointly decide who did what. Each job was rated by duration, difficulty and cake.

'Cake?' I asked, and smiled – assuming a joke but Barry stayed serious.

'Cake was the amount of bonus for each task,' said Barry. 'Working the printers when they were going full blast got you the most cake. Assembly you got the least.'

'What kind of cake?' asked Guleed, because asking a stupid question often gets you the most information.

'Don't be daft,' said Barry. 'The cake was just a way of keeping score. The more tasks we done, the more the cake was worth in real money. Shared, you know, between us.'

Thus providing a productivity incentive at both the collective and individual level – Barry actually used the words 'productivity incentive' almost like a rote phrase that he'd memorised, although he seemed clear enough about its meaning.

I decided to ease back the timeline a little.

'How did you get the gig?' I asked.

'I got a text,' said Barry.

'From who?'

'Number withheld,' said Barry. 'Very popular name.'

'And what did the text say?' asked Guleed.

'"There's a job for you if you want it", and gave the address.'

I asked what the address was and Barry said it was the Print Shop. Did he still have the text? No, that was on his old phone.

'And that's all it took?' asked Guleed.

'Yeah,' said Barry, 'I suppose.'

I looked over at Maginty. According to him Barry had never held down a job in his life. He'd tried when he was younger but depression kept on getting in the way. It's hard to go to work if you can't get up in the morning.

'I'm impressed,' I said. 'It's hard to motivate yourself into a job if you've been unwell. What made the difference?'

'There was this group,' he said.

'What kind of group?'

'You know, a self-help group,' said Barry. 'People talk about their experiences and shit and you feel better.'

'Better?'

'Less alone.'

'Where did the group meet?' asked Guleed.

'At the library on the High Street,' said Barry.

'Gillingham High Street?' asked Maginty.

So not far from the Print Shop, then.

'Was this a library initiative?' I asked.

'What?'

'Was this something the library organised?'

'I know what initiative means, fam,' said Barry. 'Been on enough.'

'Then what?'

'I was at the library,' said Barry – slowly. 'On the computer. The group was online.'

'Text or voice?' I asked.

'Text,' said Barry. 'Like in a chat room.'

'And what did the group talk about?' asked Guleed.

'I don't know . . . shit, everything,' said Barry. '*Star Wars*, Paris, who liked bananas and why. I don't remember most of it. I do remember laughing so hard once they nearly threw me out of the library.'

We asked after names but of course they were all online tags – still, Silver's analysts could have a fun time doing traffic analysis. And one tag did jump out – that of JadeInSecret, who I suspected might be the Jade from the Print Shop's medication whiteboard. I decided to wait before I asked, because Barry was in full flow.

Barry was amazed. He'd done group therapy on the NHS and he supposed some of it might have helped, but he'd never felt 'better' the way he did after a session. And unlike those sessions in 'meatspace', this felt entirely personal.

'It was about me, about what I needed,' he said.

I was thinking of William Lloyd's unrecorded chats at his terminal and started getting a horrible cyberpunky *Neuromancer*-esque vibe from the whole set-up. So I asked if he had any proof that any other of the chat-room folk were real.

'Yeah,' he said, and then the doorbell rang.

Maginty stepped into the hallway to deal.

'Are you expecting anyone?' asked Guleed.

'I don't know,' said Barry. 'Is anyone ever expecting anyone?'

Whatever we were expecting, what we got was a tall, thin white woman with mousy blonde hair cut into a bob to frame a sharp-featured face with startling green eyes. She was wearing a plastic trench coat over a green polo neck jumper and black leggings. She was frowning and rummaging in a baggy burgundy faux leather shoulder bag while Maginty tried, unsuccessfully, to block her advance into the living room.

Then, with a triumphant grunt, she retrieved an official ID card and waved it at Maginty.

'Julie Hunt,' she said. 'Kent and Medway NHS and Social Care Partnership Trust. What are you doing with my client?'

Maginty explained that we were merely taking a statement and there was nothing to be worried about.

'This is a vulnerable individual,' she said. 'He shouldn't be interviewed without an appropriate adult.'

'We can formally arrest him if you like,' said Maginty. 'Finish this off at a police station.'

Hunt gave him a bad look and then turned to call to Barry over our heads.

'Barry? Are you okay with this?'

Barry stared at her in confusion.

'It's me, Julie Hunt,' she said. 'Are you okay with this?'

'We're talking about the Print Shop,' he said.

Julie Hunt perched on the arm of Barry's chair. I felt Guleed shift her position in response – so that she could intervene quickly if the woman misbehaved.

'As long as you're cool,' Hunt said to Barry.

Barry bobbed his head.

'I'm good, good,' he said.

'You said you knew that the chat-room people were real,' said Guleed. 'How did you know that for certain?'

'Because I met them,' he said.

'Have you offered your guests tea?' asked Hunt.

'Tea?' said Barry.

'Would you like me to make some tea?'

Barry nodded.

'Yes, please,' he said, and Hunt rose and squeezed past Maginty, heading for the kitchen.

I asked Barry where the meeting had taken place, and he named a nearby pub whose name caused Maginty to mutter under his breath.

That bad, I thought.

'And some of them were prods at the Print Shop,' he said.

'Which ones?' I asked as casually as I could.

'I can't remember,' he said. 'Jade knew who everyone was – that was sort of her job.'

'Can you remember any of them?' I said. 'Perhaps their nicknames?'

'Not really,' he frowned and then brightened. 'Why don't we ask Jade?' he said and, straightening up, looked over our shoulders and called, 'Jade! Who was at the Print Shop?'

A little belated light in my head went *ping*! But much too late.

I turned to warn Maginty, just in time for Jade, aka Julie Hunt, to walk up to him and throw a kettle's worth of boiling water in his face. He floundered backwards yelling as Jade threw the kettle at Guleed's head. Maginty's eyes were squeezed shut, so he didn't see as Jade calmly transferred a kitchen knife from her left hand to her right and stabbed him in the chest.

The blade boinged off his stab vest in an almost comical way so Jade turned on Guleed, who was lunging to her feet.

It was the worst kind of police aggro you could think of short of facing down a street full of Millwall supporters after a disappointing showing at the Den. Cramped quarters, one officer down, one distressed and possibly violent male, one armed and definitely violent female and two of you in plain clothes with nothing in the way of pepper spray, extendable batons or stab vests to stand between you and a long lie-down in casualty.

Barry jumped to his feet and, without getting up, I jammed my leg in front of his shin and, lurching forward, I tried to grab hold of his arm. I was trying to yank him off his feet but instead he just pulled me to mine. Jade stabbed at Guleed's face. Guleed turned, got both hands on Jade's knife arm and slammed her shoulder into the woman's chest in a move that was way more to

301

do with officer safety training than any martial arts her fiancé was teaching her.

'Leech!' screamed Jade, but Guleed threw her weight backwards, driving the other woman into the door jamb.

Maginty was shaking and making a low keening noise. I recognised that as the sound you make when you're desperately trying not to scream. His hands were up by his head, but he'd balled his fists to stop himself from touching the scalded skin of his face.

'You leave her alone!' yelled Barry, and careened forward.

There was a horrible crunching, tearing sound and he came staggering back with blood pouring from a deep knife wound in his shoulder.

Jade stared in horror at the mess it was making of Barry's new shirt.

'That's your fault!' she screamed at Guleed. 'That's on you! You c—'

Guleed had taken the opportunity to slam Jade's wrist against the wall, causing her to yell and drop the knife. I tracked it as it fell behind the sofa – always keep your eye on the weapon. You don't want your attacker picking it up and you definitely want to know where it is when people start asking you questions about appropriate levels of force.

Which was what I applied to Barry's legs to make him sit down hard on the floor. Guleed herself was a model of self-restraint when she pulled Jade off balance, hooked her knee and dropped her on her back. The woman managed to get a couple of obscenities out before Guleed had her flipped over and pinned her with one knee on her back.

Barry was plucking at his reddening shirt and I decided to take the risk and aid Maginty. I grabbed his fists in one hand, told him to stay still and conjured a water bomb over his head and let cool water slosh down across his face.

'Oh, thank God,' he said. 'That feels much better.'

The skin on his left cheek was already beginning to blister.

'Just don't touch it, mate,' I said.

'I'm bleeding,' said Barry in a quiet voice.

'He's going to die,' said Jade. 'And it's all your fault.'

I turned my phone on and called 999.

'Well, that went tits up remarkably fast, didn't it?' said Maginty.

CHAPTER 14

PERFECT ORGANISM

To say that Kent Police were incandescent would be an amusing understatement. Fortunately, since I was still a lowly DC, I tucked myself under the mighty wings of Detective Chief Inspectors Nightingale and Seawoll. Guleed, being a sergeant, had to step up and shoulder her share of the responsibility. I'm sure she bore it with stoic fortitude. I made a mental note to lend her my copy of Marcus Aurelius.

While she faced the music the following morning, I was safely back at my fake job. With my fake boss and my fake friends.

'Why didn't you invite us?' asked Victor at morning snacks.

'Invite you to what?' I asked.

'To the party in the park,' he said.

'Because nobody told me about it until it had already started,' I said, and asked whether Everest had worked out who had been secretly chatting with William Lloyd yet.

'Have not,' said Everest, gloomily contemplating

a peanut butter flavoured Kit Kat. 'Thank you for reminding me.'

'I don't suppose it was possible for Deep Thought to be talking to him, was it?' I asked.

'Who's Deep Thought?' asked Everest.

Shit, shit – of course, Skinner hadn't told them. I was beginning to lose track of who knew what.

'Ah,' I said, not trying to hide my dismay. 'Shit, I shouldn't have used that name. You didn't hear it, okay?'

Victor leaned closer and wiggled his eyebrows.

'Yeah, but what is it?' he asked.

'A digital personal assistant.' I lowered my voice. 'Like Alexa and Siri – only better.'

'Hard to be worse,' muttered Everest.

'That's Skinner's secret project?' said Victor – he seemed disappointed.

'What were you expecting?' asked Everest. 'Starships, electric scooters, a pneumatic transport system?'

'Could it have been Deep Thought talking to him?' I asked.

'What are you thinking?' asked Everest.

I was thinking of Barry and Jade's chat room and the fanatical violence of Jade's attack on us in Barry's flat. Jade wasn't stupid. She must have known that assaulting three police officers was only going to end one way. Just as William Lloyd must have known, with his plastic machete and one-shot pistol, that he was going to be captured or worse.

The prisons are full of people with poor impulse control and a lack of foresight. But this was different – these attacks had been more like those undertaken for political or religious motivations, where the perpetrator has convinced themselves that they are less important than the cause they are fighting for.

'Maybe it said something?' I said. 'That set him off?'

'Not a chance,' said Everest. 'People do what they want – they only blame machines when it all goes wrong. And the only way an algorithm could access William Lloyd's terminal would be if someone with SysOp authority gave it access.'

'And who would that be?'

Everest spread his hands and stared upwards in pious respect.

'Either Skinner or someone with access to the top floor,' said Victor.

Skinner was out of the building, so I asked Dennis Yoon and Declan Genzlinger, since they worked on Bambleweeny's lower floor. But their best bet was that Skinner kept ultimate authority to himself.

'He's a hands-on kind of guy,' said Dennis.

Guleed was equally unhelpful when I went for an early lunch at the safely halal Nando's on City Road. I reckoned this was far enough past the roundabout that the mice wouldn't go there, but in any case what could be suspicious about having a cheeky Nando's?

'Julie Hunt was not helpful,' said Guleed. She had apparently adopted the 'no comment' school of conversation at the start of the interview and stuck to it with frustrating consistency. 'It was creepy, really,' said Guleed. 'It was like a robot.'

'Hold that thought,' I said. 'What about our Barry?'

Barry Collard's cut had proved deep, but had missed anything vital. Once he was out of the local casualty he'd been escorted to UCH for a brain scan where, much to Dr Walid's mixed relief and disappointment, there were no signs of hyper-thaumaturgical degradation – one of the key signs that someone's brain has been damaged by using magic.

I asked whether they'd scanned Julie Hunt, but she'd refused to give permission for further tests and we couldn't force them without a court order.

'Which we wouldn't get,' said Guleed. 'Nightingale has declared them non-Falcon so we're moving them out of the new cells and back into a normal custody suite. They're going to charge Julie Hunt with aggravated assault and obstruction, for the moment.'

Assaulting a police officer in the execution of their duty always counts as aggravated assault, although I was surprised they weren't going for actual and/or grievous bodily harm.

'That's just to keep her banged up while we find out what else she's been up to,' said Guleed.

That she'd been up to something, nobody had any doubts about. Especially since Barry continued to sing for his supper.

'Actually quite hard to shut him up,' said Guleed, who was carefully rearranging her chicken breast pitta to suit some personal but exacting standard. 'It's clear that, while the Print Shop didn't have a manager, Julie "Jade" Hunt was the manager they didn't have. We're tracing her background, but it looks like she was getting her instructions over her phone – and there's no sign of that.'

They hadn't traced the other people named on the whiteboard – JC, Solid and Yax – yet. But the feeling was that, given they all cheerfully worked at the Print Shop, they were probably Medway locals.

'Kent Police are working that lead,' said Guleed. And, picking up her pitta, she took a big bite.

'Do we know what they were making?' I asked, and then had to wait while Guleed finished chewing and swallowing.

'According to Barry,' said Guleed, 'plastic toys.'

'Don't tell me – great big model dragonflies.'

'Amongst other things.'

'What other things?'

Guleed wiped her fingers and checked her notes.

'Spider thingies.'

'Oh, great.'

'Plastic guns and plastic bullets,' said Guleed. 'Although they didn't have to assemble those. We showed Barry a picture of the "pistol" William Lloyd fired at Skinner and he gave a positive identification.'

'Lovely.'

'And squiddy things.'

'Squiddy things?'

'That's what he said. "Squiddy things" with pointy heads and tentacles.'

'How big were the squiddy things?' I asked and Guleed, whose mouth was full again, held her hands about a metre apart.

Somebody had done some powerful magic inside the Print Shop. It could have been that person or persons unknown had magically acti-vated what was almost certainly a collection of drones. The dragonflies we knew from South Tottenham. The spiders were obvious. And the squiddy things . . .

I sighed – people have far too much time on their hands.

Barry hadn't seen or experienced anything like what we'd seen that night in South Tottenham.

'He thought they were rubbish toys,' said Guleed. 'Even when they put the batteries in, they didn't work.'

No. Because the batteries were only there to power the microprocessors, which in turn were 'sacrificed' to drive the drones. That stage of the manufacturing process must have taken place out of Barry's sight. As did the pickups.

'Every time they finished a batch,' said Guleed, 'they stacked them on those wooden racks we found and left them there overnight. In the morning they were gone.' She picked up her corn on the cob and pointed it at me. 'What does that suggest to you?'

'Somebody else came during the night and magicked them,' I said.

'Is that a real term – "magicked?"' asked Guleed.

'And it's spelt with a "k", too,' I said. 'But the technical term is actually "enchanted". Only the trouble with that word is that everyone starts thinking glass slippers and spinning wheels.'

Guleed explained that Kent Police had, after a great deal of moaning, started looking at CCTV footage from the surrounding roads to see if they could spot a van coming in to make the pickup. There were no council CCTV cameras covering the High Street and, *quelle surprise*, all of the privately owned cameras that might have had the Print Shop in view were inoperable or didn't keep their image data for more than a week.

We weren't going to catch them that way.

'This is getting really messy,' I said. 'There's too many things going on we don't know about.'

'How unusual is that for us – seriously?' said Guleed.

As a security measure we left Nando's separately,

but I was passing through the Old Street underpass when someone called my name – it was Leo Hoyt. He'd been behind me.

'Where have you been?' he asked.

I told him Nando's, in case he was following me. But if he was he didn't give anything away.

As we walked back to the SCC I asked if he liked tentacle porn, and he said he could take it in small doses but he preferred his fantasies to be vaguely human.

'That's just speciesist, that is,' I said.

'Yeah, you would say that, wouldn't you?' he said. 'What with you being sensitive about that sort of thing.'

I considered asking what that was supposed to mean. But I wanted him distracted, not focused on me. So I made a thing about making him agree that whatever was on the next illicit USB, he would be the one to scan it. He said fine, whatever, but diverted back on to my investigation into William Lloyd's little breakdown.

I didn't blame him – it was the most interesting thing that had happened recently – but still . . . I also noticed him watching as I stashed my outside phone in a locker. To keep him happy, I asked if he wanted to sit in while I interviewed some of the mice who'd known William Lloyd and used that as an excuse to find out where Terrence Skinner was currently located. Johnson informed me that Mr Skinner was currently in the south of France 'on business'. Scheduled to return two days hence.

'Do you need to get in touch?' he asked, but I said it could wait.

I started carrying out the interviews as cover, but didn't learn anything that Belgravia hadn't got from their initial investigation. I also noticed Leo Hoyt casually passing by the meeting room I was using – he waved when I caught him looking the second time. Coincidence? I should fucking cocoa.

I was wondering if I could make use of his suspicious nature by getting him to bring me a drink when I got an outside call on my babelphone.

'Peter,' said Stacy. 'Is that you?'

I thought the switchboard must have routed her through to me by mistake, but when I offered to switch her to Johnson she said no.

'I wanted you,' she said, and there was a reluctant pause. And with personalities like Stacy's that's never a good sign.

'I need a favour,' she said, and there was definite strain.

'Sure,' I said, with a completely false confidence.

'Only Tyrel can't know,' she said. 'Can I trust you on that?'

You can trust me, I thought, but really you shouldn't.

'Sure.'

Stacy filled me in and it was every bit as awful as I thought it was going to be. I found Leo and asked if he could cover for me.

'What is it?' he asked.

'Family emergency,' I said, and patted my stomach.

He waved me away and I headed for Kingston as fast as Transport for London could take me.

Kingston nick is one of those functional 1960s nicks, a big steel-framed concrete office block set edgewise to the road so that it presents a cheery windowless façade to the general public. It also stands next to the Hogsmill River path and boasts a sad strip of gravelly faux Zen garden which isn't fooling anybody – especially any passing Buddhists.

I'd spent the journey in trying to think of something convincing I could say to prise Oliver out of custody. He'd been picked up during a stop and search and had been, allegedly, found carrying an illegal bladed weapon – Stacy hadn't specified what kind.

Getting him out shouldn't be too hard – it was getting him out without a pending court case that was going to be a trick. Kingston didn't have the same reputation as some nicks that shall remain nameless, so it was entirely possible that Oliver had actually been carrying a knife when he was searched. And that was the problem. Police don't like knives – getting shot is a remote possibility, whatever the tabloids say. But getting stabbed? When you're a response officer, that can happen ten minutes into your shift while you were still wondering where you were going to stop for refs. One minute you're thinking coffee and bacon sandwich, and the next you're lying in casualty with the word 'perforated' being written down on the clipboard at the end of the bed.

Face that sort of tension for a couple of years and you start to have views on the subject.

I still didn't have a plan beyond claiming I wanted to recruit him as an informant. Which, by the way, is a terrible plan. Not least because the use of CHIS, or Covert Human Intelligence Sources, is tightly regulated.

I needn't have worried, because as I crossed the bridge I ran into Stacy and Oliver leaving the station in the company of somebody I recognised.

He was a tall, handsome white man in an old-fashioned Armani suit in black wool, with a mass of chestnut hair that fell below his shoulders. He was shaking hands with Oliver and Stacy, but turned as I approached and gave me a big friendly smile.

And with that smile came a rush of sensations – cricket and beer, bicycles and evensong, the clink of a pianoforte and smell of clean upholstery. His name was Emanuel Hogsmill and he was, amongst other things, the *genius loci* of the river we were standing next to.

'Peter,' he said, holding out his hand. 'How nice to see you.'

I shook hands to be polite, but my first question was what he thought he was doing.

'Just a little bit of legal business,' he said. 'Beverley asked me to have a look at the case.'

I looked over at Oliver and Stacy, who both had that stunned expression people get when their local river god has been making themselves charming. It wears off. And often, if you're lucky, overexposure renders you immune.

But sometimes it doesn't.

'How is Beverley?' he asked. 'You must come up to the Spring Court after the twins have sprung. If you don't present them, the Old Man will be most put out.'

Extended families, I thought, the same the world over.

I said I'd be sure to tell Beverley.

'I won't keep you any longer. Give my regards to your lady,' he said and, after saying goodbye to Stacy and Oliver, headed down the river path in the direction of the Thames.

'You had *him* as a lawyer?' I asked Stacy when the glamour had worn off a bit.

'You know how it is, Peter,' said Stacy. 'When you're on the job you hate the twisty fuckers, but when you're facing a panel suddenly they're the best thing since sliced bread.'

'So he got you a caution?'

'Nah,' she said. 'Charges dropped. They even had the arresting officer come in and apologise.' She frowned to signal her disapproval. 'That wouldn't have happened in my day.'

'Wow,' I said.

And, to test how deep the glamour had been, I asked if she remembered his name.

'Of course. It was Hogsmeade,' said Stacy. 'Emanuel Hogsmeade – no, wait, that's Harry Potter, isn't it? Hogsmill. I remember now because it's the same as the river. I suppose his family must be local.'

'Oh, definitely local,' I said.

'Well, he is a solicitor,' said Beverley.

'I looked him up,' I said. 'He was articled in 1876.'

'That explains why he's so good at it, then, don't it?' Beverley leaned back in the sofa and lifted a foot into the air. 'You promised.'

I sat down on the pouffe, grabbed her foot and dug my thumb into the smooth skin of the arch. Beverley gave a happy groan and flexed her perfect toes, although I noticed that she'd got hard skin on her heels just like the rest of us common mortals.

'And *you* promised,' I said, meaning that she wouldn't use her 'natural persuasiveness' to mess with the criminal justice system.

'I didn't, though, did I?' she said. 'I merely asked a legal acquaintance to take an interest. For all you know he did it with charm and legal acumen.'

'Even so—'

'There,' said Beverley suddenly. 'Harder, there, harder, oh yes.'

'Even so,' I said, although Beverley had her eyes closed. 'It's not right.'

'Peter,' she said. 'It's an ecosystem, a network of patronage and intersectional power relationships. If Oliver had been a proper Oliver with double-barrelled parents and a serious melanin deficiency, chances are he wouldn't have been stopped in the first place and probably would have been let off with a caution in the second.'

Not with his record, I thought. But that was probably me missing the point.

'No parent's going to let their child get mulched by the legal system, are they?' she said. 'Not if they can do something about it. Well, Oliver is lucky – he has Stacy and Tyrel. And now he has me.'

'Doesn't make it right,' I said.

'It is what it is,' said Beverley, and presented me with her other foot.

Later I dreamt that the Bulge was singing to me in two-part disharmony, only for me to wake up and realise it was my phone.

I grabbed it and answered and a familiar American voice said, 'Hi, can I speak to Detective Constable Peter Grant?'

'Speaking,' I said cheerily, and wondered what the hell was going on.

'My name is Kimberley Reynolds from the FBI,' she said. 'I'm not sure if you remember, but we worked together on the Gallagher case a few years back.'

'Of course – Agent Reynolds. How can I help you?'

'I'm making an official request for assistance from the Special Assessment Unit,' she said.

Which meant she must have gone through the official liaison at the NCA before she phoned me. Which explained the text from Silver which simply said 'Call me'. So Skinner had gone officially official. And, from what Reynolds had told me about her place in the FBI hierarchy, this meant the shit was falling from quite a height.

'What's the nature of the request?' I asked.

'The current status of an American citizen, and whether they're currently engaged in illegal activities.'

'Are these illegal activities of a special nature?'

'We believe so.'

'What's the individual's name?'

'Terrence Skinner,' said Reynolds. 'The tech entrepreneur – have you heard of him?'

'I believe I have,' I said. 'I thought he was Australian.'

'Naturalised in 2007,' said Reynolds. 'Is he the subject of an investigation?'

'He's certainly a person of interest,' I said. 'I think we should continue this conversation from a secure location.'

'Well, don't dawdle,' said Reynolds. 'You're going to want to hear this.'

★　　★　　★

Driving through London at four in the morning is always eerily quick. Your London commuter brain is telling you *hours*, but you do the trip in less than thirty minutes. I crossed Waterloo Bridge with low clouds and drizzle turning the floodlights of the South Bank and Westminster orange and green under a sullen red sky.

The brand-new vehicle gate on Bedford Place had an equally new intercom entry box bolted next to it at convenient van driver's height, but it currently had a plastic bag taped over it to show it was inoperative. I got out and used the key and drove in.

To my surprise, the building materials had been cleared out of the rear courtyard and the Portakabin moved to allow easier access to the new loading ramp leading down to the basement. There was even room in the garage between the Jag and a brand-new modified Sprinter. Although I noticed the van hadn't been painted yet.

As I climbed the spiral stairs to the Tech Cave, I checked to see if Molly was watching me from an upper window. Nightingale swears she actually does sleep, but I've never seen any proof.

I flipped the master power switch as soon as I was inside and pulled a Coke out of the fridge to serve as a coffee substitute while I waited for my PC to boot up. As soon as Skype was running, Reynolds's call flashed up.

'What was all that about?' I asked when I saw her face.

'Skinner's been connected to another case,' she said.

At 10.15 on a Monday morning in August 2015, one Anthony Lane walked into the offices of an obscure tech start-up in San Jose carrying a concealed handgun. He talked his way past the receptionist before using the threat of force to gain access to the secure area at the rear and then, once he was in, opened fire. One person was killed instantly, two others were wounded and Lane himself was shot eight times in the back by a responding police officer. The attack barely made the news, being just one of several hundred to several thousand – depending on where you set the parameters – of active shooter incidents so far that year.

'It wasn't on my list,' said Reynolds, 'because the perp was dead.'

Agent Reynolds, in her capacity as special agent in charge of weird shit at the FBI, had spent a hefty chunk of the last two years interviewing surviving shooters to see if there was a super-natural explanation for the increasing number of mass shootings in the US. The survey had yielded a grand total of one possible possession by a bear spirit. But because the project was ongoing, it gave her official permission to stick her nose into any case that vaguely matched the criteria.

'So what caught your attention about this one?' I asked.

'Your friend Terrence Skinner bought the

company,' said Reynolds. Because this was a semi-official contact, she was calling me from her cubicle in FBI HQ. I got an impression of dimmed lights and hush; it was after eleven in Washington DC. 'Canned all the surviving staff, liquidated their property assets and closed them down. Now, why would he do that?'

'Because they had something he wanted?'

'I sent you some crime scene photographs. Have you got them yet?'

I found them in the inbox of the email account I keep just for this purpose. They had that over-saturated look that crime scene pictures always have, the blood splashes being a particularly lurid red. But fortunately the bodies had already been taken away. Instead the floor was scattered with yellow evidence markers. The room was obviously a lab or a workshop with workbenches along one wall, storage racks at the back and an easy to clean blue and green tile floor. Water had washed in from the far end of the room, diluting the blood pools at the edges, and there were scatters of broken green glass littering the floor. Managing that scene must have been a laugh, I thought.

'Go forward a couple,' said Reynolds, and picked up a white and blue coffee mug with FBI written in big yellow letters on the side.

I clicked forward and didn't need to be told when to stop – a close-up of the racks at the back revealed a clear plastic shield, pockmarked with what I assumed were bullet impacts, and behind the shield a dense cube of brass and steel gears – the Mary Engine.

'And a week after Skinner buys up the company, somebody tries to "carjack" him.'

Which Reynolds thought unlikely, given that carjacking, like most car crime, is a crime of opportunity. To her it seemed much more like a deliberate but botched murder attempt.

'The perp walked up to the car, a Tesla Model S, at an intersection and fired three times through the closed driver's side window,' she said.

All three shots miraculously missed, and Skinner's compulsive flooring of his accelerator and the Tesla's mad acceleration meant he shot out into the intersection before his attacker could adjust their aim. Ironically he narrowly missed being T-boned by a semi, which would have finished the job nicely.

While Reynolds had been giving her opinion on the carjacking, I'd been clicking through the pictures looking for a closer view of the rest of the shelving. When I found it I zoomed in – luckily the images were high-resolution, so I got more than just a pixelated blur. There was more broken glass on the tops of the shelves and remains of what must have been glass jars the size and shape of a demijohn. I knew this because (a) two of them had survived the shooting intact and (b) I'd seen identical jars in a cellar under a house in Chesham.

They were the Rose Jars – where ghosts could be imprisoned and kept for years.

'You're going to tell me that Andy Lane was shooting at the equipment, not the people,' I said.

'Spoiler,' said Reynolds. 'I re-interviewed the surviving witnesses and they agreed that *Anthony* Lane opened fire at the Mary Engine and the jars on the rack. Before you ask, they were both interns and didn't know where the items had come from.'

The dead guy, a certain Branwell Petersen, MIT graduate and former Microsoft employee, had died, the witnesses thought, because he stepped between the shooter and the Rose Jars.

'The interns said he threw himself into the line of fire,' said Reynolds. 'As if his life was less important.'

The official report claimed that the two interns had subsequently been wounded when Anthony Lane turned his gun on them, but Reynolds thought they'd actually been hit by stray rounds from the responding officer.

'Name of Lisa Perez, aged thirty-six, married, two kids,' said Reynolds.

Perez, a twelve-year veteran of the SJPD with a good record and reputed to be steady and reliable, had stepped into the company's front office in response to a complaint from the neighbouring business and had just asked to see whoever was in charge when she heard gunshots from the rear of the premises. Fearing an active shooter, Perez called it in and immediately investigated.

'Now this is where it gets hinky,' said Reynolds. 'According to her report, Officer Perez entered the lab and found Anthony Lane reloading his handgun. She ordered him to drop the weapon and, when he refused to comply – and indeed completed his reloading – she opened fire.'

'Eight times?' I said.

'For one thing, Peter,' said Reynolds, 'when engaging an armed opponent you shoot them until they fall down. However, reading between the lines on the follow-up report, it was obvious to me that Officer Perez emptied her magazine and continued to pull the trigger for some time after it was obvious the incident was over. I believe the two interns were wounded by rounds from her weapon, but the SJPD glossed over this aspect of the case because in any event Officer Perez retired with a "service-related disability" less than a month later.'

Perez had been diagnosed as suffering with PTSD.

'It was the first time she'd ever shot anyone,' said Reynolds. 'It's a traumatic thing even if it's a righteous shoot – but I don't need to tell you that.'

So, probably it was the normal reaction to having violently killed a fellow human being. But Reynolds didn't like 'probably'. Which is why she managed to wangle an interview with Officer Perez, who was initially reluctant to talk but relented when Reynolds made it clear that she understood some things that were 'difficult' to include in a report.

'Some of the material Dr Walid sent me was a lot of help,' she said. 'You must thank him for me.'

Officer Perez told Reynolds that she saw something, something she couldn't describe, something that filled her with such fear – *terrified* was the word she used – that she emptied her magazine at it.

'What does this remind you of?' asked Reynolds.

'The petrol station in Cleveland,' I said.

'The Cleveland gas station,' said Reynolds.

The shooting death of John Chapman, former associate of Martin Chorley, at a petrol station in Cleveland, Ohio. I'd assumed he'd been killed by Chorley because he knew too much. But the man himself had denied it.

'I've seen panic fire before,' Reynolds had said. 'And this was strictly spray and pray.'

Chapman had been accidentally shot by responding police officers who reported a similar level of incomprehensible fear. Or, rather, didn't report it until Reynolds had turned up and ferreted it out of them.

'Perhaps we're dealing with a type of *Fae* that uses fear as a defence,' said Reynolds.

'Why not a practitioner?' I asked.

'It seems too reactive,' she said, and she had a point. Practitioner magic was all about thought

325

and control. This fear projection did seem reactive. 'And it didn't do the perp much good, now, did it?'

Assuming that Anthony Lane, our gunman, had been the source of the fear. I pointed this out and we knocked it back and forth, but agreed we didn't have enough data to be sure.

'Another thing you might find familiar,' said Reynolds, 'was Lane's profile.'

'Don't tell me – mild-mannered, apparently normal. Friends and family baffled?'

'Yep,' said Reynolds. 'Worked at the 7-Eleven on McLaughlin Avenue – less than five hundred yards away. Never showed any interest in guns until he drove to Reno the previous weekend and bought his Glock at a local gun store.'

In other words, a similar profile to William Lloyd, who also gave no indication he was about to go postal until the day he did.

'Do you know if he'd joined any chat rooms or had spent time on social media?' I asked.

'What – you mean more than anyone else?' said Reynolds.

'You can ask your friends at the NSA,' I said. 'They're bound to have the metadata.'

Reynolds put down her coffee mug and leaned in closer to the screen. I noticed then that the mug had life-sized fingerprint smudges painted on the side.

'Hey, guys,' she said. 'How about it – you can get favours on both sides of the pond.'

We gave them a couple of seconds to reply but of course they didn't. The first rule of Big Brother is that Big Brother is never watching you when you want him to.

Work pretty much covered, I gave Reynolds the Bulge update and she told me she'd leased a new car, a proper off-road SUV this time. We promised to keep each other, and presumably the NSA, regularly updated and hung up.

There was a scratching at the door and when I investigated I found Toby sitting on his haunches and looking at me with an expectant expression. I glanced over to the first floor opposite and saw that the lights in the breakfast room were on. Toby obviously needed me to open a silver salver and liberate some sausages.

When I'd first arrived at the Folly, Molly had insisted on cooking breakfast for twenty instead of an actual complement of three – not counting Toby. Since then the numbers of people demanding bacon, sausage, eggs and kedgeree have fluctuated, culminating in Operation Jennifer, where we must have had more than thirty people eating in shifts. It was during that period that fruit and baked goods first appeared, so that it is now possible, against all police tradition, to eat a balanced breakfast. There was a flare-up again when we had the builders in, which also saw the introduction of *zacuscă?*, sheep's cheese, *popara* and – my personal favourite – a sort of open-topped sandwich with cold meat and salad.

At some point Molly had learnt how to manage her supply to match demand, so I was pleased to note that we were back down to just the five salvers and one table set with cutlery.

Toby bounced around my feet as I hunted for the sausages, but looked disappointed when I put some on a plate under the table. Still, he nommed them all up, I noticed. There was a pot of tea waiting on the table, kept warm by a crudely knitted blue and white tea cosy with a bobble on the top.

I poured myself a cup and considered Deep Thought.

It had to be one of three things. A genuine Artificial General Intelligence. An intelligence that used to be a real person housed, somehow, inside a contraption constructed by mashing up a Mary Engine and one or more intact Rose Jars. Or, finally, a fake run by Skinner. The last would be a scam to create false value for the Serious Cybernetics Corporation, so that a larger competitor could be lured into buying the SCC at a hugely inflated price. According to Officer Silver, this sort of thing was currently all the rage in Silicon Valley.

The last seemed unlikely – Skinner didn't seem to be the type. Hype his product beyond its actual capabilities, maybe. But run a long con on this scale? Besides, if he was truly looking to generate false value, then he should at least be hinting at Deep Thought's existence.

I wasn't qualified to tell whether it was a real AGI – it passed a rough approximation of a Turing Test with me, but as Everest and Victor would no doubt love to point out, that actually proved nothing except that Skinner might have produced a very sophisticated person emulator.

I poured myself another cup of tea.

So it could be a ghost, revenant or some other incorporeal entity trapped inside the Mary Engine or a Rose Jar – or a combination of the same. A ghost would be sad but harmless. But a revenant – something that could eat ghosts, and directly affect people's minds? That could be really dangerous. According to the literature, the bloody things entrenched themselves if left in place too long.

I heard running feet and Foxglove charged into the breakfast room, naked except for a white sheet that she held over her head so that it billowed artistically behind her. She did a circuit of the room and then charged out again with Toby barking at her heels.

Molly appeared suddenly behind me just as I raised my teacup and almost caused me to spill tea down my front. She whisked away the teapot and went gliding off. In the distance I could hear Toby barking as he and Foxglove did a lap around the second-floor balcony.

Nightingale once had a friend called David Mellenby, who was the closest thing to a modern research scientist the Folly has ever produced. I have his unpublished notes and, while much of the maths is beyond me, he did record his ideas in a sort of waking dream journal – bits of which I understand.

He postulated that there were other planes of existence which he called *allokosmoi*, from which the various supernatural types, including practitioners, drew their power and their influence. He speculated that if a revenant stayed in a fixed location, then that place would start to overlap with the particular *allokosmos* from which it drew its power. I think he thought *vestigia* were a boundary effect of this overlap. I'm not sure if he was right about that, but it would certainly explain invisible unicorns and many other instances of weird shit.

Molly placed a fresh pot of tea on the table – this one had an orange and brown knitted tea cosy in the form of a broody hen.

'The builders uncovered a chest while they were finishing up,' said Nightingale from the doorway. 'Judging by the tea cosies and other things, I think it must have contained items from the downstairs mess hall.'

Which was a polite way of saying the servants' quarters.

Nightingale sat down and paused while Molly fussed around him laying out cutlery, and a fine white porcelain cup, saucer and milk jug. I thought of Beyoncé Knowles and the over-sugared latte and smiled.

'You seem remarkably cheerful for this time in the morning,' he said.

'We have to do the raid tonight,' I said.

'Ah,' said Nightingale, pouring a cup of tea. 'I see. What's your thinking?'

'Someone, or something,' I said, 'is using the internet to assemble an army of magical drones. We've identified one manufacturing cell, but we can't be sure there aren't more.'

'Agreed,' said Nightingale, and thoughtfully stirred his tea.

I read him into the briefing I'd got from Reynolds, and he drew the same conclusions I did.

'I believe that there is a better than even chance that the "something" doing the organising is located on the closed top floor of Bambleweeny,' I said. 'We need to get in there and find out, one way or the other.'

'This makes sense, of course,' said Nightingale. 'But why the urgency? Surely, if you're right about this Deep Thought, then caution would be advisable.'

'The situation is too unstable,' I said. 'I have two suspects under my roof who even as we speak are probably plotting to double-cross me. At work, Leo Hoyt is definitely getting suspicious. But, most importantly, the Print Shop in Gillingham was wound up voluntarily. I think that means their preparations are done, and whatever they wanted those drones for is about to happen.'

'You want to seize the initiative?'

'Yes,' I said. 'Our one advantage is that they seem to have no idea we exist. If we act now we might be able to roll them up before they know what's hit them.'

Nightingale frowned into his teacup.

'Perhaps,' he said.

'What have we got to lose?' I said.

Nightingale looked up and gave me a strange, sad smile.

'Oh, everything, Peter,' he said. 'But then, such is life.'

CHAPTER 15

A STRANGE GAME

It was go to work in black that night, although most of it was really dark blue. And as casual as we could get, because – amazingly – when going equipped it's better not to look like you're planning a burglary. Believe it or not, the police are trained to spot such subtle signs as balaclavas, nylon climbing harnesses and big shoulder bags that go 'clonk' when you put them down.

We arrived separately using three different Tube stations and rendezvoused inside a green late-model Transit van that I told Stephen and Mrs Chin I'd stolen earlier from a building site that had shut up for the night.

For all I knew, this was true. Because Silver had supplied the vehicle, and God knows where she got it from. For extra verisimilitude it came with a ramp attachment as if I truly intended to move something bulky, say a mechanical computer and a couple of Rose Jars. I told them we had to wait in the van until at least 1 a.m.

'Why the hell are we here so early?' asked Mrs Chin.

'This is a big crime,' I said. 'The police will pull footage from every CCTV camera in a five hundred metre radius. This looks less suspicious.'

'Apart from the bit where we all climb into this van,' said Stephen.

'Ah, but Mr Skinner didn't want any cameras pointing at his secret lift,' I said. 'So this is a general blind spot. And, ditto, none of the Vogon cameras cover this area either.'

'There'll be something,' said Stephen. 'A segregated closed circuit system linked to the top floor – at minimum.'

'We snuff those on the way in,' I said. 'And since we were going to have to sand everything once we were up there anyway, that'll take care of any recordings.'

'Sand?' asked Mrs Chin.

'Destroy with magic,' said Stephen. 'What happens to silicon chips if you cast a spell too close to them.'

Mrs Chin nodded and glanced at her watch.

'More than two hours?' she said.

'If we want to be safe, yeah.'

'The problem here,' said Mrs Chin, 'is that it may be okay for you young people but some of us are going to have trouble holding our pee for that long.'

'Got you covered,' I said, and held up two empty two-litre Diet Pepsi bottles.

'That's not going to cover it,' said Mrs Chin, so

I showed her the nice clean medical funnel I'd brought along to avoid spillage.

'First working bathroom we find is mine,' said Mrs Chin.

Obviously variable bladder capacity had been a failure in my contingency planning but there wasn't anything we could do about it now.

Stephen unfolded the stepladder I'd brought so that Mrs Chin could sit in comparative comfort while me and Stephen sat on the floor with our backs against the side of the van. With Mrs Chin perched above us, I had a terrible urge to put my hand up whenever she asked a question.

Partly for its entertainment value I pulled out my Airwave and set it to cover NI (Islington nick) and City.

'What's that?' asked Mrs Chin.

'Police scanner,' said Stephen.

I interpreted a couple of incidents for them – the assault near Liverpool Street station, the noise complaint in Hoxton, the constant moaning by overworked response officers and, reading between the lines, the gnashing of teeth by their skippers because they didn't have enough manpower.

'Skippers?' asked Stephen.

'Sergeants,' I said.

'They don't get a lot of action around here, do they?' said Mrs Chin. 'New York is much livelier. Or at least it used to be.'

'Oh, yes, Mrs Chin,' said Stephen in a mono-tone. 'Tell us about the good old days.'

'Do you get a lot of action in New York?' I asked. 'Our kind of action, that is?'

'When I was a junior we spent most of our days underground,' said Mrs Chin.

'Still do,' muttered Stephen.

'There's a whole world down there,' she said. 'Subways, sewers, steam tunnels, the old rivers. A whole population that went underground during the winter – vagrants, criminals on the run . . .'

'Mutant turtles?' I asked, and Stephen sniggered.

'You joke,' said Mrs Chin. 'But personally I wouldn't have been surprised. Vampires were a problem, of course – they always are. You burn out one nest and another would pop up. Got real bad in the '70s until a bunch of homeless vets went after them with homemade napalm and flamethrowers – quite a war by all accounts.'

'You didn't intervene?'

'I was a teenager at the time, but the Association stayed out of it,' said Mrs Chin. The Association being the New York Libraries Association, the militant magical wing of the New York Public Library Services. 'Although we're all members of the Green Machine as well.' That being the AFSCME, the union that most mundane librarians belonged to.

The war had raged until the early 1980s, when things had gone creepily quiet. But there was much less in the way of vampire incidents after that.

'Still get them, though,' said Stephen.

The most dangerous thing Mrs Chin had personally dealt with was a possessed shade at the notorious Willowbrook State School on Staten Island – which I had to look up later.

'When you say shades, what do you mean?' I asked. 'Do you mean *Fae*?'

'I mean everything that's not normal,' said Mrs Chin.

'Like New Jersey,' said Stephen.

Mrs Chin nodded at me.

'He knows what I mean,' said Mrs Chin. 'He should do, considering his domestic arrangements.'

But yes, I teased out of Mrs Chin, the shades were what we would call the *Fae*, or rather anyone who inhabited the demi-monde for anything other than style reasons. Shades were tolerated in New York – who wasn't? But part of the Librarians' job was to keep an eye on them.

'What about the rest of the States?' I asked.

She confirmed that the Bureau of Indian Affairs held down the reservations, but she seemed to think the FBI dealt with the rest of the country. Which probably would have come as a surprise to Agent Reynolds, all on her lonesome in the Office of Partner Engagement.

I wanted to ask about the rivers, but the Airwave, which had been merrily squawking away in the background, said, 'Two seven eight show state thirteen.' Followed immediately after by the response: 'Confirmed two seven eight state thirteen.'

This was the signal that Silver and Nightingale were in position. I waited a couple of minutes before checking my watch and telling the others it was time.

Outside the van the air was moist and cold, and after a quick shufti to make sure no one was watching, we scuttled down the slight ramp to the entrance.

First up was the mechanical lock on the metal roller door that guarded the loading bay. Stephen did that with a neat little spell which, as far as I could tell, disassembled the lock from the inside. While he did this, I threw an infrared chip killer at the CCTV camera concealed in the door frame. By the time Mrs Chin strolled along we had the door up and open with a theatrical flourish.

'Thank you, boys,' she said as she walked inside.

Inside was a two-metre-deep loading bay complete with concrete dock at a convenient height for access by a large two-axle lorry. I leant the metal stepladder against the dock and held it fast while Mrs Chin daintily climbed up. Stephen vaulted up in one fluid motion and examined the closed heavy-duty doors of the goods lift.

'Now what?' he asked as I hauled up the stepladder.

I pressed the lift call button and the heavy doors opened and we stepped inside. The interior was your standard metal box with a non-slip corrugated floor and heavy rubberised padding on the walls that rose to waist height. The floor was scuffed and the padding had been scraped so hard in some places that the metal was showing through.

What there weren't were any floor selection buttons, although there were two red domes containing CCTV cameras mounted at either end.

Stephen brushed his hand across the blank panel where the buttons should be – there wasn't even an intercom grille, alarm button or fire safety override key. The Fire Brigade would have had a fit if they'd found out.

'It's a very elegant system,' I said. 'If you want to go up you have to call someone on the top floor and they press the button to activate the lift mechanism.'

'So you have a man on the inside?' asked Mrs Chin.

'I wish,' I said, and told them to stand flat against the walls.

In the old days lifts had hatches in the roofs to allow nervous Edwardians the prospect of escape if trapped. In these days of health and safety gone mad, it's generally considered safer if members of the public stay in the nice safe metal box rather than expose themselves to limb-mangling heavy machinery and fatal falls down adjacent shafts. The hatch is still there. It's just that it's now bolted down from the top – nice big bolts, though, so the Fire Brigade can open them quickly.

Or a bright young wizard with a new spell can punch them out one after another. Especially if he has the blueprints and knows exactly where they are. Stephen snorted as the locks fell into the cab and I *impello*'d the hatch up and to the side.

'Show off,' said Mrs Chin as I positioned the stepladder under the hole.

I paused to pull on a pair of workman's gloves, with reinforced panels on the fingers and palms, over the latex pair I was already wearing. Then I climbed up the stepladder, reached up and pulled myself into the darkness.

I flicked on my penlight and flashed it around the lift shaft. This was where things could have taken on the definite contours of a popular edible fruit but luckily, built into a shallow recess, was an emergency ladder vanishing up into darkness. I hadn't been certain it was going to be there.

'It's a good thing I'm wearing my sensible shoes,' said Mrs Chin as she poked her head up through the hatch. She reached out with her arms and snapped her fingers.

'Get a move on,' she said, and I grabbed her arms and pulled her up and then stooped to help Stephen in turn. I pointed out the ladder.

'You go first,' I said. 'Mrs Chin goes next and I replace the hatch and follow after.'

Stephen started uncoiling the nylon rope he had wound around his waist.

'What happens at the top?' he asked.

'It's a standard lift door,' I said. 'Can you handle that?'

Stephen said he could, and stopped to help Mrs Chin secure the rope around her waist.

'If you get tired,' he said, 'hold the rope and I'll pull you up.'

'Stop fussing,' she hissed. 'I was doing this before your mother was born.'

Stephen swarmed up the ladder and by the time I'd replaced the hatch – so that from inside the lift, at first glance, it would look intact – the pair of them were vanishing into the gloom four metres above.

I followed and only caught up when Stephen reached the top set of doors. I felt that little tingle, like pins and needles, that I recognised as part of Stephen's *signare*. There was a very mechanical *clonk* sound and light flooded in as the doors opened.

Getting out was easier than I expected since, strangely, the designers had put in a shelf and handgrips to assist transfer from the ladder. Just another example of lunatic health and safety, I thought as I stepped onto the top floor of Bambleweeny.

It was brightly lit and mostly empty but for a

cylindrical cage three metres across that rose from floor to ceiling. The uprights were made of blue steel with two distinct and separated layers of fine copper mesh. Extending from the base for two metres all around was a thick rubber flooring.

Mr Faraday, I presume, I thought.

'Don't touch the cage,' I said. 'It might be electrified.'

The floor was clear for another couple of metres around the insulation mat and then there was a double row, each side, of the same boring beige cubicles as on the floor below.

'Is it in there?' asked Mrs Chin.

Me and Stephen crept forward – craning our heads to check the cubicles – until we were close enough to peer through the fine mesh. The Mary Engine looked as it had in the eBay pictures I'd first seen of it, a steampunk Borg cube of steel and brass gears and ratchets. It stood on a thick plastic table and there was a white box attached to one side – an electric engine to turn the crank, I assumed. Next to it were two large jars filled with cloudy amber liquid connected to the Mary Engine by curly red insulated wires with bulldog clips at either end. As I moved around the cage I saw that there was a desk supporting a bog-standard tower PC with a flat screen, mouse and keyboard. An Ethernet cable snaked out the back and up to what I assumed was an adaptor fixed to the side of the Mary Engine.

Having confirmed the presence of the Mary Engine and the Rose Jars, it was time for my sudden but inevitable betrayal. Me, Nightingale and Silver had worked out several contingencies, of which the simplest would be to flash my torch out of a west-facing window.

'Right,' I said, 'we check the rest of the cubicles, dismantle the cage, grab the goods and out.'

Mrs Chin came to stand beside me.

'What about your algorithm, Peter?' she said, and I could feel her shifting her weight – balancing on the balls of her feet. 'The one that was supposed to make this all worthwhile?'

I clocked Stephen casually moving around the curve of the cage – splitting my focus.

I crouched slightly as if drawing attention to the PC next to the Mary Engine.

'It's in that, isn't it?' I said. 'We take it with us.'

Never mind Stephen, I thought, Mrs Chin will be the real threat. I can probably get a strike in if I surprise her, but after that it's anyone's guess. Still, one of the alternative plans to alert Nightingale and Silver was to make as loud a noise as possible.

As an organisation we like to play to our strengths.

I decided on a big snapdragon for distraction and a shield slam as follow-up. I was clearing my mind when somebody else interrupted.

'Oh, look,' said a voice, 'it's the Pink Panther.'

And Leo Hoyt, sitting on an operator's chair, pushed himself backwards out of a cubicle near the back of the room.

I straightened up, but before I could speak my arm went dead. I turned to look and saw that Mrs Chin had grasped my wrist with the finger and thumb of her left hand. Her right hand was held up beside her face with the little finger extended, as if she were drinking tea with the Queen.

I felt the numbness rushing down past my elbow – there was no pain but it was terrifying – and I tried to break my own balance so that I'd fall away from Mrs Chin and break her grip.

'Stop that,' she said. 'Or I stop your heart.'

Human beings are really difficult to directly control by magic – Dr Walid has postulated that the human central nervous system generates its own autonomic magical resistance as a function of evolving in a world where potential predators can do magic. In order to partially paralyse me like that, Mrs Chin had to be a very highly trained practitioner. A true master, in Nightingale's terms. An utter pain in the arse, literally, in mine.

I wasn't sure she could stop my heart, but I decided to err on the side of caution and stopped moving.

'What's going on?' said Leo, scrambling off his chair.

'Stephen,' said Mrs Chin. 'If you don't mind?'

I recognised the spell as the same *impello-palma* combination he'd used on me at the London Library. Leo went over on his back with a shocked grunt.

'Stay down, Leo!' I shouted. 'Wait for assistance!'

'Good advice, Leo,' said Mrs Chin. 'You listen to your friend.'

I tried forming a spell – the first long, complicated one I could think of. In this case *telescopium*, which was Newton's own creation and had largely gone out of fashion with the invention of the binoculars. Mrs Chin sensed me, of course, and sent a pulse of pain down through my wrist into my left leg. This is the standard technique for subduing an experienced practitioner – you keep disrupting their concentration. You can use cold water, loud noises, electric shocks or, in this case, magically induced pain.

I groaned theatrically and hunched down with the pain, which allowed me to get my left hand into the top pocket of my trousers.

'Oh no, you don't,' said Mrs Chin, and another pulse of pain made me spasm upright. Too late for her – I had my screamer in my hand.

'What is that supposed to be?' she asked, shifting position so she could see my left hand.

'Thermal detonator,' I said, and held the screamer up in what I hoped was a threatening gesture.

'You're fucking kidding me,' said Stephen.

'No, seriously,' I said. 'It's built around a stripped-down L84 grenade with a clockwork timer to make it magic-proof.'

'Why would you even make such a thing?' asked Mrs Chin, with a note of horrified curiosity.

'We use them on vampire nests,' I said.

Stephen looked interested. Mrs Chin's gaze stayed fixed on me. That's the trouble with direct control spells – you have to maintain them. Postmartin calls it the 'control fallacy' and says that it's a common fault of powerful practitioners.

'That makes sense,' said Stephen.

'Does it?' asked Mrs Chin.

'Yeah,' said Stephen. 'The amount of times I've had to lug gas around the Subway to clear nests.'

'Can I point out this is ticking,' I said. 'Literally.'

'You're going to tell me it's got a dead man's switch,' said Mrs Chin.

'It's essentially a hand grenade and I've pulled the pin,' I said.

'Stephen,' snapped Mrs Chin. 'Get rid of it.'

There was a weird pulse down my arm, not painful but shocking in its intensity, and my left hand popped open against my will. As the screamer began to fall, Stephen snatched it with *impello* and propelled it straight at the window. It should have bounced – modern office windows are double-glazed, heat treated and shatter resistant. But instead Stephen melted a small hole through both panes and out it flew into the street below.

I glanced at Stephen, who waggled his eyebrows to show that he knew how cool that was.

We waited for the bang, but of course nothing happened.

'Must have been a dud,' I said.

Another pulse down my arm shut me up while Stephen rolled Leo over on his front and secured his wrists behind his back with a cable tie. Mrs Chin continued to control me while Stephen did the same to me. Then I was made to sit on the floor next to Leo, who had struggled into a sitting position.

'I have no doubt you're capable of breaking those ties,' said Mrs Chin. 'But in the time it takes you to do that I will break both your legs – *capisce?*'

'*Si, baroni,*' I said.

'We're not here to hurt anyone, but this is too important to let you get in the way.'

'What's so important about it?' I asked.

'Nice try,' she said, and walked back to where she could keep a beady eye on me and Leo while still supervising Stephen as he started to methodically cut a hole in the side of the Faraday cage.

'The police are on their way,' said Leo. 'I hit the panic button as soon as you came up the lift.'

I wanted to tell him that they were already

here, but I wasn't ready to surrender what slim advantage I had. I did tell him to keep his head down and to run like fuck if he got the opportunity.

'Wait,' he said, putting one and one together and making three. 'That means . . .' he began, but clamped his mouth shut when he saw my expression.

'Yes,' I said. 'And the Pink Panther is the diamond, you twat.'

The Mary Engine was a dense cube sixty centimetres on each side. Given that it was made of brass and steel, we'd assumed it was going to be heavy. To that end Stephen had purchased a reinforced nylon bag with a rigid base and heavy-duty castors. Used by roadies, he explained, for moving amplifiers around. He had to use *impello* to get the Engine into the bag. Once he had it zipped up and had dragged it clear of the cage he looked over at Mrs Chin, who nodded.

'Do it,' she said.

Stephen made a needless theatrical gesture and the two Rose Jars imploded, the murky fluid inside cascading down onto the rubber matting. There were no sparks, so I guessed the Faraday cage had been passive rather than active.

Mrs Chin gave me a stern look.

'And remember,' she said, wagging her finger. 'The shades are never truly your friends – they all want something.'

In the bag, so to speak, the Mary Engine would

have been a bugger to move even with me and Stephen handling it. As it was, Mrs Chin had to divide her attention between keeping an eye on us and giving the occasional push.

Which was probably why Nightingale chose that moment to make an appearance.

He walked quietly up from the direction of the lift wearing his sturdiest navy blue worsted Detective Chief Inspector suit and introduced himself. Or at least he tried – he actually only got as far as, 'Hello, my name is Thomas Nightingale . . .' when Stephen tried to throw a cubicle at him.

It was a clever move, because the fabric-covered chipboard, backed up by the weight of a desk, a computer and an in-out tray, came flying in from behind Nightingale. I gave him A for effort, and Nightingale gave him a complicated variant on *impello* that threw him in my direction.

For boring historical reasons, I've practised quite hard recently learning various techniques for dealing with bound hands. A quick bit of spot heat and a twist and I got to my feet just in time to give Stephen a good kicking when he landed in front of me. Unfortunately, when I went in for a restraint he managed to get his arm around my neck and tried to put my head through a cubicle wall. We were in a sort of weird crouching grapple when two sudden bursts of *vestigia* startled us. One had the distinctive twist and punch that Nightingale gives his spells, but the other was like a crowd shouting at a football match.

Me and Stephen were so surprised that we forgot we were supposed to be fighting and stared at where our two teachers were facing off. I've seen Nightingale fight masters before, and that had involved a lot of flash and a ton of property damage. This was nothing like that; each faced the other like boxers sparring in a ring, their weight shifting from foot to foot, hands held in loose fists, eyes fixed on their opponents.

I could feel multiple *formae* piling up around each of them, but there wasn't even a ripple in the air. This was speed chess with an invisible board. And when both of them released their spells, I swear I felt the building creak under the strain. Neither waited for the other to follow through and the *formae* flickered past my senses too fast to even separate one from another. Nightingale's right fist clenched slightly and Mrs Chin opened her palm. I think there were at least two more passes, and both rocked back on their heels before shifting stances again.

Nightingale was grinning – a wide smile of unselfconscious pleasure – and we heard a wheezing sound that I realised was Mrs Chin laughing.

'Wow,' said Stephen in wonder, and he punched me in the bollocks.

I curled up around the pain, but I've been in too many fights not to use the motion to get my leg hooked around the back of his knee. He went over backwards and I rolled behind the wall of a cubicle and used a chair to pull myself to my feet.

Stephen came after me. He knew he had to keep the initiative, but I was swinging the chair the other way so that he ran right into it. As he staggered back, I followed through with a freezing water bomb to the head to disrupt any magic he was planning.

I caught sight of Leo sensibly stumbling towards the relative safety of the far end of the office and returned my attention to Stephen, just in time to get one of his nicely calculated *impello-palma* to the stomach.

As Nightingale always says, never take your eyes off your opponent – and Stephen would probably have put me down with the next spell if there hadn't been a sinister 'pop' from back where the old folks were fighting.

And a concussion wave blew us and every loose bit of furniture five metres further down the office. I found myself, with no intervening period of consciousness, in the dark and wedged under a sheet of plasterboard. I have, for both personal and operational reasons, a slight phobia about being buried under rubble. So I was probably a bit more forceful than I might have been getting the stuff off me. There's a spell that dates back to the Victorian era called the *coffin bell*, designed to allow a skilled practitioner to dig himself out from his own grave. It's a fourth order spell, so I reckon you'd have to be a pretty good practitioner to be able to cast it after being accidentally buried alive. I also have doubts about whether it could shift four cubic metres of loose earth, but it certainly made short work of the pile of office furniture I was under.

The lights were out, but there was enough reflected street light for me to see the room. Because I've learnt to respect Stephen's ability to sucker-punch me at every opportunity, I immediately shifted position and did a visual sweep.

Whatever had gone 'pop' had cleared a circle in the middle of the room. The Faraday cage had resisted being blown down, but the copper mesh had been stripped off the steel pylons – they would still be digging fragments out of the wall weeks later. Beyond the immediate radius of complete destruction the cubicles had been knocked over, rather than flattened, and they seemed intact at the far ends.

At the centre of ground zero was the nylon carry case containing the Mary Engine. Amazingly, the bag was intact but judging by its malformed, half-crushed shape its contents were not. Next to it someone had placed a miraculously spared office chair on which Mrs Chin sat with her hands primly clasped in her lap. Behind her, as per regulations when dealing with dangerously Falconcapable prisoners, stood Nightingale.

'Ah, Peter, excellent,' he said. 'Would you be so good as to check for casualties?'

PART IV

CYBERDYNE

I'm sorry, I couldn't find 'a good song' in your music.

Siri

CHAPTER 16

NICE JOB BREAKING IT, HERO

I found Leo Hoyt, dazed but unharmed, tucked into the far corner. I cut the ties on his wrists and told him to stay put until someone came and got him. Judging by the state of the room, that somebody would probably be the fire brigade. Then I went looking for Stephen, who had been half buried – but unlike me he was pinned under a heavy wooden desk. Once I established he wasn't being crushed, I decided to leave him for the fire brigade, too.

'I think the building has been compromised,' said Nightingale, when I joined him and Mrs Chin.

He pointed a hand at the ceiling and I saw that the hanging tiles had been blown away, revealing the actual concrete roof which was marked by an alarming star-burst of cracks. Positioned, I noticed, right over the squashed remains of the Mary Engine.

'Did you do that?' I asked Mrs Chin.

'Patricia Chin,' she said formally. 'Chief Librarian, 020.131.'

What with giving the fire brigade and the

London Ambulance Service priority, finding an alternative access to the emergency stairwell, and then making sure Mrs Chin and Stephen were led out separately but with appropriate Falcon-capable escorts – i.e. me and Nightingale – it took two hours to quit the building. By that time Tyrel Johnson had turned up along with Bradley Michael Smith, and a couple of other SCC employees were out the back. I got a glimpse of Johnson's face as I accompanied Stephen to the prisoner transfer van. He didn't look happy.

The van with Nightingale and Mrs Chin arrived at the Folly first, which meant we had to park in Bedford Place while it manoeuvred in and then out of the Folly's courtyard. While we waited, Stephen sat quietly with his handcuffed hands in his lap. I sat opposite and kept my eyes on him. I had no doubt that he was perfectly capable of blowing the doors off the van if he wanted to, but he stayed suspiciously subdued even when it was our turn to unload.

In a nice purpose-built nick, your prisoner vans back up to a rear door carefully recessed so that the suspects are funnelled into the building. It's as much a psychological ploy as anything else – resistance is futile, and all that. Retrofitting a building that had been designed as a gentleman's club in the middle of central London meant compromises – starting with the fact that we could only unload one prisoner van at a time.

We were still short of uniforms, so it was Guleed

who threw open the van's back doors and grinned as I helped Stephen out.

'Welcome to the Folly,' I said, but if he knew the name he gave no reaction.

I led him down the brand-new access ramp to the basement where a large steel door had been set into a reinforced concrete casing. On the other side, where the Folly's small gym used to be, was a little vestibule with clean whitewashed walls, a second fuck-off steel door, and on the other side of that, our brand new PACE-compliant custody suite. You could still smell the fresh paint.

As the designated Falcon-qualified officer I had to continue with Stephen to the search room, where he surrendered any personal possessions, assured me he wasn't carrying anything up his bum – we took his word for it – and stripped him down to his knickers so he could be inspected under UV light. There was a long painful-looking scar on his upper left arm and a puckered circular scar on his stomach.

'Not a bullet hole,' he said.

'No?' I asked.

'Crossbow bolt,' he said.

Because he was only our second paying customer, he got a choice of brand-new alternative raiment and went for the grey tracksuit bottoms with matching grey sweatshirt, all still in their plastic wrappers. Once he had some paper slippers on he was ready to meet his new best friend and guardian of his well-being – the custody sergeant.

Probably the only advantage of belonging to an organisation that is being relentlessly downsized in the name of austerity is that if you do have a budget, it's easy to pick up some talent. In this case, Sergeant Anthony Finnegan, who was a large, imposing white man with no neck and, in a savage response to a burgeoning bald patch, no hair. We picked him because his performance reviews were littered with words like 'solid', 'dependable' and, more than once, 'unflappable'. When, as the final part of the interview process, Nightingale demonstrated how unexpected magic could be by conjuring a werelight in front of Finnegan's face, he'd merely nodded.

'You learn something new every day,' he'd said.

He was one of four custody sergeants we kept on the books for twenty-four-hour cover, although we lent them to various other London nicks when our cells were empty – which up until now had been all the time.

Finnegan was still processing Mrs Chin when we emerged from the search room.

She'd opted for the stylish navy blue tracksuit bottoms and a soft cotton smock and was explaining that no, she had no allergies or urgent medical needs, but she did want a lawyer and a phone call.

Finnegan explained that once she was processed all that could be arranged, and the sooner she was processed the sooner it would all happen.

'I could call the American embassy if you like,' I said.

Mrs Chin shot me a poisonous look.

'Where's your master?' she asked me.

'Gone back out,' I said. 'Why? Are you ready to answer some questions?'

'No,' said Mrs Chin with a tight smile. 'And much as I appreciate the change of clothes, I believe it's time Stephen and I were leaving.'

She raised her right hand, little finger extended – and nothing happened.

In the Newtonian magic tradition you don't actually have to make a gesture to cast a spell – it's all in the way you line the *formae* up in your head – but everyone does, even Nightingale.

Mrs Chin's gestures became more emphatic, but you don't get to be a master of the forms and wisdoms without being quick on the uptake. She gave me an accusing look.

'How are you doing that?' she asked.

'Wouldn't you like to know?' I said.

The answer, of course, was that I wasn't doing it at all.

Along with the gym and the showers, we'd sacrificed the Folly's underground shooting range to install a custody suite of six modern cells with toilets, one medical examination suite, an exercise room, prisoner showers and, located at the north end of the suite so it could have windows into the front area, a large airy studio. Here Foxglove, when she wasn't running naked through the Folly or sketching people in the park, worked and slept. And generated a sort of field that negated magic. We call it the MSA – the Magical Suppression Area – and we'd put in some work hours testing its limitations, although none of us had any idea how it actually worked.

Now, my theory was that this field was a boundary effect caused when Foxglove draws one of David Mellenby's *allokosmoi*, specifically the one colloquially known as Fairyland, closer to our reality. But I haven't devised a way of testing that hypothesis yet. At least, not a safe one.

Still magic, like policing, has always been much more about the practice than the theory.

Mrs Chin and Stephen exchanged horrified looks and for a moment Mrs Chin looked like a frightened old woman – but only for a moment.

Been there, I thought, done that, read *The Silmarillion*.

Mrs Chin took a deep breath and then nodded at Stephen, who sighed. After that the pair allowed themselves to be fingerprinted, cheek-swabbed and photographed but refused to answer any questions beyond their names.

Once Stephen and Patricia Chin were safely banged up, I went upstairs, wrote up my notes and changed into my emergency work suit. I looked at my face in the mirror as I attached my clip-on tie. Judging by my expression, I wasn't happy about something.

My shrink has 'suggested' that it might be 'useful'

if I were to spend more time exploring where my emotions originate. This has always struck me as good advice, so having determined that I was, in fact, discontented, I set out to track down the source.

After popping downstairs to check that Foxglove's Magical Suppression Area was still working, I went looking for answers – starting with what was left of the top floor of Bambleweeny. I arrived via Clare Street and slipped in through the police cordon – I wasn't ready to run into Everest or Victor. And I certainly didn't want to meet Johnson just yet.

The fire brigade had declared the building structurally sound, forensics had finished their sweep and the three computers with intact chipsets had been carted off for analysis. The rest of the electronics had been powered up during the fight and their insides reduced to a fine glittery sand.

'That last blow was deliberately noisy,' said Nightingale. 'Mrs Chin was making sure that nothing electronic survived.'

He was stalking around the middle of the room, slowly retracing the fight from Mrs Chin's perspective, stepping where she stepped and holding his arms as she had. Occasionally he would rewind, reversing his steps, before making the same move again – it looked a little like minimalist t'ai chi.

'That last spell was completely out of character,'

he said. 'Loud, flashy, destructive. Pointless.' He stopped moving and straightened up. 'She was the best practitioner I have ever fought, Peter.'

'Better than you?' I asked.

'Overall, who can say?' he said as he checked his cuffs. 'In combat magic – no. Although we were close enough that I believe she initially thought she might win. It was only when it became clear the outcome was inevitable that she changed tactics.'

He looked at the pattern of cracks in the ceiling and down at the matching set on the floor. At the precise centre there was a rectangle of un-damaged carpet tiles where the Mary Engine had sat in its bag.

'She destroyed the Mary Engine so we wouldn't get it,' I said.

'Yes,' said Nightingale. 'It might be wise to find out why.'

'She doesn't seem keen to talk to us,' I said. 'And Stephen even less so.'

'Perhaps your Mr Skinner can enlighten us,' said Nightingale.

But Mr Skinner didn't want to talk to us either, and Silver, who'd already had a go, warned us off making another approach.

'It's possible we might be able to salvage our investigation,' she said, 'But Skinner's going to be on his guard now – we need to calm things down.'

It was sensible advice. While we hadn't

recovered the Mary Engine, or the Rose Jars, or the *Enchantress of Numbers* music book, they were definitely no longer missing – so that had to be something. Right?

I was missing a night's sleep by then, so in the absence of any useful work I went home. Beverley was out at a lecture, so I flopped down on the bed and went out like a light.

The next morning I had one of those vivid half-dreams you can get when you've just woken up to the happy revelation that you don't have to get out of bed just yet and you have time to snuggle up to a friendly neighbourhood river goddess and go back to sleep.

I was back on the top floor of Bambleweeny, only it had been redesigned by Ken Adams, the Faraday cage replaced by a useless Perspex cylinder enclosing a clanking mechanical Difference Engine from which a tangle of fantasy lab glass-ware sprouted into two huge jars the size of telephone boxes. Around the cylinder were arrayed ranks of fridge-freezer-sized, reel-to-reel magnetic tape drives and amongst them men and women, many I thought I half-recognised from the SCC, all dressed in Lycra catsuits, wandered with clip-boards or stared at blinking lights.

'So we meet at last, Mr Bond,' said a voice.

The huge jars were filled with a swirling mixture of amber and yellow liquids and curled inside each, like a wizened foetus, was the shrunken body of a man. In my persona as James Bond – as played

365

by Colin Salmon – I stepped forward and one of the curled figures lifted its head to stare at me with glowing red eyes.

I got the strong impression that the man in the jar was about to tell me his dastardly plan, but my bladder woke me and I had to get up. Once I was in the bathroom I thought I might as well have a shower, and after that I was up and ready for action. It might have been a Saturday, but below the rank of chief inspector weekends are an entirely notional concept.

Also that day, I was back on the job as proper police which, as any modern copper will tell you, starts with an hour in front of an AWARE terminal catching up with your emails and trying to interpret the gnomic and often contradictory directives that flow downhill from senior management.

Then I had a meeting with the duty solicitor, who'd been drafted in to represent Stephen and Mrs Chin.

'I didn't even know there was a station here,' she said.

I explained that we'd been reactivated due to the general sell-off of police assets – an explanation she found all too plausible. You can always get on the right side of legal aid lawyers by having a mutual moan about austerity. It's one of the many ways that adversity helps bring people together.

I then had a meeting with the CPS about what

to charge Stephen and Mrs Chin with, in which we decided that obstruction, fraud and various immigration offences would do to keep them banged up for the duration.

What duration that was depended on them, and so far it was going to be the maximum the law allows followed by deportation.

I spent the rest of the day up in Hornchurch being debriefed by Silver's mob. One of the advantages of the circumstances surrounding my particular covert operation was that I was able to keep my notes up to date during the course of the investigation. My main problem during the debrief was explaining the difference between a pen and paper RPG, a console-based JRPG and a board game such as *Firefly*. And why the gaming sessions had served as an important intelligence-gathering platform.

'Couldn't you have got them drunk?' asked one of the interviewers.

'Trust me,' I said. 'This was more effective.'

Silver herself was off at an inconveniently scheduled wedding, but arrived back in the evening to tell me to go home and take the next day off. Which suited me perfectly right up until the moment I got home and Bev told me that Skinner had fired Tyrel Johnson for cause.

'It's not fair,' she said. 'They needed his salary.'

I wouldn't count on you bowing out gracefully, Silver had told me. *These operations always end messily and nobody likes to be betrayed – however good the cause.*

'Did you know that before Tyrel got that job they were this close—' she held her finger and thumb a centimetre apart – 'to selling their house?'

Unwisely I asked whether social services didn't pay them to foster, which got me a glare, the cold shoulder and the growling Bulge. Although the last one might have been hunger, since I was still cooking dinner at the time.

'You've seen those kids,' she said. 'They need special care and that *costs* – you know that.'

I wanted to say it wasn't my fault, but it sort of was – or at least close enough for me to feel guilty about it.

'You lot are always complaining that everyone expects you to be social workers,' she said. 'You saw what happened with Oliver – you know with boys like that it's one slip and they're sucked into the prison ecosystem. They don't get second chances.'

She wasn't mollified even when I plonked a hill of rice topped by my mum's patented groundnut chicken – spontaneous tongue combustion guaranteed – in front of her. Although the Bulge stopped growling.

'Is he going to be charged with anything?' she asked.

'Tyrel?'

Beverley waved a half-eaten drumstick at me.

368

'Yes, Tyrel,' she said.

'Not that I know of.'

'One slip,' muttered Beverley and then louder. 'I liked them.'

'Maybe you should visit,' I said.

'I did,' said Beverley. 'But Stacy told me to go away.'

'Go away?'

'I'm paraphrasing.'

'And you didn't just charm your way in?' I asked, which got me a hard look.

'That wouldn't have been proper,' she said. 'There's limits.'

'On me too,' I said, and she nodded sadly.

We ate in silence for a bit until Beverley finished her plate and asked if there was seconds. Force of habit meant I'd cooked enough rice for three times as many people and the fridge held a stack of Mum's Tupperware. A couple of these regularly arrived with my mum's twice-weekly visits and despite our best efforts, we were falling behind. To deal with the overspill, Maksim was planning to install a second freezer cabinet in the laundry room next to Beverley's biological sample fridge – the one with the yellow and black biohazard sign on the front.

I microwaved the backup beef knuckle and cassava leaf soup, poured it over another small hill of rice and placed it before my beloved – who was suitably grateful. Outside it started to rain, and I scraped my leftovers into the organic recycle bin and rinsed my plate before putting it in the dishwasher.

Policing doesn't really deal in aftercare – at least not for the victims.

Beverley dropped a denuded knuckle on a side plate and sighed.

'We can sort something out later,' she said. 'Once the dust has settled.'

I started rooting in the fridge for the chocolate cake I'd cunningly hidden in amongst the plastic containers and felt better. Sometimes, when all else fails, a vague aspiration will see you through.

Well, through to morning anyway.

Ten minutes later Guleed called to say that Leo Hoyt had been found dead.

CHAPTER 17

I DON'T BELONG TO ANYONE
ANY MORE

His body was found on Whitmore Road in Hackney, wedged between two parked cars. He had been discovered mid-evening when the owner of one of the cars tried to drive it away and hit an obstruction.

I recognised the location from Leo Hoyt's file as being less than twenty metres from his home address – an ex-council flat on the Colville Estate that had once belonged to his granny. She'd stayed in London when the rest of her family moved to Essex, bought her flat in the first throes of Right to Buy and left it to Leo in her will.

It was also less than five metres from where the Whitmore Road crossed Regent's Canal.

Belgravia MIT were handling the case and if they wanted me contaminating their crime scene they would call me. Besides, Nightingale had already done an initial Falcon assessment which included popping down to the nearby canal moorings to see if anyone had seen anything unusual, or whether anyone unusual had seen anything at all. He promised to let me know if he uncovered anything pertinent.

'But in the morning, Peter,' he said.

It's hard to detach from a case. So over the years I've developed various techniques to help me sleep. In this instance I adopted the 'very boring but necessary book' method – what with my preparation for a sergeant's qualification I was spoilt for choice. But in the end I settled on *The Role of the Father in Child Development*, which one of Beverley's big sisters had given me – I suspect ironically. The joke was on her, because as I settled down with Beverley beside me I barely made it through the preface before dropping off.

It's much harder to keep your detachment at a post-mortem if you know the corpse personally, even if you didn't like them much. So I let Guleed make the trip to the Iain West Memorial Forensic Suite and watch Leo Hoyt be unzipped, but I did agree to meet her at Belgravia nick since they were handling the case.

There's something very comforting about an outside inquiry office when a case has pushed you off balance. You're surrounded by loads of coppers working the phones or the computers, tracing, interviewing, eliminating and grinding down leads until either they vanish or the truth is revealed. Or at least something close enough to the truth to get you a result.

It's like the sea washing onto a beach, soothing, regular and unstoppable.

When I'm working at Belgravia I share a desk with Guleed, so while she was enjoying Leo Hoyt's post-mortem I logged into HOLMES and started going through the action list to see if anything popped up. I started with a keyword search for any mention of Leo Hoyt. Most of them were in the reports I'd written for Silver, but I read them anyway. When I'd finished all that, I felt a weird little discontent like an inaccessible itch. But it wasn't until I was tracing the reconstructed time-line of our raid on Bambleweeny that I realised what it was.

There was no record of Leo calling the police.

'Don't worry,' he'd said to me. 'I hit the panic button.'

But not the one installed by the security company the SCC had contracted to wire up the alarms on every floor except Bambleweeny. Nor, according to the interview Guleed had conducted with Tyrel Johnson, had Leo contacted him. I even called CCC and asked them to check their records in case he'd made a direct 999 call. They had no record of any 999 calls until the flurry that followed Mrs Chin's explosive demolition of the Mary Engine.

So what panic button did he push? And to who, or even whom, was it connected?

Guleed arrived bearing coffee and demanding fritters. I opened the plastic container I'd brought specially and offered the contents to Guleed, who immediately popped a whole one in her mouth and chewed slowly. Post-mortems, however fresh the corpse, leave an unmistakable and persistent smell in the nostrils. Guleed and me had recently discovered that slowly eating one of my mum's cowpea fritters served to completely obliterate that horrible combination smell of disinfectant and off meat. True, it obliterated the rest of your sense of smell as well, but that was a small price to pay.

I have to hide them from Beverley, though. Otherwise there'd be none left for operational use.

'They think he was electrocuted,' said Guleed, when she'd finished swallowing. 'But they're not sure.'

There'd been two contact burns on Leo's neck, as if he'd been tasered. But no gross physiological damage to any organs that Vaughan could find.

'Your boss said he could sense a faint *vestigium* consistent with the drones that attacked you in South Tottenham,' said Guleed. But *vestigia*, like most physical evidence, was subject to cross-contamination and was often ambiguous. And, unlike most forensic evidence, it was definitely, definitely not admissible in court.

'He also wants to see you at the Folly when you finish here,' she said. 'It's all go in the magic police.'

Together we went through Leo Hoyt's timeline, working back from his death.

'He walked down from Dalston,' said Guleed.

There had been a timed and dated receipt from the Tesco Express on Kingsland Road – they found a plastic bag with the purchases underneath a nearby car.

'One loaf extra thick sliced white bread, one pint of Tesco own brand semi-skimmed milk and a 700 ml bottle of passion fruit and mango flavoured alcopop,' said Guleed sadly. 'Made with real fruit juice.'

According to the electoral register he lived alone, and there was no sign at his flat that he had regular visitors.

I pulled up Google Maps and marked the location of the crime scene, the Tesco Express and the Serious Cybernetics Corporation. Leo Hoyt's flat was roughly fifteen minutes' walk southwards from the Tesco and about twenty minutes' walk north of the SCC. You might hop on a bus up the old Roman road to Dalston if you wanted to visit Ridley Road market, but a Tesco Express? They were located all over London – there was one less than a hundred metres from the SCC itself on City Road. Nobody has a favourite Tesco Express.

'Unless he fancied someone in the shop,' said Guleed.

So checking that possibility went on the action list.

Guleed listed his known friends, the majority of them dating back to his schooldays, and their known addresses and I marked them up. Most of them still lived in Essex, although two of them had moved further afield – to Chester and Hastings. All of them would have to be talked to and calling them went on to the action list. Stephanopoulos was likely to bounce some of the routine interviews back in our direction, so we both laid plans to be out of the office when she came in on Monday.

Dalston has two Overground stops, Dalston Kingsland which connects to the east-west route from Stratford to Richmond, and Dalston Junction that runs south across the river. We were going to have to check the CCTV at both stations and when I say 'we', I of course mean some freshly minted DCs attached to Belgravia MIT. They'd work backwards from the timestamp on the Tesco Express receipt, and if they spotted him emerging from the station we'd know which train he came on. And once they had that we could, hopefully, track him back to where he got on.

Guleed made an appointment to meet with Seawoll and the case manager to discuss the new actions, and then wrestled the container of fritters from my grasp.

'You've got an unlimited supply,' she said.

So, bereft of fritters, I schlepped over to the Folly to see what my governor wanted.

On my way in I took the opportunity to ensure the MSA was still in place. After all, this was its first extended test. And it relied on Foxglove, who had an alarming tendency to run out of the Folly and chase down random passers-by who she thought had interesting faces. I'd installed some Mark II magic detectors around the custody suite, just in case. But, having watched the fine control Mrs Chin exercised in her craft, I wasn't sure she couldn't stealth her way past those if she chose.

Once I'd confirmed both she and Stephen were still safely banged up, I went in search of Nightingale, who I found in the number two teaching room – the one he and Abigail had transformed into a metal workshop. Besides the forge, the centrepiece here was a thick oak workbench which had been scored by over a century of careless metal bashing. Nightingale had cleared this and laid out what I recognised as the remains of the Mary Engine.

He grinned when he glanced up.

'Excellent,' he said. 'Come and have a look at this.'

I joined him in front of the table and he asked me whether I could sense any *vestigia*. I let my finger brush against a beautifully tooled steel and brass camshaft – there was a trembling, almost imperceptible, chime that I recognised as Mrs Chin's *signare* and the clockwork tick and willow tree smell that was pure Nightingale.

But nothing else – no other *vestigia* at all.

To be thorough I checked all the assembled

pieces, and bent down to get my face as close as possible.

'Oh, shit,' I said as the implications sank in.

'Precisely,' said Nightingale.

Metal retains *vestigia* very well. And, never mind what it was built for, the Mary Engine had been around enough magic to pick something up.

'I don't suppose the *vestigia* could have been hoovered up?' I asked.

Revenants and vampires, in their quest to sustain themselves, could suck all the *vestigia* out of a locality. Along with, in the case of vampires, all the life as well.

'That's always a possibility,' said Nightingale. 'But in this particular instance I think not.'

'Which means this was – a decoy?'

'Yes, I believe so.'

And realistically only one person could have arranged to have a decoy in place on the top floor of hyper-secure Bambleweeny.

'Skinner,' I said. 'So he knew I was a plant?'

'Did he?' said Nightingale, falling unconsciously into his teacher voice. 'It's never wise, Peter, to assume that events revolve around oneself. We've seen ample evidence Skinner was up against formidable opposition. He may have instituted the deception right from the start. The real Mary Engine may never have entered the building on Tabernacle Road at all. He may have been as utterly surprised at your disclosure as Mr Johnson was.'

'But the effect is the same,' I said. 'Whatever the intention, and whoever the target was, the decoy worked on both of us. And the Librarians.'

'And presumably whomever was the original target.'

'Bugger,' I said.

'Quite,' said Nightingale.

Because Skinner was currently untouchable – hidden behind a wall of lawyers and accountants, many of whom were currently resident in other countries. In time Officer Silver could probably chip away at the money fortress, but her Judicial Disposal was over the policing event horizon and accelerating.

Needless to say, we were not going to be her favourite people.

'Well, you know what you do when you need to look something up,' I said.

Nightingale's lip twitched.

'You ask a librarian.'

My attitude to modernising the Folly was that if you were going to break with tradition you might as well go all the way. So instead of the scarred laminated table so beloved of the Metropolitan Police and television crime dramas, our interview room was large, airy and devoid of tables of any kind. Instead, three metal chairs are bolted to the ground facing three equally bolted down chairs. The suspect – sorry, the interviewee – sits in the middle chair while their brief and/or appropriate adult sit on either side. With no table to hide behind, the interviewee's body language is on full display. So any compulsive leg twitching, foot tapping or other obvious tell can be assessed by the interviewing officer. Just to add insult to injury, the middle chairs are placed five centimetres forward of the others – to make the subject feel that little bit more exposed. Or at least that's the theory.

It didn't seem to be working on Mrs Chin, although the duty solicitor, a pinched-faced white woman in a smart but easy to maintain navy skirt suit, obviously resented not having somewhere to rest her notepad.

Once we'd finished the preliminary sparring, I brought out a heavy-duty clear plastic bag and held it out for Mrs Chin to see. Inside were a selection of bits from the Mary Engine.

'Do you know what this is?'

Mrs Chin sighed, glanced over at her solicitor and said, 'No comment.'

I held the bagged remains out until they almost touched Mrs Chin's knees. The solicitor frowned at me and made a note, but Mrs Chin only looked puzzled.

'That can't be,' she said, paused, and then reached out to brush her fingertips across the plastic surface. She glanced up and gave me a sharp look.

'This is not good,' she said.

'Why?' I asked.

Mrs Chin was silent for a moment before turning to her solicitor and asking her to leave. Having had long experience with police methods, the woman was reluctant to abandon her client and in the end it took Mrs Chin's best librarian glare to drive her off.

Once the solicitor was gone, Mrs Chin turned to me.

'Have you heard of the Rose of New Orleans?' she asked.

'Only that the Rose Jars are named after her,' I said. 'And that she was active in London in the late eighteenth century.'

'That's it?' said Mrs Chin. 'That's all you Brits know?'

'That's all I know,' I said. 'I make no claims for anyone else.'

'Well, she was a woman of colour,' said Mrs Chin. 'Why should she be remembered here?'

As opposed to the statues erected to her all over the States, I thought, but I kept my mouth shut because knee-jerk nationalism is something you're supposed to keep out of the interview room.

'Her name, as far as we know,' said Mrs Chin, 'was Rosemarie Louise Moreno.'

Born in New Orleans to a prosperous 'free coloured' family sometime after 1750, she was definitely educated in Paris and inducted into the *Académie Royale de Philosophie Occulte*. Founded in 1682, it had – unlike the Folly, its British counterpart – enjoyed official royal patronage. Or at least enjoyed it until the royals had their heads cut off.

'In a hundred years only twelve women were ever admitted to the Academy,' said Mrs Chin.

Rosemarie Louise Moreno was resident in Paris until the French Revolution shut the Academy down, after which the Librarians believed she surfaced in London.

'Or to be precise,' said Mrs Chin, 'a certain Rosemary of New Orleans is mentioned in the letters of Elizabeth Montagu.'

The original bluestocking and famous society hostess. Certainly, this Rosemary was the right age, nationality and colour – coincidence? The Librarians didn't think so.

They also thought she had brought certain techniques to London from Paris.

'Some argue that she was building off her New Orleans magical heritage,' said Mrs Chin. 'But it's much more likely that it was knowledge developed at the Academy.'

Knowledge that was lost to the French when Napoleon reconstituted the *Académie de Philosophie Occulte* in 1804, but without its female members. And presumably never gained by the Folly because they were a bunch of stuffy white aristocrats.

I personally think Mrs Chin would have been surprised by the collection of chancers, quacks, mountebanks and dilettantes that coalesced into the Society of the Wise around the same period.

But I wasn't in that interview room to discuss comparative historiography.

The knowledge brought over by Rosemary included the eponymous Rose Jars, although Professor Postmartin, who we outsource our erudition to, pointed out later that we had evidence of their use decades prior to the French Revolution.

Rosemary was also a known associate of Mary Somerville, which gave her a direct connection to Ada Lovelace and Charles Babbage. The Librarians believed that the secret knowledge she held had been passed on – specifically relating to the construction of the Mary Engine.

'Secret knowledge of what?' I asked.

Mrs Chin hesitated and then came to a decision.

'How to make magic,' she said.

'In what sense?' I asked, although I had a pretty good idea already.

'In the sense of making magical power,' said Mrs Chin.

'So you think the Mary Engine is a . . . what?'

'A machine for generating magic in industrial quantities,' said Mrs Chin.

I thought of Martin Chorley scrabbling around with his ludicrous schemes to generate magical power from ancient gods and enchanted tower blocks, and all the time he had the key to his mad ambition in a lock-up in Marble Arch.

You had to laugh.

'This isn't funny,' said Mrs Chin.

'It's a London thing,' I said.

Mrs Chin rapped her knuckles on the remains of the fake Mary Engine like an angry teacher.

'If this is a fake, then you have to recover the original,' she said. 'If you won't let us keep it safe, then you should destroy it yourself.'

'Why?'

'Are you stupid?' she asked. 'How do you think they made those drones?'

And suddenly I saw the whole operation in my head. The drones were manufactured off site at the abandoned internet café in Gillingham. Then, after the likes of Barry and Jade had left for the night, person or persons unknown tooled up with the Mary Engine in a van, zapped magic into the drones, loaded them into the back of said van and away they went.

I know they must have done the zapping at the Print Shop because the *vestigium* had still been so vivid there. But why? Why not pack up the drones in the van and take them back to base to be zapped? Why risk taking the Mary Engine out?

And magical power, as far as our limited understanding went, wouldn't animate a drone – you'd need a proper spell for that. A string of *formae*, *adjectiva* and *inflectentes* that used magic to change the physical world.

A string of operations like you'd find in a computer program, I thought. And had we been living in a rational world a light bulb would have appeared above my head.

'*The Enchantress of Numbers?*' I asked. 'A program?'

'That was my theory, yes,' said Mrs Chin. 'I assume the drones were enchanted using a similar program, although I've never heard of an enchantment that could make an automaton walk – let alone fly.'

'That knowledge might have come from tenth-century Baghdad,' I said.

'Interesting,' said Mrs Chin. 'What makes you say that?'

I was tempted to tell her that we had a book in *our* library that had to be restrained from roaming around the Folly on its own, but I didn't trust her enough to be giving away state secrets just to big up my ends.

'I might tell you,' I said. 'If you promise to be good.'

Mrs Chin sniffed.

'There's another thing,' she said. 'We have a letter from the Rose herself in which she urges Ada Lovelace to dismantle the engine and burn the plans.'

'Does she say why?'

'As I remember the quote,' she said, 'Rosemarie writes *you may believe yourself to have created an engine of the spirit but I fear that you have instead opened a portal into darkness.*'

'A portal into darkness?' I said.

'That bit I'm sure of,' said Mrs Chin.

I thought of the horrible dead fish *vestigium* that had clung to the drones, the Print Shop and, worst of all, the demon trap I'd stepped on in Tottenham. Maybe it tapped into one of the *baccaliaos allokosmoi* – the dimension of rotting seafood.

'Just because the *vestigium* stinks doesn't mean it's a portal into darkness,' I said.

'Because what would the Rose of New Orleans know about anything?' said Mrs Chin. 'She was only the foremost practitioner of her generation.'

'Are you willing to share that letter?' I asked.

'A copy, sure,' said Mrs Chin. 'Assuming you ever let me out.'

'Sooner,' I said. 'Rather than later. Especially if you help us get this sorted.'

'I shall be co-operation itself,' she said.

It was a stupid question but I had to ask her whether she knew the current whereabouts of the Mary Engine. She made it clear that even if she did know – and I can't imagine why would she have gone on a raid with me if she had – she wouldn't tell me.

'I thought you wanted it destroyed,' I said.

'I'm not sure I trust you to do it,' she said.

I called the solicitor back in and terminated the interview. The solicitor wanted access to the PACE mandated recording – particularly the bit she wasn't in the room for – but I said that would be up to Mrs Chin.

And then I walked away with the cheerful step of a police officer who's just made a tricky ethical question somebody else's problem. When I checked my phone there was a message from Silver to call her back. I paused at the custody desk and rang her on my mobile.

'September Rain has been detained at Gatwick Airport,' she said.

'Why?' I asked.

'I issued a stop order on her,' said Silver, and pointed out that Ms Rain had been practically living in Terrence Skinner's pocket since they'd both arrived in the UK. 'If anybody knows where the bodies are buried it will be her.'

'Can I interview her?' I asked.

'That's the plan,' she said.

CHAPTER 18

AN EXTENSION OF THAT QUALITY

We let Border Force hold her until Monday morning, at which point a couple of Silver's officers picked her up and brought her to the Folly. While she was in transit we had a pre-interview strategy meeting in the breakfast room which included Stephanopoulos, Silver and Guleed – it's amazing how easy it is to persuade senior officers to attend meetings when Molly does the catering.

We decided that we would play it talkative cop/silent cop, with Guleed playing the role of the quiet cop who watches the proceedings with a sinister knowing expression. You can guess who got to be the mouthy one.

September Rain had the same duty solicitor as Mrs Chin and she was probably wondering what dreadful sin she'd committed in a previous life to end up back in this strange nick, with its uncooperative American prisoners and no bloody place to rest your bloody notepad.

September was attempting to lounge comfortably in a seat that had been specifically designed to make that impossible. Since we weren't looking for any forensics we allowed her to wear clean clothes from her luggage, a pair of skinny jeans and a plain black sleeveless blouse. To minimise her tells she'd jammed her hands into her pockets and crossed her legs at her ankles – it made her look like a sulky teenager.

'You were stopped at Gatwick Airport prior to your boarding a flight for Mitchell International Airport in Milwaukee,' I said. 'Why Wisconsin? I thought you were from California?'

'No comment,' she said.

'You don't have any family in Milwaukee, do you?' I asked. 'Brothers, sisters, cousins – friendly neighbour with a beard?'

We knew she didn't, because Reynolds had sent me her known associates list the week before, along with Bradley Michael Smith's and all the other American members of Total Executive Cover.

'There was a flight to New York less than two hours later and another to Los Angeles an hour after that,' I said. 'Both had seats available. Wouldn't either of those be more convenient? You didn't book any connecting flights, so what was your plan? Buy one when you got there or travel on by road?'

Reynolds had assured me that, while September had attended a very comprehensive bodyguard course, she didn't have any military or police experience. Certainly no interview or interrogation training – looking cool in shades, defensive driving and knowing when to take a bullet for your principal was a completely different skill set.

'You were actually in a taxi heading for Paddington when you made the booking,' I said. 'You then switched destination to Victoria to catch the Gatwick Express.'

She glanced away, but the room was designed to drag the interviewee's gaze back to the interviewer.

'You know what that sounds like to me?' I said when she was looking at me again. 'It sounds like someone catching the first possible flight to the States – wherever it was going, and whatever airport it was leaving from. Well – maybe not Southend.'

I leaned forward a bit – keeping eye contact.

'You should have caught the Eurostar,' I said. 'You could have turned up with thirty minutes to go and been in Paris or Brussels in less than three hours, and then you'd have the whole Schengen area to lose yourself in.'

A little crease in her forehead.

'You know what the Schengen agreement is, don't you?'

Her lips thinned as she stopped herself from answering.

'I totally understand,' I said. 'You're an American, this is your first trip abroad. Your instinct was to go straight back home to the good old U.S. of A. Like I said, totally understandable. You weren't thinking straight, were you?'

Definite flinch this time. And the creases between her eyes deepened.

'But here's the thing,' I said. 'I've seen you in action, so I know you don't panic when the shit hits the fan and that you have physical courage.' I saw just a hint of a smirk – everyone likes praise. 'So what terrified you to the point where you ran for home? Not a threat to yourself, because you'd stand your ground. And not a threat to somebody else because, you know, same. Not a physical threat at all, in fact.'

A definite increase in tension around the mouth, and the eyes flicked to the left again. You can read a whole pile of books about tells and micro-expressions, but it's never going to be an exact science on account of everyone being uniquely different from everyone else. Still, that flick to the left betrayed her.

'You consider yourself an honest type of person, don't you?' I said. 'Straight shooter, say it as you see it, call a spade a spade, give the dog a bone, get the job done, do an honest day's work for an honest day's pay – so what did Terrence Skinner do, September? What did he do that had you running for cover?'

There'd been a little jump on Skinner's name.

'Inappropriate sexual contact?'

Another frown, because a female bodyguard knows how to deal with that sort of thing – especially in Hollywood. In the pre-interview discussion Stephanopoulos and Guleed thought

391

it was unlikely. We had a very good idea what had caused September Rain to quit the employ of Terrence Skinner. But having a good idea is not the same as knowing for sure – let alone having evidence of it.

'We've had your FBI file sent over,' I said, and that provoked an actual physical start.

I wondered what she'd done that she thought the FBI might be interested in, or how surprised she'd be to know that it was mostly gossip from the LA office that Reynolds had hit up a few old mates for. Facebook and Amazon most likely had better files on September than the FBI had – although that was probably about to change.

'So I know that some of your former clients haven't been beyond a bit of recreational drug use, occasional rages and sexual assault allegations,' I said.

September gave a little shrug and tilted her head slightly to the left.

Her contract with one client had finished when he was arrested for sexual assault. Ultimately the charges had been dropped and Reynolds said that her contact in LA was adamant that September might have been a witness, but had refused to answer questions. Loyalty, or a fat termination fee plus NDA – nobody was sure.

'So a bit of drugs, violence and rape wasn't going to bother you much, was it?' I said, and she flinched again. Not so professionally impassive that she didn't want me to think she stood aloof during an actual attack.

'Pride,' Stephanopoulos had said. 'She doesn't want you looking down on her.'

'I understand totally,' I said. 'Professional ethics and all that, isn't it? You couldn't grass up your client but at the same time you didn't want to be party to anything worse. You must have loved Skinner when you started working for him. I mean, he's bad news for crabs and personal data protection, but he's not a noted groper or fighter.'

I paused to make sure she was following my logic. You can be too clever during an interview and a common tactic for interviewees is to zone out and stop listening. Varying the pitch of your speech helps, as does working in tandem with another officer – me and Guleed have a nice line in this, of which mouthy cop/thoughtful cop was only one of many variations. Although Stephanopoulos has banned us from using the one where we both pretend to be speaking Wakandan.

'Has he ever made a grab?' I asked.

'I'm not his type,' said September – finally.

'What is his type?' I asked.

'Petite, Japanese, passive-aggressive,' she said. 'He learnt Japanese so he could hit on the booth bunnies at trade shows.'

'Really?' I said, hoping to strengthen the engagement. 'Did it work?'

September gave me a contemptuous look, tinged with a bit of disappointment.

'Of course it worked,' she said. 'These billion-aires always get what they want – in the end.'

Interesting, I thought – a little bit of class warfare.

'Not always,' I said as primly as I could.

'Tell that to Jeffrey Epstein,' she said, which meant nothing to me at the time.

'So what did he do?' I said, meaning Terrence Skinner – but looking back at the transcript it was obviously ambiguous. Still, just as you can outsmart yourself you can out-stupid yourself. The key to success then is your follow-through.

'Sex trafficking of minors,' she said, which sounded unlikely for Skinner so I guessed she meant this Epstein person.

'Japanese minors?' I asked, because a little bit of deliberate misunderstanding can smooth the way to the truth.

'What?' September seemed genuinely confused.

'You said Uncle Terrence was trafficking minors,' I said.

'No,' she said – outraged.

'Because you wouldn't put up with that, would you?'

'What do you think?'

What I thought was that I needed to get the interview refocused.

'I think it was murder,' I said.

This time she flinched back in her chair hard enough for her ankles to uncross.

'I think you know he murdered someone, but

you only found out afterwards when it was too late,' I said. 'Instead of reporting it to us, you decided to get the hell out of Dodge. Was that your professional ethics? Client confidentiality?'

September looked deeply unhappy at that.

Guleed crossed her arms, which was her signal to me to shut up for a bit.

September frowned at her, then at me, and then turned to look at her solicitor.

'My client—' started the solicitor, but September interrupted.

'I didn't know anything for certain,' she said. 'It would have been pointless to call the police, and frankly I didn't want to get involved.'

'Why don't you tell us what you do know?' said Guleed. 'And then perhaps we can send you on your way.'

September opened her mouth, but her solicitor coughed and put a hand on her shoulder.

'I'd like a word with my client first,' she said.

So we suspended the interview while they had a chat and headed out to the custody desk, where Foxglove had persuaded Sergeant Finnegan to pose heroically in the manner of a seventeenth-century monarch. We took the opportunity to pop upstairs for coffee and cake and, to prove that we weren't heartless, brought some down to use as a reward if September co-operated.

The solicitor was obviously not that happy with the idea of trusting our integrity, not even after I gave her a cupcake with pink icing and smiley face made from Smarties. Still September, like most people, needed to sing. Because then it stopped being her problem – didn't it?

'He got a text that upset him,' she said.

'Where was this?'

'In the penthouse,' she said.

'When?' I asked.

'Last Saturday, early evening.'

'When early evening?'

'About 6.30.'

I deliberately paused to make a note.

'So about this text?' I asked.

'It came in on a cell phone I didn't know he had,' said September. 'It seemed to upset him.'

'Upset him how?' I asked.

'He doesn't normally show emotions,' she said. 'He's like you Brits, only the Australian version. So when he started saying the C-word – I was shocked.'

I exchanged looks with Guleed – September obviously didn't know Australians as well as she thought she did.

'What did he say?' asked Guleed. 'What was the context?'

'There wasn't any,' said September. 'He just kept saying the C-word over and over again, under his breath – "cuntcuntcuntcunt" – like that.'

Then he'd stepped out onto the balcony and dialled a number on the mobile – which September thought was probably a cheap burner – and closed the sliding doors behind him.

'He didn't want me to overhear him,' she said. 'But I can lip-read so I knew what he was saying.'

'And what was he saying?' asked Guleed quickly – possibly to stop me from asking September the hows and whys of her learning to lip-read. It's not a common skill amongst the non-hearing impaired – I made a mental note to ask her as a follow-up.

'He said, "But he was helpful," and then, "Are you sure?" I think that was a question, but I missed the next bit because he turned away.'

'Did he turn back?' asked Guleed.

'No, he put the cell phone away and stood out in the cold for at least ten minutes,' said September.

She thought he might have texted someone before he came back in and gave September her instructions.

Skinner fished yet another burner phone from a locked drawer in his desk and handed it to September. She was to wait until it was time for her regular run up the canal and hand the mobile over to Leo Hoyt, who would be waiting for her at Camden Lock.

It was a good plan. Skinner's penthouse flat stood right next to Regent's Canal and the towpath formed a convenient pedestrian shortcut all the way to Camden and as far as the Islington Tunnel in the east. The tunnel was inaccessible to foot traffic but beyond it the canal ran further east –

right past Whitmore Road, where Leo Hoyt had been found murdered.

September Rain frequently went for runs along the towpath when she was off duty. These were carefully noted in the surveillance logs of the team that Silver had watching Skinner, but the budget didn't stretch to following September when she went jogging.

'Did you make the rendezvous?' asked Guleed.

September said that of course she had – in fact she'd had to wait around a bit because she'd done the distance in record time. When Leo Hoyt turned up she handed over the burner phone and then jogged back the way she'd come.

'How did he seem?' I asked.

'Pleased with himself,' said September. 'I think the boss had offered him Tyrel's job.'

I thought of the contents of Leo's shopping bag – the booze – a celebration perhaps. The route made sense now – Camden Road Overground station to Dalston Kingsland, into the Tesco Local for a celebratory bottle of Hooch Tropical and off home with a skip in his step.

And a murderous drone zeroing in on the mobile phone Terrence Skinner had given him.

'And that was the last time you saw him?' I said.

'Yes.'

'Did you see or hear anything else on the towpath when you ran back?'

'Like people?'

'Like something else. A drone, or more than one,' I said.

I was thinking that poor Leo was found less than ten metres from where the Whitmore Bridge crossed Regent's Canal and that, after dark, you could have as many drones as you like zip along the canal – through the Islington Tunnel – to hover in ambush under that bridge.

'No,' said September. 'A couple of guys on bikes is all.'

We asked a couple more questions, partly to nail down the timeline but mostly to change the rhythm of the interview.

'This all seems very innocuous,' said Guleed. 'I don't really understand why any of this would make you run for home. Are you sure you weren't just homesick?'

September visibly bristled, as Guleed had intended her to – now she had something to prove.

'He was waiting for me when I got back, stopped me before I could have a shower to check that I'd handed over the phone,' she said. 'He was sweaty and nervous, which wasn't like him. When he went back to the top floor I followed him up and slipped into the kitchen – fixed myself a smoothie.'

There must have been something in my expression, because she chuckled.

'In case he caught me,' she said. 'I know, right? As if I was a kid again.'

And like a kid eavesdropping on her parents, she didn't understand half of what she heard and was disappointed by what she did.

'He said, "He's in position, so we can get on with the transaction." Then a pause and then he asked whether it was necessary.'

'Whether what was necessary?' asked Guleed.

'What do you think he was talking about?' said September. 'I didn't know, not then. I didn't figure it out until the next morning when Bradley called to tell me Leo was dead and even then . . .' She looked away – avoiding eye contact. 'I woke Terry up and told him and he sighed. Like it was bad news he was expecting. That's when I knew.'

She'd been right. It wasn't much in the way of evidence. But now we knew what we were looking for – two burner phones, drone sightings, a reason for Terrence Skinner to want someone as innocuous as Leo Hoyt dead – we had a chance to latch on to a line of inquiry. Policing is about moving from the unknown to the known and then further – to the provable.

So we went back to the conversation.

'Did you overhear anything else?' I asked.

'He said, "It should be ready soon,"' – but she didn't know what 'it' was or how soon 'soon' was. The conversation had obviously gone round and round on those points. Was 'something' really necessary and 'it would be ready soon'. Skinner's tone had been placating, wheedling.

'Not his usual billionaire self,' she said.

'When did you decide to make a run for it?' asked Guleed.

'I was planning it as soon as I saw his reaction yesterday morning,' she said. 'After he went out I gave it half an hour, grabbed my stuff, and got out.'

'Why did you wait half an hour?' I asked, to cover my surprise. Because, according to Silver, Skinner was still safely tucked up in the penthouse.

'I wanted to make sure he was clear of the area,' she said.

'Any idea where he went?' I asked.

'Why?' said September with a sly smile. 'Don't you have him under surveillance?'

'We're the police,' I said. 'Not the security services.'

September shrugged.

'Same difference,' she said.

The observation room was right next door to us, but I would have thought that the double course of solid red brick between would have muffled the sound of Silver yelling into her phone more than it did. I did my best to ignore it.

'So where do you think he went?' I asked.

September thought he'd gone wherever it was he went whenever he went without her.

'I wasn't happy about letting him out of the perimeter, but it was only once or twice a week and I assumed it was a sex thing,' she said, 'You can't argue with clients when it's a sex thing – they just get stubborn.'

Guleed was the one wearing the Bluetooth earpiece connected to the observation room, so I assume it was Silver who prompted her to ask how Skinner left the penthouse unobserved.

'There's a third exit out through the building next door,' said September.

Silver had already ordered her team to arrest Skinner before me and Guleed were out of the interview room. But it was too late – he was gone.

Nightingale headed with Silver to the penthouse to cover any Falcon aspect, while I went with Guleed to Belgravia to feed the voracious maw of HOLMES on the off chance that it might reciprocate and spit out something exciting. We were soon generating actions with gay abandon. Mostly this was door to door, or rather mooring to mooring – inquiries along Regent's Canal asking bemused boat owners and runners whether they'd seen or heard anything in the hours before Leo Hoyt's murder. This was going to be man-power intensive and I added an action for myself to see if I couldn't locate the Goddess of the Canal. After all, it was her who had provided me with that first drowned drone down by Skinner's penthouse.

Before I could set out to look for her, I got an email from Reynolds containing scans of Anthony

Lane's manifesto – the one he'd had on his person before murdering Branwell Petersen and shooting up his lab in San Jose. Stained with his own blood, parts of it were illegible. But fortunately the FBI labs had managed to bring out the obscured sections and provide a transcript.

The opening paragraph started *A LINE MUST BE DRAWN*, all in caps before settling down to three or four pages of what would have looked like deranged gibberish – to someone who hadn't spent just over three years learning magic. With that knowledge, the writing ceased to be gibberish and became merely deranged.

According to Anthony Lane, God gave the gift of spirit not just to man or living things but to all creation. So that everything – rocks, trees, my dad's stereo – was imbued with a sort of consciousness. Postmartin has explained to me that such a belief system is called *animism* and is very widespread, especially in those places where the locals were sensible enough to eat any missionaries before they could open their mouths. My mum, once you're past her surface Christianity, believes in this stuff. And I personally don't so much believe in it as have to massage its feet when I go home at night.

Certain people were selected by God to be custodians of the world. These people were given great gifts, again in capitals – *GREAT GIFTS*, to *DEFEND* the natural world order. But *MEN* had taught themselves to *MANIPULATE THE*

SPIRIT OF THE WORLD and have used that knowledge to *USURP* the *NATURAL ORDER*.

There then followed a long list of calamities that Anthony Lane blamed on those who *USURPED THE NATURAL ORDER*, including but not limited to the current drought in California, over-population, illegal immigration and the opioid addiction crisis in the American Midwest. They were *LEECHES* who sucked the very spirit from the world.

At no point did Anthony Lane refer to these *LEECHES* as practitioners, or even wizards or witches, but it was clear from the third paragraph on that that was who he meant. I wasn't sure what my exact role in the misselling of Fentanyl was supposed to be but I'm sure, if he hadn't been shot dead, Anthony would have told me. Probably at great length.

The last half of the manifesto dealt with the imminent arrival of *LATE STAGE USURP-ATION* in which the leeches would apply industrial processes to their misuse of the world's spirit and *STRIP-MINE THE VERY SOUL OF THE PLANET*.

Reynolds had noted that analysis of Anthony Lane's social media accounts had found that these phrases had been frequently used in conver-sations he'd had with others on Twitter, Facebook and, dating as far back as 2007, LiveJournal. All of the associated accounts had, suspiciously, been closed within a week of the San Jose attack. The

FBI's counterterrorism analysts' general assessment was that there were more than a hundred active adherents – that was the word the FBI used – adherents to the doctrine of the ASU – Against Spiritual Usurpation. Reynolds said she'd got the impression the Counterterrorism Analysis section hadn't taken it very seriously.

While I read it through again, I had two thoughts. One was that magic on an industrial scale was exactly what the Mary Engine was for, and two: 'leech' was what Jade had shouted when she tried to stab us up in Gillingham.

Which was contradictory, weren't it? Because Jade had been definitely engaged in some late stage usurpation, what with the Print Shop's mass-producing magical devices. Whoever had demon-trapped Stephen's flat and set the drones on us at Mrs Chin's place had access to the Mary Engine. And presumably the only person with a Mary Engine was Terrence Skinner – current location unknown.

And if Skinner had known about Stephen, why had he let him run around inside the Serious Cybernetics Corporation?

This was assuming there was only one Mary Engine – not a safe assumption at all.

One thing I was fairly certain of was that wherever Skinner had been sneaking off to, that was where he'd stashed the Mary Engine. Silver had a bunch of her officers running down Skinner's tangle of shell companies looking for properties,

Guleed was organising a CCTV search around the penthouse to see if we could follow Skinner that way, and Nightingale would be canvassing the demi-monde.

So I decided to see if someone had already done the work for us.

I went back home and did something I hadn't done in a long time – I put my uniform back on, including my Metvest. True, it remained as scratchy as ever and as stylish as a church hall disco, but just then nothing could have fitted me better. I was done fucking about in the shadows – it was time to get legal.

Then, literally armoured, I drove over to the Johnson house and rang the bell.

Stacy answered the door.

'Fuck off, you fucking cunt,' she said.

'Did that ever work on you?' I asked.

'No, but I wasn't a fucking cunt,' she said. 'Was I?'

'I need to talk to Tyrel,' I said.

'That's Mister fucking Johnson to you,' she said, but she hadn't shut the door in my face. Which meant she was going to let me in, eventually, after she'd had her say.

'I'm not being funny,' she said. 'But it's Bev I feel sorry for. How she can stand to be around such a lying, duplicitous sack of shit is beyond me.'

'That reminds me,' I said, and held up a plastic shopping bag.

She wanted to carry on swearing but she also wanted to know what was in the bag.

'What's that?'

'It's the root ginger you liked,' I said.

'Don't want it,' she said.

'It's not from me,' I said. 'It's from Bev.'

'Fine,' she said, and held out a hand. 'Hand it over.'

Once she had the bag, she turned on her heel and walked away.

'Tyrel's in the living room,' she said over her shoulder.

Johnson wasn't happy to see me, either. But at least he didn't call me a cunt.

He was lying on the sofa in a pair of blue tracksuit bottoms and a red T-shirt, legs crossed at the ankle, head propped up on a cushion so that he could see the TV.

'Why are you in uniform?' he asked.

'I missed it,' I said. 'Don't you?'

'I loved being spat at,' said Johnson. 'And the trousers never fit properly.'

I didn't tell him that *my* uniform trousers, along with the shirts, had all been slyly tailored by Molly when I wasn't looking and fit perfectly.

'Do you want a drink?'

'I'm on duty,' I said.

'Well, I'm not,' he said. 'So I'll have a large one. Scotch.'

I poured him a large one into a cut-glass tumbler and handed it over. Johnson waved me into a chair. I wasn't used to wearing so much kit and the belt dug into my hip when I sat down. Johnson saw my discomfort and laughed as I adjusted the strap on my pepper spray.

'You look like a bargain carousel at the pound shop,' he said. 'Is this supposed to impress me, or remind me how lucky I am to be out of the Job?'

'To be honest,' I said, 'I have no fucking idea.'

Johnson rotated his legs off the sofa and sat up.

'You know that Somali DS, right?'

'Sahra?' I said. 'Sahra Guleed? Worked with her loads of times.'

'That's a good interview technique she's got,' said Johnson. 'A bit wasted on me, though.'

'Why's that?'

'I didn't know anything, did I?' he said. 'Didn't know about you, your bloody accomplice or even that Skinner was up to no good. He was a rich man, so of course he was up to no good. But it was a good job so I wasn't paying proper attention.'

'That's not true though, is it?' I said. 'I know you know something.'

'What makes you think that?'

'Because you're police.'

'Ex-police.'

'Good police,' I said. 'Too good not to know something.'

'What is it you think I know?'

'I don't know,' I said. 'That's why I'm asking.'

'And why should I tell you?'

'Because then you'll know I know you're a good copper and we can get past this and do some good together.'

'Which will be what?'

'Only one way to find out,' I said.

'Actually it was Leo who sniffed it out,' said Johnson. 'Boy had a real talent. Sniffed it out and brought it to me and I was wondering what to do with it when you made the whole thing irrelevant.'

'So what did Leo sniff out?'

'Skinner has a warehouse down in the Medway Ports,' said Johnson. 'Kept it right off the books.'

CHAPTER 19

THE LOOT BOX

I'm an inner London boy born and bred, so I didn't grow up amongst hypermarkets and shopping malls. Industrial parks to me were repurposed warehouses or box sheds crammed together on reclaimed railway land. Gillingham Business Park, on the other hand, was a sort of garden-suburb industrial stroke retail park. Once you turned off the A2 it was a network of tree-lined two-way roads, except instead of rows of identical semis you had huge business concerns instead – retail towards the front, increasingly industrial towards the back.

We'd already pinpointed the location on Google Maps so it was an easy matter to cruise slowly past, as if we were lost amongst the maze of identical leafy streets and mini-roundabouts.

Skinner's warehouse, like most of the rest of the business park, was what architects and builders call a crinkly tin shed. Basically you slap down a concrete base, assemble a steel portal frame and hang composite insulated panels from it to form the envelope. Bish, bash, bosh. Instant warehouse, factory, retail outlet. You can make them as big or as small as you like – this one was medium, a hundred metres long, thirty wide and two storeys high – sandwiched between a Parcelforce depot and an empty lot.

After a quick drive past, we doubled back and stopped across the road in a car park attached to an ice-skating rink. Unlike the rest of the car parks, which were employee only, this one was open to the public so we wouldn't stand out and get spotted. Well, probably wouldn't.

From our position we could see the front of the warehouse. Unlike most of the industrial units, where the staff car park and the entrances were on the long side of the building, Skinner's warehouse had its main entrance at the narrow end facing the street. There was no visible signage indicating who the building belonged to – obviously if you didn't know what was there, they weren't going to tell you. Outside we could see a black Range Rover with illegally tinted windows, a dark blue old model Ford Transit van, an Audi and a VW Polo.

We were too far away to clock the indexes, so I got out of the Asbo and stepped far enough away so that I wouldn't sand the electronics or Guleed's phone, and cast *telescopium*. This shaped the air into lenses to form a crude telescope – modern wizards prefer using binoculars, partly because it's less of a faff but mostly because it's not possible to set yourself on fire by accident when using them. I noted down the licence plate numbers, got back in the Asbo and emailed them off to the inside inquiry office to check.

The Range Rover and the Transit van were registered to the Serious Cybernetics Corporation, and the other two were owned by a retired schoolteacher in Dunfermline and a solicitor in Preston.

'What do you want to bet that those are duplicates?' said Guleed.

If you want to drive around in a stolen vehicle without getting stopped or picked up on ANPR then the best way is to attach fake plates. If you're clever, you pick an index belonging to some blameless low-risk individual who drives the same make and model as your stolen car. There's a lively market for suitable numbers on the so-called 'dark web', or if you're a traditionalist you can pick an individual and steal a car that matches theirs.

While I'd been scoping the cars, I'd noticed that the empty lot wasn't totally empty. A row of three articulated lorries were parked close to the fence line. Each one had a dented shipping container mounted on its trailer, with its rear end pointing at the warehouse.

The empty lot was a large expanse of cheap gravel mottled with weeds and wild grass that had obviously been empty for years. Waiting in vain for that lucky customer who was looking for some light industrial space close to the Medway Ports.

Guleed nodded at the articulated lorries.

'I wonder what's in those,' she said. 'They look like they're lined up with the loading bays.'

It was true. Unlike the main entrance, the warehouse's big freight doors were in the side facing the empty lot. There were three of them, and they lined up with an articulated lorry each.

'Could be a coincidence,' I said.

'Yeah,' she said. 'But we're going to have to check them anyway – before we do anything else.'

'Let's go and have a bit of a look, then,' I said.

But Guleed wasn't happy about us being out the front and leaving the rear of the warehouse unsupervised. Neither of us wanted to call in the cavalry until we were sure that the cattle baron and his henchpeople were in residence, so we compromised and called PC Maginty, of the Gillingham Safer Neighbourhood Team, instead.

'He is the closest, after all,' I said.

His neighbourhood must have been unusually safe because he picked up on the second ring and agreed immediately to help.

'He's got the Falcon bug,' said Guleed when I told her. 'Once you have a taste of it, you start gagging for more magic in your life.'

'Is that so?'

'You should know,' she said. 'You're the poster boy for it.'

While we waited for Maginty, we rooted around in the stake-out bag for snacks. Unfortunately, my suspension followed by my stint undercover meant I hadn't done any proper surveillance for a while and the score was meagre.

'Percy Pig?' asked Guleed, holding up the pack.

'I got them for Brent,' I said.

Fortunately, there was a packet of Marks & Spencer ginger nuts and two bottles of lukewarm Highland Spring.

'They're not thrilled,' said Guleed suddenly.

'What?'

'Michael's family in Hong Kong,' said Guleed. 'They're not thrilled. About the melanin thing.'

'Ah.'

'Not that anyone said anything,' she said. 'Nobody . . . objected. Certainly not in front of me. Not in English anyway but, you know, there was that ripple when I was introduced. That hesitation – you know?'

'Yeah,' I said. 'That.'

'Like they were all carefully reviewing their next words just in case something slipped out. Something unfortunate.' She sighed. 'And my problem is that I don't know whether I want to put up with that – whether I *can* put up with that.'

'Do you love him?'

Guleed looked shocked.

'Say that again.'

'Say what?'

'That. That word.'

'What? Love?'

Guleed laughed.

'I've never heard you use that word before,' she said. 'At least not seriously. Who are you, and what have you done with the real Peter Grant?'

'Stop avoiding the question,' I said.

'What was the question again?'

'Do you love him?'

This time Guleed covered her mouth to smother her laughter.

'It's not that funny,' I said.

'Not for you maybe,' she said. 'But for everybody else . . .'

I waited with as much dignity as I could muster.

'Yes, I love him,' she said finally. 'Does that make a difference?'

'What do you think?' I said, which is my shrink's favourite comeback.

'I didn't ask him to convert, you know,' she said. 'He volunteered – I'd have married him in a registry office with no fuss.'

'I bet your parents would have loved that.'

'They love him more than they love me,' she said.

'Maybe his family will get used to you.'

'You mean the same way they would chronic back pain,' said Guleed.

I was about to say that they might actually change, when a blue Hyundai pulled in beside us. Maginty had brought along his skipper – a short, round Asian sergeant by the name of Yasmin Mahmood.

'I don't trust him out on his own,' she said, after we were introduced. 'He's been led into bad ways.'

Given that Maginty still had sterile dressings on his forehead and right cheek, I didn't think I could argue.

As police, we are perfectly entitled to stick our noses in where we're not wanted. However, because Terrence Skinner and God knows what in the way of destructive Falcon material might be in the warehouse, we didn't want anyone inside to clock that we were sniffing around. The problem was that with the expanse of weed-strewn emptiness around the lorries it was going to be hard to get close without looking suspicious.

'That might be why they're parked where they are,' said Guleed.

But luckily, as police, we also knew that people in general wandered through life in a state of blissful obliviousness, and that if you were swift and didn't act suspiciously you could cross thirty-odd metres of open ground without drawing attention.

Nine times out of ten.

As we strolled across, Guleed asked me whether me and Beverley were going to get married.

'That's a good question,' I said. 'We've talked about it, but there's problems.'

'Like what?' Guleed sounded sceptical.

'Ceremonies,' I said, 'can be dangerous things around people like Bev. We don't want to get hitched and then find it's necessary to spend every second Sunday outside the New Malden branch of Dreams scattering rose petals into the culvert to keep the relationship going.'

'Is that sort of thing likely?'

'I don't know,' I said. 'Neither does anyone else.'

'Seems far-fetched,' she said. 'Why don't you just say you don't want to get married?'

'Let's just say we want to take it slowly,' I said.

'Slowly,' said Guleed. 'You're having kids!'

'All the more reason to wait until they're old enough to express an opinion,' I said, and Guleed snorted.

'I'm going to hold you to that,' she said as we fetched up at the rear of the first artic.

We'd brought a bolt cutter, but in any event the rear door was unlocked – although I had to perch on a narrow ledge along the back to get it open. The container was only half full and my penlight illuminated a wall of all too familiar greasy grey-green plastic. As I climbed inside I sensed an equally familiar *vestigium* – the same rotting fish smell like a *plateau de fruits de mer* that had been left in the sun for three days straight.

What appeared to be a solid wall of plastic wasn't, of course. I could trace the outline of a mechanical torso, the lines where one drone's wings fitted between another's legs. It was a three-dimensional puzzle constructed out of drones – they seemed dormant at first, but as I got closer I heard a noise. A high-pitched fluttering buzz like the wings of a fly vibrating against a window pane.

I estimated that half the length of the container was packed with sleeping drones. A solid forty cubic metres of the fuckers. I backed slowly out of the container and climbed down onto the gravel.

'And?' asked Guleed.

'We call everyone in,' I said.

It took them an hour to arrive, which gave us plenty of time to check the other two containers. The middle one was empty but the third was completely packed.

'What are they for?' asked Guleed, as we walked away even more briskly than we'd approached.

'Nothing good,' I said.

While we waited for Nightingale to arrive, Guleed ferreted out the site manager and extracted everything she knew about the warehouse.

'Which was not much,' said Guleed. The building was leased by a company called ThisIsNotABanana, which we found out later was one of a series of shell companies designed to obscure the real owner, Terrence Skinner, and keep it at arm's length from the Serious Cybernetics Corporation.

'She did say that it had its own electrical substation,' said Guleed. 'Although why they'd need one I don't know, unless they're growing dope or something.'

Guleed hadn't spent the last month embedded in the upper tech industry like I had, so I explained.

'A lot of computers,' I said. 'And their air conditioners.'

'And for that they need a whole substation to themselves?'

'A *lot* of computers.'

'To do what?'

Which was the same question Nightingale and Stephanopoulos asked when they rocked up with a couple of vans of TSG and the local duty inspector, who was there to make sure us Londoners didn't do anything elitely metropolitan on his manor.

I gave them most of the options, but left out Bitcoin mining. Because not only would the explanation of why that uses huge amount of power have taken about three hours, but also because I was a bit hazy on the details myself.

I explained Plan A, which went down about as well as I expected.

'Absolutely not,' said Nightingale, but I could see Stephanopoulos had given it more thought.

'Peter's right – it is what it is,' she said. 'We have to try it his way in the first instance.'

Nightingale gave me a narrow-eyed look.

'If needs must,' he said. 'But I want you to be cautious.'

'Hey,' I said. 'Cautious is my middle name.'

'But your first name is Never Knowingly,' said Stephanopoulos. Which got all the laughs it deserved.

But first we wanted a quick look at the Transit van parked outside, so I took Guleed. Or rather, given that she was a skipper, she supervised my initial approach.

'You're thinking the Print Shop?' she asked as we walked across the staff car park.

'Why else would they use an antique?' I said.

Something with no microprocessor to sand, and thus safe to use around high-intensity magic. At some point, I thought, we're going to have to start tracking thefts of old vans – I mean, why else would anyone steal one?

This specimen was well kept, with a recent paint job and unworn tyres. We strolled up until the side of the van hid us from the main building and I peered in through the passenger side window. The interior trim was ragged, the seat covers torn and held together with duct tape. I craned my head to see over the seats into the back, but all I could make out was a rumpled lump.

On really old model Fords you used to be able to open the doors with a house key, but unfortunately this particular one came from a more recent and less enlightened time. Still, on the off chance,

I tried the sliding door in the side. And, to my surprise, it opened.

Inside a tarpaulin was draped over a suspiciously cubed shape. While Guleed kept watch I lifted the tarp to reveal the faceted steel and brass corner of the Mary Engine. Judging from the scratching on the cast-iron frame this one had seen some use recently. I leaned in and pressed my fingertips against the cool metal – the surface was greasy with light oil, and beneath that I sensed the creaking mechanical rocking motion of a Newcombe Steam Engine.

And, behind that, a horribly familiar sensation like wriggling cilia and the stench of rotting shrimp.

This was definitely the original Mary Engine, the one Skinner had brought over from the States, and if it was stashed out here in the van, what the fuck was in the warehouse?

I snatched my hand away and slid the van door closed.

'Did you bring your knife?' I asked Guleed.

'They're bound to have spotted us by now,' she said as she handed me a bone-handled fisherman's clasp knife that she swore she only used for getting the stones out of horses' hooves.

'Can't be helped,' I said, and carefully punctured first the front and then the rear left-hand tyres. The trick is to turn the blade so it slips between the radials rather than cuts through them.

I handed Guleed back her knife and she examined the blade critically.

'Whatever happens,' I said, 'we can't lose this.' I pointed at the Mary Engine.

Guleed nodded and put away her knife.

'Good luck,' she said as I adjusted my suit jacket into respectability.

'Right,' I said, suddenly dry-mouthed. 'Let's get on with it.'

The main entrance was a pair of innocuous double doors, made of metal and painted with white enamel. A sign attached to the right-hand side said that visitors should use the intercom. This was a silver speaker grille and button recessed into the metal wall beside the door. There was no company logo or helpful name, not even a unit number to aid deliveries. Serves them right if their pizza never arrives, I thought.

I pressed the button and, while I waited, I checked and counted at least three CCTV cameras covering the door.

The only reason Seawoll and Nightingale were letting me try Plan A was because Plan B involved a protracted siege, and Plan C involved us going full Nightingale. And for that we'd need authorisation from the Commissioner and possibly, since we were on Kent Police's turf, the Home Office as well.

There was a buzz, the door opened and I stepped through.

Into a small antechamber with bare walls and ceiling of cemented concrete blocks; the air was close and unventilated and the only other break in the wall was another reinforced composite security door opposite the entrance. Written on the door in small unfriendly letters were the words: DON'T PANIC!

And underneath: THIS DOOR WILL NOT OPEN UNTIL OUTER DOOR IS CLOSED.

There was no visible keypad, retina scanner, lock or even a doorbell, although two Perspex domes in the ceiling marked the presence of more CCTV cameras. Like the secret lift back at the SCC, the security here relied on someone inside letting you in.

The entrance closed behind me with the clatter of electromagnetic deadbolts.

Someone or something? I wondered.

Whichever it was, they made me wait at least a minute in the dead air of the antechamber before the inner door buzzed and opened inwards. Lights flickered on, revealing a long corridor lined with rigid metal fencing. The roar of the heavy-duty air conditioning gave away the room's function – beyond the metal fences were rows of what looked like high-end music centres mounted on shelving units. These were what Everest and Victor would call HPC platforms – High Performance Computing. This was either a server farm or a data storage facility, the sort of thing City firms use to back up their data. At this level of computing, Victor had told me, you didn't measure things in kilobytes or MIPS.

'You have to assume they're running the latest kit,' he said. 'So you measure everything in kilowatts of IT load.'

Hundreds of kilowatts, thousands in a room like this.

And there was room for another floor above my head.

There were gates through the fences halfway along the corridor. Locked, but again with no key or touchpad. I paused to watch the unblinking blue lights arrayed across the faces of the black boxes. Victor or Everest probably could have made a guess as to their make and purpose, but all I saw was an enormous magical accident waiting to happen.

Skinner had made his fortune designing servers, and for all we knew the whole of London's internet depended on these machines. One magical 'incident' and it was goodbye Netflix, Pornhub and online shopping. And the economy would take the kind of hit that registers on the quarterly GDP figures.

Which was why Plan A involved me walking in and having a chat with Skinner.

The world is full of rooms like this, for data storage, server farms or internet backbones, although 70 per cent of internet traffic passes through Loudoun County in Virginia. Reynolds says she thinks that's so spooks from the NSA don't have a long commute when installing yet another tap.

I'd said that I was fairly certain that you didn't use a long cable to tap the internet and she shrugged, and we waited a couple of seconds in case whoever was monitoring us could break into the Skype call and put us straight.

The wall at the far end was covered in foam cut into egg-crate shapes to act as sound baffling. The wide door set into the wall was similarly covered, making it hard to spot from a distance. There was yet another press-button intercom which gave me a static shock when I used it.

The intercom hummed and crackled. Then there was a *thunk* from behind the door and it started to slowly retreat into the wall. I went to step through and stopped – the wall was at least half a metre thick. The door had to be dragged all the way out by hydraulic arms on the other side and then ponderously swung aside.

'Stand clear of the moving doors,' said the intercom, followed by something that would have sounded like, if a person not a machine had made it, a snigger. As I walked through I stopped to examine the wall. It was composed of layers of different materials of different thicknesses, like the composite armour you find on modern tanks – thin layers of metal, thick planks of yellow pine and a couple of thicker layers of what looked like insulating foam. If I'd sat down to design a wall for protecting electronics against serious magic abuse, I'd have come up with something like that.

Good, I thought, I don't need to be as careful as I thought I did.

'Glad to be of service,' said the door as it started closing behind me.

The room I'd entered took up a quarter of the warehouse and was open all the way up to its steel rafters. The walls were lined with the same foam soundproofing as the wall I'd just walked through. The floor was an expanse of thick wood planking polished to a high sheen, surrounding a dais on which sat a plinth topped by an array of modern stainless-steel musical pipes. It was an honest-to-God organ – or rather, I saw as I looked closer, a modern streamlined copy of an automatic fairground organ. One that had been stripped of its baroque gilt decoration which had been replaced by matt black metal grilles and smooth grey panels with aluminium trim. There was no keyboard. Instead I could see what looked like a Mary Engine embedded behind a clear glass panel at the centre, while at its head, one on each side, were two demijohn-sized glass jars filled with a cloudy red liquid – the Rose Jars. A rack of HPCs, like those in the first room, stood either side of the organ and in front of the left-hand rack waited Terrence Skinner.

He should have been wearing a black roll-neck jumper with a faux military insignia on his chest, but obviously Skinner hadn't been reading the script and had turned out for the final confrontation in jeans, black Nike trainers and a loose blue pinstripe collarless shirt. He was, at least, sitting in a swivel chair in front of the steady unblinking lights of the HPC rack. But he didn't say, 'Ahh, Mr Grant, we meet again,' which showed a shocking lack of etiquette on his part.

'Hi, Peter,' he said. 'Come to see the start of the new world?'

'I don't want to be a downer,' I said. 'But I'm here to talk about Leo Hoyt.'

'What about him?' said Skinner casually, but the heel of his right trainer started to tap on the polished wood surface of the dais.

'We need to clarify a few things,' I said, and walked up to join Skinner on the dais.

'We talked about this,' said a voice from nowhere. 'This is the response we anticipated.'

The voice was an attractive tenor with a mid-Atlantic accent coming, I realised, from multiple speakers positioned in and around the organ. I used its arrival as an excuse to peer curiously at the machine.

'For someone who just wants to clarify a few points,' said the voice, 'you've sure brought a lot of cops.'

There was another glass panel next to the Mary Engine, lit from the inside by the shade of blue light that is now compulsory for all high-tech equipment from the Sonic Screwdriver on down.

'We weren't sure what we might find,' I said, and crouched down to look through the glass.

Inside was a music book, identical, I assumed, to the one stolen from Henry 'Wicked' Collins in January, connected to a reader much like the one cobbled together by Mrs Chin. Only this one was beautifully put together out of brass and mahogany.

'You already had a copy of *The Enchantress of Numbers*,' I said. 'Where did you get it?'

'Branwell Petersen had it,' said Skinner. 'I bought it with the rest of his lab equipment. Didn't realise its importance at the time, though.'

So Petersen had had all the pieces of the puzzle when Anthony Lane graduated from mashing the caps lock to pulling the trigger. Eat hot lead, you *USURPER OF THE NATURAL ORDER*!

'As I indicated earlier – we discussed this,' said the voice, which I was assuming belonged to Deep Thought. 'This one is as bad as the Librarians. They're just looking for an excuse to shut you down.'

So you know about the Librarians, I thought. Interesting.

I shifted to the left and tapped the glass in front of the Mary Engine. Close up I could see that it was as clean, as pristine and as streamlined as the mechanical organ it was part of.

'Is this a copy?' I asked.

'More like Mark II,' said Skinner. 'We reverse-engineered the old one and built that one from scratch. With better tolerances, mind you – the old one used to stick.'

'Where's the old one now?'

Because I wondered whether Skinner knew about the van and its trips out to the Print Shop to activate the drones. And if he didn't know? What would that mean?

'Terrence,' said Deep Thought, 'this man does not have our best interests at heart.'

'In pieces,' said Skinner. 'We had to take it apart to see how it worked. It's in storage now. What has this got to do with Leo?'

'I don't know,' I said, and brushed my fingers across the glass again. There was no *vestigia* anywhere in the vicinity. I wondered if this was another fake – another decoy – and whether Skinner knew. I stood up and drifted towards the right-hand Rose Jar – the one furthest from where Skinner was sitting. 'Where is it now?'

'Over there,' said Skinner.

He jerked his thumb at where stacks of white plastic storage containers were stood in rows against the wall. They, along with the plastic garden furniture, sofa bed and the neat pile of pizza boxes, eliminated what was left of the James Bond villain vibe.

The Rose Jars were set high and further back than the front of the organ – making them hard to get close to.

'Why both jars?'

'That was the design they used in San Jose,' said

Skinner. 'Didn't want to mess with it until we knew how it worked.'

'How does it work?'

'Not sure yet,' he said. 'I think the jars create a multidimensional operating space that allows a consciousness to develop free of the normal hardware restrictions.'

It sounded plausible to me, and for all I knew that's how they stored ghosts.

'Did Leo know about this place?' I asked.

Skinner hesitated.

'I don't know,' said Skinner. 'I think he might have—'

The voice interrupted.

'What he knew was irrelevant,' it said.

'Speaks to motive,' I said, and managed to get myself a good look in the jar. There was a glow, and a fluting *vestigium* like the sound of a finger tracing the rim of a wine glass.

I was a little bit disappointed.

It was just a ghost.

Part of me had wanted a working Artificial General Intelligence – one that at least wouldn't keep trying to make me watch Adam Sandler movies.

'So who's in these Rose Jars, Terry?' I asked. 'What spirit have you got putting the intelligence into your artificial?'

'This is where people like you go wrong,' said Skinner. 'You look at a Rose Jar and think, "Wow, it's got a ghost in it," when you should be thinking "That device can hold an entire human personality."'

'So, no ghosts,' I said.

'I am not a ghost,' said Deep Thought – the accent had slipped westward, California at a guess. 'I am as much a fully self-aware person as you are.'

'In that case, Mr Deep Thought, I am arresting you for the murder of Leo Hoyt,' I said. 'You do not have to say anything.'

'Are you nuts?' asked Skinner.

'Hey, Terry,' I said, 'if he's as much a person as I am, then he's subject to the law. Which means it will harm his defence if he doesn't mention something he relies on in court. Anything he does say may be given in evidence.'

'Have you finished?' asked Skinner.

'Not quite,' I said, and slapped my hand on the side of the organ. 'You're nicked, sunshine.'

Skinner's mouth worked – he obviously wanted to say something clever, but all he managed was, 'This is so fucking pathetic.'

'And I'm having you for conspiracy and aiding and abetting,' I said.

'Aiding and abetting what?' he asked.

'Poor little Leo Hoyt, you cunt,' I said, surprising myself. 'We know you used a burner and we know the cell tower. It's only a matter of time before we have the metadata for all the calls and texts. We have a witness – so you're done, mate.'

'I don't know what you're talking about, *mate*,' said Skinner.

Actually, I doubted we could make September testify in court and the chances of getting the phone data were slim at best. Still, tech types always overestimate the efficacy of technological solutions. And Skinner must have been spooked because he took a step away from me and almost fell off the dais – catching himself just in time.

'Nothing to do with me,' he said.

'Really?' I said. 'Why don't we ask Deep Thought here?' I turned to look at the pair of Rose Jars. 'You know something, don't you, Deepy? You've been a busy little unincorporated spirit, haven't you? Recruiting your little network, sending out your van.'

'What van?' asked Skinner.

'The one outside with the fully operational Mary Engine in it,' I said. 'Where did you think those drones came from?'

'What van?' said Deep Thought. 'What drones?'

There was a sudden grinding noise from the left wall. I looked and saw bits of the foam sound-proofing had started breaking away. Judging by the shape and position, this was one of the freight doors – rolling up. As it rose, chunks of foam fell to litter the floor and grey light washed in through the widening gap. The electric motors driving the slats were whining in protest, but the sound-proofing had obviously been glued directly to the wall without a stiffening layer of plasterboard.

'Deep Thought,' said Skinner in his best talking-to-Siri voice, 'deactivate the freight doors.'

'It's not me,' said Deep Thought.

Skinner turned to me.

'Are you doing this?' he said.

The door had risen high enough that I could see the articulated lorries lined up in the empty lot. It didn't take a genius to see that the next stage would be to have several metric tonnes of plastic killing machine swarming out of the lorries and in through the freight door. But why? What did either Skinner or Deep Thought think they would achieve?

I looked over at the two Rose Jars and the penny dropped.

'God, you guys are dumb,' said a voice that was probably, all things considered, not Deep Thought.

'Who said that?' asked Skinner in a high querulous voice.

Later I reckoned he'd worked it out too, but in that moment he didn't want to admit it to himself.

'I'm the man from pest control,' said the voice. 'Here to stamp out all the leeches.'

'He's in my head,' said Deep Thought, in an oddly calm voice. 'There's a whole part of me that's not me.'

'That's because you're the ghost of Branwell Petersen,' I said. 'Which makes *you*—' nonsensically, I turned to face the second Rose Jar – 'Anthony Lane.'

Skinner looked at me, his face pale and terrified.

And I saw him put it all together, just as I had thirty seconds earlier. The Rose Jars had been empty when Anthony Lane turned up to put an end to Branwell Petersen's little experiment. The Mary Engine must have been running, spinning magic out into the environment, so that when they died their personalities had been imprinted inside the jars.

'That name means nothing to me,' said Deep Thought. 'I remember my first conscious thought – here. I awoke here. I am Deep Thought.'

'Pathetic, isn't it?' said what I assumed was the ghost of Anthony Lane. 'They upset the natural order of things and they have no idea what they're doing.'

Outside I heard a couple of big diesel engines firing up.

'So did you kill Leo Hoyt?' I asked, to distract Lane.

'Oh fuck,' said Skinner in a resigned tone. 'There must have been enough of a pattern to form a personality, but without memory. Still, not a total waste of time – we're still talking about a self-aware construct.'

'He was a loose end,' said Lane to me. 'It was easy enough to convince Crocodile Dundee here that he was a threat.'

There was a disappointingly muffled *crump* sound from outside. I'd been hoping for a bigger bang, but it wasn't a real explosion.

'What was that?' asked Skinner.

'That was a couple of phosphorus grenades going off inside a pair of shipping containers,' I said, and started edging casually towards Skinner. With the freight door open I was less than five metres from escape.

'That's unfortunate,' said Lane. At least I think it was him.

'Now, I want everyone to remain calm,' I said but just then the organ started to play 'Oh, I Do Like to Be Beside the Seaside' in full brass band oompah-oompah mode and the freight door started to grind downwards.

I would have liked to ask Lane what his plans for all those drones had been, but Skinner had grabbed a monkey wrench from somewhere and was running towards the Rose Jars. His logic was obvious – if Lane was a stored ghost, then smashing his jar would finish him off. I assume he knew which jar to smash, but before he got halfway across the dais a drone dropped down from the rafters. There was a bang as the drone fired and the jar on the left shattered, fragments of glass and cloudy red water spraying across Skinner, the organ and the HPC units. Skinner yelled something and swung wildly and managed to hit the drone square on. It went arcing across the room to smash into the foam soundproofing with a dull thud. Two more drones were dropping from the ceiling – I got one with a fireball but missed the second, which shot around behind the organ. Distracted, I wasn't fast enough to stop Skinner swinging his monkey wrench around in a full arc and smashing the last Rose Jar.

'Armed police!' I shouted at him. 'Drop the weapon and put your hands on your head!'

Skinner gave me a look of stunned incomprehension and kept the wrench. What I hoped was the last drone came buzzing around the side of the organ and I zapped it with another fireball. In my excitement I overdid it and the plastic dragonfly shape disintegrated like a TIE fighter.

Skinner's eyes practically bugged out and he quickly dropped the wrench and put his hands on his head. I ordered him off the dais and got him to kneel down in an open patch of flooring.

There was a clank as the freight door whirred down the last half metre and closed.

I pulled out my phone and thumbed it on. While I waited for it to boot up, the organ crashed into the final chords of 'Oh I Do Like to Be Beside the Seaside' and then mercifully shut the fuck up.

I used a plastic tie to secure Skinner's hands behind his back, just in case he got any funny ideas. Then I punched Stephanopoulos' number on my phone and told her that the building was secure.

'See how it bloody is, Peter,' said Skinner bitterly. 'The dead hand of the past – always dragging us back down.'

He probably would have continued, but he realised I wasn't paying attention. Instead I was listening to a rhythmic grinding sound like a washing machine made of gears. I hopped back onto the dais and found the sound was coming from the Mary Engine. I crouched down and looked inside – through the outer layer of machinery I could see camshafts and flanges turning.

'How do I turn this off?' I asked Skinner.

'It shouldn't be turned on,' he said. 'It has an isolated power supply.'

The grinding rhythm was picking up and the gears and shafts were visibly turning faster.

And there was the spoilt fish *vestigium* that I had come to know and love.

I stepped away sharply and ran around the back to check there wasn't a power cable I could pull out. There was no exposed cabling. Everything had been boxed away into conduits – you couldn't fault their health and safety standards.

I called Stephanopoulos and told her I needed the freight door open. Immediately. I didn't catch her reply because my phone squawked and died. I looked over and saw all the blue lights on the HPC rack had gone out. The grinding sound was rising in pitch – the washing machine full of gears was ratcheting up into its spin cycle. I briefly wondered what would happen if I threw a high-powered masonry breaker spell into the

Mary Engine, and then decided that it probably wouldn't be wise to be in the same postcode when I did it.

I ran to Skinner and pulled him to his feet.

'This is all your fault,' he said as I dragged him towards the freight door.

The grinding noise had become a metallic screech. The air was suddenly full of the reek of dead fish, and as I turned to look back it seemed that darkness was beginning to crowd in from the corners of the room.

A portal into darkness, the Rose of New Orleans had written, and I realised that this was an *allokosmos*, an alternative cosmos, pushing into mine.

And there was something in that darkness – I could feel it. A sort of gleeful madness, a wild and vicious enthusiasm. I decided I was probably going to have to risk taking out the Mary Engine after all.

Behind me there was a shriek of shearing metal and the freight door rose half a metre. Guleed rolled through the gap and jumped to her feet.

'Need a hand?' she shouted over the scream of the Mary Engine.

'Yeah!' I said. 'Grab him and run away. Go sharp left and keep going.'

'Until when?'

'I have no fucking idea,' I said.

There were deep shadows moving in the darkness

and an impossible wind brought a charnel house reek to our noses.

The freight door wrenched itself upwards. I didn't need to sense the tick, tick precision of Nightingale's *signare* to know he was doing it. Guleed ducked under the edge, dragging Skinner with her – I heard her yelling at everyone to get clear.

'Peter!' said Nightingale from outside, in as urgent a tone as I've heard him use.

I told him to hold the door where it was.

'And get ready to drop it as soon as I'm out,' I said.

I'm not sure, but I think I heard him sigh.

And suddenly something was looking at me out of the darkness – huge and cool and unsympathetic.

God, I hope I make my sanity check, I thought, and threw the biggest skinny grenade I could conjure at the Mary Engine.

Then I ducked out into the grey Medway daylight.

Nightingale gestured with his hand and the freight door slammed down behind me. I took off to the left along the side of the warehouse – hoping that the half a metre of magic-resistant wall might provide a blast shadow.

Ahead I could see Guleed, Skinner and half a dozen TSG officers legging it as fast as full riot gear would allow. They'd all worked with us before, so they knew not to hang around when the wheels came off.

Nightingale kept pace with me.

'How long?' he asked.

The skinny grenade was one of the first things I invented when I became an apprentice. Skinny comes from *scindere*, one of the *formae* used in the spell – it makes what is basically a big time-delayed fireball stick to whatever I threw it at. Nightingale didn't approve, because apprentices, especially early on, are supposed to concentrate on precision and correct forms. And, to be fair, I've had to do quite a bit of remedial work over the months to correct bad habits I'd fallen into.

Also, I've never managed to get the timer to work with any kind of precision.

'About—' I said, and then the warehouse exploded.

Or rather didn't.

Nightingale flicked up his shield behind us – he can do that while running, the show-off – but there was no blast. At least no physical blast. Instead, a great pulse of *vestigium* rolled over us and it was as if my ribcage and head rang like a bell made out of hamburger. I stumbled, but Nightingale grabbed my arm and kept me steady.

We reached the road where Guleed, Skinner and the panting TSG officers were waiting.

'Not again,' said Guleed, looking over my shoulder.

I turned, but as far as I could tell, apart from a

plume of white smoke rising from the far end, the warehouse was still upright.

'You know what they say,' I said. 'Any building you can walk away from . . .'

CHAPTER 20

DON'T GET DISTRACTED BY
THE SUBTEXT

You'd be amazed how often the police never get to the bottom of a case. You can investigate a crime, identify a suspect, and put together enough evidence to send them up the steps to await Her Majesty's pleasure and still never know all the whys and wherefores.

That the ghost of Anthony Lane piggybacked on the fake personality of Deep Thought to gain access to the workers in Bambleweeny is undisputed. He probably suborned William Lloyd early on and used him to gain wider access to the internet and set up the Print Shop. There were others involved – a joint effort by the NCA and the Folly identified three more SCC employees who helped move equipment in and out of Bambleweeny. Getting in and out was easy because Deep Thought controlled access to the hidden freight lift and what Deep Thought controlled, so did Lane. All three employees claimed they thought they were following legitimate instructions from management – and I tend to believe them.

What we don't know is where Lane learnt how

to manipulate people so completely. I'd have sworn he was a lone madman with a manifesto when he murdered Branwell Petersen, so I reckon he must have had access to skills and techniques from outside. I'm guessing that the badly named Against Spiritual Usurpation is a real group, and planning its campaign against *LEECHES* and *USURPERS* – wherever they may be. Although, fortunately, that campaign is mostly Reynolds' problem, not ours.

To add to her woes, we asked her to pick up the Librarians and take them home. She said that she was doing these repatriation flights so often that the check-in staff at Dulles had bumped her up to business class. Using evil European-style red tape as an excuse, we fixed it so she stayed over two nights, which gave me a chance to show her around the changes at the Folly and introduce her to Foxglove. Reynolds took notes on practitioner containment and the subsequent portrait *American Woman With a Notepad and a Small Annoying Dog*, acrylic on canvas, currently hangs in the breakfast room. After that, Beverley had her round for afternoon tea and Bulge appreciation.

'Are you two going to get hitched?' she asked.

'It's complicated,' said Beverley.

The next day Nightingale and I escorted Reynolds, Mrs Chin and Stephen to the airport, where they caught a scheduled flight back to New York. It was our treat, and although we shelled out for premium economy seats, the Librarians didn't seem at all grateful to be travelling with an FBI agent.

'Don't think we will forget this,' said Mrs Chin, as we waited in the secure departure area Border Force maintains at Heathrow.

'Good,' I said, and deliberately leaned into her personal space. 'You came to my city uninvited and put members of the public at risk. You tell all your friends and allies and whatever else that they don't come to my city without asking permission first.'

Mrs Chin sneered at me – it was a good sneer, and I was almost convinced.

'Is that clear?' I asked.

She jerked her head in what might have been a nod. I gave it the benefit of the doubt and stepped back.

Terrence Skinner remained our problem. He retreated back into his billionaire's money cocoon and defied us to make something of the scant evidence we had. His legal team even demanded the return of any materials seized at either the SCC or the Gillingham warehouse. Where the Mary Engine and associated organ had stood, there was nothing but a twisted, half-melted mass of metal and plastic, although interestingly the wooden dais was scorched but relatively undamaged. The *vestigium*, that vomit-inducing rotting prawn aroma, coupled with the sensation of millions of little feelers exploring your skin, was so strong that even non-practitioners were creeped out. Even if they didn't know why.

The hundred million quid's worth of HPC in the rest of the warehouse had made it through relatively unscathed, so me and Frank Caffrey cut out a chunk of the composite wall under the guise of taking evidence and carried it away for further study. You never know when a bit of magical shielding might come in handy.

Thinking of the way the darkness had fixed me in its gaze, I felt that the added protection might be needed sooner rather than later.

After a long and acrimonious three-way discussion between Silver, Seawoll and the CPS, it was decided not to charge Terrence Skinner. The murder of Leo Hoyt would remain an open case until such time, as Seawoll put it, 'We can nail that smug bastard against the wall.'

I'm not holding my breath, but I am maintaining a watching brief. I know what the demi-monde is like. And Skinner has acquired a taste for it – he'll never go back to being a straight tech-bro now.

Meanwhile, some other people seemed gloriously unaffected.

Like Everest and Victor, who I met up with at the Paradice Board Games Café in Bromley which has coffee, snacks and big tables you can play games on. They even have a large selection of games you can borrow if you didn't bring your own. Which was just as well because when I was younger I never had enough money, and now I have enough money I have other things to spend it on.

'You're a Cylon,' said Everest.

We were playing *Battlestar Galactica,* which is a cooperative game where the gimmick is that at least one of the players is secretly a Cylon who wins by destroying the Battlestar. The other players have to identify the Cylon before it can carry out its dastardly yet strangely non-specific plan.

'That's outrageous,' I said.

Oliver Partridge gave me a suspicious look. I'd brought him with me so that Tyrel and Stacy could have a romantic night in. Part of my penance for having got Tyrel fired – although I still don't think it was my fault. Beverley was keeping Keira entertained at Wandle's latest pop-up boutique – now currently in Summers-town – doing what, I didn't like to speculate.

Victor moved his Admiral over from Colonial One.

'So is it true?' he asked.

'Of course not,' I said. 'I am not and never have been a Cylon.'

'That Skinner integrated a ghost into his IT architecture.'

'How would I know?' I said, looking at Everest, who was frowning at the board. 'I'm just here to keep you guys safe.'

'But not employed,' said Victor.

'We've already been headhunted,' said Everest

without looking up. 'And why would it be Peter's job to keep us employed?'

'I really think you're a Cylon,' said Victor.

As it happened it turned out that Oliver, the cheeky little git, had spoofed the Loyalty Deck so that we'd all been playing Cylons right from the start.

There was really only one place secure enough to store the original Mary Engine. So, once we'd cleared the cells and put them back to standby, me and Nightingale wheeled it down a short corridor with a grey steel door at the end. There were multiple overlapping circles scored into the metal.

Nightingale put his hand on a seemingly random section of the door, there was the merest suggestion of magic, and the door swung ponderously inwards. Disappointingly, it was less than three centimetres thick. But then I suppose its physical mass was probably the least of its defences. Likewise the room beyond was just that – a room. The walls were lined with shoulder-high, grey steel filing cabinets, each drawer with a label in faded type on card – EB1945/1, EB1945/2, EB1945/3 . . . The walls were of unpainted brick and it was lit by a pair of bare bulbs hanging from the ceiling at either end. There was plenty of room in the corner to stash the Mary Engine, and Nightingale waited patiently while I checked yet again that the locking bar that prevented the engine turning was in place.

We still hadn't located whoever it was who had reverse-engineered the Mary Engine for Skinner, which meant that somewhere out there were people who knew how to build one from scratch. Our only hope was they didn't know what it was for.

Once something is known, it's almost impossible to retain control. I looked around at the filing cabinets and wondered what secrets they contained. A large chunk of Nightingale's peers had died to recover those cabinets. I wondered why they'd never been opened – or destroyed.

'You never had any plans to use this information,' I said. 'Right?'

Nightingale put his hand, gingerly, on top of one of the filing cabinets.

'Right?' I said again – louder than I meant to.

'No,' said Nightingale. 'To what end, Peter, would I turn it?'

'I don't know,' I said. 'That's what worries me.'

'No,' said Nightingale. 'Never again.'

'So why don't we just burn it?' I said.

'I did give serious consideration to doing just that, but Harold talked me out of it.'

Professor Postmartin was against the destruction of historical records on general principle, but he had a specific objection in this case.

'The Germans may have kept meticulous records. But Able Company—' the strike team assigned to take the camp headquarters and research labs – 'didn't have time to keep the filing

448

intact. Everything was carted away willy-nilly and dumped in the gliders.'

As a result the forbidden material, the product of the obscene experimentation by the *Ahnenerbe*, was mixed up with routine camp records – including those of the prisoners.

'He said that we needed to keep them against the day when no one was alive who remembered what happened,' said Nightingale. 'He said this would be their only chance of a memorial and an explanation of how they'd lived and died.'

'It all happened seventy years ago,' I said. 'That day is tomorrow – at the latest. And what did happen to the inmates? Do you know?'

'Baker Company was assigned to liberate them,' he said. 'But they were the weakest – we assumed that the Germans would put the bulk of their defence around the manufacturing complex.'

Instead Baker ran head first into the men and tanks of the SS Panzergrenadiers in at least company strength. And amongst them there were things that were not men and not tanks.

'They never got near the barracks,' said Nightingale. 'They were thrown back upon our landing zone and we had to commit our reserves to stop them from being overrun.' His fingers drummed on the filing cabinet. 'The Germans didn't seem to care about defending the plant at all, but they fought like mad to stop Able Company flanking them and reaching the barracks. It was as if keeping us away from the prisoners was all that mattered.'

And so Operation Spatchcock came apart and Britain left the cream of its young wizards scattered amongst the broken trees of the Grosse Ettersburg. There was no mass prisoner breakout, no British-aided disruption behind German lines, or any of the foolish advantages the planners thought they might win. Only the Black Library. Bought at such cost to the British and their allies.

'What happened to the prisoners?' I asked.

'We think the vast majority were murdered,' said Nightingale.

One of the British survivors, Hugh Oswald, had been with Patton and the Third Army when they liberated nearby Buchenwald. There was nothing left of the plant or barracks but scattered rubble and nightmare *vestigia*. There were mass graves, of course. There were mass graves of prisoners all over Germany and occupied Europe, and once you were shot in the head and dumped in a pit nobody could tell a wizard from anybody else.

'I was ill for most of the latter part of 1945,' said Nightingale. 'So I saw none of the aftermath myself. At least not in Europe.'

He made an after-you gesture at the still open steel door.

'Perhaps it will be a suitable project for my retirement,' he said as we left.

'And when will that be?' I asked.

Nightingale touched the door again and then stepped back as it swung closed.

'I think that rather depends on you,' he said. 'Don't you?'

A couple of nights later I woke up in the middle of a summer's day with dust motes dancing in the sunlight pouring in through French windows and the light summer curtains rustling in the breeze. Outside I could hear birdsong, much louder than normal, and smell distant woodsmoke. Beside me, Beverley had kicked off the duvet and lay dark and perfect across the white sheets.

But there was a white man beside the bed, a pale hand resting on Beverley's stomach. He was half naked and swirls of blue paint ran up his arm, across his shoulders and down his chest and belly. He had a long face with a straight nose and a wide mouth that was crooked into an expression of mingled joy and grief. When I tried to scramble out of the bed, he held up his hand to stop me and put his fingers to his lips. Then he smiled and I recognised the smile.

This was the old god of the Beverley Brook from ages past – a son of Old Father Thames, dead for over a hundred and fifty years. Killed, if you believed his brothers, by the tide of filth poured into the river by the thoughtless denizens of London.

Never mind that development on the South Bank had barely reached Battersea at the time.

He looked down at Beverley's face for a moment, nodded, and then looked back at me. Gravely he bunched his fist and thumped it on his chest and then, without any fuss at all, he vanished.

Taking the summer's day with him and leaving me in the dark with rain against the window and Beverley a shadow in the darkness. It might have been a dream, but I've learnt to distinguish the two.

Beverley shifted and rolled onto her side. I put my hand on her – it was like touching a radiator. So far her pregnancy had been free of any medical complications, but this felt like a terrible fever. I switched on the reading lamp and said her name.

When I shook her shoulder she opened one eye and gave me an annoyed look.

'What is it?' she asked.

'Are you alright?' I asked.

'I'm fine,' she said. 'Apart from being awake.'

'You're burning up,' I said.

Beverley touched her own cheek with the back of her hand.

'Huh,' she said. 'Yeah, it's a hot flush.' She snuggled back into her pillow.

I touched her shoulder and found her skin temperature felt normal again. She took my hand and drew me down until we were spooning.

'Tyburn said this might happen,' she said sleepily.

The air in the room was cool against my legs and back. I let go of Beverley long enough to hook the duvet and draw it up over us.

'How often did she say it happened?'

'Not that often,' said Beverley. 'Until the last week before she popped. Then she said they turned off the central heating and let her warm the house. Said it saved tons off her gas bill.'

'Did she say if anything else happened?' I asked. But Beverley was fast asleep.

TECHNICAL NOTE

The 3-D printing in this book represents what was available during the period it was set, as do the drones and other bits of technology. 3-D printing is what they call a rapidly evolving technology and nobody really knows what its ultimate impact will be – certainly not me. Anyone tries to tell you different, feel free to hit them with a selfie stick.

Peter not only misquotes Sir Walter Scott: *O, what a tangled web we weave when first we practise to deceive!* But to add insult to injury, misattributes the quote to Shakespeare. This is entirely the fault of Captain Jean-Luc Picard.